P9-DOG-646

The Atomic City Girls

(Courtesy of the Department of Energy)

The Atomic City Girls

Janet Beard

wm

WILLIAM MORROW
An Imprint of HarperCollins*Publishers*

This is a work of fiction. Names, characters, places, and incidents are products of the author's imagination or are used fictitiously and are not to be construed as real. Any resemblance to actual events, locales, organizations, or persons, living or dead, is entirely coincidental.

P.S.™ is a trademark of HarperCollins Publishers.

THE ATOMIC CITY GIRLS. Copyright © 2018 by Janet Beard. All rights reserved. Printed in the United States of America. No part of this book may be used or reproduced in any manner whatsoever without written permission except in the case of brief quotations embodied in critical articles and reviews. For information, address HarperCollins Publishers, 195 Broadway, New York, NY 10007.

HarperCollins books may be purchased for educational, business, or sales promotional use. For information, please e-mail the Special Markets Department at SPsales@harpercollins.com.

FIRST EDITION

Designed by Diahann Sturge

Library of Congress Cataloging-in-Publication Data has been applied for.

ISBN 978-0-06-266671-0

18 19 20 21 22   LSC   10 9 8 7 6 5 4 3 2 1

In memory of my grandmother Eunice Beard

Acknowledgments

MY FIRST AND ALWAYS MOST ENCOURAGING READER WAS MY dad, Bill Beard, to whom I owe limitless thanks.

I was lucky to meet Raelee Chapman in the early stages of writing, who not only provided excellent criticism but also organized a writing group and insisted they read my entire first draft. Many thanks to her and those other readers, Katie Snell, Nick Smith, Melody Ellis, and Emma Rooksby.

Meghan Formel and Erin Coffey read later drafts and both gave excellent advice. I am also grateful to those who assisted me as I found my way in the publishing world, including Michelle Andelman and Victoria Lowes.

I am endlessly indebted to my agent, Rayhané Sanders, for her enthusiasm, tenacity, and wisdom. And I am beyond grateful that she found the perfect editor for this novel, Lucia Macro. Huge thanks to her and everyone at William Morrow who has helped turn my words into a book.

Thanks always to my husband, Declan Smithies, for understanding and supporting my need to write.

Though the characters in this novel are fictional, the real people who worked on the Manhattan Project in Oak Ridge inspired them. I hope I have done justice to their memories.

(Courtesy of the Department of Energy)

The Atomic City Girls

Prologue

November 1942

THE NEWS THAT JUNE'S GRANDFATHER WAS BEING EVICTED HAD come from her older sister Mary, who worked in town at Langham's Drug Store. She rushed past June, who was reading a schoolbook in the living room, to find their mother Rose in the kitchen. "Mama, I got a telephone call at work today."

"A telephone call? Who on earth was calling you?"

June put down her geometry book and twisted around in her chair. Her mother was peeling potatoes at the sink. Mary stood beside her, acting all tall and important like she had ever since she finished school and got a job in town. "A man from the Army."

Rose put down her knife. "What does the Army want with you?"

"He was looking for you, Mama. He was calling about Grandfather Foster."

Rose's face tightened. "I don't understand . . ."

"The Army is buying his house. He has to leave in two weeks; he has no choice."

"The house in Bear Creek Valley?"

Mary nodded. "The man couldn't tell me what they need it for, except it's to help win the war. He'd been to see Grandfather but said the poor old man didn't understand when he tried to explain what was happening." Mary's tone softened. "The Army man said he kept saying it was 1924. Grandfather must be losing his mind."

Rose let out a loud breath. "I suppose we have to go get him, don't we?"

"He said we should make arrangements."

Rose turned from her daughter and gripped the counter in front of her. "June!" she cried out, without looking up. "Go fetch your daddy!"

June leapt off the chair and ran out the front door toward the barn. She was a loose-limbed sixteen, still more girl than woman, and young enough to run from place to place. Her brown hair wrapped around her long neck as she sprinted through the field, white skirt whipping at her legs.

She'd always known her mother hated her grandfather, though the reasons had never been fully explained. Her mother hardly ever spoke about her life before meeting June's father. The one thing June was certain of was that her grandfather Jericho was a drunk. She'd heard enough whispers between her parents and seen enough of Jericho himself to be sure of it. Jericho never had been what a grandfather was supposed to be, and they'd only ever been to visit him four times. He had a long beard and always wore overalls, living alone with his dogs in the tiny dirt-floor cabin where Rose had grown up. The dogs had snapped at June when she was little, and her grandfather did nothing to stop them. He didn't talk to her or her sister much, and when he did, he was surly and serious, as though they'd done something to make him angry. Rose told them he didn't like children, but he didn't seem to treat her parents much better. Rose was tense around him and unsmiling; June's father Frank strained to make conversation.

June heard her mother tell her father about the phone call in hushed tones, her arms crossed and head bent under the burden of the news. Frank took it in slowly. "Reckon we can make a room for him in the attic."

"Where are we supposed to get a bed for him?" Rose protested.

"We can load up the furniture from the house in Bear Creek Valley and bring it over here."

"And what are you going to load it onto? Your back?!"

Mary spoke up then, and June realized she was the only one not invited to the conversation. "The Army man said if we could find a truck to borrow, he'd give us the ration stamps for gas."

Frank cleared his throat. "Reckon Hank Lawson could loan me his truck."

* * *

JUNE JUMPED AS soon as she heard the engine of the truck grumbling in the driveway the next morning, and Rose looked up, too. "Go on, then," she said to June, who turned and ran to the front of the house.

She'd only ever been in a car a handful of times before, when her uncle came to visit and took them out for drives. She walked to the passenger-side door and peered inside. "Better put on your sweater," said Frank. "Gets cold in there with that broke window."

The truck rumbled as her father put it in gear. June sat up straight and tall, peering down at the ground through the broken window. They began to move, and she felt a small thrill. As they headed out of the hollow, Ronnie Lawson ran out to the road and waved. His round cheeks were flushed and his dusty curls flopped in the air as he ran beside the truck. She waved back at him as they passed.

June looked up toward the sky. The leaves were mostly gone from the trees, but a few brilliant reds and yellows stood out against the bleak November landscape. As they picked up speed, a cold wind whizzed through the broken window, and June shoved her hands under her legs to keep them warm.

Frank was silent. After a while, June turned to him. "What do you think it will be like having Granddaddy around?"

"We'll manage all right. Just one more mouth to feed. He probably don't eat too much, though."

"What about Mama?"

"She'll get used to it."

"What do you think the government needs Granddaddy's land for?"

"Hank said he'd heard they were building a demolition range."

"What's that?"

"For trying out weapons, I reckon. Practicing."

June shivered. It didn't seem right that the Army could take a man's house from him. She supposed they must need the land for a good reason, wartime and all, but it didn't seem fair to force people to take in crazy old grandfathers.

They had to drive through Knoxville to cross over the Tennessee River. June was always impressed by the city, small as it was. The tall buildings, movie theater, and department store might as well have been in New York or Chicago for all she knew. Women in fancy hats walked alongside men in dapper suits, and everyone looked rich and busy and alive, like they were on their way to do something important. Not like back home, where there were no buildings or people, just familiar trees and country and cows.

By the time they got to Bear Creek Valley, June's feet were numb with cold. Frank parked at the bottom of the hill, and they looked up at Jericho's tiny cabin. It was so different from their two-story farmhouse that she could hardly imagine her mother growing up here.

Jericho's hounds appeared on the porch, barking loudly. June's frozen feet thudded on the ground as she hopped out of the truck, sending a shiver up her legs. She followed her father up the hill and stood behind him on the porch as he knocked on the door. "Jericho! You in there?"

The old man opened the door and peered out at them. His overalls were covered in dark stains, and his beard went halfway down his chest. "What you want?"

"Jericho, it's me, Frank." The old man stared blankly. "Rose's husband."

"Rose?" Jericho looked skeptical. "Rose who?"

"Your daughter."

"What'd she go and marry you for? You look like a darned fool."

"You know me, Jericho. You've known me for years."

"Ain't never seed you before in my life. But you might as well come on in, if you like." He opened the door wide for them.

A dank smell assaulted June as she walked through the doors. The dogs ran in after them, still barking intermittently. It was dark inside, but she could make out the outlines of a few pieces of homemade furniture—a table and chairs, a rocking chair in the corner. There was a brown jug on the table beside a jar of pickles, a guitar lying against the wall. A fire was burning, and June went to it, eager to warm her feet.

"Jericho, we've come here to help you move. You're going to come live with us and Rose. We don't have much time, so we need to pack up whatever you want to bring with you."

"What you talking about?! I ain't moving nowhere."

"You have no choice. The Army is evicting you from your land."

"I don't give a goddamn about the Army!"

Startled by the profanity, June turned from the fire. Frank put his hand on Jericho's shoulder. "I'm sorry about this. I know it's not what you want. But we're going to help you."

The old man stared up at Frank distrustfully, but he didn't move his hand. "June, why don't you start collecting your granddaddy's things?"

She didn't want to move away from the fire and, to be honest, was scared of looking too closely at the interior of the cabin. Luckily, Jericho didn't own much. She began by taking down a few pictures on the wall beside the fireplace. One was a cross-stitch sampler her grandmother must've made before she died. "Cleanliness is next to Godliness," it proclaimed, though the thick layer of dust covering the frame mocked the sentiment. Beside it were two photographs. One showed Jericho when he was younger, though not much different in appearance. He was wearing a hat and overalls with a darker but just-as-long beard, standing in front of the cabin.

She wondered if they were the same overalls he was wearing today. The other photograph was a formal portrait of her grandmother, who looked stern in a black dress with the high collar of a long-ago era. June took the pictures down carefully. The walls behind them were covered in old newspapers. Bits of ancient news and advertisements peeled off in her hands: "President Coolidge announces . . ." "Harmon's soda for a delicious . . ." ". . . destroyed by floods."

Frank cleared his throat. "I'm going down to the truck to bring up some feed sacks and egg crates for packing."

She shot her father a panicked look, terrified to be left alone with the old man. But Frank paid her no mind and went out the door. Jericho stayed seated at the table, a dog curled at his feet. He bent over to speak to it. "We gonna go hunting later, girl. Catch ourselves that fox we saw yesterday."

A few minutes later, she heard an extra set of footsteps join her father's over the porch. Frank came in carrying the crates, followed by another man in work pants and boots. "June, this is Leonard McMahon. He lives up the road here."

"Nice to meet you," said Mr. McMahon. "How you doing, Jericho?"

"Why won't you'uns leave me and my dogs be?"

"We're helping you pack," said Frank, in a patient tone not unlike the one he'd had to use with Rose last night. He turned to June. "Here, you can load up everything looks worth saving in this here crate."

She took the crate and began stacking the pictures. Mr. McMahon stayed and helped them pack up Jericho's few motley possessions. The old man watched them suspiciously but didn't make a fuss. They were able to pack up the house quickly. After Frank and Mr. McMahon had carried the wardrobe, rocking chair, and table down to the truck, they sat on the porch to take a break. June brought them water from the springhouse in two cups she'd found in the kitchen and given a quick scrub.

"Your family got somewhere to go?" Frank asked Mr. McMahon.

"We'll be staying with my sister for the time being. She lives about fifteen miles from here." Mr. McMahon shook his head slowly. "You know it weren't ten years ago we got kicked off our land when they built Norris Dam. Government man came around that time, too, and told us they were fixing to buy our house and we had no choice but to move. My old farm is at the bottom of Norris Lake now. At least TVA gave us some time, helped us move. This time round, we find a sign tacked in our yard telling us we got two weeks to move. How's a person to find a new piece of land in two weeks? What am I supposed to do with my cattle or the hay in the barn? And the Army ain't paying half of what the place is worth. The timber alone is worth more than they done give us for the whole farm! So many folks round here been kicked off their land that property prices in Anderson County have shot up, and we can't afford nothing."

McMahon spat emphatically on the ground. "I just don't know what Mr. Roosevelt wants from me. I done sent two of my boys off to fight his war and now he has to take my farm from me, too! You a farmer, Mr. Walker, so you understand."

"You work a piece a land for years, the government can't put no price on that."

"For men like us, our land is everything."

"We're mighty thankful to you for helping us today—and for getting the news to us."

"That were my wife's doing. Lucky thing I weren't in the house when that Army feller came back asking about Mr. Foster's family. I'd warned him not to step on my property again—and it is still my property for another week." He finished off his water in a big gulp and stared out toward Pine Ridge, where the sun was beginning to set.

"It's a good valley," he said, his voice soft. No one spoke for a long moment as the light began to fade.

(Courtesy of the Department of Energy)

Chapter 1

November 1944

THE BUS TO OAK RIDGE WAS PACKED WITH OTHER GIRLS JUNE'S age, along with a few soldiers and laborers in the back. June had sat in the front by a window to watch the farms and trees pass by, but nerves kept forcing her to look around. The recruiter in Knoxville had pointed the bus out to her, yet she was terrified that she'd gotten on the wrong one. None of the buses in and out of Oak Ridge were labeled because officially the city didn't exist.

June had felt sophisticated and grown-up this morning, with her hair curled and her mouth painted red, even though she was wearing one of her sister's hand-me-down dresses. She was on her way to her first job, paying seventy-five cents an hour. Now panic rose up in her belly. Everyone else seemed so calm. How did they know they were headed in the right direction? She looked over at the bus driver, a wide man with a roll of fat at the back of his neck in between his hairline and his shirt collar. She could ask him if she was going to the right place. That's what Mary would do. Mary had no fear of talking to people. June turned to the middle-aged man sitting beside her. His head was tucked into the *Knoxville Journal*. "Roosevelt Makes History" read the large headline, and below, in smaller print, "Elected to Record Fourth Term." Of course June already knew that.

The last time she'd come out this way was two years ago to move her grandfather out of his house. Since that afternoon, they'd heard lots of stories about what was happening in Bear Creek Valley. The Army had built a city, folks said. Mary had been working in Oak Ridge for almost a year and assured June there were plenty of good jobs for the taking. Her sister lived in a house with five other young women. There was no room for June at the moment, so she was going to have to live in a dormitory. June didn't really mind, though. Mary got on her nerves more than ever now that she was going steady with a sergeant.

A tall fence topped with barbed wire ran along the road, and June could see buildings beyond it in the distance. A sign in front of the fence read MILITARY RESERVATION. NO TRESPASSING. The bus slowed and finally stopped, stuck behind traffic. She craned her neck to see out the front. The cars were stopped at a large gate and lookout tower, where a soldier stood, holding a rifle.

They sat in traffic for twenty minutes. Once through the gate, the bus wound past endless neighborhoods of houses and trailers, all newly built. She couldn't believe that this was the same land on which her grandfather had lived. It was a large town now, an expanse of buildings and homes that went on as far as she could see. Some neighborhoods were obviously not yet finished. An entire subdivision was made up of only chimneys, which would presumably become whole houses one day, and another was filled with tiny aluminum trailers. The cars on the road kicked up clouds of dust, which seemed to have landed on everything in sight. The bus drove into a business area, with various shops and people coming and going, waiting in lines—young girls, soldiers in uniform, and workmen in plainclothes. It was startling these days to see so many young men in one place.

When the bus driver dropped them off in front of a large white building, he announced, "All new employees report to the front desk." She was in the right place.

June was sent to a place called the bullpen, the training center where new employees had to wait while their security clearances came through. A throng of other girls sat in a white-walled room with a blackboard at the front where a tall man in a gray suit took roll just as in school and handed out a general information bulletin to them. "You are now a resident of Oak Ridge," it read, "situated within a restricted military area . . . What you do here, what you see here, what you hear here, let it stay here."

"Welcome to Oak Ridge," said the man. "You are all going to be working at one of our plants here on an essential wartime project. We are going to train you, but we cannot tell you what you are working on. It is a matter of national security. But I promise you, ladies, that it is of the utmost importance. If our enemies succeed in this endeavor before we do, God have mercy on all of us."

The man's tone softened. "You will work six days a week, ten-hour shifts with an hour lunch break. Shifts will rotate around the clock. It will be hard work, but you can rest easy at night knowing that you are helping to bring an end to the war."

He passed around a drawing of some kind of a machine with knobs, meters, and levers; none of it meant anything to June. "This is a drawing of the machines you will be operating. The machines may look confusing, but your job is very simple."

A stern man in Army uniform came in. He walked quickly to the front of the room and began talking. "I'm going to tell you a story about a girl who was working here at Oak Ridge. She knew she wasn't supposed to tell anyone about what she was doing here. But she decided to write a letter home to her mother describing what the town looks like. She mentioned how many dormitories there were, how many houses she supposed had been built in the last month, how many cafeterias there were." For a moment, he silently paced across the room.

"Another story. A man working in a plant went to Knoxville on his day off. Ran into an old friend in a tavern, who asked him where he works. Now, this man also knew better than to talk about his job. But he told his old friend that he worked at the Clinton Engineer Works in a plant and went on to describe what it looked like." He shook his head, as though marveling at the man's idiocy.

"A schoolteacher here struck up a conversation with an acquaintance, another Oak Ridge woman she met in church. Began telling this woman about some of her students, where they're from, what their parents do. Little did this woman know that her friend was reporting back to Army Intelligence. Her friend knew that by having this sort of conversation, the schoolteacher was putting our project at risk, as well as the lives of our boys overseas. The man in Knoxville didn't know that a secret agent overheard him at the tavern talking to his friend. And the girl who wrote the letter to her mother didn't know that all mail going out of Oak Ridge may be examined."

He stopped pacing and faced them head on. "You are living on a military reservation. Everything about this place is secret. The most inconsequential detail could provide important information to our enemies if it fell into the wrong hands. It is up to you to keep your mouths shut. And it is also your responsibility to report anyone who breaks security."

He swung around and pointed to a girl in the front row. "Would you turn in your father?" He turned to a man behind her. "Your mother?" Turning again. "Your brother? Remember friendship, even family ties, are no excuse. If you know of someone breaching security, it is your responsibility to the United States of America to report it."

June had a terrible impulse to giggle. This always happened to her when she was nervous in quiet, serious places. She'd burst out laughing at a church revival once and came dangerously close to giggling at her own grandmother's funeral.

The man produced a piece of paper from his pocket and held it in front of them. "This is the Espionage Act. It says . . ."—he cleared his throat and began reading—"'Whoever, with intent or reason to believe that it is to be used to the injury of the United States or to the advantage of a foreign nation, communicates, delivers, or transmits, or attempts to, or aids, or induces another to, communicate, deliver, or transmit, to any foreign government . . .'"

He went on and on. June couldn't follow the words; all her energy was going toward suppressing the anxious laughter building up in her chest. She bit her cheeks to keep from smiling and stared down at her hands. She knew she must be visibly trembling and could feel her eyes begin to water with the strain.

The man put the Espionage Act down and looked solemnly around the room. "People will ask what you do here. Don't worry about being rude. If someone asks what you're making, tell them lights for lightning bugs or holes for doughnuts."

She lost control, and a muffled giggle escaped.

The man turned to her, and June prepared for him to yell. But instead he smiled. "That's right. It sounds silly. But it's better to sound silly than put our boys' lives in danger."

She smiled back, the laughter gone. The man handed out declarations of secrecy, which everyone had to sign. When they finished, he sent them across the street for lunch.

The cafeteria was bustling. June piled mashed potatoes and meatloaf onto a plate and looked for a place to sit. It was like high school, except there were three times as many people in this room as there had been in her entire school. The tables were full of people talking and laughing with friends. She wondered where Mary was, wishing for the comfort of a relative, or anyone to eat lunch with, really. Finally resigning herself to being alone, she sat at the end of a long table and ate in silence.

When she was done, she wandered back to the bullpen and found the room for the next training lecture, "Young Woman's Guide to Oak Ridge." A lumpy woman in her fifties sat at the front of the room, wearing black-framed glasses and a shapeless brown dress. Gray curls formed an orb around her head. She opened a large handbag and took out a pile of pamphlets, which she began passing around the room.

The pamphlet was called "Between Us Girls and the Gatepost." June opened it and saw a drawing of a pretty young girl sitting at a desk. A man stood over her as though trying to get her attention, but she was engrossed in typing.

"My name is Mrs. Ransom," announced the woman in a honeyed voice. "I'd like to welcome all you young ladies to Oak Ridge. I'm going to tell you about working here, woman-to-woman. For how many of y'all is this your first job?"

June raised her hand, as did most of the girls. "You're going to have a wonderful time working here, I guarantee. But you will have to work hard. And there is some advice I want to give you about the workplace." She said it as though she were just a good-natured woman who went around dispensing free advice to younger ladies.

"The first thing we're going to talk about, which I'm sure is on all your minds, is what to wear." This wasn't on June's mind at all. She'd never had much choice in what she wore; she was usually in dresses she'd sewn herself from whatever fabric was available, or hand-me-downs from Mary.

"The word I want you all to keep in mind is *decorum*. Don't wear too much makeup. Don't wear dresses that are too short. Don't expose your midriff." She put her hand across her own midriff to demonstrate, and June had a horrible unbidden image of what it would look like bare.

"Imagine your mother is here to keep an eye on you, and don't wear anything she wouldn't find appropriate." Her voice was losing its sweetness.

"You will be working around a lot of men, remember, and you don't want to distract them. Don't flirt on the job. There will be dances where you can have fun; save your flirting for then. You have a responsibility to our boys overseas to work as hard as you can and not do anything to keep the men around you from working hard, too. You don't want innocent boys to lose their lives because you're wasting time flirting."

Mrs. Ransom paused. When she spoke again, the sweetness had returned. "But that doesn't mean we don't want you to look attractive! You also have a responsibility to keep yourselves looking neat and pretty. Your appearance should reflect well upon the Manhattan Engineer District as a whole. Suits are always a good choice, as are sweaters and skirts. Tailored dresses are fine, especially if you can sponge-press them yourself in the dormitory."

June owned only five dresses, and they were basically all the same shape. She'd never even seen girls in short dresses or with exposed midriffs. And the thought of flirting mortified her.

* * *

It WAS TWO more days before June got her security clearance and was finally allowed to leave the accommodations in the bullpen to move into the dormitory. She was praying for a nice roommate.

The first thing she noticed about Cici Roberts was that she was tall. She stood straight with perfect posture, her navy jacket emphasizing her wide shoulders, which somehow did not look manly, but rather elegant. She carried herself as though she ought to be wearing a crown instead of the small hat that was perched on the dark brown waves of her shining hair, which perfectly framed her stunning face. Her lips were large and round, painted a deep red. She was unarguably beautiful, majestic, out of place in the drab, militaristic dorm room. Cici looked as though she had never darned a sock or weeded a vegetable garden or scrubbed a floor. She belonged in large rooms with high ceilings, sipping from porcelain teacups, ordering servants around.

And then she spoke. Her voice was coated with sugar, bourbon, and a sprig of cool mint, a perfect southern accent that to June was more recognizable from the movies than from anyone she knew in East Tennessee. Cici drawled out her words so that it didn't much matter what she was saying; you listened to every note for its music. "Hello there! You must be June. I'm Cici Roberts of Nashville, Tennessee. It is such a pleasure to meet you. Why, you are just adorable! I'm so happy we're living together and know we will be the best of friends."

June shook Cici's long, cool hand. "Pleased to meet you," she replied, suddenly ashamed of her own hillbilly twang.

"Here, this is your cot," motioned Cici, and June put her bag down beside it. "Isn't this room just awful? I've tried to pretty it up a bit." There were postcards decorating the wall over Cici's bed. "But I'm afraid there's only so much we can do."

Cici sat on her bed and June did likewise on her own cot. "Where are you from?" Cici asked.

"Near Maryville."

"Never heard of it. Is it nearby?"

"Not too far off. My mama grew up here in Oak Ridge."

"That so? Hard to imagine what this place used to look like."

"It looked about the same as every place else round here." June looked around the room to a third bed. Cici followed her eyes.

"One other girl is living here." Cici gave a quick look at

the door and whispered, "I hate to say anything unkind, but between you and me, she's just trash."

June wondered what qualified this girl as trash but was afraid to ask. Cici went on: "The dorm is all right, though. They don't allow men inside—what a nuisance! You should see them all huddled out front on Saturday night, waiting for their gals. The canteen across the street is a decent place, good coffee. We have it all right here. I'm sure you got the security talk in the bullpen. Let me tell you, they mean it. A girl living down the hall got fired last week. Folks said she wrote too much about town in a letter she wrote to her boyfriend overseas."

"It doesn't seem right they can read our letters."

Cici shrugged. "It's security, is all."

"How long have you been in Oak Ridge?"

"Just two months, and they have flown by. Work keeps you busy, and the rest of the time we're busy having fun. There are dances here almost every night—it's like heaven. And the men! There are more men here than any other place in the country right now, except Army bases. But these men aren't headed overseas next week; they're staying right here! I mean, you have to be careful, of course. Some of them only have one thing on their minds, if you know what I mean." She arched her perfectly formed brow. June nodded.

"Why, we should go out tonight to celebrate your arrival!" Cici beamed. "I bet you could pick up a soldier at the dance."

June winced at this last comment. "Oh, I hardly know how to dance."

"I'll teach you! A pretty thing like you would have no problem getting a boy to teach you, either."

"Maybe I could just watch you dance."

"Nonsense! Being here is a golden opportunity; you mustn't waste it. We will find you a soldier tonight."

"I had a soldier," she snapped, her voice louder than she meant for it to be.

Cici's face deflated. "Oh."

"My fiancé was killed three months ago."

"Oh, you poor thing. I'm so sorry, and me going on this way."

June hadn't meant to blurt out about Ronnie that way. "It's all right. I know you didn't mean anything by it."

"Of course. I shouldn't have pestered you like that. But still, you should come to the dance. It's a whole heap of fun, even if you're not looking for a man."

"I'd love to." June felt tremendously glad to have a friend and something to do tonight. But the dance made her nervous, and she was glad to have an excuse not to flirt or try to catch a soldier's eyes. With that feeling of gladness came the dull pain of guilt, which had become all too familiar.

Ronnie Lawson had lived next door to June her whole life, and they'd been best friends. They saw each other almost every day, running around the woods after school, going to the creek to swim in the summer. A couple of years ago, though, something had changed. Ronnie began to act awkwardly around her, going off to play with other boys that summer and teasing her in front of everyone when they were back at school. One day his taunts about how skinny she was were too cruel. She cried all the way home from school, and Mary found her sulking in the barn. When she told her sister what had happened, Mary acted as though it were the most natural thing in the world, her best friend's betrayal. "He probably just likes you," she said.

"Likes me? He sure doesn't act like it. We always liked each other; we were best friends!"

Mary laughed at her, and June felt her already injured pride take another small blow. "Silly, he doesn't just like you as a friend anymore. I'll bet he's sweet on you. He just doesn't know how to tell you, so he's being mean. I remember boys doing just the same thing to girls when I was in school." She made it sound like that was so long ago, when she'd only just graduated from high school that spring.

June thought her sister was crazy at first, but slowly she did begin to notice things. Ronnie sometimes stared at her in class. One day, she was almost certain, he followed her home from school, walking a distance behind her as though trying to hide. By the next fall, he'd asked her to go steady, and how could she say no?

At first June had been terrified of Ronnie's visits. But by spring, she was used to them. She felt comfortable in Ronnie's arms, happy when he arrived on the porch, but never desperate to see him again, never fiery with desire. He only ever pecked at her mouth or cheek, thankfully not trying to go any further. He seemed to think she was too shy and proper to open her mouth or kiss him back. Maybe she was, yet she couldn't dispel the feeling that if it had been another boy kissing her, she would want to throw her head back, open her mouth to him, and kiss him the way the stars did in the movies.

It was two days before their high school graduation when Ronnie came by to ask if she wanted to go on a walk. June looked to her mother for permission, who nodded, smiling.

"I'll come back to help you with supper," offered June.

"Take your time."

Ronnie was silent as they set out across the field toward

the stand of woods behind his house. He wasn't a talkative sort, but June didn't mind silence. As they neared the forest, she spoke up. "Mama wanted me to invite you and your family over for dinner after graduation. Do you think they'd like to come?"

Ronnie stopped walking. He shook his head. "I can't. I'm catching a ride with Ollie to the bus that afternoon. We're headed to basic training in Alabama."

The words physically impacted her before she could even think through their meaning. She felt as though her head momentarily filled with hot air. "But . . . it's so soon."

"I told you I was going to enlist as soon as we graduated."

She stared at his chubby pink face, still so childlike, not the face of a man who could fight in a war.

"I want to ask you something important," he said, thrusting his hands into his pockets, his face growing serious.

June was scared of what the question might be, and looked down.

"June, I want you to marry me when I get back."

He was facing her now, holding both her hands. She felt cold, even though the air was heavy and hot, and had the desire to run as far as she could.

There was no deciding. She knew the only answer she could give was yes, so she opened her mouth and let the word squeak out. He looked so happy that she couldn't help but smile. His arms enveloped her with a new urgency and passion, his mouth fell on hers, and this time she turned her neck up and kissed him like Vivien Leigh.

"I love you," he whispered in her ear, his breath hot against her cheek.

"I love you, too," she heard herself saying.

But even as the words hung fresh in the humid air, June was certain that she did not love him, not the way a woman is supposed to love her husband. She loved Ronnie as her best childhood friend, but she felt no passion for him as a lover, no desire to spend the rest of her life at his side.

As he walked her back to the house, she realized that the mystery of her blank future had, just like that, been filled in. She would go on living here, on a farm, with Ronnie. Her life would resemble her mother's. It seemed simple and, instantly, unavoidable. And the thought of it made her want to cry.

Ronnie's mother had her over for dinner the night before he was to leave. Suddenly graduation day, which she had looked forward to all year, had become an afterthought, just something else that was happening the day Ronnie left for basic training.

Ronnie lived with his mother and little sister Evie. His father had died of a heart attack a year ago, and his older brother was already overseas. The four of them sat around the table eating a feast of ham, mashed potatoes, green beans, and rolls. Maggie Lawson stared at her son as he ate, and June tried not to notice the terror in her eyes.

"Reckon it'll be even hotter than this in Alabama," Ronnie spoke in between chewing great mouthfuls. Neither his appetite nor his spirits seemed to be affected by his impending departure.

"Don't suppose the Army will give you food this good," said June, smiling appreciatively at Mrs. Lawson.

"They'll give you Hershey bars!" said little Evie.

"I'd rather have Mama's shoofly pie."

Everyone was grinning at Mrs. Lawson, but the poor woman could hardly bring herself to smile back.

"Make sure they take care of you," she said finally.

Ronnie was all confidence. "The Army takes care of its men."

After dinner, he wanted to take June on a walk down to Gregory's Pond. That night his kisses were filled with passion, and his hands touched parts of her they'd never dared go near before. She let them. A feeling of duty had fallen over June ever since Ronnie had asked her to marry him. She didn't seem to be choosing or participating in anything; she just responded however she thought he wanted her to.

Again, his hot, urgent whisper was at her ear, "If you're going to be my wife, it wouldn't be a sin for us to . . ."

He couldn't say the words, but she knew what he meant. And even to this one last outrageous request, she couldn't say no. The boy was going to war, she figured, she had to make him happy on his last night home. And besides, it was over quickly.

Four months later, he was dead.

It had been an afternoon in September when Evie came running over and found June on the porch of the house, shelling peas. As soon as she saw Evie sobbing on the drive, June knew what had happened. It was so fast. Just the day before, she'd gotten her first, and now only, letter from Ronnie after he'd shipped out.

June went with Evie to the Lawsons' house. Mrs. Lawson was crumpled on the kitchen floor in her worn blue apron, curled in a fetal position, moaning. She was a stocky woman, but appeared small and compact, as though tragedy had shrunk her. June didn't know what to do, what to say, but Evie was watching, expecting June to somehow help her mother. June got down on her knees beside the woman and touched her shoulder. "It's June, Mrs. Lawson. Evie told me."

As she said this, her voice cracked, and she felt hot tears spill over her eyes.

Mrs. Lawson became quiet. She sat up and looked at June, taking her hand. "Oh, poor June. You loved him so much. You loved my boy." She embraced June, who was sobbing now herself, partly at the loss of Ronnie, partly at the tremendous guilt of knowing she hadn't ever loved him like she should.

And so the past two months had been full of this gnawing sadness and unrelenting self-hatred. She went through her chores on the farm, more obsessed with Ronnie than she ever had been when they were courting, the perfect image of a miserable young war widow. She cried into her pillow at night, stayed quiet at the dinner table, and spent inordinate amounts of time to herself, walking the paths they used to go down together.

Finally her father suggested that it might do her good to get away from the farm. Why didn't she go work at Oak Ridge with her sister? The idea suited her well enough; she liked the thought of working, and hoped it would distract her from herself.

Because beneath her grief, deeper down than even the guilt, was another feeling, one she wouldn't dare name or even allow herself to think before trying to shake it loose.

Relief.

* * *

June was able to follow her roommate to the bus stop on her first day to be sure she was going to the right place. They had to wait in a long line to get aboard and were forced to stand when they finally got on the bus. Cici grabbed hold of a leather strap hanging from the ceiling, and June looked around for something similar to grab on to. But before she'd spotted anything, the bus began to move, and she felt herself lurch backward into a seat.

It was just after seven A.M., and clouds of dirt kicked up by cars and buses glowed in the morning light. People were marching up and down the boardwalks or standing at bus stops. Even a group of children waited by the side of the road. The bus wound through town into a less developed area to the south, then around the base of a ridge and into another valley. June thought she recognized it as Pine Ridge, near where her grandfather's house had been, but it was too hard to tell with all the construction. As they turned into the valley, another large watchtower appeared, like the one at the entrance, and beyond that, a huge complex of buildings. Vast warehouses connected by parking lots spread out into the distance. The hillside above the valley was treeless and scarred with a large muddy gash. Cranes and trucks appeared to be hard at work building even more facilities there. The scene was stark and industrial and covered in brown dust.

Everyone had to line up to go through "clock alleys." June had been to a training the day before, so she knew to clock in at the alley for her craft, which was operation, since she would be operating a machine. Cici got in the line for operation as well, and June was happy that she didn't have to strike out on her own quite yet. Posted on the wall over their heads was a stern warning: "Employees shall clock in and out only in the alley designated. Employees punching cards in any other alley will be subject to Immediate DISMISSAL." After clocking in, they had to present their badges at a security checkpoint. Here Cici left to report to her job. "Good luck! I'll see you at home tonight, and we'll celebrate your first day."

She gave June's hand a quick squeeze and walked away, tall and perfectly proportioned. After going through two more security checkpoints, June was sent to a training room. Five other girls from her previous training session were already waiting. A woman stood in the front of the room with a brown clipboard in her hand and a serious expression. A poster behind her read: "Everyone pays a loafer's wages. You with hard work, your sons and brothers with LIVES."

The woman began calling out names and ticking them off one by one on her clipboard. June was called out last. The woman put the board down. "I'm Miss Collins, your floor supervisor here at Y-12. I'm going to take you to your cubicles. You should have been trained on the basics of this in the bullpen. Your job is to operate a machine. You will be working in the same cubicle with the same machine every day. Your job is simple, but it is of vital importance. You must be diligent and alert. We cannot tolerate mistakes. You will watch the meters and adjust the dials to make sure they stay in the right range."

Miss Collins marched them deeper into the building. Long rows of lights shone down from enormous high ceilings, illuminating metal equipment. Industrial noises screeched and echoed in the distance. Miss Collins stopped in front of a row of tall machines, each with a female operator perched on a stool in front of it, spaced about ten feet from one another. "These are your cubicles," she said, and began pointing out where each of them should sit. The "cubicles" were actually large metal boxes that reached all the way to the ceiling and were covered in meters, knobs, and levers. June had been given a diagram of the machines in her training, so she was familiar with the design. Still, the scale of the operation was a surprise.

Those sitting at the cubicles got up to let the new workers sit down. June looked up at her cubicle as she sat and noticed that "General Electric" was etched into the metal. She stared at the array of levers and knobs.

"You've been trained on how to turn the knobs?" asked the dimpled girl who had given June her stool.

"Yes."

"Okay. Why don't you give it a try?"

June looked at the meters and then gave the knob a slight turn to the right. The needles on the meters responded, pointing upward where they should be.

"Good job," said the girl. "It's not too hard; you'll get the hang of it fast. The tricky thing is not getting bored. You have to find things to occupy your mind, you know, or you can go crazy staring at these meters."

"Thanks," said June, and the girl moved off down the hallway. She'd been on the night shift, which someday June would have to work as well because shifts rotated.

June watched the meters carefully and adjusted the dials every time they started to veer in the wrong direction. Miss Collins wandered up and down observing the girls, and June felt herself sitting up straighter on the stool as Miss Collins walked by. It was simple enough; occasionally she had to adjust the levers as well, but after half an hour, she was already beginning to feel as though she had mastered the machine. There were switches she didn't understand, labeled "Tank Operation," "Vacuum Operation," "Heater Operation," but they had been told to ignore them. The knobs and meters all indicated different numbers, and the girls were supposed to keep them at the right numbers, though they had no idea what they meant.

Soon her mind began to wander. She was still staring at the meters, but it was becoming increasingly difficult to *think* about them. All sorts of other thoughts were creeping in, taking over. She could feel the itchy wool of her skirt through her cotton slip. She wondered how the other girls were doing, if their machines were just the same as hers or different. Occasionally she even looked over to see what they were doing, but always turned back to her machine as soon as she spotted Miss Collins. She wondered if Miss Collins had a beau or even any friends, for that matter; she seemed so stiff and serious. But that was probably just because of the importance of her job. Maybe outside of work, she was friendly.

She wondered what Mama and Daddy were doing back at the farm right now. What would she be doing if she were there, too? A cold wave of homesickness washed over her, and she tried to stop thinking about it. *Homesick* was an appropriate word. When she thought about home, an actual physical sensation overwhelmed her, a longing she could feel in her stomach. She saw the sun rising behind the house, her bed laid out with one of Grandma's quilts; she thought of Mama taking biscuits out of the oven, Daddy wolfing them down at the table. Even the thought of her crazy grandfather Jericho talking to his hound dogs made her heart swell up into her throat. She tried to focus on the meters.

At least she had Cici to be friends with. They would go to dinner at the cafeteria together tonight and maybe to a movie afterward; June would suggest it. Cici seemed to know about all the dances going on; maybe tagging along with her room-mate wouldn't be so bad. She wondered why Cici didn't like Lizbeth, their other roommate. June had only met her once, but she seemed nice enough.

There was so much noise in this room, and June wondered what was responsible for it. What was this machine doing? What did the meters measure? What did her knob control?

She heard loud, fast footsteps behind her and turned to see a thin man with dark hair and glasses, young but important-looking in a brown suit, walk through the hall. His eyes met hers, and she turned back to the machine, ashamed to have been caught neglecting her duties. For a moment she felt glad that he had looked at her, then immediately embarrassed and ashamed by her gladness. What would a man like that, prob-ably some sort of top-level official who could walk through all the different areas of the plant, want with her? Besides, she had no right to want men to look at her anyway, and with that thought, her mind turned, as it always did, to Ronnie.

Where was he now? She wanted to believe in heaven but couldn't quite picture it. Could Ronnie see her now? Did he know what this machine was doing? Could he read her mind? The thought shook her, forced her to look away from the me-ters, down at her hands. She was lost in her guilt, imagining that if Ronnie could see her now, he'd know for sure that she didn't love him. Ronnie had been killed in Saint-Malo, France. They had an atlas at home, and she had found it on the map of Europe, so far away that it hardly seemed real. She and Ronnie had been in French class together just a year ago, learning the language of this country where he had gone to die. She thought of Ronnie's mother, huddled on the floor, sobbing. She would write Mrs. Lawson a letter.

There must be so many Mrs. Lawsons all across America. Not just America, of course—all over the world. And to think of the places where bombs were being dropped, where Hitler had invaded. . . . June felt lucky to be here in America. Why should she be spared when so many were suffering, dying? What would she do if she were a man and had to go fight? She couldn't imagine it; she would be so scared. How did they know what to do in battle? She knew, of course, that they were trained, but how could you ever know what to do when people were trying to kill you? Was it different for men? Did they have some innate understanding of how to fight, how to kill?

When her shift was finally over, June turned the machine over to another girl. It felt wonderful to be off the stool, and she couldn't wait to get home and talk to Cici. In the back of her mind, she wondered how in the world she would do this again all day tomorrow, and the day after that, but she pushed that thought away, as she'd been pushing her thoughts away all day long, and paid attention to how glorious it felt to not be staring at those meters.

She followed the other girls through the clock alley and back out to the bus stop. A bus was waiting, already crowded with other workers whose shifts had just ended. This time June knew to find a strap and hold on. Just as the bus began to lurch forward, the man in the brown suit jumped aboard, barely keeping his balance as he climbed the steps and grabbed the strap next to June's. She faced out the window, but he only had room to stand sideways, facing her. As the bus turned out of the parking lot, she struggled to keep from leaning into him, aware that her shoulder was grazing his chest. She stared down at his shoes, the leather deeply creased and covered in dried mud. The bus came to a sudden stop, and her body tensed as she tried to keep herself from falling into him. She felt her shoulder make contact with his body. "Excuse me," she murmured.

"Certainly." His voice was deep and assured. She looked up and met his dark eyes. His stare felt intense, and she looked down again quickly. She could feel the warmth of his body next to hers and realized her heart was beating hard and fast.

(Courtesy of the Department of Energy)

(Courtesy of the Department of Energy)

Chapter 2

SAM CANTOR HAD ARRIVED IN OAK RIDGE ONE YEAR EARLIER. He'd been waiting for months for his assignment, watching as one by one his colleagues in the physics department at Berkeley all went off to work for the Army. When he finally got the order to report to Tennessee, it had been a relief. He was only twenty-nine and could feel the judgmental stares of strangers wondering why he wasn't in uniform. At least now he would be a part of the war effort. During the long train ride to Knoxville, he watched as soldiers piled off and on at every stop, kissing girlfriends and mothers good-bye, slapping fathers and brothers on the back with fragile bravado. Sam wondered which of these leave-takings would turn out to be tragedies and judged himself for cowardice cleverly disguised as intellect.

Sam piled into what the private cheerfully called a "stretch car" to make the journey from Knoxville to the Clinton Engineer Works. A Chevrolet had been cut in half and some boards and pieces of sheet metal nailed across its midsection to create an elongated vehicle that looked like something out of a Looney Tunes cartoon. Sam sat on the boards between two other men also reporting for employment at the CEW. While the feeling of their hot bodies pushed up against his was deeply unpleasant, he consoled himself with the thought that they would be the first to be flung out on the side of the road if the car fell apart.

The odor of unwashed bodies mingled with that of gasoline. Despite the proximity of his neighbors, though, Sam was cold, unused to the damp eastern climate after three years in California. He ached with tiredness, days of inadequate sleep taking their toll. First there had been the train ride, then the last two nights at the Andrew Johnson Hotel. The place was overflowing with out-of-towners looking for work in Oak Ridge, and Sam was forced to share a room with three other men, one a genuine hillbilly who didn't seem to own shoes. Sam himself was in ragged shape, worse than usual—and usually his clothes needed mending and his face shaving. He was pale and thin, and his too-long brown hair curled at the ends. A pair of thick round glasses magnified the dark circles under his eyes. He needed a cigarette badly. A hot bath and a clean bed wouldn't be bad either. Above all, he needed a stiff drink.

"Is tha-it ee-it?" The man to his left seemed to be speaking, but Sam couldn't decipher a word through the man's piercing twang.

"Is tha-it ee-it?"

"What?" asked Sam helplessly.

"Tha Clinton Engineer Works."

The man to Sam's right leaned over him. "Yes, sir, I do believe that's it."

Sam looked up from his companion and saw they were approaching a tall fence covered in barbed wire and a concrete tower, from which a man with a large rifle looked down. The stretch car stopped behind about twenty other vehicles all waiting to enter. When the car finally made it through the security gate forty minutes later, they drove into a massive construction site. Workers climbed on huge piles of wood and metal, the road was clogged with trucks going in both directions, and the damp air was heavy with the stinging sweet smell of asphalt and lumber. In the midst of the cranes and half-built buildings stood a large billboard with a picture of three monkeys with their hands on their eyes, ears, and mouth, respectively. The sign commanded: "What you see here, what you hear here, what you do here, let it stay here."

Around a bend, they came upon a community of trailer homes, row after row of nondescript white boxes winding around a semicircle. There were no trees in this newly constructed area, just prodigious amounts of dirt. Newly paved roads wound up a hillside covered in small prefabricated homes. Farther on was something of a town with a market, pharmacy, and cinema constructed around a small cement plaza, and beyond this loomed the Hill, where a broad white building housed the CEW administrative offices.

The stretch car stopped in front of a wooden boardwalk, but it was impossible for Sam to get out without placing his foot in a trough of mud. As he felt his one pair of shoes being sucked into the muck, he tried to focus on the positive—he was finally out of the car.

Inside, a large reception area resounded with chatter and the sound of high heels clicking on tile. After waiting in a long line, Sam spoke to a receptionist with blond curls. She told him he would probably be kept here for two days as he underwent orientation and security procedures and filled out paperwork. "But I've been filling out paperwork for two days already in Knoxville!" he snapped.

The blonde was unfazed. "I'm sorry, sir, but it's Army procedure. Fill these out," she said as she thrust a stack of documents toward him, "and take them to Mrs. Hawthorne at the other side of the room"—she pointed—"and she will take care of you. Welcome to Oak Ridge."

He sat on a hard wooden chair and faced the forms. *Name:* Samuel Abraham Cantor. *Date of Birth:* December 14, 1913. *Place of Birth:* Brooklyn, New York. *Previous Employer:* University of California, Berkeley. *Position Held:* Assistant Professor. He had provided the information on countless forms already.

A wide smile was stamped across Mrs. Hawthorne's face. "Mr. . . . oh, excuse me, *Dr.* Cantor. Welcome! Here's some information for you about life in Oak Ridge"—she pushed a number of brochures at him—"and Manhattan Engineer District procedures." She winked. "Don't worry, Dr. Cantor, you're almost done with the paperwork. Just as soon as we get your security clearance, we'll send you on a quick tour. For now I'd like you to attend a lecture on safety and security just down the hall here."

He felt around his pockets for a stray cigarette for the fourth time since leaving Knoxville. There still weren't any. "How long until I get my housing assignment?"

"With any luck we'll have that all set up in the morning!"

"Where will I stay tonight?"

"In the guest house, Dr. Cantor. It's lovely, I assure you."

After the safety and security lecture, there were similar presentations on first aid, Tennessee driving laws, and most useless of all, Tennessee customs and folklore. "Welcome to Tennessee," said the serious-looking man lecturing a room of thirty-odd new employees, "the Volunteer State, so called because of the many brave Tennesseans who volunteered to join the Texans in their fight for independence."

Sam's eyelids slowly descended. He bit his tongue to try and keep himself awake as the man discussed the Tennessee state bird and told a story about Davy Crockett. Behind him, a large poster inquired, "Are you really doing your part for security??" Sam squinted at the other audience members. The worker beside him was wearing dirty coveralls, a pack of cigarettes sticking out of his chest pocket. Sam stared at the cigarettes, full of longing.

It was seven hours before he finally got a smoke, bummed from the engineer who was to be his roommate for the night. The young man was thrilled to find out that both he and Sam had grown up in New York City. Sam didn't particularly feel like reminiscing about Coney Island and egg creams, but he desperately needed a cigarette, so he gave in to his roommate's excitement. They puffed by the window of their small but hospitable room.

"You oughta see what they call spaghetti here. What I wouldn't give for a meal at my cousin Eddie's restaurant on 187th Street! You ever been up that way?" his companion asked in a Bronx accent.

"I'm afraid not."

"I miss the old neighborhood. My whole family lives there, you know? And it's where I went to school, where I went to church. You Jewish?"

He asked the question innocently, but Sam still paused before replying, "Yes."

"Yeah. I miss all the Jews in New York. Funny, huh? Guess I'm just real homesick."

Sam said nothing but drew on his cigarette. The boy lacked menace; he seemed genuinely nostalgic for Jews. Sam's silence didn't seem to worry him. "You understand a word these folks are saying?"

"Not a damn thing," said Sam. He leaned back in his chair, stretching his legs.

"I never heard an accent like it!"

"Say, Mikey, you know where we can get a drink around here?"

"There's beer at the canteen, but that's all. It's a dry county, haven't you heard? Prohibition never ended in Tennessee."

"Damn! I could sure use a drink right now."

"I know what you mean. But be careful—you can get arrested if you're caught bringing liquor in through the gates. This is the honest-to-God Bible Belt. You're not in Flatbush anymore!"

Sam sucked at the end of the cigarette until it tasted terrible, not wanting to let it go. Grudgingly, he stubbed it out and tossed it from the window.

His security clearance came through the next day, and Sam got his promised tour from Private John Bagger, who hardly looked older than fifteen, with a small round face and ears too large for it. He drove Sam around in an open-top car and told him about the Manhattan Engineer District's amazing achievements in building this town out of nothing. "Just one year ago, sir, this land was empty except for the occasional farm or cabin. There was only one paved road on the whole reservation! Now there's a fully functioning city." They passed a few makeshift buildings that were hardly more than shanties, with sloping roofs and noticeable gaps in the walls.

"There's certainly a lot of dirt."

"Yes, sir! The construction has kicked up a lot of mud, as I'm sure you've noticed. I hope you've got a good pair of boots!"

Sam looked down at his once-black shoes, now caked grayish brown.

"We're driving on the main street of Oak Ridge, Tennessee Avenue. To our right are brand-new residential communities. You'll never get lost here because of the clever system of street names. The avenues are named alphabetically from east to west after the states of the union. For instance, Arkansas is the easternmost, next over is California, and so on. Then any street that turns off of one of the avenues has a name beginning with the same letter, A for Arkansas, C for California—"

Sam couldn't bear any more and cut him off. "Yes, I see. That is terribly clever."

Private Bagger had turned onto New York Avenue so Sam could get a better look at the homes. The yards were covered in mud and they all looked eerily similar to one another, but not altogether awful. An effort had been made to leave some trees standing in the midst of the construction. Still, the winding cul-de-sacs and rows of identical houses had the look of children dressed up in adult clothing. They wanted to be a real neighborhood but hadn't quite managed.

"You may notice that the houses all have a similar look; that's because they are prefabricated for us. We call them cemestos, because they're constructed of a mixture of cement and asbestos. A new house goes up in Oak Ridge every thirty minutes."

"Well, that explains the noise." Sam had spent another sleepless night in the guest house.

They drove down the hill, out of the cemesto houses and into a neighborhood of trailers. "We have a wide range of dwellings, depending on people's position in the MED, the size of their family, and the length of their stay here."

Private Bagger pointed to a barbed-wire fence and gate off to the left. "That's one of the prohibited areas. You have to pass through a security gate to enter the CEW from the outside, and once inside, you'll have to pass through another gate to get to the prohibited area where you work. It's very important you keep your badge with you at all times!" Sam had been given a badge with his picture, a payroll number, some letters representing the restricted areas where he would be allowed to work, and the Roman numeral IV, which gave him access to all the information about the site where he was to be working for the Tennessee Eastman Corporation, though the various other work sites were still restricted.

"And here on your right is the dormitory where you'll be staying—"

"Excuse me, did you say 'dormitory'?"

"Yes, sir, this is it right here." Private Bagger pulled the car up in front of a four-story rectangular institution.

"There must be some mistake. I'm not supposed to be staying in a dormitory."

"Well, that's what it says here." The boy tapped the file beside him. "I'm sure it's just temporary. With so many people coming and going, it can take a while to make housing arrangements."

Private Bagger was already leaping out of the car, grabbing his suitcase, but Sam was paralyzed with rage. "Please take me back to headquarters."

Private Bagger's face seemed to grow even smaller with distress. "I'm sorry, sir, I'm under orders to drop you off here."

Sam jumped out of the car and grabbed his bag from the boy's hand. "Thank you, Private. That was a very informative tour."

"You're welcome, sir. Hope you enjoy your time in Oak Ridge."

Sam approached the front desk, explaining to the woman there that this must be a mistake, but she assured him that it was not. "You're lucky, Dr. Cantor. Last week we were squeezing them in five to a room."

He left his bag at the dormitory and walked back toward the administrative building at a quick, determined pace. Lack of sleep compounded his already acute sense of injustice. He was irrational with exhaustion, ready to take on the entire Army if need be to get himself a private room for the night.

He wound up back in line behind the blond receptionist. "There's been a mistake with my housing assignment," he sputtered as soon as he reached her. She cut him off immediately.

"You'll need to speak to Mr. Newman. He's in charge of housing. Down this hallway . . ."—she pointed—"third office to the left. Knock on his door, and I'll let him know to expect you."

He did as he was told. A hearty voice called out, "Come in!"

"Hello, I'm Dr. Samuel Cantor," he began calmly, formally, preparing to build into an impassioned rant.

Mr. Newman, an imposing figure in a gray suit, half rose and extended his hand. "Doug Newman. Pleased to meet you. Have a seat."

Sam sat across from him, balancing his hat on his knee. He could hear the sound of hammering coming from the construction outside. Mr. Newman leaned back in his chair. "So, Dr. Cantor, how can I help you?"

"There's been a mistake with my housing assignment. I've been told I'm to stay in Dormitory Two with three other men in my room. This is unacceptable."

Mr. Newman nodded sympathetically. "I'm sorry to hear about the situation. As you can see, and hear, we are in the midst of an unprecedented building project. Now, I work for the Roane-Anderson Company. Have you heard of it?"

Sam shook his head, and Mr. Newman continued. "We're a new company that the Army has hired to run this town." Mr. Newman took a cigarette case out of his breast pocket, and Sam couldn't stop his eyes from widening at the sight of it. "You smoke?" Mr. Newman asked and held out the open case for him.

"Thank you," said Sam as he eagerly grabbed a cigarette. "I haven't had a chance to buy a pack since I got here." He felt around his pockets for a match, but Mr. Newman had already struck one and was holding it out for him. Sam met the flame with the end of his precious cigarette and inhaled deeply.

Mr. Newman lit his own cigarette and leaned back again. "So, Dr. Cantor, part of our job—our biggest job, really—is sorting out adequate housing for all of the employees here at the Clinton Engineer Works. To tell you the truth, the Army has hired more people than we have room for at the moment."

Sam tried not to be distracted by the glorious jolt of tobacco. "Mr. Newman, I am a highly respected scientist. The government is entrusting me with resources and top-secret information. They cannot expect me to live in a dormitory like a college freshman."

"I understand your frustration, Dr. Cantor. Let me assure you that an effort will be made to rectify this. In fact"—he began shuffling through a stack of papers on his desk—"I have the paperwork here to assign workers to ten new trailers, and I'm going to make sure that you are placed in one of these."

Sam remembered the depressing rings of trailers. "Thank you, sir."

"It will probably be a week until these are up and running. Can you manage in the dormitory until then?"

Sam clenched his jaw. "I can manage. But I want your company to know that I think it's a fine way to greet the scientists you have working here—by throwing them into accommodations that are hardly better than barracks!" He stood to make his point fully dramatic, took a final drag of the lovely cigarette, and stubbed it out in Mr. Newman's ashtray. "Thank you for the cigarette and your help."

"You're welcome, Dr. Cantor." He stubbed out his own cigarette as Sam started out the door.

"Oh, and one last thing," said Mr. Newman, and Sam turned back. "We have better men than you, Dr. Cantor, living in Army barracks in far more godforsaken spots than Oak Ridge." His face was still friendly, but his voice was cold.

* * *

SAM WALKED SLOWLY back to the dormitory, the anger and adrenaline gone, replaced by a great tiredness. It didn't matter if anyone was in the room or not when he got back, he was going to sleep. He could sleep for two days if he wanted; he didn't have to start work until Tuesday.

"Sam!" he heard someone call out, and he stopped, wondering who might know him in this foreign place. He turned and saw Charlie Stone crossing the muddy street toward him, smiling and waving.

"Sam, it's so good to see you! I'd hoped you'd make it out this way." Charlie patted him on the back, and Sam shook his hand heartily.

"Sure is good to see a friendly face!"

"When did you get here?"

"Just two days ago. Is this place as awful as it seems?"

Charlie laughed. "It grows on you." Sam looked skeptical. "Truly, you'll see. There's a certain charm to frontier living. Say, can I get you a cup of coffee? I was just headed to the canteen."

Charlie led him to a cafeteria near the town site. The two men had been friends in graduate school at Princeton in the thirties. Charlie had been the nicest guy in the physics department.

The cafeteria was bustling, and the strong aroma of bacon alerted Sam to the fact that he was hungry. "They serve breakfast all day here, and the place is open twenty-four hours to accommodate all the different shifts," explained Charlie.

Sam got a plate full of eggs, bacon, and biscuits the likes of which he'd never seen before. They were dense yet fluffy, dripping with butter. He crunched into the bacon with the unavoidable guilt that came from disappointing his mother, but it passed quickly.

Charlie sat across from him with a cup of coffee and a tuna sandwich. "How long's it been? The last time I saw you was back in Princeton . . . in what? Thirty-nine?"

"That sounds right. How have you been? How's Ann?" Ann was Charlie's wife, a thin but pretty girl from old Boston money.

"We're well. Moving here has been . . . a challenge for her. But listen, Sam, could you do us a huge favor?"

"What?" Sam asked through a gluttonous mouthful of eggs.

"Would you move into a house with us? We're on a waiting list to get one, and since we don't have children, it would help if we had a boarder."

Sam swallowed and looked up. "Are you serious? I'm supposed to be living in a trailer; of course, I'd be thrilled! Are you sure it would be all right?"

"Yes, yes! You'd be doing us a favor. Really, I don't know how long it will take us to get a house otherwise."

"Well, if Ann will have me, I'll do it."

"Ann will be delighted."

"You've made my day, Charlie!"

"Wonderful, then it's all settled. So what took you so long to get here, Cantor?"

"Security clearance took forever."

"I see. And that wouldn't have anything to do with past bad behavior?"

"Who knows? They interviewed every member of my family they could get their hands on—scared my poor aunt half to death. She thought I'd become a spy. Apparently, it's very

suspicious to U.S. Army Intelligence that I have so many rela-
tives in Germany. Never mind, of course, that all those relations have either fled or disappeared."

Charlie nodded solemnly. "Well, thank goodness you're
here now. We could use you."

"Is there anyone else here we know?"

"Will Kellerman's here. Some other names you'd probably
recognize, but none of the old gang."

"Most are in New Mexico, I guess."

Charlie shook his head and whispered, "Not here." In a
normal voice he said, "I wouldn't know." His friendly eyes
widened meaningfully. He looked down at the table and
picked up Sam's battered hat. Its edges were frayed and the
top drooped, pathetically. "I know there's a war on, but can
we get you a new hat?"

Sam smiled. "I'll see what I can do." He gathered the
remainders of eggs and biscuit crumbs up onto his fork and
shoved them into his mouth.

(Courtesy of the Department of Energy)

Chapter 3

$\mathcal{D}$ESPITE THE FACT THAT HE WAS WEARING ALMOST ALL THE clothes he owned and was further wrapped in two blankets, Joe was cold. Each breath he took sent icy air tearing into his nose and chest. The woodstove in the middle of the room couldn't combat the wind ripping through the plywood walls of the hutment, nor could the thin, flannel blankets.

The door opened, and a blast of air assaulted him. It was Ralph, finally coming home from the rec hall. Joe watched him walk to the cot to take off his boots. As he started to take off his jacket, Joe whispered, "Ain't no point. You're gonna need that on to get through this night."

"I'm hot." Ralph hung the jacket on a clothesline strung up across the room.

"You're crazy." Joe rolled over in his cot to face the wall, the weak heat from the stove now on his back.

Sometimes it was no use talking sense to Ralph. Still, the boy was his only real friend here at Oak Ridge, at least the only person he'd known long enough to trust. They'd come up from Alabama together a year and a half ago to work in a labor gang. Now they shared a hutment with three other men. The plywood box could hardly be called a house. It was sixteen feet by sixteen feet, and their cots and chairs filled the room right up. There were no windows, just pieces of wood on a hinge you could open in summer. It had been hot when they arrived in July, hotter than Alabama if that was even possible. The colored hutments were built on the lowest point of land in Oak Ridge, a swamp overridden with mosquitoes. They had to keep the windows open at night, and the mosquitoes were as much residents of the place as he and the other workers living there. Those first nights had been sleepless, too, but it was because he couldn't stop sweating or scratching the great pink welts on his legs and arms.

Joe tried to remember that heat, the awful insects humming above his head, and wondered if it was worse than this November cold. But summer seemed like a dream, impossible to recapture. At least now he'd gotten used to things. Those first months he had thought he wouldn't be able to stand being away from his wife Moriah. On those sleepless, sweltering nights, he'd had half a mind to walk right out of the wretched hutment and hitch a ride down to Alabama where Moriah and the children were waiting. Now he knew he could stand it a little longer, make more money, get Moriah up here just as soon as possible.

Thirty-eight dollars a week, weather permitting. That was what had brought him here in the first place and that was the reason he stayed. They got fifty-seven and a half cents per hour for forty hours, eighty-six and a quarter cents per hour for overtime, and as long as it didn't storm, he could work eighteen hours overtime. Joe had always been a hard worker.

He was six foot two with strong, long arms, toughened by years of work, and was proud of his ability to provide for his family. That was all a man needed, really, and it kept him out of trouble.

The labor gangs were working on huge buildings, bigger by far than anything Joe had ever seen. Whatever it was the Army was building here, it sure made an impression. He didn't have any experience doing construction but was a fast learner. These days, the foreman had him mixing and pouring concrete, endless amounts of the stuff. By the end of the day, every muscle in his body called for a reprieve, his back ached, and his shoulders felt pinched with pain. But he'd never been one to complain about hard work. What bothered him most about the job was the landscape. He missed the country. He felt as though he might as well be on Mars, looking around at the sprawling mass of beams and frames and half-finished factories. Steel, concrete, men in hard hats, and mud as far as he could see in any direction. It oppressed him. It was unnatural and ungodly, and he missed the fields, the trees, birdsong, and animal noises, rather than the relentless hammering, drilling, and rumbling of engines.

When he wasn't working, he kept to himself or palled around with Ralph. They got plenty of food in the colored cafeteria, though you had to be sure to get there before they quit serving. There were always two choices, "not spicy" or "spicy" for the folks from Louisiana who liked that sort of thing. He'd tried the spicy food once, but it just burned his mouth. The not-spicy food kept his belly full, but what he wouldn't give for some of Moriah's fried okra and collard greens.

He wrote to her and the children every day as best he could, though his spelling wasn't good. He'd never got past the fourth grade in school and knew he got things wrong. But he had to stay connected to them, and in return they each sent him little notes and drawings. He kept them all, neatly folded in his footlocker under the cot. He put everything of value he owned, which wasn't much, in the locker, because there was no lock on the hutment. Be charitable to all men, but don't trust any of them, his father had always said.

He went to church regularly, though he made it a point to stay away from the holy rollers in town. Joe had always taken his spirituality seriously and never trusted fanatics, the roadside prophets too easily overcome by the Holy Spirit, and there were plenty of that type here in Oak Ridge. Ralph still came to church with him, but the boy seemed to seek out trouble. Ralph had always been hot-tempered. He'd shown up one day about five years back on the Hopewell farm, couldn't have been older than fourteen, with the nastiest broken arm Joe had ever seen. Said he was looking for work, but he could hardly stand with the pain in his arm. Joe figured he must have been running from trouble, but something in the boy's firmly set lips moved him. He brought Ralph home, and Moriah took care of him, setting his arm in a splint. It was never quite right, but he was strong and made up for it with his good arm.

Ralph went to church with them and became a favorite because of his strong tenor. Reverend Clayton said Ralph had the sort of voice that brought sinners back to God. He still didn't drink or gamble, at least not that Joe knew about, and that was saying something in this place. Wasn't much else to do, and the rec halls were filled with illegal hooch and poker games. Joe stayed away from that stuff, but occasionally he went with Ralph to the rec hall. It was little more than a barn. Sometimes a screen was pulled down to show race films. Other times he played checkers with Ralph or the other men. But he always kept an eye out and made sure both of them got out of there if things turned rowdy. Just last week a man had been stabbed in the hutment next door over a five-dollar gambling debt. Folks had too much time on their hands. That and they weren't allowed to live with their women, which stirred up trouble.

In any case, it wasn't drinking or gambling that worried Joe about the boy; Ralph's real problem was his temper. After a year, he finally told Joe why he wound up on the Hopewell farm. His stepfather had been hitting Ralph's mother until the boy got in the middle. He'd beaten the man badly and hadn't waited to see what shape he'd be in when he regained consciousness.

"Joe?" Ralph whispered. "You awake?"

"No, sir. I'm dreaming of a furnace."

"It ain't right."

"What?"

"This ain't no fit place for a man to live. We were better off working in the fields."

"We could hardly feed ourselves."

"At least we ain't have to answer to no one but Mr. Hopewell. Here we've got the whole Army against us."

"It won't last forever, Ralph. War'll end someday. Least you ain't fighting."

Ralph had tried to enlist, but the Army wouldn't take him on account of his arm. Sometimes Joe thought the boy would have been better off serving, with all that fight inside of him. But selfishly, he was glad Ralph was here. Even though he was just a boy, he was a good friend. Hot-headed, yes, but

Joe knew if he or Moriah were in any kind of trouble, Ralph would be the first person there to help them.

Ralph rolled over, away from him. The boy got big ideas from the colored newspapers his friends in the rec hall gave him. Sometimes he'd read them aloud to Joe. He read haltingly, betraying his lack of education, but far better than Joe could read to himself. Last summer the papers had stories about Negroes rioting in cities and often getting killed. Ralph would get too worked up reading about it to keep his voice steady and finally would put the paper down to go outside and walk or smoke. Ralph wore a Double V pin on his jacket, which he'd ordered from the *Pittsburgh Courier*. The two V's stood for Double Victory—democracy at home and abroad. Joe told him it would only draw attention to him, but Ralph just laughed in a bitter way and said white folks wouldn't know what it meant anyway.

Joe didn't worry too much about the things Ralph said. He was just a kid, after all, didn't have the same worries Joe did trying to feed three children. Joe was forty-eight and had worked for Mr. Hopewell as long as he could remember. This was his first time out of Alabama, and sometimes he missed the red dirt of the farm so much that he felt his chest tighten—strange because he'd always cursed that piece of land where he had been born and stuck his whole life. But it was home, and miss it he did, just as he missed the little cabin where he had grown up and where his own children had been born. Shabby as it was, it was a real house, suitable for a family. Moriah would be in the wooden bed at the back now, asleep under one of her quilts with little Ben in her arms. The girls would be sleeping in their bed across the room, the only time they were ever quiet. If he had been there, he would kiss their soft cheeks, tiptoe over to his bed, and slide in behind Moriah and Ben, wrapping her in his arms. If it was cold in the cabin, they would keep each other warm. If he was feeling hopeless, she would put her warm hand on his cheek, talk to him in her rich, soothing voice until he was calm.

In a moment, Joe was asleep, still shivering but dreaming of Moriah.

Then before he knew it, the alarm was ringing—a harsh, tinny sound. At home in Alabama, Joe would wake up naturally at dawn with the sun's rising and the rooster's crowing. It wasn't like he'd enjoyed waking up so much back then, but it was more peaceful than greeting the day in this plywood box with that awful little clock blaring at him.

It was his and Ralph's week on the early shift; the other men in the room stayed still or groaned or rolled their heads under their pillows. Joe silenced the alarm and swung his legs over the side of the cot. He went over to a washbasin and braced himself for the touch of icy water. The joints in his fingers ached as he slid his hands into the bowl and splashed his face, as quickly as possible. That woke a man up.

He and Ralph would get breakfast in the cafeteria, then head to their gang. Joe looked forward to breakfast, mostly because the cafeteria was well heated, and he would be comfortable for the first time in twelve hours. Then it was back out into the cold to work, but labor kept a body warm.

Ralph was still in bed. Joe gave his shoulder a squeeze. "Ralph!" he said in a loud whisper, trying not to disturb his roommates.

Ralph didn't respond, and Joe shook him hard. "Wake up, boy!"

Ralph let out a little moan and rolled over. Half asleep like this, he looked like a child.

"Come on," Joe whispered more gently. "Let's get some coffee and grits in you, and you'll feel better."

Ralph didn't say a word on the way to the cafeteria. "You shouldn't stay out so late," chided Joe.

Ralph hunched into his jacket, hands dug deep into the side pockets.

The sun was just rising up over the ridge in front of them, bright but not warm. Joe watched his breath cloud in front of his mouth as he spoke. "Got to take care of yourself, Ralph."

Ralph sighed. "Yes, sir, I hear."

Joe doubted his lectures ever did much good, but he suspected the boy appreciated them, despite his surly attitude. Ralph's daddy had never been around, and his stepfather had obviously been no-account.

The colored cafeteria was crowded with all the men on the early shift filling up for the morning's work ahead of them. Sure enough, the room was sweltering with radiator heat and the crowd of bodies. It was loud, too; the walls echoed with conversations, laughter, even a harmonica coming from somewhere—too much noise for that time of the morning.

They got platefuls of biscuits and gravy and mugs of black "coffee"—not real coffee but an earthy-tasting substitute. It was hot at least, as were the biscuits, even if they were dry and crumbled at the touch. The gravy was thin, with only a couple of puny pieces of sausage bobbing in it, but the food would keep him going till their next meal in five hours.

Ralph gulped down the fake coffee but only picked at his biscuit. "Aren't you hungry?" asked Joe.

He shrugged. Times like this, Joe wanted to shake some

sense into him. Why was he always so sullen, making himself so miserable? If a man puts a plate of hot food in front of you, you eat it, simple as that. "You ain't sick, is you?"

"Nah, I ain't sick." Ralph took a big bite. You just had to nudge him, like a child.

"Got a letter from Moriah yesterday. Ben learned to say 'Daddy' when she showed him my letters."

Ralph had a soft spot for the children. He almost smiled.

"Where were you last night, anyhow?"

"Rec hall."

"Playing checkers?"

Ralph shook his head. "Talking." He leaned into Joe and spoke in a low voice. "Some men here got real big ideas."

"What sort of ideas?"

"Ideas about how we can change things." Ralph leaned back, as though to let that sink in.

Joe was suspicious of this sort of talk. "You getting into trouble?"

"No, sir." Ralph stabbed some biscuit and shoved it into his mouth. "It's not like that. These are good folks who think we deserve to be treated better for helping our country fight this war."

A bell went off, which meant it was six fifty, time for the men to go meet their crews. Everyone began getting up, the room loud with the sounds of trays being slammed down and chairs sliding against the rough floor. Ralph stood, and Joe followed.

"Just be careful," said Joe. He couldn't help but sound disapproving.

They would be pouring concrete that morning, laying the foundation for yet another new building. He and Ralph met the rest of their gang, and they were all loaded into the back of a bus to drive across the reservation to the site. The buildings being built were giants; for the life of him, Joe couldn't work out what in the world the Army would do with such monstrosities. He looked out over what had been fields and farmland when he first arrived—familiar and so much more fathomable to him than these warehouses, factories, and endless parking lots. Plenty of folks would no doubt marvel at the sight of a city being built practically overnight. It did give you a sense of man's capabilities. Maybe that was what got Ralph so riled up about this place. For a young man, Joe reckoned it would be hard to look around without thinking about what was possible, what men could accomplish, and what a man could do for himself.

The spot where they'd been working all week was at the bottom of a steep valley. It was as though they were filling the valley right up with their construction. He was glad to have a chance to do his part for the war effort, not because of patriotic feelings exactly, but more because he knew so many young men who were off fighting, boys from his church back in Alabama and some of the other field hands from the Hopewell farm. Even young Teddy Hopewell had died in Italy. Moriah had written to Joe after Teddy's death, distraught. She'd looked after him as a child.

Once he was working, Joe's mind wandered less. He became focused on the task at hand, which was a relief because it took his mind off the missing—missing Moriah, missing the children, missing the country. The morning would pass by quickly enough this way, and soon enough another day would be gone. He'd be exhausted, but one day closer to having enough money to send for his family.

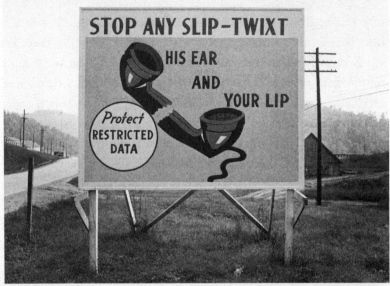

(Courtesy of the Department of Energy)

Chapter 4

_F_OR CICI ROBERTS, THE WAR HAD BEEN AN OPPORTUNITY, AN IN-
ternational crisis disruptive enough for her to undergo a personal transformation. In 1942, she had been a sharecropper's
daughter, beautiful but with a bleak future of poverty, hard
work, and harder religion in front of her. A year later, she had
run off to Nashville with a boy she knew from grade school
who had just enlisted. He wanted to marry her, but as soon
as she got to town, she found a room to share with another
girl and a job as a hostess at a hotel restaurant downtown.
She was hired because she was pretty, and the rich ladies
who came to dine there liked to be surrounded by pretty
things. She listened carefully to them and their debutante
daughters. As Cici seated them at perfectly set tables, she absorbed the way they held themselves, the formation of their
vowel sounds. At night, she would lock herself in the hallway bathroom at her rooming house and practice talking like
those Nashville ladies.

By the time she heard about Oak Ridge, her transformation was almost complete. No one ever had to know that her daddy was a sharecropper; she spoke and carried herself like a plantation heiress. What Cici lacked, of course, was actual money. But she recognized a prospect to fix that at the Clinton Engineer Works. Cici loved everything about Oak Ridge—she didn't even mind the mud. She could be whomever she pleased in this strange new town full of people passing through, people from all over who didn't know anything about her or care where she came from. She loved the boys and the parties and the dancing. She loved roller skating and listening to records and how everything here was different from Perry County.

She had to be careful with the boys. It was fun to flirt and be admired, but she always kept her ultimate goal in mind: finding a husband with money. So many girls got swept away at the sight of a uniform, but just because a man was a hotshot in the Army now didn't mean he'd amount to squat when the war was over. Wars can't last forever, and you had to think long-term. It was lovely to be making seventy-five cents an hour, but it wasn't enough. Cici had glimpsed what life was like for the truly wealthy, and saw no reason why it shouldn't be like that for her, too. Her mother had always told her that working hard would get her anything she wanted, but her hardworking mother's body was worn out at forty, and her mother's future held nothing but more work. Cici wasn't going to waste her life working hard; she would use the gifts God had given her, her striking good looks, and see that they secured her a future with as little work in it as possible. She made sure to tell everyone she could that she was here to do her part for the war effort. What she carefully implied was that she had no need for the money she made working in the factory. Her time and energy were being donated as an act of charity. One of the most important lessons she learned in Nashville was that money (or at least the illusion of money) attracted more money.

Cici asked the right questions of her suitors, subtly did her research. You had to find out his plans, what kind of family he was from. She carefully strung along as many boys as possible at a time, giving each just enough attention to keep him wanting more, but not so much that he would get the wrong idea. You couldn't let them get too far; it was important to have a sterling reputation so that when you found the right one, he would marry you. Of course there were older men at Oak Ridge, too, men who already had money. But Cici found that pursuing those types was tricky; they didn't tend to socialize with the young people at the dances and the bowling alley. Besides, most of them were married, and if they weren't, you had to wonder why not. She'd gone on one date with a bald engineer who spent the whole time telling her about his three beloved pet turtles he'd had to leave back in Pennsylvania with his mother. He hadn't tried to kiss her or even hold her hand once all night, which was just as well.

She had meant it when she told June that they'd be best friends. Her new roommate seemed sweet, and to tell the truth, Cici needed a friend. She'd never been good with other girls. Boys she knew how to talk to, but girls always seemed jealous; or maybe it was because she could be a little mean. She was competitive when it came to men, but you had to be, especially in times like these, when there were hardly any of them to go around. But June was perfect; she was mourning a dead fiancé and plain and shy, anyway. Cici was feeling happy and charitable. Things were going so well for her in

Oak Ridge that she ought to share her happiness by reaching out to help this new girl.

She could have nothing to do with the other roommate, Lizbeth, however. It was such a horrible coincidence. She'd recognized the girl as soon as they met; Lizbeth had lived a town over from Cici growing up, and she remembered her from summer revivals. Lizbeth had never let on that she recognized Cici, so it was quite possible she didn't remember. Still, it made Cici nervous; she'd told everyone she met here that she was from Nashville, and Lizbeth might figure out the truth. Cici tried to stay away from her and always treated her coldly. She felt bad about this, but it couldn't be helped. Besides, everyone over in Lewis County was trash. Luckily, Lizbeth didn't spend much time in the dorm. Cici usually had the room all to herself when she got home from work. Today, though, June was there, eagerly waiting for her, like a little dog.

"Hi, Cici!" June called out as she came through the door. "I'm so glad you're home. I've been dying to talk to someone all day!"

Cici began peeling off her boots. "The work's pretty boring, huh?"

"I thought I was going to lose my mind! What do you do to make the time go by?"

"I don't know," said Cici as she sat down on the bed. "Think about what I'm going to do when I get off work, I guess."

"Do you want to go get some dinner?" June asked.

"Yes, just give me a minute to put myself together."

Cici had put a small mirror on the wall over the dresser the girls shared. She went to it now and examined her face to determine what needed to be done. Powder, definitely; the wintry weather was turning her face red. A bit of eye shadow, but not too much; she wanted to look polished, not garish. And lipstick, always.

June was chatty all through dinner. She talked about her family back on their farm and all the mud and dust in town and how many choices there were in the cafeteria. She ate as she talked, wolfing down macaroni and cheese. Cici was surprised to see such a skinny girl eat so much. Some girls are just lucky, she supposed; though really, June was too thin, scrawny, like a tomboy, and she had hardly any bust. Cici was lucky in that department. She had a full bosom, a tiny waist, and long, long legs.

When they finished eating, Cici suggested they go bowling. June giggled. "I've never been bowling!"

"Oh, June, that's so cute! You're such a sweet country girl." Of course Cici had never been bowling before she moved to Nashville either.

All the way to the bowling alley, June kept talking. "So do you work at the same kind of machine as me, turning the knobs and watching the meters?"

"Yes. Don't worry, you get used to it."

"Do you ever wonder what the machines are doing?"

"June, it's not safe to talk about that kind of thing!" Cici looked around to make sure no one could hear them.

"No one's around. Don't you wonder?"

"No! And you shouldn't wonder either."

Finally June was quiet.

The bowling alley was crowded, and Cici looked for boys they could play against. Bowling was an excellent chance to show off your figure while acting helpless—troubled by the heavy ball, confused by the score pad. Of course June really was troubled and confused by it all. She looked a bit stunned by the noise and commotion. Cici went first and showed her how to hold the ball. But June's first attempt wound up in the gutter—and her second, third, and fourth. She was getting discouraged and Cici was getting bored when a group of four soldiers took the lane beside them.

June sent her fifth ball immediately into the gutter and trudged back to try again. Cici saw the boys looking over at them. June plopped the ball right into the gutter again and gave Cici a miserable look. Cici went to the front of the lane and stood up straight with the ball in front of her, chest forward, head high. She didn't have to turn around to know that at least one of the soldiers was taking a good look. Gracefully pulling her arm back, she released the ball. Five pins went down. As Cici waited for her ball, she told June, "Don't worry. You'll get the hang of it. It just takes practice, is all." Then she scored a spare.

June clapped for her politely, then got up to face failure once again. As she walked forward, Cici turned around toward the soldiers, who were still setting up and lacing their shoes. "Say," she said loudly, and all four of them turned. "I don't suppose any of you could help my friend? It's her first time bowling, and I think she needs a good lesson."

They all scrambled to speak at once. "I could show her!" "I've been bowling for years." "Anything for you, gorgeous."

Cici smiled graciously. "Why don't we all play together?" she asked. By the time June came back to sit down, their game was over, and Cici had moved into the boys' lane.

Two of the boys were demonstrating their bowling technique to June, while the other two were staring at Cici. "Poor thing," she said, watching her friend, and in a loud whisper continued, "she just lost her fella overseas." She hoped this would quickly circulate through all four soldiers, while she made up her mind which one to go after. The two boys nodded solemnly and gave June sympathetic looks when she came back to sit down again.

By the end of the evening, June had learned to bowl, and Cici had made a date for Saturday night with the best-looking soldier of the group.

* * *

JUNE HAD AN alarm clock, but her eyes flipped open automatically anyway at 6:29. She blinked in the darkness. She'd been dreaming about work, the meters and the dials. But there was something else in her dream that gave her an uneasy feeling. She tried to recapture the images before she was too awake to remember. She'd been in Y-12 on her stool, turning the knobs, but someone else had been there, too. Ronnie. It came back to her in a flash, and she wished she hadn't remembered after all. Ronnie had been alive and talking to her, trying to distract her from her work, teasing her like he always did.

Ronnie was gone, she thought. How far gone? she questioned the darkness around her. *Gone,* echoed the dark corners of the room. *He is dead, and you didn't love him,* and she knew then that this thought had lodged in her brain and would come up again and again for the rest of the day.

The problem with the work was the monotony. She tried to force her thoughts in positive directions, but it was a struggle with no distractions, nothing to focus on. She tried to plan a birthday present for her mother or imagine a radio drama in her mind. A wealthy New York socialite on a pleasure safari in darkest Africa is separated from her much older husband and the rest of her party save for the rough and worldly adventurer who's been leading them through the jungle. How were they separated? Perhaps a lion attacked their camp in the night. She saw blood and bones, ripped shreds of clothing, and winced, not wishing such a gruesome fate on the socialite's dull but kind husband. Maybe a tribe of cannibals captured the lady and the adventurer, though of course he would arrange for their escape in no time. Coming up with details helped kill the time. On the evening of the capture, the socialite would be wearing a smart khaki suit, with a wide collar and pleated skirt. She was an icy blonde with blue eyes. The adventurer was dark, of course, strong and wild-eyed. Clark Gable. The radio drama now a cinema spectacular. The cannibals were dancing and chanting around the two of them, who had been tied to a tree. But Clark had already managed to undo the knots in the ropes binding their hands.

Then it was lunchtime, and June let the blessed respite of conversation, giggling, and gossip wash over her. By evening, the socialite and Clark Gable would be making love on a steamer bound for New York, the husband having conveniently succumbed to an unidentified tropical disease as they'd made their way through the jungle. (Much more humane than death as a lion's dinner, June thought.)

By June's fourth week at work, she barely registered the meters at all. She kept her eyes on them constantly and somehow her mind identified where they were pointing, but it had become subconscious; turning the knobs, an automatic reflex. She got into a routine; the first few hours would be interminably long and she'd alternate between making up grand stories of adventure and counting the minutes, happily marking the hours as they passed, eagerly calculating when she had made it halfway to lunch, two-thirds of the way to the end of the day. Lunch would refresh her spirits, and every day when she left, she'd feel a great surge of relief, as well as the smaller, dull dread of having to do it all again tomorrow.

Not that it was always boring. Occasionally the machines would start going haywire, the meters flipping back and forth wildly. Her mind would snap back into focus, her daydreams ending abruptly, and she'd have to devote herself to keeping the controls steady. Sometimes this lasted for hours.

They had been told not to wear hairpins, and on June's third day, it became obvious why. One girl had forgotten, and when she sat down at her cubicle, the pins actually flew out of her hair. She began screaming, and Miss Collins rushed over and told her to hush. "Everyone, get to work," she growled as the girl whimpered.

A thought occurred to June that day—magnets. Her mother had a jewelry box with a magnetic lid, and June had played with it as a child. The way the lid grabbed a needle from her fingers was not unlike how the machine yanked out the girl's hairpin. It was like they were dealing with giant magnets.

In less hectic moments, it was a struggle not only to keep her thoughts in line but sometimes just to stay awake. She frequently let Cici talk her into staying out too late at dances and could never sleep quite through the night in their little dorm room. If the sounds of the other girls didn't keep her awake, the sounds of the town would. Some nights she could hear construction noises off in the distance, and every night she could hear the roller rink, which was just next door. Since people worked around the clock, everything in Oak Ridge was open twenty-four hours, including the roller rink. As she stared at the meters after a sleepless night, her eyelids would feel heavy and begin to drop over her eyes. She would open them as wide as she could and stare straight ahead until they started drooping again. At all costs, she had to avoid letting her head nod. If Miss Collins saw that, she'd be in hot water for sure.

But as the days passed, work became more bearable. Time didn't seem to drag as much the more time went by. The girls became less shy around each other, and before and after work they talked and laughed like old friends. Most of them were local girls like June, and this was their first time away from home. Sally, a plump redhead with rosy cheeks, was stationed at the next cubicle down from June, and they usually sat together at lunch. It was a casual friendship; Sally loved to laugh and gossip. Before June had even figured out who the other girls were, Sally was already filling her in on their backgrounds and love lives. When it came to her own love life, Sally was shy, and June suspected that she'd never had a boyfriend.

The girls ignored the training talk they'd been given in the bullpen and flirted whenever a male was present. There were usually engineers and scientists in the lunchroom, and though they kept to their own tables, the more outgoing girls always found a way to strike up conversations. June and Sally stayed in the corner, far away from the action and free to observe. June was developing a deep respect for Cici's talents as she watched these less skilled young ladies bat their eyes and giggle in such an obvious way. Cici somehow never looked like she was the one pursuing a conversation; even if

June knew Cici'd had her eye on a fellow, she always made it seem like he was the one seeking her out. Compared to her, the girls at work overdid it and looked desperate. Not that the men seemed to mind. For the most part, they delighted in the female attention.

"Afternoon, Dr. Thomas," Mary Lee, one of the worst of the flirts, would say to the same tall engineer every day at lunch. Her smile showed off badly crooked teeth, but he didn't seem to mind.

"How are you today, Mary Lee?"

"Not too bad, I reckon. You save me a spot over there?"

Every day he saved her a spot, and she slid beside him on the end of a table filled with his colleagues. They watched her with bemused smiles, nudging one another, chuckling. "Ooh, I'm getting awful thirsty!" Mary Lee said one day. "Can I have a sip of your Coca-Cola?"

Dr. Thomas slid the bottle over to her. She leaned over the table, pursed her lips on the straw, and sucked in an over-the-top way, so that her cheeks became hollow. When she removed her mouth, the straw was painted in bloodred lipstick.

June watched from the line. She walked quickly past their table with her tray to find Sally, and as she did, she noticed for the first time that Dr. Thomas was wearing a wedding ring.

Not all men responded to the likes of Mary Lee. Some of the older married men kept to themselves, away from the girls. One man in particular always ate alone, the same dark-haired scientist June had noticed on her first day. She often saw him in the corridors or the lunchroom and had overheard someone call him Dr. Cantor. He seemed important, or maybe it just looked that way because of how he always ate alone, apart from his nudging, chuckling colleagues. No girls ever bothered flirting with him, though he was handsome in a thin, disheveled way. But something in his demeanor signaled that he was too serious for flirting, and they would only be wasting their time. June would watch him eat a tuna sandwich, quickly with determination, as though, like someone out of a propaganda poster, he couldn't wait to get back to his work. He must be very smart and well educated. She wondered if he had a girlfriend and where he was from. What did a man like him do when his shift was over? Surely he didn't go bowling or to the roller rink. It was even hard to imagine someone so somber at the cinema, but then again, everyone went to the pictures, didn't they? What would it be like to run into him outside of the cavernous factory? He would never speak to her. Why would a man like that ever speak to her? Why was she even thinking about it?

Even though work was getting better, come the end of her shift, June was always ready to leave. Her main objective when she was outside of Y-12 was to try to forget about the place until the next day, and her favorite method of forgetting was the movies. She had been to the cinema only a handful of times as a child; the fact that she could go whenever she wanted in Oak Ridge was thrilling. As soon as a new picture arrived at the cinema, June had to see it. Even when the movie wasn't very good, she was happy to be there. She loved everything about the experience. A big marquee over the theater read: RIDGE THEATRE: PERFECT PICTURES FOR PARTICULAR PEOPLE. She would settle into the velvet seats and enveloping darkness and get lost in the flicker of images on the screen, the beautiful stars in their beautiful gowns, the dancing or shooting, depending on whether it was a musical or a Western. Most of all, she loved not having to think about dials, meters, war, or Ronnie.

Cici didn't share June's enthusiasm for the cinema. She preferred dances, bowling, roller skating—any activity which could be combined with flirting. June didn't mind; she liked to be alone at the movies. Besides, most nights she accompanied Cici anyway, except for when her roommate had dates. June liked the dances more than she had expected. There was a heady excitement to being in a room with so many young people, listening to fast-paced swing music. Cici was always fun, full of energy, jitterbugging, bringing over boys. They were always nice to June but clearly more interested in Cici. But June's feelings weren't hurt; it was a relief to not have to worry about flirting, which she didn't know how to do anyway. Occasionally a boy would ask her to dance, and she found it wasn't as scary as she'd initially thought. Most of them would lead her along, spinning her once in a while, smiling when she went off in the wrong direction, and she always wound up laughing. Besides, the music was so infectious that she couldn't help but move in time to the rhythm. Almost every evening was occupied by such parties or movies, and June enjoyed the constant motion of it.

Cici had a strict regimen for attending dances, which she tried to teach to June. It was essential, she said, to bring a nice pair of shoes to change into out of your boots once you got to the dance. June still had only one pair of shoes and was planning to spend her first paycheck on desperately needed boots to contend with the Oak Ridge mud. Cici, meanwhile, confided that she had saved up two weeks' worth of salary to purchase her collection of makeup, perfume, nail polish, and curlers. She would spend a good fifteen minutes applying makeup before she went out, which June found incredible, since Cici was so naturally good-looking. She said as much to Cici one evening, and her roommate laughed. "You may think I'm beautiful, but this takes work."

The bulk of Cici's admirers were soldiers stationed here in Oak Ridge, so there was no fear of them having to go over-seas, at least for the time being. Cici didn't seem to spend much time with any one of them; she was always searching for someone better. The only one so far who had made an impression on June was a soldier named Bob. He'd brought Cici a Hershey bar when he took her out, which she later gave two-thirds of to June, because she said she didn't want to lose her figure. June devoured the chocolate, which only soldiers could get their hands on these days, and thought to herself that if she were Cici, she'd seriously consider marrying the man.

Other than going to the movies or dances with Cici, June spent most of her free time in lines. The lines that stretched along the boardwalks at Williams Drug Store and the A&P were more like huge human chains, the likes of which she had never seen before. Of course, once you got in the store, there was no guarantee that they would have what you wanted to buy. Because of the rationing, Oak Ridge couldn't keep enough products for its booming population. June then had to stand in another line to drop off her laundry, which Cici warned her would take a week to get back. June would rather have just done her own laundry, but she would have to use the sink in the dormitory bathroom, which was tiny. Besides, there was another line of girls waiting to use it. The cafeterias had lines, too, especially when shifts changed, and everyone in town headed for supper at the same time. Cici complained about the food, but June was in awe of the different choices she could have every night of the week. She'd never eaten spaghetti before, and delighted in twirling the strands around her fork and slurping down the red sauce.

On Sundays, church services were held all day long in Oak Ridge. One week she had the wild idea of not going. It was such a strange feeling to know that she didn't have to go to church; no one was here to make her or look down on her if she didn't. But it was sinful to take such pleasure in the idea of missing church, so she went to the Chapel on the Hill, which held worship for many different faiths. When she got there, a Lutheran service was beginning. She was going to leave, but the usher insisted that all Christians were welcome. Afraid to seem rude, she stayed and sat in the back of the chapel. At first the service was mostly familiar Bible passages and prayers, but then it came time to take communion. June froze in her seat, unsure of what to do. The congregation was going up row by row and kneeling at the front of the chapel, and they all seemed to know the procedure. As the usher approached her row, June panicked and bowed her head in prayer, pretending not to see him.

At the end of the service, June slipped out quickly to make her way home to the dorm and Cici and probably another dance at the canteen. She wearily thought of the rut she was in: picking up Cici to go to the cafeteria, setting her alarm and getting up in the morning, sitting at her cubicle, staring at the meters, the war continuing on and on, Ronnie still gone, still dead. It wasn't that this was a bad life—her job was fine, and so was the town. But sometimes the same walks and bus rides every day, the same thoughts going through her head, the routine of doing her hair, making the bed . . . sometimes it just felt unbearable. She knew she had nothing to complain about, really, so she felt guilty for feeling as she did, but if she was honest with herself, though she didn't think she was unhappy, she couldn't quite say she was happy either.

As soon as she got home, June noticed that Cici was acting strange. She was sitting in front of her mirror but not applying any makeup or doing her hair, just staring absently at her face.

"Do you have a date tonight?" asked June, trying to sound cheerful.

"No." Cici didn't look away from the mirror.

June laid her pocketbook on her bed and sat. "Do you want to go to the canteen later?"

Cici turned away from the mirror slowly to face June. "I don't think so. I feel . . . tired. Do you mind?"

June actually felt relieved. "No, that's fine. Maybe I'll go to the cinema. Or is it too late?"

"Or maybe we could just go for a walk or something? Would you mind that terribly? I don't feel like being alone tonight."

It was surprising to see Cici this way. She was usually so controlled, so put together, like a picture of a lady in a magazine, hardly real. They walked along the boardwalks, past the canteen and rec hall where they usually went to dance. Even though it was after midnight, there were still people out in the streets, others like June and Cici, just getting off the evening shift. A sliver of moon shone from behind the clouds, and June shivered in the cold night air. It was winter now, and Christmas was just a week off.

"You think it's safe to walk around at night like this?" asked Cici.

"I reckon so. Lots of folks are out and about."

"Did you hear about that girl in Lafayette Hall? They say she was murdered."

"What?"

"The girls at work told me about it. Her boyfriend strangled her. My friend Jill was in the room right next door when it happened."

"That's awful!" June was taken aback, but she wondered if this was true or just gossip. "How'd he get into the dorm?"

"Must've slipped past the front desk. Worst part of it, security took away her body, and they haven't told anyone what happened. It's like she never existed. She just . . . disappeared."

They walked along the boardwalk in silence for a moment, past trailers stretching on as far as the eye could see in either direction. "Do you ever think about dying?" Cici stopped in front of a small patch of woods left standing between the trailer park and a housing subdivision.

"Sure. I think about Ronnie a lot. I wonder where he is, and if I'll ever see him again."

Cici nodded, but her gaze was fixed on the trees in front of her. "You heard the news from Europe?"

"Yeah." June hadn't had a chance to listen to the radio news that day, but she had seen the headlines and heard folks talking on the bus. The Germans had launched a surprise offensive, and there had been heavy fighting. People had thought the German army was in bad shape, that it was only a matter of time till the Allies made it to Germany. But this meant more bloody fighting. It felt like the war would never end.

Cici dug her hands into her coat pockets. "I used to work

in a restaurant in Nashville, and we kept pictures of all the boys from the neighborhood who were overseas, you know, under this big flag. Whenever a boy died, me or one of the other girls had to return his picture to his family. We had to return so many pictures."

Cici started walking again. "Let's go home. I'm worn out."

They walked silently toward the dorm. It was unusual to spend a quiet moment with Cici. June wondered about her fancy way of talking and dressing; it seemed strange that she'd ever worked in a restaurant. The way Cici went on, June assumed she had come from a well-off family. But if she'd had to work as a waitress, maybe she wasn't as rich as she acted. Cici never did talk about her family or the past. And occasionally she said things that confused June. One of the boys she'd been talking to at a dance a few days before had made a joke about Brutus and Julius Caesar, when his friends all got up to dance without him. Cici had clearly not understood what he was talking about. June had read Shakespeare's play in high school and would have thought Cici'd done the same if she went to a fancy Nashville school.

Cici had become her best friend, that was for sure, but sometimes June wondered if it hadn't been by default. Cici could be selfish; she ignored June when she was focused on boys, then used June to get their attention when it suited her. She had a habit of laughing at people, which could be cruel, and didn't seem to spend much time considering what it might be like to be less beautiful than she naturally was. But at other times, when she chose June to confide in or spirited her away on an adventure, it felt wonderful. Everyone looked at them, because Cici was beautiful; everyone, other girls and all the boys, wanted to be at their table, because Cici automatically gave it an air of glamour and elegance. In those moments, June felt so special. She'd look over at Cici, and Cici would wink back, and the world would know they were best friends.

(Courtesy of the Department of Energy)

(Courtesy of the Department of Energy)

Chapter 5

CHARLIE AND ANN HAD BEEN OFFERED A TWO-BEDROOM HOUSE just one month after adding Sam to their application. It was perched on the side of a hill covered with identical structures; each resembled a small child's drawing of a house, a plain white rectangle with a slanted roof. The only accessory was a small porch, just big enough for a bench, which jutted out beside the doorway. Besides one tree that had been spared by the construction crew, the yard consisted entirely of mud. Charlie had carried Ann over the threshold even as she yelled at him, "I have my boots on! I can walk through a little mud," laughing all the while. Sam had volunteered to help them move; his own possessions were easily hauled over from the dorm in one trip.

When Charlie let her down in their new living room, Ann sighed. "How will I ever keep these floors clean?"

"We can leave our boots by the door," suggested Sam.

"Somehow it doesn't work," replied Ann. "We tried everything in the trailer. Sometimes I think the mud actually has a mind of its own and crawls into the house." Ann was thin with sharp features that could look severe when her expression was serious. But when she smiled, which luckily was often, her features relaxed, and her face became welcoming.

"It's cold in here!" said Charlie. "Better go take a look at the furnace."

"I'll do it," volunteered Sam. "You finish up with the moving." Sam went past the utility room, which housed a coal furnace, and out a back door to the coal box. He opened it, began loading coal into a small bucket, then hauled it inside to the furnace.

It was wonderful to be out of the dorm. Every day he got new roommates, and they had gotten progressively worse. Last night two of them stayed up until two playing cards, while the third snored at an inconceivable volume. As if that weren't enough, his room was flooded with light at night because of the construction going on down the road. On his way to the bus stop in the morning, Sam would see the shells of new buildings that had literally gone up overnight.

Ann stuck her head in the utility room. "I hope you can eat supper with us tonight, Sam. I think we should have a celebration."

"Sounds great, Ann."

She flitted off, looking far too delicate in her white satin blouse for this dirty town. Sam slapped his hands together to knock off the coal dust and looked around. Charlie and Ann had managed to bring some nice things with them that made the house look livable. Charlie was hanging up framed prints of flowers in the living room while Ann arranged a lace tablecloth on the dining table. Their efforts at decorating were endearing, though completely foreign to Sam, who had never bothered to do a thing to his apartment in Berkeley during his years of living there. He went down the hall to his room. It was small but comfortable, furnished with a simple dresser, table, and bed. He unpacked easily, flopped back on the bed, and stared up at the ceiling, beginning to relax for what seemed like the first time since he'd arrived in Oak Ridge.

On the first day of his new job, Sam had spent ten minutes wandering through a sprawling parking lot—buses snaking in and out—before he found the sign for Y-12, the facility where he would be working. A distressing number of people were already waiting. Bus service in Oak Ridge was free, but everyone had to show their badge as they got on to prove they were allowed into the Y-12 area. Sam stood in the midsection of the bus as he watched the Negroes make their way past the sign that read COLORED. This was his first time in the South, and though he hadn't exactly spent his youth palling around with the locals in Harlem, the explicitness of segregation here startled him. Charlie had told him that there was a whole other section of housing that hadn't been on his official Army tour, where the colored construction workers lived in tiny shacks.

Sam looked out the window at a train carrying an endless line of identical trailers. It was starting to rain. The bus wound through the security checkpoint, and he finally saw Y-12, a series of large, warehouse-looking buildings.

The plant was designed to enrich uranium. For the weapon the Army was trying to make, the uranium isotope U-235 was required, and needed to be separated from U-238. The top physicists in America had spent the past few years trying to figure out the best way to do this. At Berkeley, Ernest

Lawrence had designed the calutron, which used magnets to get the job done, and this was the method employed at Y-12. Sam had worked with him, experimenting and designing the prototype for what would now be used on a massive scale here in Oak Ridge. He could hardly keep from running straight into the plant, he was so excited to see what they'd been working on for so long.

Once he made it through security, Sam reported to his new supervisor, Dr. Armstrong, a stocky man of about forty, who gave Sam's hand an aggressive shake and led him down a long corridor. "It's good to have you here, Dr. Cantor. As you can see, the facilities are operational, but we're having a lot of difficulties."

He opened the door to his office for Sam and closed it behind them. "Please sit down. In a nutshell, we've been asked to achieve the impossible here. We've built an enormous facility without knowing how it's going to operate, and so far it's been little short of disastrous. You've been briefed on the plant's operations?"

He had. The day before, a thick envelope marked Top Secret had been hand-delivered to him, which included a blueprint of the entire Y-12 facility and outlined its operations.

"We're adjacent to the Alpha 1 building now," continued Dr. Armstrong. "Would you like to take a look at the racetrack?"

"Yes, sir."

"You might want to leave your watch here. The magnets can destroy it. And if you have any other metal on you . . ."

"I don't think I do." Sam laid his watch on the desk.

The uranium began the enrichment process in the Alpha buildings, which were referred to as racetracks because of

their ovular shape. This racetrack contained ninety-six calutrons. In the calutron, a vaporized sample of uranium was
bombarded with electrons and became ionized. Next, the
ions were injected into a vacuum chamber, accelerated, and
sent through a strong magnetic field, which forced them into
radial paths. The lighter U-235 traveled on a smaller radius
than the heavier U-238, and in this way, the isotopes could
be separated.

Dr. Armstrong took Sam into a nearby building, which
looked like a typical factory from the outside. After passing
through two more security checkpoints, they went into the
production area, and Sam got his first look at the racetrack.
The calutrons were arranged around a powerful electromag-
net in an oval for maximum efficiency. The oval was about
forty yards long and twenty-five yards across.

"Come on, I'll take you for a closer look." Dr. Armstrong
led him to one of the calutron inspection windows. Behind
heavy glass Sam saw it—the strange blue glow that he knew
to be uranium. It was beautiful.

Next, Dr. Armstrong led him up a staircase to the catwalk above the racetrack. Large steel beams rose above them.
Stepping onto the catwalk, Sam felt a tugging at his feet like
he was walking through chewing gum. Dr. Armstrong saw
his look of alarm and shouted, "The nails in your shoes are
being pulled by the magnets."

He could look down on the calutrons now, though there
wasn't much to see. It was what was going on inside them
that was miraculous. When they descended, Dr. Armstrong
took him out to the operating cubicles, a long hallway filled
with control panels, where young women sat on stools, carefully monitoring the dials. At Berkeley, graduate students had

been in charge of operating the calutrons. These girls looked like they belonged in the halls of a high school rather than at the center of the world's most sophisticated scientific operation. They ignored Sam and Dr. Armstrong and stayed focused on the controls.

As they walked back to Dr. Armstrong's office, the older man seemed to perceive Sam's thoughts. "We need manpower to run the facility, but obviously, there aren't any men around. So we have eighteen-year-old girls out there operating these things."

"Do they have any inkling of what they're dealing with?"

"Of course not. Even if we wanted to explain it to them, do you think these girls would understand? Most of them come from local communities and have no more than a high school education, which is substandard at that. So we tell them to watch the meter and adjust the dials to keep them in the right spot. They do as they're told. We haven't had any problems yet, except with the occasional girl crying when the magnets pull her hairpins out."

They arrived back at Dr. Armstrong's office, and he ushered Sam inside. "Let me tell you, Dr. Cantor, these girls are the least of our problems. Building the facilities has been a challenge every step of the way. The amount of money already spent here is staggering. Have you wondered, for instance, how we ever got enough copper to produce the electromagnets?"

"How?"

"We didn't. Instead of copper, we've used silver. Fourteen thousand tons of it borrowed from the U.S. Treasury."

"My God."

"I cannot stress to you enough how high the stakes are here. The government has invested a monumental sum of money and manpower in this project. And as I'm sure you know, we have every reason to think that Hitler has done the same." Dr. Armstrong had worked himself up. His blue eyes glistened, and Sam could hardly stand to hold his stare.

"I'm ready to help in any way I can."

"Good. We're losing far too much material, and what we're producing isn't enriched enough. The racetracks are in constant peril of breaking down. We've already had vacuum tanks leaking. Mistakes have been made at all levels of operations: electrical circuits have shorted, and welds have failed. I'm afraid you have climbed aboard a sinking ship, but I hope we can bail ourselves out yet."

"These sorts of problems had to be expected with a project of this scale."

Dr. Armstrong gave him a bemused half-smile. "As far as the Army is concerned, problems are never expected. Now, I know you're probably disappointed about not being down in New Mexico with the big shots designing the weapon. But let me assure you that Y-12 needs a physicist like yourself with experience in the rad lab. If we don't sort things out here, our boys in Los Alamos won't have anything to make their bomb out of. We have a research wing in this building, and I am putting you in charge of the laboratory there. I promise you, Dr. Cantor, the next few months are going to be very busy."

Sam felt like a soldier with a mission. To be given a research project of this scope was thrilling. What did it matter if he was living in a dorm as long as he had a laboratory? He would essentially live in the lab anyway, and he wanted to start this minute. He had the wonderful certainty that he was doing the very thing that he was born to do.

The conviction stayed with him throughout his busy first

day. It kept him happy and focused as he went about his work, sure of himself and what he was doing. It wasn't until late that night in his dorm room that he began to doubt. He lay in bed, unable to sleep. Images of softly glowing uranium plasma danced in his head as he contemplated what building this bomb would mean. It was by no means the first time he had thought about it, but it also had never seemed so real as it did today, standing face-to-face with one of the most expensive government projects in history, all aimed at gathering a handful of uranium isotopes. Dr. Armstrong worried that Y-12 would never be functional, but Sam didn't doubt for a minute the project would succeed. There was a certain momentum to something this big. With these many minds, this much effort, a bomb was inevitable.

* * *

SAM HAD FALLEN asleep without meaning to in the peaceful quiet of his new room at Ann and Charlie's house. He was awakened by the sound of Ann screaming. "It's loose, Charlie! Do something!" Sam felt around the unfamiliar nightstand for his glasses and leapt off the bed, heading toward the living room. He stopped abruptly in the hallway when he saw a live chicken, hopping and flapping around the living room. Ann was squealing by the front door, while Charlie stalked the bird from behind. "Sam!" called out Ann. "Do you know how to kill a chicken?"

"I'm from Brooklyn," was all he could manage.

Charlie lunged forward and grabbed the bird by a wing. It made a terrible squawk, and he grabbed its leg. "Get a knife, Sam," he commanded, "and meet me out back."

Sam opened the kitchen drawers in search of a knife, still groggy from his nap. He saw steak knives, butter knives, nothing really appropriate for killing a chicken. "Here!" Ann called out. "We hadn't unpacked it yet." She appeared in the kitchen, holding out a butcher knife for Sam. Dutifully he took it and went out back.

Charlie was standing by the coal box, holding the chicken as far out in front of himself as possible. He gave Sam a desperate look. "I think we chop its head off."

"Why do we have a live chicken, Charlie?"

"Apparently, that's all they had at the market. Ann wanted dinner to be special, and she somehow managed to carry this thing all the way home. Then it got loose, and well, you know the rest."

They stared at the mass of feathers and flesh. Sam wished he'd ignored the shouting and stayed in his room. "Why don't you hold it down on the ground?" he ventured.

"All right."

Charlie bent his long legs and hunched over to place the chicken on the ground. Sam stood over it with the knife, took a deep breath, and whacked at the creature's neck. A spray of blood spurted up into his face. "Goddamnit!"

Sam wiped his face with his hands. Charlie was still holding the now-headless creature down as it lurched and kicked out its final moments. "What do we do now?"

"I guess we have to get rid of the feathers."

"Jesus Christ."

When they got the bird to a state they hoped would no longer horrify Ann, Sam went to the bathroom to scrub off the blood and feathers. He never wanted to see a chicken again. Nevertheless, after a couple of hours, a delicious smell began to waft from the kitchen. Sam helped set the table, and he and Charlie sat across from each other until Ann brought it out, placing it proudly in the middle of the table: a lovely hump of bronzed, dripping meat. There were carrots and mashed potatoes, too, all served on elegant plates.

"It looks marvelous," said Sam.

"Certainly better than when we left it," said Charlie. He stood and dug the same knife he had used earlier to dispatch the bird into its roasted flesh.

"Well," said Ann, "this is real country living, after all, I suppose!"

"I can't believe you made it home with this thing," Charlie spoke with affection.

"I was determined to have chicken. And when I asked the man at the store for one, he went to the back and brought it out. At first I panicked, but then I realized lots of people must kill chickens every day for dinner."

Charlie sat back down and raised his water glass. "A toast! To our new house!"

They clanked glasses. Sam dug his knife and fork into the meat; it was delicious. "It's good to have a home-cooked meal."

"Poor Sam," said Charlie, pointing at him with his knife, "needs a woman to look after him."

There had been a woman in California off and on, a secretary at the university who had been conveniently married to an accountant Sam had never met. He didn't have to worry about marrying her or making her think he wanted to marry her or any of that. Bored with her accountant husband, she had pursued Sam, another handy aspect of their relationship, since he had never been particularly adept at wooing women.

Back in college, he had passionately chased after one girl for almost two years, but her unrelenting rejection had dampened his romantic spirit. There had been dates and a couple of minor courtships in graduate school, but they had been achieved only with great discomfort. All ended badly. "I'm afraid that's too great a task for any woman," Sam replied.

Ann's brow furrowed. "Nonsense! I'm sure you'd make someone a lovely mate. And this is the perfect place to look. They say when the facilities are all up and running, we'll have eight women to every one man here in Oak Ridge."

"What, you think I should marry one of these local girls?"

"There are girls from all over," replied Ann. "Secretaries, teachers, I've even met a chemist."

"Ann is vice-president of the Oak Ridge Woman's Club," explained Charlie. "And she sings in a choir."

"I had no idea we had clubs and choirs in Oak Ridge."

"Well, we're only just getting going, of course, but you'd be surprised at what goes on. There's a real thirst for community involvement, maybe since the community's so new."

"Take a look at the *Oak Ridge Journal,* Sam. You'll get a real laugh from the list of organizations. There's a folk dancing group, a rabbit breeders association . . . What do you think? Ready to take up an extracurricular activity?"

"I've got plenty to keep me occupied at work."

"Oh, come on, Sam!" said Ann. "You can't work all the time!"

"I don't know," said Charlie. "He came pretty close at Princeton."

"I'm just doing my part for the war effort," said Sam.

Charlie hooted. "Sam Cantor, patriot! I like it."

After dinner, they drank tea in the living room and listened to the news on the radio, mostly reports of the Allied bombing of Berlin. When Ann retired to her bedroom, Charlie took Sam's teacup from him, placed it on a shelf, and asked, "Shall we continue celebrating?"

"What did you have in mind?"

Charlie opened a trunk below the shelf, dug through it, and pulled out a bottle of Johnnie Walker. Sam sat up, astounded. "You rascal! How did you get it here?"

"I smuggled it in. I've only had the nerve to with this one bottle, and look, I've drunk hardly any of it after getting it in." Charlie poured a slug into each of their empty teacups and replaced the bottle in the trunk. "I rolled it up in the middle of Ann's undergarments, hoping that would dissuade security from taking too close a look."

Sam sniffed the whiskey appreciatively, letting it tickle his nose for a long moment. "I didn't know you had it in you, Charlie."

"To the future." Charlie held out his glass.

Sam raised an eyebrow. "The future." He took a long sip and felt the sweet familiar burn slide down his throat.

Charlie went over to a record player and put down the needle. Big brassy jazz suddenly filled the room. The sound perfectly matched the buzz in Sam's head. A trumpet wailed out, and he took a second sip.

Charlie sat and leaned in toward him. "What do you think? Ann's a light sleeper, so I don't want to talk too loudly. But what do you think? Is this going to work?"

"What?" asked Sam, completely absorbed in the music and his scotch.

"This!" Charlie motioned around them with a sweep of his hands. "Can we do this thing?"

Sam caught his drift. "You mean build a bomb?"

"I haven't said the word since I got here. The security talks really get to you, don't they? I mean, for all I know, you're an undercover security agent."

"Please, don't be ridiculous. For all we know, Ann is."

"I'm fairly certain we're working in different areas. I'm at X-10."

"I'm at Y-12." Perhaps it was the whiskey, but he actually felt his heart rate speed up a little. Charlie was right; the security talks did get to you. He'd been told so often not to talk about what he was doing that he felt nervous even here. "Let me guess," Sam said. "You're working on a graphite reactor."

"We just went critical."

Sam sipped his whiskey. The graphite reactor was designed to turn uranium into a new element, plutonium, which could also be used in a bomb. The Army was trying more than one method to get what it needed.

"We're a pilot program," Charlie went on. "There's a facility going up in Washington State just to produce plutonium."

Sam drank a final gulp of whiskey. "Yes. To answer your question, Charlie, yes, I think we will definitely do this thing. God forgive us."

"I was afraid you'd say that." Charlie poured more drinks. They sat there for some time silently, sipping their scotch, listening to the trumpet shriek and sputter.

(Courtesy of the Department of Energy)

Chapter 6

JOE COULDN'T SEE RALPH ANYWHERE IN THE REC HALL, BUT HE did find the boy's friend, Otis, leaning against a wall, smoking a cigarette. As best Joe could tell, Otis was always in the rec hall. He reckoned the young man must work some time, but Joe never saw much evidence of it. As usual, Otis was immaculate, dressed like he was on his way to a nightclub— shiny suit and tie, polished shoes, fedora tilted back on his head, carefully crafted mustache traversing his face. You'd think he was a gangster or a musician the way he presented himself, not a construction worker. Otis came from Memphis and had a citified walk and talk that left Joe feeling dizzy. He was always smiling, but not in a friendly way, more like he was laughing at you.

"Evening, Joe." Otis sneered at him.

"Evening. Have you seen Ralph?"

"Yes, sir. He's with Shirley." Otis's suggestive tone somehow made the girl's name sound indecent.

"I see. They at one of them meetings?" Ralph had taken to attending the Colored Camp Council.

"No, sir. They're going for a walk." He made the word *walk* sound even worse than *Shirley*.

"What you make of Shirley?" Joe asked Otis. She was a girl from Atlanta Ralph had been chasing for months now.

Otis shrugged. "She a fine-looking woman."

"Besides that."

"Does there need to be a besides that?"

"You ain't go in for them meetings, do you?"

"Only meetings I attend be about cards or dice."

"Ralph gambling, too?"

"Ain't you worry, preacher man. He on the straight and narrow." He grinned. "Despite all my best efforts."

Joe felt foolish for trying to talk to Otis, for thinking he cared about Ralph as anything more than an impressionable country boy he could impress with his Memphis swagger. He said a quick good-bye and went back out into the cold November night.

Shirley had first come on the scene a few months ago. It had already been summertime hot even though it was only the first week in June, and Joe and Ralph had started their shift in the thick heat of midafternoon. Their crew was digging trenches, laying pipes, and then digging some more, and after five minutes in the early summer sun, the men's shirts were dripping with sweat. Joe knew how to take his mind off the heat—he'd spent his life sharecropping in Alabama. The key was to find a thought or song or Bible verse to focus the mind on, away from the discomfort, the aching back, the burning feet. Some men in the crew sang out loud and that was a help. Joe couldn't carry a tune, but he liked to listen, and the music helped the time pass.

The sun set, but the air stayed sultry. They were still digging into the night—the digging, pouring, lifting, building, none of it ever enough for this city in progress. An hour before the end of their shift, Joe heard a rumbling in the distance and felt a slight movement in the humid air. He knew the storm would cool them down, which was almost worth getting soaked for.

Men hooted and hollered in the rain. The dirt became mud in a matter of minutes, and the foreman shook his head helplessly. "Go on home," he shouted over the storm. "Shift is almost over, and it's no use getting anything done now."

Ralph began walking fast toward the bus stop. "I'm starving," he muttered. Ralph still ate like a growing boy.

"Hopefully, we'll miss the rush on the bus," Joe said.

A couple of white laborers were already waiting at the bus stop. Ralph, Joe, and three more men from their crew hung back from the white fellows. They couldn't have been any wetter submerged in a bathtub. Joe kept his hand around the wad of money in his pocket to keep it as dry as possible.

All the seats on the bus were full, but it wasn't bad compared to what they were used to at shift change. They often had to wait for two or three buses to go by before getting on. Of course they had to let the white folks on first, and some bus drivers didn't even stop if they saw only Negroes waiting.

The white men got on, and Joe and Ralph followed. The back of the bus was already filled with straphangers, so they stood in the middle with the others from their crew. The bus lurched forward. Joe thought about what he would get for supper in the cafeteria. Beans and rice again, probably, which was fine with him, as long as it was hot.

A big crowd was waiting at the next stop—the shift must have ended. The bus driver, middle-aged, scrawny, with brown stubble on his face, stopped and turned back slowly to look at Joe and the other men from his crew. "You boys best get off and make room for these here passengers."

Joe looked at Ralph, whose whole body tensed. "Sir, we *are* passengers," the boy replied, calm, cool.

The bus driver was chewing gum. "You colored boys best get off and make room for the white passengers."

"Get off the bus, niggers!" a man shouted, Joe couldn't see who. He was already moving, dragging Ralph with him toward the door, following the other Negroes. Joe knew exactly what would come of trying to stay on that bus, and he feared Ralph didn't fully comprehend it. The boy had fought his stepfather, sure enough, but it seemed he didn't yet know that no luck could be depended on to save you in a struggle, especially when faced with twenty white men slicked with wet and hate.

"I will report this to the Army!" Ralph shouted as Joe got him off the bus. The other Negro men shook their heads at him, and the whites in line watched them walk off with confusion.

"Army don't give a shit, son," said one of the men from their crew, and Ralph kicked a Coke bottle hard as he could— the glass smashing loud enough to be heard over the pounding rain.

They walked a mile in silence, rain pelting them the whole way to the cafeteria. Ralph stopped at the door.

"Ain't you coming in?" asked Joe.

Ralph shook his head.

"You need to eat."

"Ain't hungry."

Ralph turned and walked away. A couple of the other men from their crew laughed. "I sure am!"

"Let's get out of this rain!" said another.

Joe held the door for them, still watching Ralph disappear into the storm.

The rain had cleared up by the time Joe finished supper, but he was still sopping, his damp shirt clinging to his skin. He was desperate to go back to the hutment and change into dry clothes but figured Ralph had gone to the rec center and wanted to check on the boy.

He could hear voices and music spilling out of the center as he approached—laughter, hoots, Billie Holiday crackling out of a speaker. The storm had gotten folks excited. Inside, it was hot; a feeble ceiling fan twirled above them, no contest for the fifty-odd bodies mingling in the humid space. Most men sat at tables playing cards. A few took turns at the two punching bags in the corner.

He found Ralph sitting at a table across from Otis. Smoke from their cigarettes billowed upward. Otis was laughing at some just-told joke, but Ralph didn't appear amused.

"Well, if you ain't as wet as Ralph here!" said Otis, leaning back in his chair to make room for Joe to sit.

"Got caught out in a real frog strangler."

Ralph let out a short, angry laugh. "Got throwed out into it, you mean."

Joe shrugged and reached in his shirt pocket for a cigarette.

"Welcome to the U.S. Army, son. At least we ain't getting

shot at in Normandy. I'd just as soon not die for the privilege of getting throwed off a bus to serve my country."

Ralph's jaw twitched.

"Anyone want a Coca-Cola?" asked Joe.

Otis smiled, as though he'd told a joke. "Sure, Joe."

What did that grin mean? Joe had a mind to slap it right off Otis's face. When he returned with the Cokes, Joe slammed Otis's down in front of him hard, though he didn't seem to notice, taking a big swig from the bottle. Otis then pulled a glass bottle out of his pocket, winked at Joe, and poured a clear liquid into the soda. "Want a little taste?"

Joe shook his head, and Otis's taunting grin returned. "I forgot. You're a good, churchgoing man. Ralph?"

Otis motioned toward the liquor.

"No thanks," said Ralph.

Otis shrugged and took a long sip. "I feel like dancing." Duke Ellington blared from the jukebox, but no one was moving.

"What do you think of them ladies over there?" he continued. "Reckon they'd like to dance?"

Both Ralph and Joe looked over. They were the only women in the room of rough characters, about eight nice-looking girls sitting around a table, sipping on Cokes. One of the girls noticed the three men staring at them and raised an eyebrow at Otis. She turned back to the others, and they all laughed.

Otis let out a low whistle. The girl sat up tall and lean, with long legs stretching out from under her red skirt. Joe tried not to stare. He tried to think of Moriah and not notice the girl's perfectly sloping breasts.

"I know her," said Ralph. "She comes to the Colored Camp Council meetings."

"Maybe I should join the Colored Camp Council!" said Otis. "I didn't know there were women there."

"She the only one."

"You know her name?"

Ralph shook his head. "Never talked to her. Just seen her around."

"Damn," said Otis. "Colored Camp Council! What goes on there, anyway?"

"Folks complain about all the things wrong with this place," said Joe. "Then write letters about it."

Ralph went to the meetings once a week and talked Joe into coming with him once. About ten men sat in a circle smoking and talking about all the things they didn't like about Oak Ridge. Joe agreed with what they said. The hutments were a disgrace, crime was out of control, and the fact that married colored couples couldn't live together was awful. But he couldn't figure out what these men wanted to do about it. Afterward he asked Ralph, who said they wanted to change things.

"How?" Joe had asked.

"We organize ourselves just like the white folks' unions. We make ourselves heard."

Joe hadn't seen this girl at the meeting, that's for sure.

"Let's ask them to join us," said Otis.

"I don't know," said Ralph, suddenly shy.

Joe chuckled. "Don't look at me. I'm a married man."

"If I don't talk to that woman in the next two minutes, some other man will." Otis took a gulp of his Coke and walked over to the table.

Joe looked over at Ralph. The man who had been itching for a fight earlier now looked like a nervous boy, his wet clothes still clinging to him. Joe tried to be encouraging. "They look like real nice girls."

"How can you tell if they're nice?"

"Reckon I can't. But they're pretty."

They couldn't hear what Otis was saying, but the girl's face was unimpressed. Her friends glared protectively at him. Otis finished, and the girl said something back to him and glanced over at Ralph and Joe.

"What you think she saying?" asked Ralph.

"I know better than to guess what a woman got on her mind."

Otis crossed back over to their table, still with a grin on his face. The girl and one of her friends followed him over. Joe figured he should stand as the ladies got near and Ralph did the same, knocking his knees on the table as he got up.

"This here's Shirley and Sarah," said Otis. Shirley was the one he was after.

She extended her hand toward Ralph. He paused for a moment, then shook it. "I'm Ralph."

"Pleased to meet you. I've seen you at the Colored Camp Council."

"Yeah, I've gone a couple times to the meetings. When it ain't during my shift."

Sarah smiled at Joe, who nodded to her, trying to be friendly. They all sat back down. Shirley hardly glanced at Otis or Joe. She was focused on Ralph. "What got you coming to the meetings?"

"Um, well, it was our foreman, Mr. Brown, who told me about it. He'd seen me reading colored newspapers on my break and asked if I was interested."

Otis tried to break into the conversation. "What's a lady like yourself doing at them meetings?"

Shirley gave him an icy look. "Trying to improve working and living conditions for my race."

Otis raised an eyebrow and grinned at Joe, who tried not to look at him. Shirley turned back to Ralph. "Where are you from?"

"Oh, me and Joe are from Alabama. We came up together for the work."

"Where you ladies from?" asked Joe.

"I'm from Knoxville," said Sarah in a soft voice.

"Atlanta," said Shirley.

"Well, you ought be careful in a place like this," warned Otis.

"I've been in worse places," said Shirley.

"Y'all work in construction?" asked Sarah. The men nodded. "We work in a laundry."

"What'd you do back in Alabama?" asked Shirley.

"Sharecropping," answered Joe. "What did your father do in Atlanta?"

"I don't know," she said, looking him straight in the eye. "Never met him. I was raised by two of my aunts. They were seamstresses."

Otis, either giving up on Shirley or trying to make her jealous, leaned over toward Sarah. "Would you like to dance?"

"No one else is," the girl said.

"Don't matter," said Otis. He stood and reached out a hand to Sarah. She giggled and he escorted her to the empty side of the room, where they started swaying in time to the music.

"You been friends with Otis long?" asked Shirley.

Ralph shook his head. "He's not so bad. We just haven't been spending much time around ladies."

She didn't reply. They all glanced over to where Otis and Sarah were dancing. Joe looked at Ralph, hoping the boy would ask this lovely girl to dance. Finally Ralph blurted out, "I don't know any dances."

For the first time since coming over, Shirley smiled. "I can teach you."

"Oh, I don't know."

"Sure I can. Do you mind, Joe?"

"No, of course not. You young people have fun. I'm gonna head on home for the night."

Ralph stood slowly and walked Shirley off to the side of the room. He began awkwardly jerking back and forth. Shirley laughed. Ralph looked up at her and began to laugh, too. As Joe watched them, he thought of Moriah at that age, so soft and firm and warm to touch. He got up to go. A night like that he worried he'd go crazy in the hutment, listening to the sound of rain pounding on the roof and the hum of mosquitoes circling his head.

And now it was almost winter; the mosquitoes were gone, and already the hutment was unbearably cold at night. The cold came earlier here than in Alabama, and of course the hutment was no better insulated now than it had been a year ago. Another season come and gone here in Tennessee. His children growing taller by the day, and he not there to see it. It drove him crazy to think about how they were changing, how he was missing it all. But being a parent meant always being nostalgic for how your children used to be. Joe missed his girls' baby coos when they became toddlers, and then missed their toddler gibberish as they learned to talk. Change was so constant with children that you never had time to catch up.

Joe needed to talk to Ralph, he decided. He should be glad the boy had a girlfriend—it was only natural at his age. But he couldn't help but think that Shirley and Otis were turning Ralph against him. It was silly, a childish thing to think. And yet it was true, wasn't it? Ralph had better things to do with his time than pal around with an old man. Joe found Otis's glamour suspicious, but the boy seemed to like it; and he was drawn to an independence in Shirley that Joe didn't understand.

It wasn't just the fact that he couldn't work out Ralph's young friends that made Joe feel old these days. His muscles ached more and more. His knees creaked, and at night, his lower back pulsed with pain as he tried to sleep. His body was wearing out, and it frightened him. He'd always relied on his strength to get by in life, whether it was in the cotton fields in Alabama or the construction sites here in Tennessee.

Joe was lying in bed, still awake, when Ralph showed up at the hutment an hour or so later. He sat up, happy to finally have some company. "You have a nice time with Shirley?"

Ralph shrugged.

"Is she your girlfriend now?"

"I don't know."

Ralph sat on his bed to take off his boots.

"You going for walks together late at night."

"Shirley and me got common interests."

"That's usually how romance starts."

"We're both members of the Colored Camp Council. You wouldn't understand."

The words stung. Joe was used to Ralph's dissatisfied tone, but it wasn't usually directed at him. "I ain't stupid."

Ralph sighed, as though Joe were indeed very stupid and it was a struggle to speak to him. "No, of course not. But you're not concerned with our work."

"I've got my own concerns."

"I know, I know. Don't you worry about it."

Joe lay back in his bed, angry now, even less likely to sleep. He tried to forget Ralph and focus on reconstructing his children's small, chubby faces in his mind. He subtracted baby fat, added height and maturity, but it was useless. He didn't know who they were becoming.

(Courtesy of the Department of Energy)

(Courtesy of the Department of Energy)

Chapter 7

CICI HAD TO WORK CHRISTMAS MORNING, BUT SHE DIDN'T MIND. June had invited her to dinner at her family's house, and she'd been glad to have the excuse to stay in Oak Ridge. She planned to stay as far away from farms as possible for the rest of her life, and she might as well be doing something useful today rather than wasting time at church or getting fat on June's mother's pie.

Anyway, Christmas had never been much to celebrate at Cici's house—if she was lucky, a few hard candies would appear in the bottom of her stocking, and occasionally an orange. A day like any other with a little extra church. Since she'd left home, Cici hadn't once contacted her family. Occasionally, in her darkest moments, lying in bed listening to the roller rink, she would think of her poor, pathetic mother. Did she also lie in bed at night, wondering where Cici had gone? Who knew? The woman had fed her and clothed her as best she could but never seemed to have the time or energy to want anything more to do with her daughter.

When her shift was over, Cici went straight to the cafeteria. Normally she would have gone home first to change and freshen up. You never knew who you might meet in the cafeteria—she'd been asked out on two dates there. But the town was dead today, and she wanted to eat quickly, by herself. The staff had tried to jolly up the dining room for the holiday. Some tinsel hung over the door, and they were serving turkey and mashed potatoes. A group of volunteer carolers stopped by as she ate her dinner. Cici smiled politely at the women as they sang "Jingle Bells," but really wished they would keep on moving.

Midway through the performance, Cici saw her roommate Lizbeth approaching her table. Cici stiffened and glared. Lizbeth didn't usually talk to her—Cici treated her so coolly that she surely couldn't want to be friends. But here the girl was, taking a seat across from her with a wide grin.

"Merry Christmas, Cici!"

"Hi, Lizbeth."

"It sure makes you miss home being here on Christmas!"

Cici sawed at a piece of turkey without looking up. "I am happy to be here, doing my part for the war effort."

Lizbeth raised an eyebrow. "Sure, I am, too, but I do miss my home on a day like this."

"I don't miss anything."

Lizbeth took a swig of milk and considered Cici. "You from Nashville, is that right?"

"Yes."

"And you don't miss living in such a big, pretty city? I used to love to visit Nashville when I's little."

"Nashville seems big and pretty only if you've never been to New York or Chicago."

"Wow. When did you go to New York?"

Cici preferred to keep her lies as unspecific as possible. "Before the war."

"Well, I miss everything. My mama and daddy, my big brothers, even the cows."

Cici was eating fast, hoping to finish before Lizbeth, so they didn't have to walk home together. The girl seemed completely oblivious to her antipathy, rambling on about her family back in Lewis County. Cici stared at her plate, refusing to look at her.

"You know, they can't even imagine where I live at now. Last week I wrote to Mama and told her 'bout how big the factory is where I work—and you know what she wrote back?"

Cici looked up, a sudden happy thought coming to her.

"She asked if it was bigger than Mr. Ingles's barn!" Lizbeth laughed aloud at the memory. "Poor Mama—the biggest building she could imagine was a barn."

"You wrote to your mother describing the top secret facility where you work?"

Lizbeth's face fell. "I just . . . I just said it was big."

"I could report you." Cici could barely suppress a smile.

"Oh, Cici! You wouldn't! You know I ain't meant nothing by it!"

The girl was more stupid than Cici had realized. "Move out."

"What? Where am I supposed to go?"

"I don't care. You must know someone you can move in with."

Lizbeth was beginning to cry. "I ain't meant no harm!"

Cici stood up. "Move out. Or I'll report you."

She turned and walked away without another look back

at Lizbeth, letting the smile she'd been holding back spread across her face. She must have looked like a grinning idiot when the tall soldier standing by the door first saw her. He opened the door wide for her. "Merry Christmas."

Cici turned her smile toward him as she walked out the door. "What's your name?" he asked.

"Cecilia."

"You make a guy homesick on Christmas!" he was now shouting after her.

She stopped and turned back. "Why's that?"

The soldier gave her a teasing half-smile. He was quite good-looking, she realized, with light brown hair and liquid blue eyes. "You remind me of a girl I used to know."

Cici raised an eyebrow. "You don't know me."

"Not yet." His grin widened. "What do you say? You don't want to spend Christmas all alone, do you?"

"You think I'm that easy to ask out?"

"No. But it was worth a shot. Come on, don't tell me you aren't a little homesick, too."

He should ask Lizbeth out, Cici thought, they could go on about missing home together. "Home . . ." Cici began. "Father would be carving the turkey, and Mother would be playing carols at the piano."

"I knew you didn't have a heart of stone! What do you say, Cecilia? I'm a good guy, I promise. Let me buy you a Coke at least."

"I have plans tonight." Cici turned back toward the board-walk, away from him.

"Oh. Can I call you at least?"

Without looking back, she said, "I'm in West Dormitory. Cici Roberts."

She took a long route home, hoping to give Lizbeth plenty of time to consider her threat. The town was almost quiet, though there was still construction going on somewhere, and she could hear the rumble of engines in the distance. She pushed her hands deep into her coat pockets for warmth. The pockets were satiny smooth inside, woolen and warm outside. She'd bought the coat two months ago—the first decent coat she'd ever owned.

The thought of that soldier lit her up. You really never did know who you might meet, and she hadn't even done her hair. It was always good to have a new prospect on the horizon. Not just in terms of her ultimate goal, but also because it gave her something positive to focus on. She tried to occupy herself with her plans, with the next thing, with the thrill of being chased, the satisfaction of conquest. Otherwise, a thing like Christmas could get you down.

By the time Cici got back to the dorm, a note was waiting at the front desk from Private Tom Wolcott. And up in her room, Lizbeth had just finished packing all her belongings into a trunk.

* * *

MARY'S BOYFRIEND BILL volunteered to drive her and June home on Christmas. June had wrapped store-bought presents for her parents in store-bought tissue paper. Mary, of course, did the same, but that hardly diminished June's pride. Bill wanted to meet their parents, and June figured he was going to marry her sister soon. Mary spent all her time with him; June had hardly seen her since she had arrived in Oak Ridge. He had a job with the Army Corps of Engineers, and looked grand in his green wool uniform with shiny brass buttons. He always went out of his way to be polite to June, which she knew was meant to impress her sister. Today he was acting more relaxed, like the brother he wanted to be. He glanced at her in the rearview mirror. "Hey, June, what's the name of that girl you always hang around with?"

"Cici. She's my roommate."

"Cici, that's right." He let out a low whistle. "That one is trouble."

Mary gently slapped his arm. "Bill! That's not nice to say. She's June's friend."

"Then June should know better than anyone. I've seen some of my boys go after her. She eats 'em right up and spits 'em back out."

June didn't really feel like talking about Cici. "She likes to flirt," she said noncommittally.

"I'll say! Hard to find a man in my company who hasn't gotten flirted with by her."

"Can we change the subject?" asked Mary.

"Sure," said Bill, grinning at her. "What'd you get me for Christmas?"

"You'll find out soon enough!" Another gentle arm slap.

June was impatient to get home. She watched houses go past, lights on, smoke spiraling from chimneys, and couldn't wait to be in her own parlor across from Mama and Daddy. As they pulled into the hollow, she smiled without even realizing it. The familiar fields and hills were covered in frost. On one side of the road, a small stream flowed at the bottom of a steep wooded hill, while on the other, rolling farmland spread out across the small valley. She knew who owned and lived on each piece of land and had been in most of the houses at some time or another. This was home. They were almost to their own farm when she noticed a figure in the yard of the Jacksons' place. She could only see his side, silhouetted against the morning sun, slumped forward on a pair of crutches. She squinted. "Mary! Is that Ollie Jackson?"

He turned to look at the passing automobile. In an awful instant, June recognized that it was indeed Ollie and that he was missing his left leg. "Oh, poor Ollie!" said Mary. "Bill, stop the car. We should go say hello."

June knew her sister was right, but dreaded getting closer to her former schoolmate. The last time she'd seen Ollie, he'd been a normal kid, playing football with the other boys. He'd also been Ronnie's best friend.

"Hello there!" Mary called out. She never seemed afraid of awkward situations. The two girls walked quickly to where Ollie stood. He shouted, "Merry Christmas!"

"Merry Christmas!" they both echoed.

"It's so good to see you, Ollie," said Mary.

"What's left of me, anyway." He said this with a smile, staring down at the space where his leg should be. June was relieved that he acknowledged it straightaway.

"How long have you been home?" June asked.

"Just a week here on the farm. I've been back stateside for a couple months, in a hospital."

"I'm so sorry," said June, and indeed, she could feel her eyes brim slightly with tears.

"Well, at least I'm alive. I'm sorry for you, too, June. We all miss Ronnie something awful."

The tears spilled over, and she felt somewhat relieved (then of course guilty for feeling relieved), knowing that crying at the mention of Ronnie's name was an appropriate response. "He sure did love you," June heard Ollie say.

She wiped her eyes with the sleeve of her coat. It was selfish and stupid for her to be crying when he was the one missing a leg. How ridiculous that he should feel sorry for her! "Thank you," she whispered.

"Your mama must be happy to have you home for Christmas," said Mary in her gentle voice.

"Yeah." He looked over at the four-room house badly in need of paint. "It's good to be home."

"It is," said June.

"We don't want to keep you from your family on Christmas," said Mary.

"It was real nice of y'all to stop by."

"You take care, Ollie," June said.

It took seeing her father on the porch, waving as they drove up, to raise June's spirits once more. As soon as Bill stopped the car, June leapt out and ran to the house. Frank enveloped her in his strong arms. By the time June was through the door, her mother had already come out of the kitchen to embrace her, bringing along with her the rich smell of roasting meat. "How is he?" she whispered in June's ear, referring of course to Bill.

"Nice," was all June had time for before the door opened, and Mary and her father came in, followed by Bill, who was carrying a Christmas wreath in one hand and playfully slapping her father on the back with the other.

"And this must be Rose," Bill said in a loud, hearty voice. June could tell that despite his bravado, he was scared.

"Pleased to meet you," her mother said as she shook his hand.

"Thank you so much for inviting me into your home."

"Of course. Any friend of Mary's is welcome here," said Frank.

"I brought this as a thank-you." Bill held out the pine-and-holly wreath to Rose.

"Isn't that lovely? Frank, can you hang it on the door?"

"Sure."

"Come on in and sit down," said Rose. "I'm still working on dinner, but there's coffee for anyone who wants it."

They sat in the living room. Like every year June could remember, stockings were hung above the fireplace, and her mother had decorated a scraggly pine tree her father had cut down in the woods behind the house. Rose brought in a tray of coffee mugs and passed them around. Frank came back in from hanging up the wreath, and they all sat in a circle, staring at Bill. "Mary tells us you're in the Army," Frank finally said.

"That's right, sir. The Army Corps of Engineers, so I'm serving right here in Tennessee."

"What exactly does the Corps of Engineers do?" asked Frank.

"Engineering projects for the Army, sir. I've been involved in the construction of the Clinton Engineer Works, where your daughters work, since it was first begun."

Mary beamed proudly at him. "Seems that's been a mighty big project," said Frank.

"I'm afraid I can't talk about it. You probably already know from the girls that we aren't allowed to talk about our work."

"That's what they said, but I thought maybe they were just trying to get us old folks to stop asking questions."

"It's true, Daddy," said Mary. "Censors check our mail. We could lose our jobs if we say too much."

"More important, we could lose the war." Bill was all seriousness when he said this, and June had to suppress a chuckle. It was like he'd stepped right out of one of the posters at work.

"We saw Ollie Jackson on the way in," said Mary.

"I know I should have written to you girls about it," said Rose, "but I just never could figure out how to put it in my letters."

"He seems in good spirits," said June.

"Brave boy," said Frank, as though it were too painful to form a complete sentence. The room was silent for a moment except for footsteps coming down the stairs. Jericho appeared, the same as ever in his overalls and long beard.

"What's all these folks doing here?"

"It's Mary and June, Jericho. Your granddaughters. And this is Mary's friend Bill."

Jericho stared at them all blankly. "Where's my dogs?"

"In the pen, Jericho. We're keeping them outside today, because we have company. You should put on a coat if you're going out." Frank took a coat down from a hook beside the door. Jericho took it from him silently and went out.

After the meal, they exchanged gifts, then sat around the parlor, drinking a second round of coffee. June wished she could stay by the fireplace into the evening and sleep in her childhood bed. But Mary was anxious to get back. "I have the worst headache," she said as they drove out of the hollow. She let out a little moan of pain. "And I'm supposed to sit for the Greeleys tonight."

"On Christmas?" asked Bill.

"They have a fancy Army party to go to."

"Why don't you have June cover for you?"

June leaned forward at the sound of her name. "Who are the Greeleys?"

Mary turned around to face her. "Bill's boss and his wife. They have three kids, four, seven, and twelve. They're good kids and real nice folks. And they'll pay you a dollar an hour."

"All right." The thought of spending the evening alone or even with Cici was awfully depressing anyway.

The line to get back through the security gate was almost a mile long. Mary held her head with one hand and continued to let out little moans. June thought she was laying it on a bit thick. She rested her own head against the window and watched the line of cars slowly snaking their way down the dusty road. One of the CEW billboards appeared up ahead: "Your Pen and Tongue can be enemy weapons. Watch What you Write and Say." It showed a cross with a helmet over it stabbed through with an ink pen.

"I'm supposed to be there at six thirty," said Mary. "Do you think we'll make it?"

"Well, there's nothing we can do to get there any faster," said Bill. "It's Christmas. I'm sure they'll be understanding."

It was six forty when they did finally get to the Greeleys'. They lived at the top of the ridge behind the town center. The hillside was covered with trees and cemesto houses and looked almost like a normal neighborhood rather than an Army reservation. As Bill turned onto the road up the hill, he asked June, "You ever been up to Snob Hill before?"

"Snob Hill?"

"That's what folks call this part of town. It's where all

the nicest houses are. You see, the farther up you go, the less mud there is."

It was true: the Greeleys had a real yard with grass, rather than the typical Oak Ridge mud pit. June could see a Christmas tree in the front window of the house.

"All right," said Mary. "I'll introduce you. Don't worry, Mrs. Greeley is nice."

Mary knocked on the door, and June stood beside her, trying to look poised and responsible. Still, it was hard not to gape at the woman who opened the door, wearing the prettiest dress June had ever seen outside of the movies. It was made of a shimmering gold that stretched all the way down to the floor. June could tell that the top was strapless, though Mrs. Greeley's shoulders were covered with a matching gold jacket. She was thin and the dress exaggerated her tiny waist, cinching in at the middle before flaring out over her hips.

"I'm so sorry I'm late," Mary began.

"Oh, don't be silly—we're running late as usual ourselves." Mrs. Greeley opened the door wide for them to come in.

"This is my sister June."

June extended her hand, and Mrs. Greeley shook it. June glanced around the immaculate living room. A gilded lamp stood over a deep burgundy sofa, and dark wooden furniture lined the walls.

"Merry Christmas to the both of you!" Mrs. Greeley said.

"We've just come from our parents' house, and I'm afraid I'm getting a sick headache. Would you mind if June filled in for me tonight? She's very responsible and works here at the CEW as well."

"Well, I don't see why that should be a problem."

As she spoke, two children came running into the living room. "Mary!" they called out. They were immediately followed by a man in uniform.

"Hello, Jason and Lucy. This is my sister June. She's going to play with you tonight."

"Hello," said June.

"I got a dollhouse for Christmas!" shouted Lucy. She didn't particularly seem to care if it was June or Mary who heard her news.

"You get home and get some rest," Mrs. Greeley said to Mary.

"All right. Bye-bye, everyone."

"June, why don't you just come in the bedroom with me while I finish getting ready?"

Mrs. Greeley led her down the hallway and shut the bedroom door behind them. She sat down at a vanity and began applying powder to her face. "I know it's awful to leave the children like this on Christmas night, but it's almost their bedtime. Anyway, we have to go to the major's party, though between you and me, they are dreadfully boring." She clipped a pair of large, sparkling earrings to her ears. "I wouldn't be so frantic getting ready, but the maid had the day off of course. Anyway, the children have already eaten, so you don't have to worry about that. Don't let them have any more candy, even if they beg. Bedtime is eight except for Jerry, the oldest. He can stay up till ten." She applied lipstick, mashed her lips together, and stood to face June. "How do I look?"

"Amazing." June meant it.

Mrs. Greeley led her back into the living room. The man was waiting for her by the door. "This is Captain Greeley; this is June." Mrs. Greeley introduced them quickly as her husband helped her into a long black coat and gave June a little nod. "We should be back around eleven. Good night, children!"

"Good night," they all called out at once, and with that, the elder Greeleys were gone. June faced the children, all three blue-eyed, well dressed, and exceptionally clean.

"Want to see my dollhouse?" asked Lucy.

"Want to see my truck?" asked the littlest one.

Jerry rolled his eyes at his younger siblings and announced, "I'm going to read in my room."

Lucy and Jason ran to find their presents under the tree. June had to give Lucy a hand with the dollhouse. It was a three-story house filled with tiny furniture. June had never seen such a nice toy in her life, or such a nice house for that matter. But Lucy soon grew tired of playing with it and demanded a game of hide-and-go-seek instead. Jason abandoned his truck in the hallway to join in, and June closed her eyes and began counting. She felt as though she was snooping, looking for the children. She opened a hall closet and saw nothing out of the ordinary, then opened the parents' closet. For a moment, she forgot about the children and just stared at Mrs. Greeley's clothes. There were dozens of jackets and dresses, all different colors, all beautifully tailored. Certainly not homemade.

Neither Lucy nor Jason wanted to go to bed when the time came, but June managed to get them washed and into pajamas by eight thirty. Lucy was still singing Christmas carols and asking her questions as June smoothed the blankets over her. "Do you work here?" asked the little girl.

"Yes."

Lucy whispered loudly, "Are you making candy?"

"What?"

"I know we're not supposed to talk about it, but some of

my friends at school think they're making candy in the factories. For the soldiers."

"That's wrong!" Jason sat up in his bed. "They're making yo-yos!"

"Nope!" said Lucy. "Daddy told me what they're really making." She looked over at her little brother, as though considering whether or not he was trustworthy, then leaned in to June and whispered into her ear, "Paper dolls!"

"That's exactly right," June told her. This seemed to satisfy Lucy, and she lay down, finally ready to go to sleep.

When June went back to the living room, Jerry was sitting on the sofa, setting up a game of checkers on the coffee table. "Wanna play?" he asked.

"Sure." She sat down on the floor across from him.

"You can go first."

She struggled to remember the rules of checkers and moved her piece. Jerry watched her intently. He had a button pinned to his shirt, which read, "A slip of the lip may sink a ship."

"What did you get for Christmas?" asked June in a friendly voice.

Jerry shrugged. "Some shirts. And a bicycle."

"A bicycle! That sounds exciting."

"Yeah, it's all right." He made his move without looking up at June and gave the impression of being completely bored.

"I'm sure you'll have fun being able to ride around town." June thought that she would like a bicycle, so that she didn't have to walk everywhere or take the bus.

"I got another present from my brother Mike. He's fighting the Japs."

"Oh. Did he send you a present from overseas?"

Jerry's face lit up for the first time, and he hopped off the sofa. "Yep. You wanna see it?"

"Sure."

"I'll be right back." Jerry ran off down the hall, and returned carrying a folded-up sheet, which he unfurled in a single dramatic gesture for June to see. It was a rectangle of a soiled white cloth with a large red circle in the middle—a Japanese flag.

"My brother got this off a Jap soldier he killed."

The flag was dirty and stained; June couldn't help but wonder if some of the dirt was human blood. It was horrible to look at, a souvenir of battle, of killing—the kind of thing that should be buried with its owner or left where it was found, far away from this American living room. Jerry's excitement over it disgusted her. "Your parents saw this?"

"Oh, yeah. Dad thought it was great. We're all real proud of Mike."

"You should treat it carefully. With respect, you know? It belonged to a soldier."

Jerry laid the flag out on the back of the sofa and sat back down. "A *Jap* soldier. Did you know they kill themselves if they lose a battle? They hold grenades up to their chests"—he demonstrated with his hands—"and explode them!" He demonstrated exploding as well, throwing his arms into the air and hurling his body back against the couch.

June couldn't stand the performance. "Why don't you put the flag away? It's almost time for bed."

"Aww, I'm not tired."

"Well, put it away, anyway, and we'll finish this game of checkers."

He slouched back to his room, returned, jumped back onto the sofa, and moved one of his checkers with barely a look at the board. "Do you think the war will still be going on when I get old enough to fight?"

"I certainly hope not! They say we've got the Germans beat—it's only a matter of time."

"It's not fair." He jumped over two of her checkers and eagerly grabbed them off the board.

"That's an awful thing to say, Jerry!" She didn't make a move, and he crossed his arms. "You'll be lucky if you never have to fight. Boys are dying every day. I just saw an old friend of mine today who lost his leg."

"But they're heroes!"

"There are other ways to be a hero. Helping people, making the world a better place."

Jerry slumped back against the sofa, unimpressed. "Maybe there'll be another war when I get older. It's your move."

She didn't care if he was only a child; Jerry had made her angry. "I'm tired of playing. It's time for you to go to bed."

"It's only nine forty!"

Before she could respond, the doorbell rang. Jerry looked at June, hopeful, but she shook her head. "Bed. Go get ready while I see who's at the door."

She felt nervous as she peered through the front window, unable to make anything out in the darkness. Who would be calling this late and on Christmas? She opened the door to reveal Dr. Cantor, the dark-haired scientist from Y-12, shivering on the doorstep in a worn coat, carrying a large envelope. He looked surprised. "Is Captain Greeley here?"

"No, he's at a party. I'm the babysitter."

"Oh. That's inconvenient. I need signatures on these documents."

"Right now?"

"The Army works around the clock."

"I'm not expecting him back for another hour or so, but I could give them to him when he returns."

Dr. Cantor studied her face. "You work at Y-12, right?"

She nodded. He thrust his hand forward. "Sam Cantor."

She shook his hand and replied, "June Walker."

"I can't leave these with you. They're top secret."

"I understand. Are you sure the signatures can't wait until the morning? It is Christmas, after all."

"Is it? I'd forgotten."

June let out a snicker. Dr. Cantor grimaced. "I'm sorry," she said. "I didn't mean to be rude. You can come in, if you like, to wait for the captain." She opened the door wider, unsure if this was the proper thing to do or not.

Perhaps he could sense her uncertainty because his own face relaxed. "No, you're right. It can wait until the morning. Sorry to disturb you, Miss Walker."

"That's all right."

"Good night. I'll be seeing you in the cafeteria, I suppose." He tipped his hat and turned back into the night. She closed the door against the cold night air, aware of a faint feeling of disappointment.

* * *

JOE HAD GOTTEN the letter from Moriah a few days before Christmas. She wrote him every couple of days, but this note was different, only three lines long:

Dearest Joe—

Our boy sick with fever.
Dr. Cox been out twice. He say prepare for worst.
Please pray for our son.

Love,
M

He must have read it a hundred times before sitting down on his cot to write a reply. Writing was always a struggle for him. He didn't know what to say, and he hardly knew any words to write, let alone how to spell them. He didn't want to write anyway; he wanted to go straight to the bus depot and head south as fast as possible to Alabama. But then he'd lose his job. He told Moriah he was praying; he loved her; God would watch over Ben. He put five dollars in an envelope and mailed it straightaway.

He was late for his shift that day. He kept Moriah's note tucked in his shirt pocket, as if maybe somehow having it close could help his little boy. He was distracted at work, slow and forgetful. Time passed slowly. Ralph was on a different crew, and he had no one to talk to. He prayed silently while pouring concrete.

Joe finally saw Ralph in the cafeteria. He felt awkward with so many other men around, so he asked the boy to step outside. They stood on the boardwalk under a bright electric streetlamp, and Joe gave him the note. He could see Ralph's breath hanging in the air as he read the letter. The boy looked up at Joe, his face stricken.

"He'll be all right, Joe."

Joe nodded. "I'm praying."

"He'll pull through, I know." Ralph patted him on the shoulder. "Come on, we should get something to eat."

Joe nodded. His stomach was growling, though he hardly had the spirit to eat. Inside the cafeteria, men's voices combined with the clank of cutlery hitting plates. The warmth of the room made Joe feel sleepy. He filled his plate with beans and potatoes. Ralph waved at someone, and Joe saw Otis waiting for them. He hated the thought of sitting with that man tonight but didn't know how to politely avoid it without making a fuss.

"I'm headed to the canteen. You boys want to come? There's gonna be a boxing match," said Otis with his strange smile.

"I'm tired out," said Joe.

Ralph glanced at him, nervous. "I'm going home with Joe."

"You don't have to," Joe tried to reassure him. "You should have fun."

"Shirley'll be there," said Otis.

That got Ralph's attention. "How do you know?"

"Ran into her and her friends on the way here. Told her we'd be there later."

"She's expecting me?"

"I reckon so."

"You should go," said Joe.

"What you going to do?" the boy asked.

"Go to bed."

Dark dreams disturbed Joe's sleep. His head and body ached in the morning. There was no new letter from Moriah. For three days, he got no news. The exhaustion, the aching, the worry quickly turned him ill-tempered. Joe snapped at a man on his crew who'd wandered off from the work site where they were laying the foundation of a house. He smoked constantly and ate little at his meals. He kept praying, though with less enthusiasm as time wore on, and more desperation, anger even. Why didn't Moriah write? He'd never doubted Moriah as a mother, but now he questioned whether he could trust her to take care of Ben all on her own. Everything she did mattered. If only he were there to help, to advise, to make sure that she was doing everything there was to be done.

Ben had just taken his first steps when Joe left Alabama. He'd been a calm baby, happier than either of the girls had been. Moriah had had an easy birth, and little Ben seemed to cry only when he was hungry. He slept easily and well. The girls doted on him, taking turns at singing him lullabies, playing peekaboo. Now he would be two and a half, walking, talking, becoming a little man. But still so small. Joe hated to think of his tiny body, writhing and sweating with fever. He would do anything to keep the boy safe. Each time Moriah had borne one of his children, Joe had felt a weight settle over him, a physical sensation pressing against his chest, full of menace. When he looked at his children, he felt love like he'd never known before, but also this suffocating weight. It was the terror of knowing that even if Joe dedicated the rest of his life to doing right by them, it wouldn't be enough. He couldn't protect them from life. He always told his children he would keep them safe, but he couldn't really. He'd been lying to them since the day they were born.

Ralph suggested they go to church together on Monday, which was Christmas. They both got off at seven o'clock and went home to change and eat before the colored service. Ralph put on a tie he'd bought in town, along with a new hat that he wore around after work these days. Joe took his own tie and hat out of his trunk. The hat was worn but sturdy. Moriah had made him the tie years ago to wear to church. As Joe wrapped it around his neck, Ralph thrust a small box toward him.

"What's this?" asked Joe.

"A Christmas present." Ralph looked up at him with boyish pride.

"Ralph, you shouldn't spend your paycheck on me!"

Ralph shrugged. "You know I don't have family of my own to buy presents for."

Joe tore at the brown paper and unwrapped the box. He popped off the lid and saw a new maroon tie. He took it out of the box and held it up in the harsh electric light. The color was vibrant. Joe had never owned a new piece of store-bought clothing before, besides shoes. "Well," he said, "ain't that nice?"

A small tree had been set up on a table in the corner of the cafeteria, decorated with gold and red glass balls. "That's an awful puny tree if you ask me," said Ralph.

"Suppose it cheers the place up, though. I wonder if Moriah got the presents I sent for the children."

"I'm sure she did. She's probably filling their stockings right now."

Joe had sent the girls a doll each and a teddy bear for little Ben a week ago.

"I sure do wish I was there tonight."

"I miss them, too," said Ralph softly.

Joe gave Ralph an appreciative nod. "How was Shirley?"

Ralph grinned. Something in his face was different from when Joe usually asked about her. "She's good. Real good."

"That so?"

"I got her a Christmas present too. Think she liked it."

"What you get her?"

"Nothing much. A bracelet. But she liked it real well."

"I'm sure she did."

The church was crowded. Men who sinned all year long in the rec hall and never set foot in the little chapel had come out tonight. Joe knew he wasn't the only one here missing a woman or children. The reverend read from the Gospel of Luke, and Joe felt comforted by the familiar words. They stood and sang "Silent Night." Ralph was beside him, singing soft but clear. The rest of the congregation seemed to fade out for Joe—he heard the boy's tenor above all others. Joe couldn't carry a tune himself and mouthed the words silently. He closed his eyes and listened as the boy sang, "Sleep in heavenly peace, sleep in heavenly peace." He must have said a thousand prayers in the past three days, but he prayed again: *Protect my son, Dear Lord, protect my boy.*

The song was over. Joe heard everyone taking their seats, his eyes still squeezed shut. He opened them and sat down. Ralph was looking at him. The boy held his eyes for a moment, silent. Ralph couldn't know what the weight felt like, the terror that death could take your child or the world could hurt him while you could do nothing to stop it from happening. But Ralph knew Joe was in pain, and his gaze held kindness and love.

After the service they went back to the hutment in silence. One of their roommates was smoking on his bed and nodded at them when they came in.

"Found that letter for you when I come in," he said to Joe,

motioning to the envelope on Joe's cot. Joe had it ripped open before he'd even finished speaking.

> *Dear Joe,*
>
> *The fever's broken. Ben drinkin broth and gainin strength.*
>
> *Sorry it take so long to write. I wanted to have good news for you.*
>
> *I got your presents for the children—they won't know what to do with such perty gifts. I also got the brooch. It the nicest thing anyone ever gave me.*
>
> *I wish I had something more to send you for Christmas but I hope the news that your son is well brightens your day. We miss you something terrible, all of us. I dream of a Christmas when we will be together again.*
>
> *Love,*
> *Moriah*

He read it three quick times. Ralph cleared his throat.

Joe looked up at him. "He better."

Ralph slapped him on the back. "I told you!"

Joe nodded and sat on the bed, still clutching the letter. "I won't go another Christmas without my family."

"I'll help you." Ralph was solemn, sincere.

"Thank you." Joe finally let his face relax into a grin. "Merry Christmas, son."

(Courtesy of the Department of Energy)

Chapter 8

AFTER A YEAR IN OAK RIDGE, SAM STILL FOUND THE WORK thrilling—perhaps more so now than ever, with Y-12 finally functioning as it should. What had once been theoretical was becoming wonderfully, terrifyingly real. This huge factory was slowly but surely refining uranium, sending off tiny precious bits of it to New Mexico in suitcases. But as the outlook of the war began to get better, the idea of this weapon seemed worse. In the beginning of the war, the physicists he knew had all spooked each other by speculating how far along the Germans had gotten creating their own atomic weapon. But at this point, Hitler's army was crumbling, and it seemed increasingly unlikely that they were racing with Germany to build the bomb. If anything, they were racing with the war itself. He knew scientists who believed the bomb would end all wars, but hadn't the horrors of the last war been supposed to end all wars? There would always be more war. How anyone could think humanity would ever give up its destructiveness was beyond him.

Max Kingsley shared his grim outlook, and they routinely wallowed in their misery over the dreadful low-alcohol "near beer" served at the taverns in Oak Ridge. Max was a physicist from England and had been working on the project before the United States had even officially gotten involved. His disillusionment was proportional to his years of service.

"Can I get you another?" Sam asked, motioning to Max's almost-empty glass. They were sitting across from each other at their usual table, hats and jackets slung carelessly on their chair backs, the ashtray between them already full.

Max shrugged. "I suppose I must." His blond hair was carefully combed across his head, a thin, slightly darker mustache balancing his face.

Sam went to the bar and brought back two beers. Max took a gulp and shook his head mournfully. "I don't know which is worse: this beer or that toxin in your pocket."

Sam always took a flask of moonshine to the canteen these days. "I don't know either, but I do know which one works faster."

Sam had stumbled upon the black market for booze one night last winter, when he found himself waiting in the usual long line to buy cigarettes. He didn't really mind the lines. He used empty time like this to ponder things that might not otherwise bubble to the surface of his mind. It could be something as simple as recalling that he had left his umbrella in the laboratory conference room the day before, or as unexpected as a memory of his grandmother's taking him to one of the Yiddish plays on Second Avenue when he was a boy. If he was lucky, his thoughts would become creative, and he would find a possible solution to the ongoing problem of leaking vacuum tanks at Y-12. Long bus rides and endless lines made him feel calm, and idleness worked a kind of magic on his mind. But this day, his thoughts kept being interrupted by a coarse young man in a dirty shirt and work pants.

"Great day, there sure is a lot a folks wantin' cigarettes!" The man shook his head at Sam. Up until now Sam had ignored him, but this was the third such comment the man had made, and it seemed too rude to pretend not to hear.

"Yes, there is."

A breeze blew through the square where they stood in front of the store. Sam shivered and flipped up the collar on his jacket to protect his neck.

"It is colder than a witch's tit out here!" exclaimed the man. The young woman standing in line in front of him raised her chin and sniffed loudly to indicate disapproval. Sam couldn't help but crack a smile. The man seemed encouraged and kept talking. "I done been here four months, and I have just about had it with these lines! I work hard during my ten-hour shift. I want to enjoy myself when I get off, not stand in no line just to get a pack a smokes!"

"Not like there's too much else to do around here for fun," said Sam, giving in at last to this stranger's desire to converse.

"Ain't that the truth! Sometimes the men on my crew go to the tavern. But they don't even serve real beer."

The line shuffled forward and the disapproving young woman got to make her purchase. "Looks like we've almost made it!"

Later, as Sam walked home along the wooden boardwalk, he heard a whistle behind him. At first he ignored it, but then he heard the whistle again. "Hey, mister!" said a man in a loud whisper.

Sam wondered if he was about to be robbed. The man from the cigarette line came out from the shadow of a post holding up a billboard. "Didn't mean to startle you. Which way you headed?"

"Just up this hill." Sam tried to sound even and calm.

"I'll walk with you. Listen, I wanted to ask. You interested in something better than near beer?"

Sam perked up. "Yeah, definitely."

"I've got a friend who could get you something. You ain't a spy, is you?"

"No, sir."

"If you're interested, meet me under this sign tomorrow night at seven, understand?"

"Yes."

And with that, the man crept back into the darkness and was gone. Sam felt like a character in a gangster movie, if the gangsters had hillbilly accents. It seemed like a terrible idea to come back tomorrow; he could be arrested and lose his job. On the other hand, he hadn't had a real drink in two months.

The next night was equally dark and cold as Sam walked toward the sign. Soft light glowed from houses. He had promised to meet Ann and Charlie later at one of the rec halls but didn't much feel like it. All the people and the laughing and the dancing—sometimes he wondered what on earth these people had to be so happy about. The girls who worked at Y-12 were all smiles and laughter as soon as their shifts ended. He hated to hear them in the corridors. They plunged him into dark moods, which gripped him and held on tight for days. He tried to keep to himself when he felt this wretched, but Ann had a way of forcing him into conversation. Once he'd foolishly told her some of his thoughts. She'd looked at him like he was a puppy with a broken leg. "Oh, Sam, sure, the world's in an awful state. Sure, the war is terrible. My two kid brothers are over there, and I think about them all the time. But we can't just give up, can we? People do what they can to keep going."

"But these girls!" He couldn't stop himself from continuing. This was another problem with the moods. When he was in a bad way, he had to stay quiet, because once he got talking, he found it hard to stop. "They're not getting by, they're thriving! The way they flirt with the men at work! The way they giggle and skip down the sidewalk!"

"Why do you think they flirt, Sam? It makes them feel alive! With so much death around us all, who can blame these young girls for wanting to feel alive?"

Sam didn't want to fight with Ann. She was too good and kind to see what he saw, and, he reminded himself, she didn't have a clue what they were really doing here. Her job was keeping the pathetic little house in order, playing the perfect little wife to Charlie. Sam didn't doubt that it was hard on her. She had been reared on maids and white gloves and coming-out parties. He admired her for her spirit, for holding a live chicken in her hand and dusting three times a day to try to rid the house of coal specks. But he didn't expect her to understand the awfulness of people.

He arrived at the billboard, one of the many signs reminding citizens to keep their mouths shut. "The Enemy is LOOKING . . . for information," it read. "Guard your talk." A large eyeball with a swastika for a pupil stared out from it. It seemed an ominous place to meet. He imagined having to call Charlie if he was arrested and how disappointed his friend would be. Charlie thought so well of Sam, always had.

He had encouraged him to be more social back in graduate school, and would take Sam along to football games and picnics with his old college pals. Charlie was oblivious to how awkward Sam felt in the midst of those old-money *Mayflower* descendants, how much they despised him for having no money and parents who'd arrived on Ellis Island just twenty-five years ago. Charlie was so unabashedly optimistic about people that he couldn't see how awful his old chums were or how useless Sam was at functioning in their world. Even now Charlie ignored Sam's dark spells. Ann tried to cheer him up, but Charlie just slapped him on the back.

He wanted to smoke a cigarette, but was afraid lighting it might attract attention. He shivered and pushed his hands deep into his pockets. His fingers found a folded piece of paper, a letter from his brother, which he took out to re-examine. He tried to remember to write Jon regularly. It was the least he could do. Jon was in the Marines and had fought at Tarawa. The last time Sam had seen him was three years ago, before leaving for the West, and his little brother had only been sixteen. The idea of him fighting was ridiculous. He watched newsreels of the Marines in action and struggled to convince himself that one of those men could be his goofy little brother. Of course Jon's letter didn't say anything about fighting. It was short, which was to be expected, full of generic pleasantries about the weather, the ocean, the other boys, the food in the mess hall. Sam was ten years older than Jon, so they hardly knew each other.

"Be sure to keep writing to Ma," Jon ended his letter, and Sam felt mildly resentful. He knew he should write his mother more often, but didn't like to have his little brother telling him so. He also knew that Jon, in the midst of fighting a war no less, likely wrote her more than he did, and that made him feel guilty.

We should have stayed in Berlin. When he thought of his mother, those were the words that echoed through Sam's head. He had heard them hundreds of times throughout his childhood, mumbled under her breath, spat accusingly at his father, or recited in commiseration with his grandmother. When his sister came down with polio, when his father lost his job, when it rained and she was caught without an umbrella, his mother always returned to the refrain: *We should have stayed in Berlin.*

When he was in a good mood, Sam's father would roll his eyes. When he was in a bad mood, he would shake his head. "What good would have come to us in Germany? I'd have been killed, no doubt, on the Western Front, and you and the children would have starved along with my sisters back in the city."

And in fact Sam's mother had spent only a few short months of her life in the city that now loomed so large in her memory. But it was the first city she'd ever seen, and it had gripped her imagination. She was only a teenager, a Polish peasant en route to America with her parents and siblings. They stopped in transit in the German capital, like thousands of Jewish immigrants before and after them. The difference for Dworja was that she fell in love not only with the city but also with Sam's father, Solomon, a Berlin native and university student who must have seemed impossibly sophisticated to her. He showed her the city, confidently speaking German, telling her of his plans to become a chemist.

Sam had often wondered how his uneducated, always worried, always nagging mother had ever been desirable enough to lure his father away from his studies to New York. At first both Dworja and Solomon were lost in New York, struggling with English and the foreign customs. But unlike his wife, Solomon became convinced of the promise of America, even if the only work he could find was in a bakery. *Study, study, study,* he told Sam, as often as Dworja mourned for the life that could have been in Germany.

Of course, 1933 was enough to overcome even Dworja's ardent nostalgia. Some small part of Solomon must have wanted to thank Hitler for finally shutting her up about Berlin. But most of him was consumed with worry for his family, particularly his beloved little sister Rachel. She had written to them every week for Sam's entire life. During the thirties, her letters became increasingly disturbing. When Solomon died unexpectedly from a heart attack in 1936, Dworja tried to convince Rachel to come to New York. But it was too late for her to get out. And soon her letters could no longer get out, either. It had been almost six years since they'd heard anything from the family in Germany.

Sam shoved Jon's letter back in his pocket and glanced at his watch. The man was late—what had he gotten himself into? This fellow could easily be a spy. Supposedly one in every four people here worked as an informant. That was how the Army kept folks in line—you really didn't know who you could trust. Mention you have liquor to sell while waiting in line for cigarettes, and the next thing you know it winds up in a report. Anyone might inform on you. Then there were professionals, of course, whose sole job was to watch for breaches in security. Sam thought he'd spotted one at Y-12. He'd seen him around for the last week, wearing a maintenance uniform, but he was never actually doing any work.

Sam heard a whistle and swung around. The man was standing in front of him, holding a suitcase. "I done brought plenty to keep you warm and happy tonight."

"How much is it?"

"Four dollars a bottle."

It seemed excessive, but Sam felt pretty desperate. Still, he figured he ought to negotiate. "*What* is it exactly?"

"Splo."

"What?"

"Hooch, corn liquor, whatever you want to call it." Sam squinted at him in the darkness. The man sighed and said in a loud whisper, "Moonshine whiskey. Homemade."

"Well, I'm not paying four dollars for a bottle of anything I haven't tasted."

"It's too risky to get it out here. You got a place nearby we could have a drink?"

Sam considered. The house wasn't far from here, and Ann and Charlie would already be at the rec center. "We can go to my room, if you want."

"Fine by me."

Sam led him toward the house. What would Ann think if she knew he'd just invited a bootlegger into her home?

"Shouldn't I know your name before I see your house?" asked the man.

"Sam Cantor." He didn't bother shaking hands, as he was now leading the man along the boardwalk.

"Pleased to meet you, Sam. I'm Homer Clabough."

Sam walked quickly for a number of reasons. It was cold, he hoped to avoid conversation with Homer, and he wanted their entire interaction to be over as quickly as possible.

"You ain't from around here, huh?" questioned Homer.

"I grew up in New York."

"New York! Imagine that! What you think of Tennessee?"

Sam struggled to think of something inoffensive to say. "Your biscuits are delicious."

"You ain't got biscuits in New York?"

"No, sir."

"Great day!" Homer spoke with a level of innocence surprising in a bootlegger.

Sam led him into the house and instructed him to wipe his boots. He turned on the light and motioned for Homer to take a seat on the couch. "I'll get some glasses."

"This is a right pretty place! Look, a record player! Did you bring it all the way from New York?"

"It's not mine." Sam set two glasses on the coffee table. "I'm just a boarder here."

Homer opened his suitcase and took out a gallon-sized glass bottle. He poured the clear liquid into the two glasses. "Here you go! Authentic splo."

It smelled like fire. Sam sipped. It tasted like fire, too. But it was drinkable, and it would certainly get the job done. "Three dollars."

Homer shook his head. "I'm sorry, Sam. I can't lower the price, even though I like you. You see, it ain't just me running this operation. I got one man on the outside brewing it, and another who gets it inside for me. It ain't no small thing getting past Army security."

Two more sips made Sam's head feel light. He was warming to Homer. "How do you do it?"

Homer shrugged. "Different ways. You sure you ain't a spy?"

"Cross my heart."

"We got a car with a special hidden compartment under the seats. Security ain't found it yet!" Homer took a swig and shook his head fiercely. "Shoo dawg!"

"So what's your job here?"

"I do construction. Union Carbide pays good, but tell you what, the real bread and butter's this here shine. I tried to join the Army and all, but I'm blind in one eye. I always done got by fine, but they didn't want me."

"You're better off here."

Homer shrugged. "Wanted to do my part, is all."

"Have you always lived around here?"

Homer nodded. "Grew up about ten miles down the road, when there weren't nothing here but some farms. Never could've imagined this. You hear tell of John Hendrix?"

Sam shook his head.

"He were a prophet lived right here back in 1915. Folks in these parts all knew about him and thought he was crazy. He would go off into the woods for days, not eating or sleeping, just praying and getting these visions. One time he went into the woods for forty days, and when he come out, he told everyone around about his vision of the future. He said that Bear Creek Valley would be filled with factories and that they would help win the greatest war that would ever be."

Sam knew he must be getting drunk, because he was enjoying Homer's story. "Is that true?"

"That's not all. He said there'd be a big city on Black Oak Ridge and named the exact spot where headquarters is located. He knew there'd be a railroad spur off the main L&N line. He said big engines would dig big ditches, and thousands of people would be running around, and there'd be lots of noise and the earth would shake."

"Wow."

"You can ask anyone from around here. They all know the story. My pappy's friends with John Hendrix's son."

"Well, that's good news, then."

"What is?"

"He said we'd win the war, right?"

"Oh, yeah! He did!"

Sam took out his wallet and handed Homer four dollars.

Sam regularly purchased moonshine from Homer Clabough now, once every two weeks, and he carried his flask with him to the canteen to help the near beer go down. He surreptitiously took a sip and offered it to Max.

"No thank you, I'm not quite that desperate yet." Max wordlessly offered Sam a cigarette from his pack, and for a moment they smoked and drank in silence. They'd developed the sort of friendship and routine that didn't require constant conversation.

A large, loud group of soldiers and girls came in. They were laughing and shouting, full of energy and abandon. The girls were wearing colorful dresses, red, green, and blue, which looked all the more brilliant next to the drab beige of the men's uniforms. One soldier went to the bar and whistled to get beers from the waitress. Another two took over a table and began pulling out chairs for the ladies, which they presented to them with a flourish. "Ah, to be young and stationed in a noncombat zone," said Max.

"We're no better. What's our excuse for not fighting?"

"Our brilliant minds. With any luck, we can kill far more people by thinking over here than by fighting over there."

The soldiers began bringing drinks over, beer for themselves, Cokes for the girls. Sam recognized a couple of them from Y-12. One was hard to forget: a real looker with dark hair, a perfect face, and an excellent figure, which she knew just how to carry. The soldiers had obviously noticed this as well; they all seemed to lean in toward her, desperate to get as close as possible. Sam recognized the girl beside her, too. She was the one from the Greeleys', and he'd often seen her in her cubicle at work. She was plain compared to her friend; her dress looked homemade. He was surprised to see her with the other girl. She hadn't struck him as the type to hang out with such a ridiculous flirt. Her big gray eyes watched the others around the table, yet she seemed to be not quite one of the group. She looked distant, thoughtful, not frivolous like her friends.

"We don't have enough fun, Sam. Look at these young people, having the time of their lives! That could be us."

"What do they have to be so happy about?"

"Well, as aforementioned, they aren't going to be slaughtered anytime soon in battle. The hundreds of young girls in town seem to amuse them as well."

"But living in this miserable place!"

"Give it time and it all becomes more bearable."

"I've been here a year."

"Well, I've been here a year and a half and have become resigned to it. After a while, Tennessee becomes inevitable. One stops fighting it, so to speak."

Sam knew he would never become resigned to life here. He had always been resistant to reconsidering negative opinions, once such opinions had been formed. He took a slug of whiskey. Max considered his friend. "You really are in a foul mood this evening, aren't you?"

"Like I said, I've been here a year."

"There are worse places to be. Battlefields, for instance."

"At least I'd be doing my duty."

Max gave him a quizzical look. "You're serious, aren't you?"

Sam didn't know if he was serious or not. He drank the beer. "It's just I get these letters from my brother. He doesn't say much about what he's seen—he can't, of course—but you sort of read between the lines. . . . He's my kid brother, for God's sake. I feel like a coward compared to him."

"Here's to cowardice." Max raised his glass.

But Sam wasn't done. "He was supposed to be the screwup. I was the smart one who aced every class in school; Jon was always getting in scrapes. A sweet, funny kid who could never stay focused or do anything right. It just doesn't make any sense."

"Of course, I understand." Max's voice had a rare ring of sincerity. "I don't have a brother, but I do have a sister whose flat was destroyed. She'd just left London the day before, thank God. But I felt it then more than at any other time, I suppose. Your family is attacked, and you are supposed to go off and fight for king and country."

They drank in silence. Finally Max spoke again. "We are fighting in our way, you know."

Sam nodded. "Yeah, I know."

The soldiers' group was breaking into spontaneous dance. They all got up and began swaying and twirling to the swing music playing on the radio, except for the quiet girl, who stayed seated. She didn't seem to mind being left behind and sat up straight in her chair, taking occasional sips from her almost-empty Coke bottle. A wild notion occurred to Sam to offer to buy her another. Idly, he wondered what she would look like with her sweater off, then immediately dismissed the thought, embarrassed at himself. Why was he lusting after this plain country girl? He gulped down his beer. "Another?" he asked, already getting up to buy a third round.

"Isn't it my turn?"

"I'm sure I owe you." He walked toward the bar, past the girl's table. As he went by, he couldn't help but look down at her. Her big eyes met his, and she smiled. He suddenly felt as awkward as if he were a teenager, and he walked as quickly as he could to the counter. What had he been thinking? She was practically a child. "Two beers," he ordered, determined to not look back.

(Courtesy of the Department of Energy)

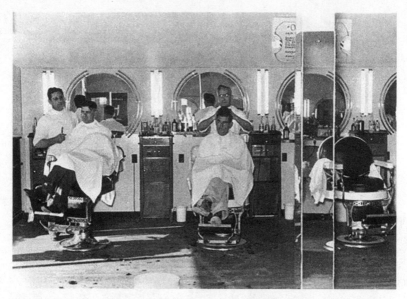

(Courtesy of the Department of Energy)

Chapter 9

CICI INSISTED ON DOING JUNE'S MAKEUP FOR THE NEW YEAR'S dance. June perched on the side of her bed as Cici carefully selected lipstick and eye shadows, holding the different shades up to June's face to choose the most flattering. Cici had been in a good mood all week, since she'd met some new soldier on Christmas and Lizbeth had abruptly announced she was moving into a shared house the next day. "I know you don't believe me," Cici said as she attacked June's face with a brush, "but I really feel like Tom is special. I think he may be the one."

June didn't believe her but couldn't reply, as she was under instructions to hold her face still so Cici could apply rouge to her cheeks. "He went to Yale—did I tell you that already?" Cici continued.

"Mmm." June tried to grunt in an affirmative way.

"His father's a banker and sounds very respectable. And Tom is so smart. You have to be to get placed in the Special Engineer Detachment, you know."

June knew because Cici had mentioned it a half-dozen times already. Most of the soldiers in Oak Ridge were in the SED. As best as June could tell, they were lucky above all else to be stationed over here instead of over there.

"Close your eyes," said Cici, and June did as she was told. She felt something smooth and cool being rubbed against her eyelids. It tickled.

"All right, look at me." June obeyed, and Cici stared at her eyes intently. "Close again. You know I've been thinking, June. Now, don't be angry at me for saying this, but I think it's time for you to start looking for a man."

June's eyes flipped open. "I'm not ready!"

"I know you feel that way now, but someday, God willing, this war will be over, and what are you going to do then? You can't be a factory girl forever. We all need to find husbands."

It seemed like enough managing to get through her time here in Oak Ridge without worrying about the future. But June knew Cici was right; her family would expect her to get married someday. "I guess I could keep my eyes open."

"Exactly! Tom has lots of friends who'll be at the party tonight. You will dance with them, won't you?"

"Sure."

"Good!" Cici gave June's shoulders a little squeeze and turned her around to face the mirror. "You won't have any problem getting them to ask you!"

June's gray eyes were framed with brown liner and accentuated with blue eye shadow. The rouge brought out her cheekbones and her round lips were painted a deep mauve. She stared at herself, surprised by what a difference Cici's cosmetics had made. She was almost certain that she was pretty.

* * *

MAX AND SAM spent New Year's Eve as they spent most evenings—slumped in the corner at the canteen. In deference to the holiday, they had started drinking earlier than usual, so that by ten o'clock, even Max had gotten tight drinking the weak Oak Ridge beer. The canteen was crowded with young people, most stopping by on their way to one of the big parties around town. They were all loud and happy, full of songs and jokes and that general sense of optimism that Sam found so baffling. As a particularly fetching group of girls walked by their table, Max suggested, presumably in jest, that maybe they ought to get girlfriends. He, in fact, had had a series of girlfriends since Sam had known him, though most of the relationships lasted no longer than a week or two. He was good-looking enough, moderately charming, and could easily wow a country girl with his accent.

"What girls are going to be interested in a couple of drunk physicists?"

"I'm serious. Most people do this. They find someone they like, get married, produce children. It makes them happy."

"There are plenty of miserable families out there."

"True, I suppose. But it might be worth a shot. Perhaps it would make us . . . care less about the world."

"Shouldn't having children make you care more?"

"Okay, it could make us more hopeful."

"It's a rotten world to bring a child into."

Max gave his friend a look. Sam could never quite tell what Max's stares meant—he seemed to have the same blank expression for rage, happiness, annoyance, or jest. "I see you are not to be convinced on this point. Fair enough."

"But don't let me stop you. Go, find a nice girl, Godspeed. Maybe you'd leave me alone."

"I know. That's my one worry. If I could be guaranteed to find a worthless, cruel woman, then I'd pursue it. But I'm terrified of winding up with a nice girl and ruining her life. What time is it?"

Sam glanced at his watch and realized he must be drunk, since it was difficult to make out the location of the hands. "Ten twenty," he finally determined.

Max slammed his beer down. "This is pathetic. Let's get out of this dump, for God's sake. It's New Year's."

"Where do you propose we go? The Copacabana?"

"The rec hall. Let's go to the dance."

"Oh, God, no. I went last year, and it was just awful."

Max stood and began putting on his coat. "There weren't nearly as many girls here last year. Come on. When's the last time you had your hand on a woman's waist?"

Sam didn't answer because he couldn't remember. "I think I'm too drunk to move."

"We're just drunk enough that it won't be too painful. In fact you might want to take a few more swigs from your flask before we go in." Max got up and handed Sam his coat from the rack.

"All right, fine, but I'm not dancing!"

"Fine, but it's the only way you get to touch a woman you hardly know without being arrested." Coats and hats in place, they wobbled out the door.

Sam had emptied his flask by the time they got to the rec hall and found it hard to focus as they walked into the large, crowded room. He was not too drunk to know he must be very drunk. Everything in the room seemed to be in motion—people, his stomach, the walls. A band was playing, and he could feel the swing music in his bones.

Max led him across the room to the far wall. "Look for a table," Max shouted back to him, but the room was packed, and he could see they weren't going to find seats. It was all the same to Sam; he felt restless, and though not sober or coordinated enough to dance, he wasn't inclined to sit still either. But Max was determined. He spotted two empty but obviously already taken seats, clearly marked by men's jackets over their backs, at a round table near the wall. Max slid into the seat nearest a tall blonde. "Mind if we sit for a minute?" Max patted the chair next to him, and Sam obediently sat down.

The blonde giggled. "Someone was sitting there . . . "

"Well, it was terribly discourteous of him to leave you all by yourself."

More giggles. Sam lit a cigarette as Max commenced his seduction. He looked around the room. There were definitely more girls here than last year; the room was overflowing with them, all wearing their best dresses, bright and colorful, sparkling in some cases, twirling and floating across the dance floor. He sucked hard on his cigarette and thought about how it would feel to have one of these women in his arms, out of her gaudy attire, naked and fleshy, her soft, smooth skin touching his, breasts and everything else. It was pathetic to be driven to self-abuse at his age, especially humiliating in his little room down the hall from the married couple he lived with, but that was what it came to every night. Max got up and winked at him as he led the blonde toward the dance floor. Sam lit another cigarette.

A few tables over, he noticed a couple of familiar girls—the brunette stunner and her quiet friend, the one from the Greeleys', June. The brunette was holding hands with a soldier while June looked on. There was something about her. She never had an empty, vapid smile on her face, like all the other girls, he'd noticed. Tonight was no different. Maybe that's what he liked about her.

* * *

JUNE KEPT HER word and danced with two of Tom's friends. One was two inches shorter than her and used this to his advantage to stare down her dress. She declined a second dance with him and was forced to dance with another, this one a foot taller and already half bald, though he couldn't have been more than twenty-one years old. He was a good dancer, or at least fancied himself to be a good dancer, insisting on twirling, tossing, and dipping June at every possible opportunity and sometimes attempting to do all three at once. Whenever she lost her balance, tripped over his toes, or thudded into his arms, he let out a shockingly high-pitched laugh. She turned down a second dance with him as well and slumped back to the table. Luckily, the rest of Tom's buddies all seemed to have dates for the night. June drank punch and watched all the graceful couples having fun dancing. She wasn't too down; it was a good party, and after all, she wasn't looking for romance. She'd bought a new dress from Miller's as a Christmas present to herself—her first ever store-bought dress. It was only cotton, but it was a bright festive red with a full skirt. A live band was playing, and she couldn't stay sad with the swinging music going. Her feet tapped under the table as she made small talk with the soldiers and their girlfriends.

Cici and Tom returned arm in arm from the dance floor. Seeing only one empty chair, he took it and motioned for Cici to sit on his lap. He grabbed two glasses of punch from the table, handed one to Cici, and said, "To 1945!"

"Nineteen forty-five!" Cici held out her glass to June, who dutifully clinked. "Did you dance with Jerry?" she asked, referring to the balding giant.

"Yes. I have the bruises to prove it."

Tom laughed. "Jerry likes to show off his skill on the dance floor. I hope it wasn't too awful."

"No, he seems nice." June hoped her tone was bland enough that they'd give up trying to match her with him.

"You must have more single friends," said Cici to Tom.

"All my friends are single."

"You know what I mean. Friends that aren't attached at the moment."

"Give it a week. They become unattached."

"Tom! Don't scare June."

June winced. "You make me sound like a charity case."

"No, of course not! It's so much better to find a fella through friends and know he's a decent guy."

"Oh, you're looking for a decent guy for June? You should've said. I'm afraid I can't help you there."

"Stop! He's just joking, June."

June looked out across the dance floor in the hopes they would stop talking about her. She noticed a figure who looked out of place. Dr. Cantor was walking toward the back of the room, scowling, completely divorced from the frivolity around him as usual.

Cici followed June's gaze. "What's Dr. Cantor doing here? He's such a snob; I'd think he had some important scientist's party to go to."

"Do you think he's a snob? I didn't know you knew him," said June.

"Of course! He never talks to anyone in the cafeteria or on the bus. Thinks he's too good for the likes of us. But look at him! He must think he's too good to bother wearing decent clothes."

His jacket was shapeless and wrinkled, it was true. June watched him get punch from the refreshment table, looking no more at ease. He seemed to tremble a bit as the woman handed him a cup.

"Looks like he's been into the gin," said Tom with a chuckle.

"Ugh!" Cici let out a loud, dismissive sniff. "He may be a snob, but he has no class. Why does he keep looking over here?"

He did seem to be looking in their direction. June turned away, embarrassed. "Maybe he saw us staring."

"I don't know," said Cici. "I think he's looking at you."

June hardly thought that was likely, but she stole a quick look in his direction just as he began walking straight toward their table. He was unmistakably headed for them, despite the fact that the dance floor was in his way. As he stumbled through the dancers, punch splashed out of his cup and dancing couples glared. He must be drunk, June thought.

"He's coming here!" Cici shrieked, as though he were a knife-wielding maniac.

He nodded at them all. "Hello again," he said, clearly addressing June.

"Hello, Dr. Cantor," she said in a soft, high voice. "This is Cici and Tom."

"Nice to meet you all," Sam said, not taking his eyes off June. "June, I was wondering if you'd like to dance."

She stared up at him in shock.

"We're in the middle of a chat," said Cici before June could respond.

"June can speak for herself, can't she?"

"We're best friends," said Cici. "I can speak for her."

Sam took a gulp of his punch and stared at June. He was swaying slightly from side to side. "If you're friends, then you'll have plenty of time to chat later. This is a party, and you should be dancing."

"I'm not sure you're in any condition to dance, sir." Tom was standing now and puffing out his chest in a show of manly protectiveness that June found alarming.

"Excuse me? Am I not young enough to dance with a pretty girl?"

June felt her cheeks flush. Tom somehow rose even taller. "What I mean, sir, is that maybe you've had too much to drink. Maybe it's time to go home."

Sam laughed loudly. "What, are you going to challenge me to a duel, soldier?"

The tension at the table seemed to drift outward, and other people were starting to stare. Tom looked like he was ready to fight, and June moved decisively, doing the only thing she could think of to defuse the situation. She stood quickly. "I'll dance," she said, aware that both Cici and Tom were glaring at her.

Sam slammed his punch glass down on the table and led her to the dance floor. They faced each other and spent an awkward moment placing their hands in the correct places.

Luckily, the song playing was slow; Sam nevertheless led her around at odds with the rhythm. June tried to stay calm and follow his stumbling as best she could. She could smell whiskey, the familiar scent that followed her grandfather, and saw that he needed a shave. He had dark eyes magnified by round glasses and was staring at her a little too intensely for comfort. But still, he was handsome, definitely different from all these young boys they usually hung around. He looked more adult, weary even, and though he might be drunk and terribly clumsy, June felt sympathetic toward him.

He stumbled badly and stepped on her toe. "Ouch!" she exclaimed before thinking.

"I'm sorry. I'm not a very good dancer."

He attempted to turn her and knocked his elbow into the back of a passing couple.

"Watch out, buddy!" an angry soldier called out.

"Dr. Cantor, maybe we should go outside."

"Why?!" He was defensive, hurt.

"Fresh air?"

"It's freezing out there. I'm having fun."

The song came to an end, but he continued moving in the same jerky way, as though he hadn't noticed. June was sure that many people were staring at them now. She leaned in to whisper to him, "Dr. Cantor, you could get in trouble with the Army if someone reports that you've been drinking."

"I've not been drinking!"

"I can smell the whiskey on your breath."

He smiled sheepishly, like a child caught with his hand in the cookie jar.

"Please, let's get out of here. People are staring, and you could lose your job."

Finally he stopped moving, though at this point the band was at least playing again. She led him by the hand to the door, deliberately not looking back to catch Cici's disapproving look. Everyone in the room seemed to watch them go. This was, no doubt, a horrible mistake. Folks in Oak Ridge loved to gossip, and she had just walked outside alone with an important man from work who was clearly intoxicated. But she felt she had to get Dr. Cantor out of there. She wasn't sure why she suddenly felt so protective of this man she hardly knew, except that he looked like he needed help, and he'd come to her.

He was right; it was freezing outside, and June realized as soon as they'd walked out onto the concrete steps that her coat was inside. She couldn't possibly face the room again just to get her coat. She sat on the concrete ledge at the top of the stairs, shivering.

"Here." Dr. Cantor had taken off his jacket and was handing it to her.

"Won't you be cold?"

He shook his head and shoved the jacket toward her. It was warm from his body, and putting it on made her feel close to him.

"Don't you have a soldier boyfriend in there somewhere?" he asked, leaning back against the side of the building and pulling a pack of cigarettes out of his pocket.

"No."

He offered her a cigarette, but she shook her head. He lit his own. "You're right. I'm drunk."

"You should go home and sober up. They say they'll throw you off the reservation if you're caught drinking."

"Why do you care if I lose my job?"

"I don't know. You seem nice."

"No, I don't." He waved the cigarette at her. "I've been awful and rude. Your friend's boyfriend wanted to punch me. And he probably should have."

"You gave me your jacket," she said, feeling foolish.

He tossed away the cigarette and sat down beside her on the ledge, so close that their arms were touching. She knew she should move her arm away, but it was warmer with him beside her. He was staring right at her face, in an embarrassing way, and she was glad of the rouge and eye shadow.

"June. . . . Is your birthday in June?"

She nodded. The music inside stopped, and they both turned at the sound of the countdown, everyone shouting, "Ten, nine, eight . . ." June thought that she should be inside with her friends at midnight, but it was too late now. Dr. Cantor began chanting along, too. ". . . four, three, two— Happy New Year, June."

Before she could reply or even knew what was happening, his arm was around her and his mouth was on hers. She tasted cigarettes and whiskey and felt his tongue brush against her own. Her mind snapped into focus, and she realized that she must push him away. She used both hands, and he looked back at her, startled.

"Dr. Cantor! What are you doing?"

"I'm sorry."

She half expected the same sheepish smile as when he'd admitted to being drunk, but this time he hung his head with proper remorse. June looked around to make sure no one could have seen.

"You should go home now." The forcefulness of her voice surprised her.

"Yes, you're probably right."

She had already taken off his jacket and was handing it back to him.

"I'm sorry if I made you feel uncomfortable, June." His face had crumpled with distress.

"It's all right. Just go home and get some sleep."

He began to walk away, and she felt deeply relieved. But he turned back. "I'll see you at work."

"Yes."

"I always see you there. All you pretty girls who have no idea you're building a very nasty bomb." He turned and walked away along the boardwalk.

June looked around for a second time to make sure no one had heard. She stood motionless for a moment. After wondering for so long what they were working on, she now recoiled from the truth. She had often thought it must be some kind of weapon, but to know it definitively was frightening.

The door behind her opened, and she turned to see Cici and Tom. "What are you doing out here?" Cici asked, her voice more annoyed than concerned.

"I just sent Dr. Cantor home."

"Did he give you any trouble?" Tom asked, beginning to puff up again.

"No, he was fine."

"You missed New Year's."

June's heart sped up despite her at the thought of the kiss. "I heard. Happy New Year."

"Happy New Year. You must be freezing! Let's get inside."

June followed them back into the crowded room. Cici nudged her as they walked back to the table. "Get yourself a soldier. A man like that can't be serious about you."

Later that night, June lay in bed with her eyes wide open,

listening to the low hum of music from the roller rink. A bomb, he had said, a very nasty bomb. It made her feel powerful, excited even, to know what so many did not, even if she was ignorant of the details.

But that wasn't all she was excited about, she had to admit, a smile lingering on her lips. He had kissed her, and she knew that the way she felt about Dr. Cantor right now was the way she should have felt about Ronnie all that time. Dr. Cantor had behaved badly, and yet she didn't care; she couldn't wait to see him tomorrow. Would he talk to her? What should she say? Would he try to kiss her again?

She couldn't sleep. Somehow, even with the terrible secret now loose in her mind, she felt too hopeful to worry, and the world was too full of possibility for rest.

(Courtesy of the Department of Energy)

(Courtesy of the Department of Energy)

Chapter 10

SAM AWOKE ON JANUARY 1 WITH A PIERCING HEADACHE AND A heavy sense of regret. He was sure he had kissed the plain girl from Y-12, and he had a horrible feeling that he had also told her something he shouldn't have about the project. His memory was cloudy. Everything was pretty much intact up until he left the canteen, but after that, he could only pull up snapshots. Max dancing with a pretty blond girl. Himself spilling punch on the dance floor. The images became increasingly humiliating. Incredible as it seemed, he must have attempted to dance. Then he remembered the cold night air, and the girl—June. The ominous word *bomb* coming from his lips. Oh God.

He spent the bus ride to work focused equally on rectifying the situation with the girl and not throwing up. He hadn't managed to get a seat and contemplated feigning illness and asking a young lady if he could have hers. He was sinking lower and lower and beginning to feel completely unfit for human contact. How could he have made such a fool of himself? He drank a lot, yes, but he usually knew how to handle his liquor. The last time he'd gotten so tight that he couldn't remember things the next morning had been years ago at a party in Berkeley, when he'd consumed most of a bottle of rum by himself. How could he have been so mad with drink to talk so loosely? And exactly what had he said? He closed his eyes and tried to push away the nausea rising in his gut.

By the time he sat at his desk in the laboratory, at least his stomach was feeling better. He sent an assistant to fetch him coffee. He told himself he must find June and apologize immediately. He would look for her at lunch—if she was working the morning shift, then she should be in the cafeteria. She could turn him in and he could be fired. That was distinctly possible. He knew nothing about her, and that was certainly what she should do, what the Army told people again and again they must do. He had to get to her first and hope that she took pity on him. But why should she? He had attacked her in the dark, after all.

And why had he kissed her? He must be more desperate for a woman than he realized. She was sweet, or at least she had seemed sweet from what he could remember. Perhaps she would be understanding. The kiss itself he remembered clearly, the taste and feel of thick lipstick, a soft floral scent, her hot tongue. To his horror, he realized he was becoming aroused thinking back on it. How much worse could this day become? His body was behaving like he was thirteen again, forced to hide humiliating bulges behind his geometry textbook in Mr. Deakin's class. He was thirty now, and this was *his* laboratory. He had to get control of himself.

The coffee arrived, and he gulped it down.

* * *

JUNE WAS SURE to apply lipstick that morning and even slipped a tube into her pocket to take to work. She borrowed some of Cici's eyeliner, too. Luckily Cici was working the evening shift this week, so she was asleep. June didn't think she would mind her using it, but worried that Cici would suspect her reason had something to do with Dr. Cantor.

She looked around the bus stop, but didn't see him. On the bus, she was fairly certain that a young man in civilian clothes whom she didn't recognize was staring at her. Was it the eye shadow? Was she glowing with excitement? There must have been dark circles under her eyes, since she'd hardly slept. She looked out the window, pretending not to notice, but felt a flush. She hoped she saw Dr. Cantor today. Even though she'd only nodded off a couple of hours ago, with all the adrenaline moving through her, she didn't feel tired at all.

After half an hour in her cubicle, though, June was yawning. She forced her mind into action to stay awake. What in the world could these dials have to do with a bomb? What was she actually doing? By the time lunch arrived, she was desperate for a break and giddy with the thought of seeing Dr. Cantor. Still, she put on a calm face as she walked to the lunchroom, not wanting to act like one of the ridiculous girls she worked with. She was startled to see him before she even entered the cafeteria, standing by the doorway. It caught her off guard, and she stared at him, unable to think of what to say or do.

He waved and motioned for her to follow him across the hallway, so she did. He waited until they were out of earshot of the girls entering the lunchroom before starting, "Miss . . ." He paused, apparently struggling for her last name.

"Walker," she said. "But you can call me June."

"June, I want to apologize for my behavior last night. I don't remember everything, but I'm fairly certain that I acted terribly."

"Don't worry, Dr. Cantor. I know that isn't how you would normally act."

He looked relieved. "Of course it's not. I made you feel awkward, I'm sure, and it was awful of me. I had far too much to drink, as I'm sure you realized."

She nodded.

"There's something else," he continued, and her heart swelled. "I think I might have spoken out of turn."

"Oh. You did say something . . ." She looked over her shoulder. No one was nearby, but she was still scared to say too much.

"Yes, I was afraid I did." He clenched his jaw and looked so upset that she wanted to reach out and stroke him, help him relax. "It was completely stupid of me. I hope you won't . . ."—now he looked over his shoulder—"tell anyone."

"No, of course not. You don't have to worry, Dr. Cantor. I'm a friend."

His entire body relaxed upon hearing this. "Thank you, June. And please, call me Sam."

It sounded so strange and casual that she smiled.

"Am I keeping you from lunch?" he asked.

"Have you eaten yet?" she offered.

"No. Shall we?"

June sat across from Sam, aware that the other girls must be staring at this unexpected coupling, some of whom might have also seen them together at the dance last night. But to her surprise, it didn't bother her at all.

She dove into her potato soup with gusto, but Sam seemed hardly interested in his. "Aren't you hungry?"

"I'm not feeling that well today." He gave her a rueful half-smile.

She leaned forward and said softly, "You shouldn't drink like that."

"I know," and his tone sounded as if he truly did.

"You really shouldn't drink at all."

His dark eyes considered her, not with such frightening intensity as last night, but still in a direct, forward way. "Tell me, June. Have you ever been drunk?"

She laughed. "No, of course not. I've never had a drink in my life."

"Then you can't very well tell me to give it up."

"You could get in trouble with the Army. And besides, you said yourself you don't feel very good."

"Yes, and I made a real nuisance of myself last night. That's all true. I clearly overdid it. But I don't see that as grounds for giving up drink completely."

The last thing she wanted to do was argue with him, so she gave a little shrug and hoped the conversation would move on.

"I tell you what. If you drink with me and don't enjoy it at all, then I'll give it up for you."

She laughed again, this time with a nervous edge. No one in her family ever touched alcohol, except for Jericho. But the chance to share more time, doing anything, with Sam was too exciting to pass up.

"Okay. When shall we do it?"

He winced. "Not tonight. Are you free tomorrow?"

She was supposed to go bowling with Cici, but could find a way out of it. "Yes."

"Then we should meet at the canteen. If you've never had a drink, you just might be able to get drunk off the beer they serve here."

For the rest of the day, she was floating above the stool at her cubicle. It was no trouble to stay awake now; she couldn't stop thinking about Sam, what they would do tomorrow, what she should wear. She replayed their lunch over and over again in her head, trying to remember his words, how exactly he had looked at her. He had a deep, rich voice, and she struggled to recall the exact intonation he used when he said her name.

Luckily, Tom was to go bowling with them the next night, so Cici didn't much care if June was there or not. June told her that Sally from work had asked her to go to the canteen with her in pursuit of a soldier she had her eye on. This had some precedent, as she had socialized with Sally a time or two, and the redhead was always pining over some boy or another. June knew Cici would never approve of her going out with Sam, let alone drinking with him. June hardly approved of it herself. She just hoped that they didn't run into Cici and Tom while they were out together.

Truth be told, Cici barely registered June's change of plans that night at all. Tom was all she could focus on these days. "It's so unfair that we can't have boys up to the room. I mean, of course, I don't want to do anything indecent with Tom! But the poor thing has to live in those awful Army barracks. I just wish I could show him some hospitality. Oh, June, it is too bad you're not coming out tomorrow. Tom's friend Stan just broke things off with his girl."

June was pleased with herself for not having to have Stan forced upon her. "I'm sure I'll meet him another time."

"Oh, you must!" Cici was in front of her mirror, putting curlers in her hair and talking to June through her reflection. "Stan's a swell guy. I think you'd really like this one."

"Mmm-hmm." June got into bed and pretended to fall asleep, imagining Sam's lips through shut eyes.

* * *

SAM WAS EMBARRASSED for feeling nervous as he prepared for his date with June. In vain he searched his room for a jacket without holes in it. He still wasn't sure why he had suggested this; the obvious reason was, of course, that he hadn't been with a girl in so long that the thought of kissing anyone provoked an erection. Still, he had shocked himself by actually asking her out. She was only a factory worker, for God's sake, and she must be very young. She looked as though she should still be in high school, with her soft face and scrawny build. There were plenty of educated secretaries around, schoolteachers, administrators, even a few lady scientists. They would be much more appropriate for him. What was he doing chasing after this simple girl?

He checked his pockets for all the requisite items—wallet, cigarettes, flask. On his way through the hallway, he gave himself a quick inspection in the mirror. His shirt was wrinkled, his tie stained, his hair badly in need of a trim. He took his overcoat from a hook by the door. Ann stuck her head out of the kitchen, where she was washing the dinner dishes.

"Headed out to see Max?"

Thinking only of how happy she would be to hear it, he said, "No, actually I have a date."

As predicted, she beamed, and Sam immediately regretted telling her. There would be questions he didn't want to answer. He lunged for the doorknob to make a hasty exit.

"Have a good time!" Ann called, but he was already out in the frigid night air.

He turned the collar of his coat up and sunk his hands deep into the pockets. He had a long walk ahead of him. Not wanting to run into Max, Sam had chosen a canteen in another neighborhood. No doubt Max would have been pleased for him; still, he wanted to keep this to himself. If he himself had mixed feelings about it, there was no sense going and telling other people, he figured.

She'd never had a drink in her life! It was sweet, really. She had the local accent for sure—a real country girl. Never would he have imagined going out with someone like her when he was back in Brooklyn. Still, the way she had handled things yesterday had been excellent, and she had a quiet reserve, which he admired.

He got to the door of the canteen, and there she was, waiting in the front, sitting by herself in a blue skirt and a gray sweater that matched her eyes. She smiled when he came in, and he smiled back, surprised by how happy he was to see her.

* * *

JUNE STARED AT the mug of beer Sam set in front of her with trepidation. He sat down beside her with his own mug and took a gulp. She stayed motionless, working up the courage to taste it. "Oh, come on," he said. "This stuff hardly counts as a drink at all."

She took a sip. It was bitter but not that bad. Another sip. Not bad at all. It tasted no worse than black coffee. She wasn't sure what she'd been expecting. "It's all right."

"See, I told you." Sam took another gulp of his drink. He was already halfway done with the mug.

"How much do I have to drink to become drunk?"

"You? I don't know. Since you've never had a sip before, you might feel a bit light-headed after just one of those. But that stuff's so weak it should take at least two or three."

She took another sip. She was becoming used to the taste and was no longer frightened. "How does it feel to be drunk?"

Sam looked thoughtful. "Depends on what mood you're in, I guess. If you're happy, then drinking can make you even happier, but if you're in a rotten mood, then it just sort of dulls the pain. Makes everything blurry around the edges. Your thoughts don't come so fast."

She took a bigger drink this time. Sam took a pack of cigarettes from his pack and offered her one. "You're trying booze, might as well go all the way and try smoking, too."

She was feeling reckless, so she took it and held it out for Sam to light.

"You have to suck on it while I light it," he said, and demonstrated with his own cigarette.

She put it in her mouth and sucked as he held the lighter to it. A scratchy sensation quickly worked its way down her throat, and she began coughing.

"Easy. Just take little puffs at first."

She didn't want to take any more puffs at all. Her stomach felt a bit queasy, and her head was a balloon. But Sam was watching her expectantly, so she took another. Without realizing what she was doing, she blew the smoke out her nose, and Sam laughed.

"I don't think I like it," she said, handing the cigarette back, unable to go on. "Where are you from?"

"New York City. But I was living in California before coming here."

"Wow. New York and California—just like a movie star."

"Not exactly."

"Still, I've never been out of East Tennessee."

"You grew up near here?"

"Yes. And my mother grew up right here, can you believe that? Where Y-12 is now, my grandfather used to have a farm."

"Imagine that."

"You must feel like you're in the middle of nowhere here."

He finished his beer. "Oak Ridge isn't exactly the middle of nowhere. But it's like nowhere else on earth. That's for sure."

"Do you miss your family?"

"Yeah. My father's dead, but Ma writes letters every week, like clockwork. I worry about her all by herself in Brooklyn, although my sister's nearby."

"When's the last time you saw her?"

"About four years ago. Before I moved to California."

June glanced at his empty glass. "Do you want some more?"

"No, I have something better." He gave a cautious look around the room and produced a silver flask from the inside pocket of his jacket.

"What's that?"

"Splo."

She laughed to hear him use such a hillbilly word. "You better be careful with that stuff."

He took a sip and squinted in what appeared to be pain. "You want some?"

"No thanks."

"That's probably wise." He took another sip and then put it back in his pocket. "You need another beer."

Sure enough, she'd emptied her glass. She wondered if she was drunk, but didn't think so. Sam was already gone to buy her another. His jacket had a hole under the arm, which she found endearing.

By the time they left the canteen, June had finished four beers, and she thought there was a good chance she had succeeded in getting drunk. She'd noticed when she went to the ladies' room that even after she'd stopped walking, she still had the sensation that the room was moving. She wasn't stumbling over anything, like drunk people in the movies, but she felt happy. Every time Sam looked at her, she couldn't help but smile. She hoped he'd kiss her before they said goodbye for the night.

"Where do you live?" he asked.

"West Dormitory."

"That's on my way home. But it's a long walk."

"I don't mind walking. I don't even feel cold." She touched her cheeks. "My face feels so hot!"

Sam gave her a worried look. "Oh, dear."

"What?"

"I think we've done it."

She giggled.

"I hope I haven't corrupted you terribly."

She walked along beside him on the boardwalk. All her nervousness from earlier in the evening was gone. She felt like she could say anything to him. "How old are you?"

"Thirty."

"Have you ever thought about getting married?"

"Not really, no. Have you?"

"Yes." She looked at the muddy boards beneath their feet. "I had a fiancé. He was killed last September in France."

"Oh, I'm sorry."

She felt a sudden desire to tell him all about Ronnie, and she never wanted to talk about Ronnie to anyone. "We grew up together. His name was Ronnie, and he was only eighteen. I mean, I'm only eighteen. But he's dead."

"It's a damn shame."

"Have you ever been to France?"

"No."

"I keep trying to picture it where he died. To think he was all alone on the other side of the world."

"Sometimes I feel like a real coward for not being over there myself."

"Oh, but you shouldn't! A mind like yours shouldn't be wasted on the battlefield. You're doing important work here. I mean, I don't know what sort of work, but I'm sure it's important."

"But I hate to think of so many good men dying. Not just men. People. My father's family in Germany . . . I have so many aunts and uncles and cousins, and who knows what's become of them."

"Your family's German?"

"Yes. But we're Jewish."

"Oh." She had never met anyone who wasn't Christian before, at least not that she knew of. "So you don't know where your family is?"

"No. But from everything I hear, it sounds like they're probably dead."

"I'm sorry. Sometimes I feel so lucky to be here, safe in America, and I can hardly understand how it is that I am safe here, when so many people around the world are dying." She worried he'd think she was foolish, but he was nodding.

"I do, too. I think, What if my father hadn't come to America? I'd still be back there. What of my brother? Why is he stuck who knows where in the Pacific Ocean, and I'm here drinking beer with a pretty girl?"

"I don't deserve it. I don't deserve to be so lucky."

"But you're hardly lucky, June. You lost your fiancé."

He gave her such a kind, pitying look that she wanted to tell him the truth.

"No. It's not like you think. You see . . ." She took a deep breath, then forced the words out quickly: "I didn't love him. Not the way a woman is supposed to love her husband. He asked me to marry him just before he shipped out, and I didn't know what to do, so I said yes. But I didn't love him."

Before she even realized what was happening, she had let out a big sobbing cry. She couldn't control herself and had to stop walking. Her humiliation only made her cry more. She squeezed her eyes shut and felt his arms encircling her. He felt warm and strong, and she put her arms around his shoulders and leaned into him, crying into the rough wool of his coat.

"I'm sorry," she croaked. "I don't usually cry like this."

"It's all right. Oh, June, it's all right. You have nothing to apologize for. I mean, you've done nothing wrong."

"I didn't love him."

"That's not your fault."

She wanted to believe he was right. The tears stopped, but she kept her face pressed into his shoulder. After a moment, he gently pushed her back and looked down at her face. She felt self-conscious and knew that the eyeliner was probably smeared all over her face now. He brought his hand to her face and gently wiped away the remaining tears. Then he tipped her chin up and brought his mouth down to meet hers.

This time she wasn't taken by surprise, and she didn't push him away. She kissed him back, not quite sure what to do, but following his lead. He grabbed the back of her head and leaned into her. He pulled his lips away for a moment and pulled off his glasses. His eyes seemed smaller but as though they could see right through her without the curtains of glass. Before she could say anything, he leaned in and kissed her again. Finally she pulled away from him.

"I don't want to go home," she whispered. She wasn't sure what she meant. It was certainly a reckless thing to say; it could be taken as an invitation, and maybe that's even how she meant it. But mostly she meant exactly what she said. She didn't want to go home. She didn't want to leave his side or for this night to end.

"Do you want to come home with me?" he asked. That almost certainly had to be taken as an invitation. She became aware of her heartbeat, aware that she was most definitely drunk. She didn't feel herself; her emotions were heightened. She wanted to say yes to him, but she couldn't say yes, could she? That was not what nice girls did. What would he think of her if she did?

Before she could say anything, he said, "I'm sorry. I shouldn't have suggested that."

"No," she said, her own mind now made up. "I'd like to."

He looked hesitant.

"Really," she said. "Unless you think that . . . you think badly of me."

"No, of course not. But I am worried that you've had too much to drink. You're not thinking clearly."

"My mind feels clearer with you than with anyone I've ever met."

He kissed her again for what seemed like a long, long time.

* * *

SAM OPENED THE door to the house slowly, motioning for June to enter. It was late enough that Charlie and Ann would be in bed. He had stressed to June that she must be quiet, and he didn't think she was too drunk to forget. The idea of Charlie and Ann realizing he'd brought a girl home was too humiliating to contemplate.

He was acting horribly. Getting her drunk and taking her home like this was fairly despicable, though he suspected that Max did this sort of thing all the time. June was sweet and would no doubt regret this all in the morning. The entire way to the house, he'd been trying to convince himself to take her home. But every time he was about to turn her around, the feel of her hand in his or the sight of the naked flesh between her scarf and coat was too much for his weak will.

His room was on the other side of the house from Charlie and Ann, thank God. He flipped on the light and closed the door behind them. She took off her coat, and he slung it across the back of his chair beside his own. She sat down on the bed and looked up at him expectantly. He wasn't sure what to do, so he sat beside her. He would tell her not to feel pressured, that they didn't have to do anything. But then they were kissing, and he lost his resolve. His hands seemed to have minds of their own and, before he knew it, were pulling her sweater over her head.

Luckily she was grinning when her face reappeared from under the cotton. He took off his own shirt and tie and kissed her again. His hands worked their way into her brassiere. Her breasts were soft and firm and fit perfectly in his palm. She didn't seem to mind his hands there; she continued kissing him, hungrily.

Now there was no turning back, and his conscience had evaporated. Her skin was so soft, still cool from their long walk outside. He couldn't get enough of touching her, feeling her nakedness pressed into his own. He laid her back on the bed, and she looked like an angel, her hair radiating from her head against the white pillow. Her mouth reached out for his, and he leaned over to kiss her.

She pulled back, and he thought she must be coming to her senses, ready to yell at him and tell him to stop. "Sam," she whispered.

"Yes?"

"I just feel like I should tell you . . . I'm not . . . I mean, it's not my first time. Does that bother you?" The look of concern on her face was so touching that he almost regained his sense of remorse.

"Of course not." He stroked her cheek for effect. "It's not my first time either."

Before his conscience reappeared, he knew he must act. As quietly and gently as he could, he began making love to her.

After two years of celibacy, it didn't take long for him to finish. He collapsed beside her, unsure of how much she'd enjoyed it. They were both trying so hard to be quiet. He held her close to him. The sensation of a body next to his own in this small bed was unfamiliar. He was drifting off, not quite asleep but dozing and content, when she whispered, "Sam, the other night . . . what you said . . ."

"Hmm . . ."

"A bomb, you said. We're building a bomb."

His eyes opened, and he snapped awake. "Yes."

"What kind of bomb? What could possibly take so many people to build?"

Briefly, he wondered if she was a spy. This was exactly the kind of thing a spy would do—get you into bed, then ask for your government secrets. But he probably did owe her some explanation after blurting it out like that. He cleared his throat. "We are building a bomb that will be a thousand times more powerful than any weapon ever created before."

He wondered where to begin, how to explain. "Do you know what an atom is?"

"A little piece of something?"

"Sort of. Did you learn about the periodic table in school?"

"Yes, the elements."

"That's right. An atom is the smallest piece of an element you can get that still has all the properties of that element. Does that make sense?"

"Yes, I think so." Her eyes were wide open, and she was staring at him eagerly.

"The center of the atom is called a nucleus, and it's made

up of parts called neutrons and protons. If you break up an atom's nucleus, energy is released. And if you can figure out a way to create a chain reaction, where breaking up one atom causes other atoms to break up as well, then you could release a huge amount of energy." It was hard to work himself back to the basics of things, and he wondered just what she'd learned about science in her backwoods high school. But she was nodding.

"That's what we're trying to do. Create a bomb that will break up atoms to release energy in a huge explosion. It will be horribly destructive—much worse than any weapon ever created."

"So that's why this town's been built?"

"You would never see this money, these resources being spent in peacetime. No government would go to this trouble to research cures for diseases or simply advance human knowledge. No, we exert ourselves to this extent only in times of war, to invent killing machines. And this, my dear, will be a killing machine worse than any that man has ever dreamed up before."

She looked frightened, and he tightened his arm around her. It was a relief for once to talk about what they were doing in plain, simple terms. But he'd gotten carried away. "I'm sorry. I didn't mean to scare you."

She shook her head. "No, I'm glad you told me. I don't care if it's a crime, I wanted to know the truth."

They were silent after that. The night was cold, but her body was warm. He couldn't tell when she fell asleep or if she was still awake as he began to drift off. Her head was on his shoulder, and he felt the gentle rhythm of her breathing against his skin.

(Courtesy of the Department of Energy)

Chapter 11

JOE HAD BEEN ON THE EARLY SHIFT ALL WEEK AND FOUND HE couldn't sleep past seven, much as he wanted to on his day off. He went out to the bathhouse and splashed some water on his face. The ground was hard and sparkling with frost, which made the run-down field of hutments look ghostly, pretty even, in the early morning light. He pulled his ragged jacket tight around his shoulders and walked toward the canteen.

He would eat breakfast and write a letter to Moriah. Sometimes he worried he couldn't quite remember what she looked like—which was crazy; they'd been married for fifteen years. He could certainly picture her face but found it harder to conjure her in action. She always had the same expression when he thought of her, shaking her head, perpetually amused and affectionate. But it had been so long since they'd seen each other, it was starting to feel like he was making her up, like she might not even exist, not really. *She might as well not exist,* he thought, and then immediately regretted thinking it.

It was good not to be working, yet the day stretched out in front of him empty and lonely. Ralph was on a different shift. He saw less of the boy these days since he'd started going around with Shirley. Joe didn't know what to make of the girl. When they first started dating, Joe had hoped a woman would settle Ralph down, but it turned out she was even more of a rabble-rouser than he was. Instead of calming him, she'd just gotten him dressing like he was off to a club in Harlem and talking more than ever about Double Victory. She was a real city girl, and Joe wondered what she saw in Ralph, fresh off the farm. It was clear enough to see what Ralph saw in her. She was undeniably lovely, with wide eyes and full pink lips. She spoke in a clear, strong voice, always confident. Bewitching, almost. If she walked right into Norris Lake, Ralph would probably follow and drown himself without thinking twice.

She was never rude to Joe, but never warm either. She'd graduated from high school a year ago and started working at the Coca-Cola factory in Atlanta. But when she heard she could make more in Oak Ridge, she'd decided to come north to Tennessee. She said she was saving up to go to school to become a teacher and told Ralph he should go to college, too. Joe laughed the first time he heard her say it. Ralph hadn't been to school since he was nine years old. But Shirley said it didn't matter, not if he was smart. Suddenly books started appearing in the hutment piled up by Ralph's bed.

It was hard for young Negroes on the reservation to date. The only place to socialize was the rec center, but this was hardly a decent place to take a lady, what with all the card games going on. Men were allowed into the women's hutment area for only a few minutes at a time. They called it the pen, and sure enough, the women were basically locked up there. No one was allowed to be out in the hutment area after curfew. So Ralph had to meet Shirley in the cafeteria or take her for a walk in order to court her. Occasionally they took the bus to Knoxville for a real date.

Not that Joe had had it much better courting Moriah back in the day. Most of their dating had been done at church. Joe had waited awhile to think about getting married. His mother had been anxious and was forever pointing out young girls in town or at church, nudging him toward them. He called on some of them, but none had tempted him to domesticity until Moriah. Something about her was different. She had opinions on most everything and wasn't shy about sharing them. The first time he spoke to her, she'd told Joe he needed to clean his boots before wearing them to church next time. Somehow this wasn't rude or off-putting; no, he'd had a clear sense then that Moriah knew better than he how he should be living his life.

In fact, it was Moriah who had first suggested that he go to work in Oak Ridge. Ralph had met a recruiter in town and had told them over dinner one night that he'd decided to go. It hadn't occurred to Joe that he could go along as well. After Ralph had left and the children were in bed, Moriah had brought him a cup of weak coffee made with grounds left over from the morning. She sat beside him on their small homemade sofa. "You ever think of working in a place like that?"

"What—in Tennessee?"

She nodded.

"I reckon I could do the work. But what about you and the kids?"

Moriah didn't say anything at first. "Thirty-eight dollars a week, Ralph says."

Joe nodded. He knew they were both thinking of what they could buy with that money, the countless problems it would solve.

Moriah put her hand on the back of his. "You know I could manage on my own."

He did. He had never doubted it, except when Ben was sick and he was mad with worry. If anything, now he had a selfish fear that Moriah and the children were doing too well without him. Of course they relied on the money he sent home, but how much of a difference did it make to the girls and little Ben that he wasn't there to tuck them in at night?

Joe looked up from his tray and saw Ralph. The boy would be eating his breakfast, then heading to work. Joe waved, and Ralph slumped over to join him. He sat down across from Joe and shoved his tray down hard in front of him. "Runny grits again," Ralph muttered. "Fourth day in a row."

"Tomorrow's Sunday. They usually give us something nice on Sunday."

"Can't wait for tomorrow, then. These are more water than grits."

Joe ignored Ralph's sullenness. Their conversations often went like this—each man pursuing his own attitude, all but oblivious to the other.

"It's warmer today. But I reckon we getting one more cold spell before spring."

"I hope it snows again."

"You crazy? Snow blows right in the hutment."

"I ain't only seen snow but two times."

"Morning, gentlemen." Joe heard Otis's voice before he even looked up, disappointed to see him joining their table. Ralph, however, seemed to perk up.

"Shirley's in line over there." Otis raised a suggestive eyebrow.

Ralph turned to see her, then immediately stared down at his plate. He never talked about Shirley and got shy whenever Joe asked about her.

"Good lord, boy." Otis laughed. "She's your girl now—you can't still be shy to see her."

As she walked over to their table, Ralph looked up from his breakfast and she gave him a sweet smile. He smiled back, and for a moment Joe could see the boy he'd been when they first arrived in Oak Ridge.

"Howdy, Shirley," said Otis in his lewd tone.

She gave a tiny nod and said simply, "Otis."

As much as Joe mistrusted the girl, he did admire her obvious disdain for Otis. He gave her an approving "Nice to see you, Miss Shirley."

"You too, Joe. Hard day's work ahead?"

"As a matter of fact, it's my day off. I don't know what to do."

"Not much to do in this place," said Ralph. "You could take the bus to Knoxville."

"What would I do in Knoxville?"

"Good question. There's not much to do in Knoxville either." Shirley was grinning, and Joe couldn't tell if she meant this as a joke. He felt like she and Otis laughed at everything, just for different reasons.

"Shirley's from Atlanta," said Otis. "She ain't impressed with our little Tennessee towns."

"You're telling me that you spend a lot of time on the thrilling streets of Knoxville?" Shirley snapped back.

"It ain't Memphis. But you can find entertainment if you know where to look."

"I'm pretty sure Joe isn't after your sort of entertainment."

If Ralph felt awkward at the tension between his girl and his friend, he didn't let on, though he did make an effort to steer the conversation back to Joe. "You could go to the movies."

"Yeah. Reckon I could."

"There's a Colored Camp Council meeting later on this afternoon," said Shirley. "Ralph and I are going. You should come, too, Joe. It sounds like you don't have anything better to do."

"Oh, no—I'm no help at those meetings."

"Just being there is a help," she insisted. "The bigger our numbers, the more powerful our voices."

Joe didn't reply. Ralph knew better than to try and get him to go back to those meetings. But Shirley was hard to say no to.

"Besides," continued Shirley, "you might find it interesting."

Joe looked to Ralph, who stared down at his grits. Otis chimed in, "It sure do sound interesting, Joe. But if you decide to skip the meeting, you can always join me for a game of dice."

Joe and Shirley both ignored him. "What do you say, Joe?" she asked.

"All right. I guess I can come along."

"Excellent." Shirley turned to Ralph. "I got a letter from my aunt Lillian. She's bought a house."

"How'd she manage that?" asked Otis.

"Years of hard work and frugal living."

"That's wonderful," said Ralph.

"Real good news," Joe added. "She must be quite a woman."

"She is. She and my aunt Gladys sew some of the most beautiful dresses you can find in Atlanta. They also raised me up from a baby."

"Was it just the three of you?" asked Joe.

Shirley nodded. "Neither of them ever married."

"Ain't you never need a man around the house?" asked Otis.

"No. In my experience, women do just fine without men." Joe's thoughts returned to Moriah.

"Well, surely, *Shirley,* you need them for something."

Otis's leer was too much for Ralph. "Shut up, Otis."

Shirley put her hand on Ralph's. "It's all right. I suppose they are necessary for procreation, but that takes only a few minutes, right, Otis?"

Joe dropped his fork, and it clattered against his plate. Ralph looked as stunned as Joe felt. Otis, however, laughed. "Suppose you're right about that."

Joe had never heard a woman talk like Shirley. No wonder Ralph was still nervous around her. Joe himself was nervous around her.

After breakfast, Joe decided to go for a walk, to get as far away from the buildings and construction as possible. The days were getting warmer, and though he kept his hands thrust into his coat pockets for warmth, the sun felt good on his back. He followed the patchworks of trees. Whenever he came to a crossroad, he turned away from whichever buildings were larger. Eventually he found an undisturbed meadow full of grass, chickweed, and henbit. No roads, no buildings, no ditches. If he stood just so, all he could see was meadow and trees, as though Oak Ridge didn't even exist. He sat on the roots of a poplar and looked up at the blue sky. Wispy white clouds swirled up above him. He could look at that sky and imagine he was home.

He met Ralph back outside the cafeteria when the boy was done with his shift. Ralph looked surprised to see him. "I ain't sure you coming."

"Got nothing better to do. Besides, your Shirley's mighty persuasive."

They walked toward the rec center. Ralph looked thoughtful. "Shirley does say whatever's on her mind."

Joe tried not to smile too broadly. "She sure does."

"I don't know what to make of it half the time."

"Girls grow up different in Atlanta, I reckon."

"Yeah. I don't know. I think it might just be Shirley."

"Be careful."

"You're always telling me to be careful. Shirley ain't dangerous!"

"All women are dangerous."

The meeting was in a small room around the back of the building, away from the noise and gambling. Shirley was already there, along with a group of something like twelve men, sitting in a circle of chairs. Joe didn't look out of place—most of them were also construction workers in work clothes and muddy boots. But he felt out of his element. The others all knew each other. Ralph was welcomed heartily as he introduced Joe around. Joe hoped that no one asked him any questions, and he could just sit back and be ignored.

When everyone had quieted down and found a seat, a man began to speak. Joe remembered Robert Wales from the last meeting Ralph had dragged him to. He was a small man, yet he carried himself in a way that gave the impression of strength—back straight, head held high, and a deep, resonant voice that commanded other men to listen. "Thank y'all for coming tonight. And thank you to those of you who accompanied me to the meeting with Roane-Anderson last week. I wish I had better news to report back. But as those of you who were there know, it was unproductive."

Ralph spoke up: "Mr. Newman denied all our requests."

There were groans and exclamations. Shirley shook her head in disgust.

Wales put his hand up to ask for silence. "His exact words were that he would review our requests."

Another man chimed in, "He said we could expect an answer in four to five months."

More groans. "Unless anyone objects," said Wales, "I think we should forget about Roane-Anderson for the time being and go straight to the Army."

"Yes, sir!" said the man beside Joe.

"I've drafted a letter to send to Colonel Hodgson." He took a letter out of his shirt pocket and unfolded it to read. "'We are sure that you, as a distinguished representative of the American Army, appreciate the great number of Negro youth fighting and giving their lives for democracy and the American way of life, as well as the Negroes here on the home front laboring to make the war effort possible. We simply request twenty-five or thirty homes to accommodate the Negro workers with families currently unable to live near the work site, constructed to the same standards as those built for white families.'"

People called out affirmations. Shirley spoke in a commanding voice, "I think you need to soften it."

Wales nodded. "You may be right."

Shirley continued, "Add something like 'we'd be grateful.' White folks like it when we beg."

"When we gonna do something about our wages?" asked the man beside Joe.

Wales looked the man in the eye. "Our wages are good, Leroy."

"Not as good as white men's wages."

"Be that as it may, our first priority has to be housing. The situation at the moment is untenable for Negro families."

Joe didn't know what that meant but could guess. There were more murmurs of agreement. Leroy crossed his arms and leaned back in his chair.

"What about the buses?" another man asked. "Half the time, they don't stop for colored men."

"That's true," said Ralph. "Maybe we should mention the buses in the letter to the colonel."

Wales shook his head. "I know the buses are a problem. But I truly believe our best strategy is to focus on one issue at a time."

Some men nodded; others grumbled in disagreement. The discussion went on like this for some time. Men brought up all the various difficulties with Negro life in Oak Ridge, and Wales tried to convince them to wait to try and solve them until the housing had been improved. Joe was impressed with his consistency. The very fact that Wales never faltered began to persuade Joe that he must know what he was doing. Finally he seemed to wear them all down. It was resolved that Wales would send his letter with Shirley's revisions to Colonel Hodgson on behalf of the council.

Joe and Ralph walked Shirley back to the women's quarters. "What'd you think, Joe?" Shirley asked.

"Mr. Wales seems like a real smart man."

"He is. We're lucky to have him."

They had to walk through the men's hutment area to get to the women's side. Ralph held Shirley's hand as they walked, and Joe tried to hang back to give them privacy. It had turned cold when the sun went down, and the streets were quiet. But as they reached the far side of the hutments, Joe could hear men shouting. Ralph put his arm around Shirley, protective. They slowed their walk as the sounds grew closer. Two men stumbled out into the street from behind a hut, in a struggle. The larger man threw a punch and knocked the smaller one back. Joe then saw that the smaller man was Otis.

Ralph let go of Shirley and ran in between the men. "Back away!" he shouted to the large man.

Joe followed. The last thing he wanted was to get in a fight on behalf of Otis, but he couldn't leave Ralph out there by himself.

"Get on out of here!" Ralph yelled to the man.

The big man considered Joe and Ralph. Otis shook himself off and walked back to join them. Otis gave his opponent his crooked smile. "You want to take another shot? Not so brave now, is you?"

"Otis!" shouted Ralph in annoyance. He turned back to the man. "I said get on out!"

"Tell your friend he best not cheat at dice no more," said the man.

"I didn't cheat!" said Otis.

"Otis, shut up!" said Ralph.

The man spat on the ground and turned to walk away. When he was a safe distance back, Ralph went over to Shirley. "You all right?"

She nodded. Joe turned to Otis. "You need to watch yourself."

"I didn't cheat!" repeated Otis. "He just don't want to pay what he owe me."

"Gambling ain't nothing but trouble, Otis," said Ralph.

Otis rolled his eyes and turned into the night. "Thanks for your help!" he shouted over his shoulder.

"Come on," said Ralph. "Let's go."

When they came to the gate to the women's area, Joe stayed back to let the young people have a moment to themselves. He was anxious to get on home and get to bed. It'd be up again at five thirty tomorrow for the morning shift. He looked over to see if Ralph was done. He and Shirley were wrapped in an embrace, mouth to mouth, arms around each other. Joe looked away quickly. A moment later, Ralph was by his side. "Ready to go on home?" Joe asked. Ralph nodded, and they walked in silence back to the hutment.

(Courtesy of the Department of Energy)

Chapter 12

THE CITY LOOKED DIFFERENT TO JUNE THE MORNING AFTER HER first date with Sam. Everything had a purpose she now understood. She saw the maintenance men and factory workers on the bus and thought, *You are all here to build a bomb.* The sprawling facilities at Y-12 made sense; her job wasn't a mindless turning of meters, but rather an effort toward a specific outcome: building the most destructive weapon in history.

It was one of those January mornings when the sun makes up for its abbreviated time in the sky by shining with exaggerated brilliance. Buildings gleamed in the brightness, people seemed encouraged by the light, and the whole scene added to June's sense of renewal. She had a strong, slightly ridiculous sense that she was changed and nothing would ever be quite the same. It wasn't just being in love, though she was hopelessly, madly, desperately in love. She also had a profound sense of hope and possibility. Sam was completely unexpected, and meeting him, loving him, was extraordinary. June had never really expected anything extraordinary to happen to her. Some children imagine growing up to be movie stars, baseball players, the president, but not June. Until today it had not occurred to her that life could hold surprises on this scale. That she could be having an affair with an important scientist—a Jew from New York—was incredible! That she could be building a bomb that would change the course of world events. That she could be in on the secret that none of these other girls turning knobs and dials had an inkling of. That someone like Sam might exist, that she could meet him, that he could want her—it was all too wonderful to believe. She wasn't naive enough to think that because he'd slept with her he loved her, and she knew men were perfectly capable of abandoning girls in these situations. But she didn't regret it. She wanted to be with him again, and as soon as possible.

She was reacting slowly at work, hardly able to concentrate, fingers fumbling, taking twice as long as usual to correct the position of the dials. She hadn't really slept. After she had dozed for maybe an hour at Sam's, he had walked her back to the dormitory, and she sneaked in as quietly as possible. Cici was asleep but must have noticed how late June was getting home. She'd already worked out her story—that she'd been with Sally in her room and fallen asleep. It was feeble, but the best she could do.

Sam was waiting for her at lunch. She was ravenous, despite her exhaustion, or perhaps because of it, and he laughed, watching her devour her macaroni and cheese. He seemed happier than normal, definitely happy to see her, and if he had any plans of abandoning her, it didn't seem like it. By now all the girls she worked with must have known something was going on between them. When lunch was over, he asked if she'd like to go to the movies with him that night. She could swear she felt her heart swelling—it was a silly notion, but she could feel it in her chest.

They began spending their evenings together regularly; usually every other night or so, they went to the movies or the canteen together. No announcement was ever made, but June soon realized they were going steady. They met for lunch in the cafeteria when she was on the day shift and ate supper together most evenings. She let him keep drinking, of course, too flushed with love to want to pick a fight. But he hardly drank much with her anyway, and she never had more than a single beer after that first night.

It sometimes amazed her how much they had to say to each other. She found herself telling him the craziest thoughts in her head, things she never thought she could share with anyone. Her wondering about Ronnie in heaven, her thoughts about the other girls at Y-12 flirting in the cafeteria, even the Hollywood romances she made up to keep herself entertained at work. He didn't seem to think she was crazy. He laughed at her in a good-natured way or listened seriously, asking her questions, surprising her with his genuine interest in her thoughts.

He talked, too. He told her stories about his family, about growing up in the city. He told her about his father, who had studied science in Germany, but when he came to New York could only find work in a bakery. Sam had just gotten his doctorate when his father died, and he was so proud that his son would become the scientist he'd never had a chance to be. His mother was still living in Brooklyn and wrote him letters in Yiddish once a week. June thought the strange script was beautiful, but Sam rolled his eyes at the letters as he translated them for her. They were mostly full of complaints—about her health, the neighbors, his brother-in-law, rationing, the heating in her apartment building. June suspected Sam exaggerated some in his translations, but she helped him come up with kind, caring replies in any case. He wrote back in English, which he said his mother should be able to read and even write, if only she would set her mind to it.

Sam also talked to her about the bomb they were making. This was only when they were alone and could be sure no one could hear them, usually in the evening in his room. She had so many questions to ask. What was she doing at her job, what were the dials measuring, what was happening at Y-12? Slowly he explained it to her, and she became familiar with all sorts of words—*uranium, enrichment, cyclotron, fission, sustained reaction,* and finally the name of the very machine she was working on, the calutron. So she came to learn that there were indeed giant magnets in the calutron, and that they were separating uranium isotopes for a bomb that was being designed somewhere in New Mexico by many of the world's greatest physicists. It didn't make the job any less boring, but it felt satisfying to know the truth. Sam explained to her that they were working on a radical new way of producing energy. A bomb was just one awful way of using energy; one day atomic energy might be used to create electricity. But in the meantime, it would be used to kill. Since she was helping build it, did that make her responsible for the lives it might take? Was she like Ronnie now, something of a soldier, at least in the respect that she was helping to kill the enemy? Men and women all across the country worked in factories building guns and planes and all other instruments of war. The planes and guns would kill people as surely as a bomb. They were all part of the war effort. Yet now that she knew the truth, her part seemed bigger than that of any riveter or welder.

This was completely different from going for evening walks with Ronnie; these were real conversations with a real boyfriend, and she felt for Sam the way she knew she was supposed to. They kissed whenever they got the chance and held hands at the movies; he even carried her over one of the giant mud puddles in front of the canteen one night. She laughed and felt foolish and was spectacularly happy.

One evening she met him at the cafeteria as he was getting off work. She was on the night shift that week and had spent the afternoon trying to get some sleep, her mind working against her as she tossed and turned, never able to get used to this schedule. The idea was that she could eat "breakfast" while he had supper, but she was light-headed from exhaustion and didn't feel hungry. "Could we just go for a walk?" she asked.

They strolled along the boardwalk. The sun was dipping toward the horizon, the air growing colder by the minute, but she didn't mind with her arm locked around his, the warmth from his body meeting her own.

"I feel lucky I don't have to work the night shift," he said.

"You are lucky. I feel like death warmed over."

"You certainly don't look it." He ground to a halt and encircled her with his arms. She tipped her head up to his, and they kissed for a long time. She no longer felt cold at all; she felt nothing but the heat of his mouth on hers.

They could hear a group of girls approaching and slowly

pulled away from each other. He looked her in the eye, in a way that made her feel as though no one had ever really seen her before, as though he knew her better than she knew herself. What did he see when he looked at her that way? Surely it wasn't the country girl who had taken the bus to Oak Ridge three months ago. She wanted to be the girl he saw, and the thought that she was thrilled her.

"You better eat something before your shift starts," he whispered.

She nodded, and they turned back to the cafeteria, hand in hand. They passed the laughing group of girls, who watched June, wondering, she knew, how a girl like her had attracted a man like that. They don't know, she thought, they can't see the June that Sam sees. It was growing dark now, the electric lights of the town twinkling before them. She wondered what he was thinking but didn't ask. He could have his own thoughts, and she could have hers; what mattered was that they were together. It was in these quiet moments that she felt herself overwhelmed with a feeling she had never known before that she could identify only as love. It was a simultaneous sense of contentment and aching for something more, joy heightened almost to sadness as she watched him, wanting him, loving him, desperate for him, praying he felt the same way.

Because she had begun spending so many evenings with Sam, she found it impossible to hide their relationship from Cici. On about their fourth date, she mentioned it casually when her roommate asked where she was headed. June was on her way out the door, all made up, and Cici was just coming home after the evening shift. There was an edge of hurt to her voice, and June realized that she was behaving strangely. They used to spend almost every night together, after all.

"I have a date," she said, watching for Cici's look of amazement. "With Sam Cantor."

"Oh." Cici didn't try to hide her disapproval. "Well, I hope he doesn't drink tonight like he did on New Year's."

"We're just going to the movies."

"Have fun." Cici didn't sound as though she thought they would.

June waved and dashed out the door. They never really talked about it again after that. Cici avoided asking June what she was up to when she went out. She was out most nights with Tom, anyway, so it didn't much matter. June would have liked to have a friend to talk to about Sam; she longed to moon over him the same way Cici did over Tom, but she could tell her friend would not be receptive.

So it remained her special, secret life. She was overflowing with secrets these days—her secret love affair, secret feelings, secret hopes. And of course the secret that could get her and Sam thrown out of Oak Ridge altogether: the secret of the atomic bomb.

* * *

JUNE WALKER CREPT up on Sam. The affair began spontaneously and was certainly motivated by lustful, animalistic instincts. That had been surprising enough, and at first he'd worried about leading her on, hurting her. But what was more shocking was his own desire, day after day, to see her. As the fog of his bodily desires began to lift, he realized that he enjoyed her company. In a simple way he wasn't sure he'd ever experienced before, her presence made him happy. Not only was he attracted to her, but he liked her. She was kind and thoughtful. He had trusted her almost immediately and felt comfortable with her, too, as though he'd known her forever. He found himself daydreaming in the lab, looking forward to seeing her after work, even wondering what she was up to at odd hours, like a lovestruck boy. It was awfully embarrassing.

She was innocent and ignorant, true, but she had an insatiable appetite for learning. He could keep her attention for hours when they were safe in the privacy of his bedroom at Charlie and Ann's. His lectures would go on almost uninterrupted, save for her questions and occasional kisses. It didn't matter if he was explaining nuclear physics or his family's history in Europe. She was endlessly interested. She was clearly infatuated but also deeply curious—not just about him, but about Oak Ridge and physics and the whole world outside of East Tennessee.

Sam enjoyed playing tutor more than he liked to admit. Talking to June was something altogether different than standing by a blackboard in front of bored undergraduates, though he was aware that she was just as young as his students back in California. It wasn't just their physical intimacy that heightened the experience. She was a blank slate; her mind was free of all but the most basic physical science she had learned in her backwoods high school. And she trusted him implicitly. She was a completely supportive audience and loyal pupil. Her eager young mind was in his hands to develop as he wished. She had opinions of her own, yes, but in these areas about which she knew so little, he found that they soon conformed to his own. He couldn't help but recognize how much he enjoyed the power, how heady it was to have such subtle control over another person.

He told her the truth, the hard scientific facts. But of course, even science could be explained to suit certain purposes, and his lessons were always peppered with commentary on his colleagues, the war, and the government. He spoke his opinions freely. He explained that in the beginning he had felt a strong sense of purpose: to build the bomb before the Germans. Most American physicists had felt this purpose; in particular, the many recent immigrants from Europe, mostly Jews who had been forced to flee Nazism. Perhaps in the face of such an undeniably evil enemy, though, they had become overly self-righteous. They thought of themselves as heroic, as doing the right thing, but he was becoming increasingly ambivalent. How could a weapon of such power be the right thing? How could more killing, undoubtedly of civilians, be heroic?

She was solemn, nodding and watching him closely with her big gray eyes. He had to give her credit; she was independent-minded enough to follow his thinking past the patriotic propaganda that surrounded them to the bigger picture of how atomic weapons could change (or, God forbid, destroy) the world.

He enjoyed spilling out his thoughts to her, holding her warm body against his, the sympathy of her mind and touch. He felt he was helping her, that with his help, June would be transformed for the better. After all, only a few months ago she had been destined to be a farmer's wife in the middle of nowhere. Already he had opened her mind to ideas she could never have dreamed before.

She was transforming him in her own way as well. He hadn't bothered buying Homer's moonshine in a month. He was spending more and more time with June, and he knew she didn't like to see him drink too much. Besides, with her there, he didn't feel the need to be drunk to enjoy himself; she was distraction and entertainment enough.

They certainly didn't spend all their time talking about physics. It was impossible for him to stay focused on any topic for more than fifteen or so minutes before the impulse to touch her became too great. They'd start necking, sitting chastely beside each other on his bed, then move on to heavier petting as arms became involved and clothes removed. A few weeks passed before they made love for a second time after that first frenzied encounter. It was difficult to find the privacy, for one thing. He wasn't allowed into June's dorm, and obviously he couldn't let on to Charlie and Ann that he was having his way with a teenage girl in their house. The first Saturday June was working the night shift and Charlie and Ann would be gone for the day, he shamelessly invited her over and they spent the afternoon together, naked for the most part, in bed.

He remembered that he had once found her plain, and it surprised him how attractive she had become to him. It was true that she did not possess the glamour of her roommate, that she lacked striking Hollywood-style good looks. Her face was expressive, though; her features delicate, the set of her jaw firm. He found her most beautiful when all her makeup was off. The natural fleshy pink of her lips aroused him, and her face without makeup was almost more naked than her body without clothes. Seeing her without lipstick was truly intimate; he knew no other man got to see those soft lips nude.

Pretty quickly he gave up worrying about the morality of the whole thing and flung himself into the affair. The one worry that they both shared was getting pregnant. June seemed to have no qualms about sleeping with him, other than the fact that she realized having his baby could be disastrous. He reassured her that he would do his best to prevent this, which mostly meant finding creative ways to avoid climaxing inside her. He didn't want to ruin this poor girl's life.

Max was the only person he could talk to about it, and even with him, it was only in vague terms. It didn't take his friend long to notice that Sam had found someone else to spend his time with. Max took a certain pride in the relationship. "I told you!" he said when Sam first confessed the affair over beers in the canteen. "I told you to get a girlfriend, and look, you went right out and did it. I had no idea you took my advice so seriously. But I must insist you name your firstborn after me."

"I'd prefer to avoid procreating at this point."

"Fair enough. Well, mate, now I'm going to have to follow my own advice, aren't I? If you're off at the roller rink half the time with your girl, with whom shall I despise the world?"

Max treated the whole thing with good-natured mockery. Talking to Charlie and Ann about it was another matter. Ann had wanted to know every last detail after that first date. He spoke casually, but they noticed the amount of time he was spending out with her. Dinners at home became friendly interrogations. Sensing that they might not fully approve of June's pedigree, Sam gave short, vague answers. But Ann was persistent and soon decided that June must come to dinner.

Sam knew June was nervous. It was charming the way she giggled for no reason as he told her a bit about Ann and Charlie on the way to dinner. They were holding hands, walking along the boardwalk. "Charlie is the nicest guy I've ever met.

He was everybody's favorite at Princeton, always hosting parties, always buying rounds of drinks. Finding out he was here was a lifesaver when I first arrived."

June giggled. "Where are they from?"

"Boston."

"And they're both your age?"

"Yes, we're all terribly old."

"Oh, no! I'm terribly young."

"You're lovely." He had to stop talking and walking momentarily to kiss her.

When they finally pulled apart, Sam repeated, "You are lovely, June Walker. And I'm sure they will love you."

When they walked into the house, Charlie greeted them in the living room. He shook June's hand vigorously, and she giggled. Sam wished that tonight of all nights they could drink with dinner. He lit a cigarette instead.

He and June sat on the sofa, Charlie across from them. "So, June, you grew up around here?"

"Yes, over near Maryville."

"And your family has a farm?"

She nodded.

"What do you grow?" Sam found it touching that Charlie was trying so hard.

"Oh, a little of everything. Corn and wheat mostly. And we have cattle, of course."

"That must have been a lovely way to grow up, surrounded by nature."

Before June could answer, Ann appeared from the kitchen. She was perfectly dressed, as usual, in a navy suit and apron.

"Hello, June!" Ann shook June's hand as well. "It's so nice to finally meet you."

"You, too." June's voice was soft, and Sam hoped she was holding up. The evening had only just begun.

"If you're all ready to eat, we can move to the table."

Ann had gone all out and set the table with the fancy lace tablecloth and candles.

She brought out pork chops with some sort of spicy applesauce, green beans, roasted potatoes, and rolls. As usual, her food and its presentation were excellent. She pulled off every dinner party, despite rationing. In fact, Sam suspected she enjoyed showing off her ability to work around the rations. She even saved her leftover cooking fat for the Boy Scouts, who had regular drives in Oak Ridge to collect fat for war glycerin production. The perfect picture of a wartime housewife.

"So how did you two meet, anyway?" Charlie asked, piercing beans with his fork.

"We work in the same place," Sam said.

Charlie smiled. "And of course you can't say any more than that. Are you enjoying working in Oak Ridge, June?"

"Oh, yes. It's great fun here. I miss my family, of course, but there's so much to do, things I could never have imagined on the farm."

Ann nodded sympathetically.

"But you must have been here much longer than me. How do you find living here?"

"Oh, besides the mud?" Ann laughed. She went on in a hesitant tone: "We like it. It was a big change for us, too, and when we got here things were much more . . . primitive than they are now. It seems like a fun place for a young person, though."

"Well, we have fun, too!" Charlie said. "Ann and I are on a bowling team."

"And I sing in a choir."

"And you have your woman's group."

"I find people here . . . very open. You know, they're from all over, all backgrounds, and everyone seems so ready to reach out and make friends, experience new things."

"You make it sound like summer camp," Sam said, shoveling potatoes onto his plate.

"Well, in some ways it is."

"Yes, top secret, wartime summer camp."

Ann rolled her eyes at him and turned back to June. "So you grew up on a farm, June?"

Sam winced to hear the conversation returning to this old material. But June managed to get through all right. She seemed to relax as the meal went on, and by the time Ann brought out apple pie, she'd completely stopped giggling. The good thing about dinner without drinks was that there was no excuse to linger when it was over, so Sam was able to initiate the good-byes and usher her out the door without too much fuss.

At first they walked toward her dorm in silence. Finally June spoke. "They're very nice."

"Yes, they are nice people."

"The food was delicious."

"Ann's a great cook. I hope you weren't on the spot too much there."

"Oh, no. I just hope they liked me."

"Of course they liked you." And again he had to stop talking and walking momentarily to kiss her neck.

Ann had gone on to bed when Sam got back, but Charlie was in the living room, smoking and reading. He looked up as Sam walked in and slammed his book shut. "She's lovely, Sam! I think you make a swell couple."

"Thanks, Charlie." He took off his coat and sat across from his friend, settling back into the sofa and lighting his own cigarette. "You know I have no idea what I'm doing."

"Well, she makes you happy, right? That's the most important thing." Charlie settled back into the sofa as if to indicate that he had issued his judgment on the matter and that was that.

It was a few days before Sam heard Ann's judgment. It was early evening, and Charlie was out. She had made tea for the two of them and they were listening to the news bulletin on the radio. Sam turned it off when the news finished and a Western came on. "Are you meeting June tonight?" she asked.

"No, she's on the night shift. I'll see her for breakfast."

"So it's quite serious between you two, isn't it?"

Sam shrugged, already not liking where this was going.

"I mean, you spend an awful lot of time together." Ann's tone was not altogether pleasant.

"She's a sweet girl."

Ann said nothing, but raised an eyebrow. Sam, who had hardly ever had a negative thought about Ann, found himself becoming angry. "What?"

"Nothing."

"It's seems like there's something you want to say."

Ann spoke carefully. "She's very young."

"She's eighteen."

"Are you planning on marrying her?"

"I don't know! We hardly just met."

Ann clenched her jaw for a moment, then spoke quickly. "This is quite a job, you know. Being the wife of a professor or researcher. There is entertaining to be done, people you have to know how to impress and talk to. Do you think she's prepared for this life? Has she had the adequate education?"

Sam saw what she was getting at. He instantly recoiled at her snobbery, though of course he had had similar thoughts about June from the beginning. "She's smart, Ann! I've been teaching her science, and I'll venture she understands more about physics than you now."

"That may very well be true, but does she know how to discuss Freud or Trotsky at a dinner party? Look, Sam, I like her! I wouldn't be saying this if I didn't like her; then I would just let you go on and do what you wanted." Ann's cheeks were flushed. The effort of this aggression, so unnatural to her, was clearly painful. She continued in a softer voice. "She's clearly in love with you. When you make a young girl fall in love with you, you have certain obligations to her. Especially if . . ."—she recoiled as though the phrase were lemon juice in her mouth—"you take her to bed." Now that she had got it out, Ann looked proud and defiant.

Sam felt too violated by this intrusion into his private life to think hard about what she was saying. "If that's all, I think I'm going to go out for a walk now."

He walked for twenty minutes before the black rage lifted enough for him to begin to think straight. How dare she, how dare she! He went over and over her words. The nerve of it! He was a grown man, and she was not his mother. She had no right to speak to him like that. Who he took to bed was his business, though he did worry how she had known that. Did she know for sure or had she just made the assumption? Had he not been quiet enough when June was over? It was too horrible to think about for long, so he returned to hating Ann. Privileged, perfect Ann. She'd been born knowing who

Freud was, no doubt. She'd never done anything inappropriate in her life and now felt compelled to pounce on him for this one possible folly. Charlie was such a good guy; Charlie didn't judge him. Who did she think she was?

Inevitably, he wound up at the canteen. Max wasn't there, so he drank by himself, stewing in his own anger, his sense of having been wrongfully accused overwhelming enough that he didn't stop for a moment to consider that she might be right.

(Courtesy of the Department of Energy)

(Courtesy of the Department of Energy)

Chapter 13

WITH SPRING CAME WINDS THAT SWEPT HAZY CLOUDS OF DUST through town. Anything left outside quickly became coated with it, and children wrote messages in the windows of parked cars with their fingers. You couldn't walk a block without getting covered in a fine film of red dirt, and Cici had learned the hard way not to attempt wearing anything white.

Nevertheless, Tom had been so insistent that she agreed to go on a walk. Some dirt in her eyes was a small sacrifice—after all, Cici had found her husband. Tom hadn't proposed yet, but she felt confident that he would soon. Married soldiers couldn't live with their wives in Oak Ridge anyway, so there was no need to tie the knot yet. But the boy was crazy for her, and was he ever a catch! Tom was handsome in a lanky way, with sandy hair and a long face. His father managed a bank, and when he reminisced about his childhood, he casually tossed off sentences like "my sister fell off her pony," "the cook had forgotten the sugar!" or "it was my last summer at our Newport house." He was bitter that the war had meant that he hadn't gotten to spend the summer before he went to Yale in Europe as his older brother had.

The big worry, of course, was that he would see through her fake pedigree. But she had gotten by so far with vague answers about her background, and Tom seemed to assume like most everyone else that she was a southern belle. No one wanted to think a pretty girl was poor. She told him that she was an orphan, which solved the problem of her parentage. His questions had led to the invention of an aunt who had raised her—Aunt Faye, whom Cici had become used to casually referencing in conversation until Faye almost didn't seem like a lie.

She implied that her family had once had money, but it had mostly been lost during the Depression. It was surprising how easily the stories came. "Father, rest his soul, wasn't a practical man," she heard herself saying as Tom helped her across a dried-up mud puddle. "I mean, I never got to know him myself. But that's what Aunt Faye always says. Bit of a dreamer. Always chasing after harebrained schemes, you know. I don't know the details, but I think he lost a pile in the crash."

"We did, too," said Tom. Cici had to stop from rolling her eyes at the thought of all the money the poor Wolcotts had lost in '29, and then no doubt promptly made back.

"It's been a struggle for Aunt Faye, raising me on her own. That's why I thought I should come out here—I know I've been a financial burden to her. Oh, and also to serve my country, of course."

"Of course." Tom shielded her with his jacket as an especially dirty gust sprayed them with dust, and she gave a mock shriek.

"My hero!" she laughed and pecked him on the cheek.

Tom had led her away from home over to the bowling alley. Cici knew he must be attempting a romantic gesture, but her fingers were growing numb and she kept slipping on the ice. Finally he found the spot he was looking for, a nondescript patch of boardwalk in front of a bus stop. He held both her hands and gave her a big goofy grin. "Do you remember?"

"Remember what?"

"This place!"

Cici looked around. Sure, she'd been through here plenty of times before, but she didn't know why it might be important. He pulled her toward him and whispered in her ear. "Our first kiss."

"Oh, of course!" They'd left the bowling alley and lingered at the bus stop together. She remembered waiting impatiently for him to work up the nerve to finally kiss her.

"I love you, Cici Roberts!" He kissed her now without any caution. As he slowly pulled his face away from hers, he handed her a small box.

"Oh, Tom, how sweet!" She pulled at the fancy gold ribbon, ripped off the paper, popped it open, and saw a gleaming ruby pendant. It was gorgeous and looked expensive.

"It's beautiful!"

"Not as beautiful as you." He kissed her again, and she kissed him back enthusiastically. A man didn't buy jewelry like this for a lady unless he was serious.

When she got back to the dorm that night, June was sitting up in her bed reading, curlers in her hair. Cici worried about her roommate these days. She'd finally shown interest in a man, but it turned out she had terrible taste. Dr. Cantor was just awful: stuck-up and strange, and he clearly drank too much. She couldn't imagine what June was thinking. The girl went out with him practically every night. Cici didn't mind so much since she was usually with Tom. But she would at least invite June out with her and Tom's friends. June never invited her out with Dr. Cantor, not that Cici wanted to spend any time with him. What did they do together? What in the world did they talk about? June would just say they'd gone to the canteen or the movies, like it was the most natural thing. Cici found it revolting.

June looked up from her book. "Hello. Have a nice night?"

Cici began unbuttoning her jacket to show off the necklace. "Look what Tom gave me!"

"Wow, it's beautiful."

Cici beamed and sat down on her bed. "Did you go out with Dr. Cantor tonight?"

"Oh, goodness, you have to start calling him Sam."

Cici scrunched her nose, not wanting to be any more intimate with him than she already was.

"Yeah. We just went to the canteen."

"Tom took me to the spot where we first kissed and gave me the necklace."

"That's beautiful."

"I think Tom wants to marry me."

"Do you want to marry him?"

"Of course!"

"Well, that's wonderful." June had put her book down on the bedside table and looked thoughtful. "Do you feel like you can tell Tom anything?"

"Anything important," she lied.

"What about your job? Do you talk to Tom about what you do here?"

"Of course not! Don't be ridiculous. You know that's il-legal. You don't talk to Dr.—Sam about it, do you?"

June looked down, and Cici had the feeling she was lying. She was not as good at it as Cici. "No, of course not. I just wondered if you ever thought about it."

"No! Besides I don't really want to talk about my job with Tom, anyway." She began taking off her boots. Honestly, June was getting odder and odder.

Cici picked up her toiletry bag and started out the door to the restroom. "Oh, by the way," June said, "the toilet down the hall is broken again."

"That's the third time in a month!"

"I know. And there's the usual sign: 'An effort will be made to attend to the problem as quickly as possible.'"

"It's ridiculous to climb up and down the stairs just to use the toilet."

"And there's nothing we can do about it. Well, good night." June turned off the light beside her bed.

Cici put on her slippers and went into the hallway to walk down to the second floor. Someday she would live in a big house with a bathroom connected to her bedroom. She could walk in there naked if she wanted, but she would probably wear silk pajamas instead. Instinctively she put her hand to her throat to feel that the pendant was still there. It was smooth and cool to the touch. Solid.

* * *

JUNE HAD SUGGESTED taking the bus to Norris Dam for a pic-nic, and Sam loved the idea. He told her he hadn't been out of Oak Ridge in a year. "I feel like an inmate sprung from jail."

"So silly! You could have done this anytime by yourself."

"Picnics by yourself aren't much fun." He kissed her cheek. They had sat in the back of the bus for privacy. It was sunny, and the trees were turning green. Each year spring was a surprise to her. Of course she knew it would come again, but still, the coming always seemed a miracle. As the bus left the gates of the CEW under the watchful eye of the guard in the tower with his rifle, she squeezed Sam's hand. For the first time, they would be together in the outside world.

The last time June had left had been Christmas. What would it be like to be headed to the farm instead of Norris? It was impossible to imagine Sam meeting her parents. They didn't know what physics was, really. They thought that the one Catholic family that had children in her school couldn't be trusted, so what would they make of a Jewish suitor for their daughter? And what would Sam make of them and the farm? She feared he would laugh at them—not openly of course, but later to himself. It bothered her how he laughed at so many things—not because they were funny but because he despised them. She doubted he realized she knew this about him; she wasn't even sure if he knew it about himself.

They never would have met if it weren't for the CEW. And even if they had met somehow, what would they have had to say to each other? If he hadn't blurted out the horrible secret that first night, would they have ever even gone out on a date? But if they were to have a future, Sam would have to meet her parents one day. The future was constantly in June's mind these days. When she felt hopeful and in love, she day-dreamed about being married in a house, their house, able to do whatever they please, make love whenever they want. She would be in the kitchen making his supper while he was reading in his study. She'd never even been in a house with a study but felt sure they'd have one. If she was feeling truly indulgent, she'd let a child scamper into the scene, a little girl with Sam's curls but her light eyes. She loved to imagine every last detail—what she was cooking, where they lived, how the house was decorated. She saw it all in cinematic glory, herself with perfect Ingrid Bergman hair and outfit, the house the sort she'd only ever seen in the movies, with open, sprawling rooms and a yard that was just for show, not for tending vegetables or animals. What was harder to imagine was how they would get there.

The dam was situated on the side of a mountain, a huge swath of concrete holding back the water. The lake above the dam looked suspended in space, on a different level from everything below the huge man-made structure. It was unnatural and ungainly and spectacular. The government had taken people's land to build the dam, just as it had for Oak Ridge, and whole farms once riverside were now lake-bottom. Now the dam generated the electricity that powered Oak Ridge.

They found a spot to picnic by the lake, and June lay back, the grass prickling her skin. He was sitting with his elbow on one knee watching her. The sun was warm on her face, and she closed her eyes.

"June?"

She was too lazy to open her eyes. "Hmm?"

"Thank you."

"For what?"

"Picnicking with me." He gently lifted her hand and stroked her palm. "I love you, June."

His tone was casual, but the words were the most momentous she'd ever heard. She kept her eyes closed, not wanting to move or speak or alter the moment in any way. The feel of his fingers on her palm seemed to send electrical shocks down her arm.

It was dinnertime by the time they got off the bus back in Oak Ridge, so they headed to the cafeteria together. As they approached the drugstore, June noticed a big group of people outside the door, not in a line, just huddled together. Everyone was standing very still, listening to a radio turned up loud. Many of the women were crying. She edged closer to hear the announcer's words. "In Warm Springs, Georgia, Franklin D. Roosevelt lies with the problems of this nation finally lifted from his shoulders, stricken late this afternoon with cerebral hemorrhage."

June put her arm through Sam's and felt tears begin to well up. She thought Sam would laugh at her for crying, but his brow was furrowed. He squeezed her arm.

The newsreader continued in his rhythmic cadence, "Franklin D. Roosevelt, the first president to be elected to four terms in the White House, has passed away and that is the overshadowing of all news events that have happened and can happen for a while."

They stayed there in the crowd for some time. It was comforting to be surrounded by others feeling the same things, even if they were strangers. Finally they continued on silently toward the cafeteria. It seemed disrespectful to eat dinner as though nothing had happened, but June was hungry. She filled her plate with spaghetti and paid the cashier. The girl took her money wordlessly, and June wondered if she'd heard the news.

She looked for a seat and noticed Cici and Tom at a table by the windows looking out over the Townsite. Cici smiled and beckoned her over. June turned to get Sam's attention, and when she looked back at Cici's table, she was sure her friend's face had fallen. At once June wished she had ignored Cici and eaten with Sam alone. But Sam was carrying his tray over to her, and there was nothing for it but to go sit with them.

"So have you heard the news?" asked June.

"Yes. I heard on the radio at the dorm before coming over here," said Cici.

"It's just awful," said June.

"He's been president for so long," added Tom.

"I remember when he was the governor before that," said Sam, "when I was a kid in New York."

"That must have been a very long time ago," said Cici.

"President Truman," June said. "It sounds strange."

"Let's hope he knows what he's doing." Sam gulped his iced tea.

"Do you have to work tonight, June?" asked Tom.

"No. It's my day off."

"We were going to go roller skating. I don't know if you two are in the mood now, but you're welcome to join us."

Cici slammed her water glass down loudly, making it difficult for the others to pretend not to notice.

"Thanks for the offer, Tom," said Sam, "but I think we'll probably just go back to my place and listen to the radio."

"We took the bus to Norris Dam today, so it will be nice to relax this evening."

"That's fine," Cici said, picking up her fork once again and violently stabbing a piece of carrot on her plate.

"How was the dam?" asked Tom.

"Lovely," June replied.

A brief silence settled over the table, but Tom seemed determined to sustain a conversation. "What exactly is cerebral hemorrhage?" he asked Sam, and Sam muttered a reply. "If these winds keep up, I don't know what we're going to do," he said to no one in particular, and no one responded.

They finished quickly, parting ways with Cici and Tom, and started the walk back to Charlie and Ann's in silence. The gusts of wind were making the spring evening colder than it should have been. Finally Sam spoke. "June, I have to say, I have no idea why you spend time with that girl. I know she's your roommate, but you don't have to hang around her."

"She's not always like that." June's voice was small and timid.

"I should hope not! She strikes me as a real phony with that ridiculous way of talking."

She knew Sam had every right to be angry, yet June felt implicated by his criticism of her friend. She tried to explain. "Honestly, there's a whole other side to Cici . . . I'm sorry she's so awful with you."

"She's awful with you, too, from what I've seen. I don't mean to hurt your feelings; I'm just looking out for you. You don't have to spend time with a girl like that."

They walked in silence, interrupted only by the rustle of wind in the leaves. June couldn't explain Cici to Sam. These days she spent hardly any time with her, yet June wasn't ready to renounce their friendship completely. Cici was still fun, and heads still turned when they went out together. But there was more to her than that, and June suspected that she might be the only person who saw beyond the beautiful surface of Cici. Yes, she acted proud, superior, rude. But June was sure that it was just that—an act. She saw Cici away from the cafeteria and bowling lanes and boys. In the dorm, when she didn't think anyone was looking, a different girl emerged. That Cici wore no makeup and had her hair in rollers. She looked vulnerable and tired, and her public bravado was replaced with an air of melancholy.

When June finally got back to the dorm that night, Cici was already there, writing a letter at the desk they shared. She looked up and asked, "Have a nice evening?"

"Oh, yes. Well, you know, the news is awfully sad."

Cici didn't reply. June knew better than to confide in her, but she couldn't help herself. "Sam said he loved me today."

Cici's eyes widened, and she put down her pen. "Oh? What did you say?"

"Nothing. Do you think I should have said it back?"

"No, of course not."

"I think he knows I love him."

"Oh." Cici's voice was thick with disapproval.

June sat on her bed, facing Cici. She felt reckless. "Cici, you know you're my best friend. I wish you would give Sam a chance."

Cici said nothing and looked down at the piece of paper in front of her.

"I know he was awful on New Year's, but you must know that wasn't normal for him."

Cici faced her head on, her eyes empty, almost reptilian. "A man like that is never going to marry you."

She picked up her pen and returned to her letter. June sat motionless for a moment before she realized she had to get out of the room. She hurried down the hall to the bathroom, struggling to keep tears from forming in her eyes.

Janet Beard

(Courtesy of the Department of Energy)

Chapter 14

As Joe wound up a ten-hour shift, he felt weary in every sense—his muscles tender, his mind exhausted by the tedium of performing the same tasks again and again.

He didn't hear at first when the foreman called out his name. One of the other men had to give him a nudge.

"Follow me to my office," said the foreman. His voice was gruff, though Joe knew by now that he always sounded that way. The foreman was heavyset with a small head, so that his face looked as if it had been squeezed together to fit onto it. But he was efficient and fair, which was all Joe could want from him. Joe figured he was about to be let go. Most of the men on his construction crew had been laid off months ago. Trouble was, they'd finished building most of what needed to be built. Joe could hardly suppress his excitement at the thought of losing his job. In two days, he would be in Alabama again. He didn't know how in the world he'd keep his family fed and clothed, but they'd be together. The thought of it sent a warm tingle through his chest.

"Have a seat, Joe," said the foreman, once they'd made it to his makeshift office, nothing more than a small hutment.

"I'm sure you know that this job is winding up." The foreman sat down across from Joe and pulled a box of cigarettes out of his shirt pocket. He extended the box toward Joe, who thanked him and took one. The foreman took one as well, struck a match, and lit both cigarettes.

"I've had to send a lot of men home in the past month." His voice was somber; he sucked on the cigarette and stared at the wall behind Joe.

"It's not a job I like, but what can you do? Construction here's almost done. Hell, I'll probably be sent home myself sooner or later." The foreman chuckled, but Joe didn't know whether or not he should laugh. He took a drag from the cigarette.

"Anyway, Joe, you're a first-rate worker, and don't think I haven't noticed."

"Thank you, sir."

"I ain't never seen you loafing on the job, and you're always first to volunteer for overtime. You're no spring chicken, Joe, but you work a hell of a lot harder than most of those young'uns out there."

"Thank you." He didn't know what else to say.

"So I've recommended to the Roane-Anderson Company that they keep you on in Oak Ridge. You're a valuable asset."

Joe was not quite sure what the man could mean.

"Construction may be over, but someone's got to clean all these buildings we just put up. You wouldn't consider janitorial work beneath you, would you?"

"No, sir."

"Great. Then you just need to go to the Hill tomorrow and talk to the Roane-Anderson folks about your new position."

Joe didn't say anything at first. The foreman looked confused. "You do want to stay in Oak Ridge, don't you?"

"Yes, sir. Only . . . do you think my wife could get a job here, too? I left her and my children down in Alabama, and I ain't seen them in almost two years."

The foreman stubbed out his cigarette in an ashtray. "I reckon that could be arranged. You just explain everything to them folks tomorrow, and if they give you any grief, tell them to speak to me."

Joe's face spread into a wide grin, and he shook the foreman's hand. "Thank you, sir. Thank you very much."

Joe felt light and young and full of energy as he walked to the cafeteria. He could hardly wait to write to Moriah and tell her to get on the next bus to Tennessee. He was overcome with a sense that life was getting better and things were turning out the way they should. They would both be earning good government wages, and the girls could go to school. Alabama, which just a few moments ago had seemed like a lost paradise, was now a place in the past. If he had his family here in Tennessee, then Oak Ridge would truly be his home.

In the mess hall, he piled an extra helping of rice and beans on his plate, wanting to celebrate. He looked forward to sharing his good news with Ralph, but for now stuffing his face would have to do! He sat and ate and must have been smiling to himself because he heard a woman say to him, "You look like you're in a good mood."

He looked up and Shirley was standing in front of him, holding her tray.

"I am, as a matter of fact." His happiness was so expansive that he was glad to share it—even with Shirley. He motioned for her to sit, and she joined him.

"Enjoying the spring weather?"

"Better than that. I just got some good news for myself. My wife going to get a job here so she can join me."

"Oh, Joe! That is fantastic news!" Shirley seemed genuinely happy for him.

He let his smile take over his face. "I can't tell you how much I missed my family."

"I can imagine. You have two children?"

"Three. I can't believe I be seeing them soon!"

"I'm so happy for you, Joe. Have you told Ralph yet?"

"No, I just found out myself."

"He'll be very pleased."

Her face was warm and enthusiastic. Perhaps he'd misjudged Shirley.

"What's your wife's name?"

"Moriah. She a good woman. Strong-willed but kind."

"That's the best sort of woman," said Shirley, grinning slyly.

"I reckon you right."

"I look forward to meeting her and the little ones."

After supper, Shirley had to go to work but sent Joe to the rec hall to celebrate with Ralph. Men and a few scattered women were playing checkers, cards, and dice, smoking and talking in the big barnlike room. In one corner, a man played the blues on a guitar, while a boy no older than ten accompanied him on harmonica. The rhythmic wailing soared right up over the muffled sound of men's voices, and the room seemed to pulse to the beat of the song.

Joe lit up a cigarette as he looked around for Ralph, careful not to look too hard at anyone. This room was full of men drunk on homemade whiskey, who would be eager for the slightest reason to start a fight. He'd known men like this all his life, though he'd tried to stay away from them. He never touched liquor himself, never put himself in a situation where a man's emotions could get the better of him.

"Joe!" Ralph called out to him. The boy was standing against the wall with Otis.

"What you doing here?" asked Ralph.

"Just came to relax a spell."

"Then you at the wrong place." Otis smiled.

Joe did not smile back. He wanted to share his news with Ralph, but not in front of Otis.

"They gonna show a picture in an hour," said Ralph, who knew Joe liked the movies.

Otis laughed. "Wouldn't count on it. Ain't no one going to get this crowd to clear out for *Cabin in the Sky*."

"I might play checkers," said Joe.

"I'll play with you," Ralph offered.

"I don't mean to interrupt."

Otis shrugged. "I'm gonna play cards anyway."

Joe watched him walk away with relief and followed Ralph to an empty table, where they set up the board.

"I been offered a new job." Joe couldn't help but grin.

Ralph looked surprised. "Doing what?"

"Janitor. And they gonna find a job for Moriah, too."

"Well, ain't that something. Moriah here in Oak Ridge! I ought to get you a Coke to celebrate."

"Don't waste your money."

"No. I's getting you a Coca-Cola."

Ralph got up. Joe watched him go and wondered if the boy would be laid off soon. He didn't want his happiness to come at Ralph's expense.

Ralph returned with two bottles of Coke, lids off. Joe leaned back for a big gulp and felt the pleasant sensation of the bubbles hitting the back of his throat. When he straightened up, he saw that Ralph was watching him. "How's that?" the boy asked.

"Nice," said Joe. "Real nice."

"You know, they may start allowing Negro couples to live together soon."

"How you know?"

"Colonel Hodgson has instructed Roane-Anderson to work with us."

"Why he want to help you?"

"Guess Bob's letter to him worked."

Joe wiggled his brow skeptically.

"Roane-Anderson be sending a representative to meet with us."

"Really?"

"Yes, sir. They coming to the CCC meeting tomorrow night."

"It'd be real nice if I could live with Moriah and the children."

"We'll make it happen."

Ralph sounded so calm and sure. Normally Joe would have laughed at his ideas, but he was in a hopeful mood, so he smiled and took another gulp of his Coke instead.

Ralph cleared his throat. "I got some news, too."

"Oh, yeah?" Joe grinned, expecting to hear that Ralph had proposed to Shirley. But the boy's face was solemn.

"I got a letter from my mama."

Joe was shocked. As best he knew, Ralph hadn't been in contact with her since he'd run off to the Hopewell place six years ago. "How she know you here?"

"Reckon one of the men in our gang know her. Told her he thought her son work here." Ralph stared down at his Coke bottle.

"What she say?"

Ralph nodded without looking up. "She says she doing good. Working as a housekeeper."

"That good."

"My stepfather gone."

"That real good."

Ralph nodded again. "When I save up enough money, I'm gonna visit her. You know I ain't ever want to leave her."

"I know, Ralph. I sure she understand."

Ralph looked up at Joe. "He ain't die that day I left. My stepfather. I always worried about that. But he ain't dead. He gone but not dead."

Ralph's eyes were wide open and vulnerable. He took a gulp of his Coke, and Joe saw that the boy's hand was trembling. Joe tried to make his voice gentle. "That real good, son. You's a good boy and we all know it."

They drank their Cokes in silence.

(Courtesy of the Department of Energy)

Chapter 15

AFTER SAM'S TALK WITH ANN, HE FELT AWKWARD AROUND THE house and spent even more time with June or Max—anywhere besides home. He hadn't eaten dinner with Charlie and Ann in weeks; though Ann still invited him, he muttered an excuse and went out. Charlie seemed pained by the whole thing, though Sam didn't know what Ann had told him. He was acting overly cheerful, always trying to catch Sam in conversation, his natural warmth turned up in a desperate effort to thaw the frost that had settled over the home. Ann acted as though nothing had happened, which irritated Sam even more. It was another symptom of her properness. Everything just so, perfectly dressed, words all well chosen. Phony.

He and June were on their way to the movies one night when they passed Charlie on the boardwalk.

"Sam! I'm so glad I ran into you." Charlie was beaming, which Sam assumed was just more overcompensation for the tension in their domestic situation. "You'll never guess who's in town—Collins!"

"Artie? You're kidding!" If Charlie had been the nicest of the graduate students at Princeton, then Artie Collins had been the funniest.

"I'm on my way now to Kellerman's house. There's an impromptu gathering. I'd looked for you at home, but you weren't there. This is perfect!"

Sam glanced at June. "Well, we were headed to a movie. Artie's an old friend. Would you mind terribly if I went?"

"She should come!"

"Oh, I don't want to get in the way," said June. "You go on. I'll be fine."

"Nonsense," said Charlie, and Sam wished he wouldn't butt in. "You won't be in the way, and we'd love your company. I won't hear of leaving you behind."

June looked up at Sam, unsure. In truth, he did think she would be in the way, or at least bored by all the physics talk and reminiscing. But after Charlie's enthusiasm, he couldn't tell her not to come. So he nodded, and they followed Charlie.

The house was almost identical to Charlie and Ann's, and they could hear laughter coming out before they even got to the door. "That's Artie for you," said Charlie. "Got the crowd going already."

Charlie knocked and someone shouted, "Come in!" Artie, jacket off and tie askew, sat in the center of a group of seven in the living room. Cab Calloway was singing on a scratchy record somewhere in the background.

"Cantor and Stone! Now the party can finally begin. How the hell are you, Sam?" Artie shook his hand and patted his back.

"Can't complain. What brings you to our fair construction site?"

"Oh, top secret government business, of course. I'm just checking up on you for Oppenheimer." Robert Oppenheimer was the scientist heading the whole bomb-building project. Sam had known him at Berkeley.

"Let me get some more seats," said Kellerman, heading off to the kitchen. His wife was sitting on the sofa with some other physicists Sam recognized, most of whom worked with Charlie. There was one woman, Dr. Elizabeth Temple, a decent scientist though not at all attractive.

"Who is this?" asked Artie, extending his hand toward June.

"My friend, June Walker," said Sam.

"Nice to meet you," said June.

Kellerman returned with chairs and said, "Artie was just telling us about life in New Mexico."

"Oh, yes. It's quite idyllic. We go horseback riding along the mesas."

"You doing any physics?" asked Charlie.

"Plenty. We're just waiting for our shipments to get in from Oak Ridge so that we can do some experimenting."

"Experimenting?" asked Sam. "Let's hope you get it right on the first go."

"Cheers to that!" Artie raised his glass of milk.

Sam had noticed that the higher up his colleagues were positioned in the operation, the more likely they were to disobey the Army codes of secrecy. Everyone resented having to work in such a scientifically unfriendly fashion and constantly dropped hints to one another.

"Presumably you can drink there at least," asked someone.

"Oppenheimer was famous for his parties at Berkeley," Sam told June. He'd always thought of Oppenheimer as a bit of a kook, really. Tall and gaunt with large dark eyes, he came from money but put on bohemian affectations. Sam had been shocked when he heard he'd been put in charge of the Manhattan Project. Lawrence or Compton at the University of Chicago would have made more sense.

"Old Oppie has changed. He's a regular slave driver these days. We eat, drink, and sleep the Manhattan Project; there's very little time for anything else."

"Except horseback riding."

"It's physics horseback riding. Oh, the secrets those mares know! They could end the war before we could, if they could just get some U-235 out of Oak Ridge."

"Watch yourself, Collins," said Kellerman.

"Well, if all the girls here are as pretty as this, then I can see why you may get distracted from the job at hand."

June giggled, and Sam hoped she wasn't too mortified by the attention.

"That's enough, Artie," said Kellerman. "While you've been trotting around on your ponies, we've been designing, building, and running some of the largest, most complicated facilities the world has ever seen."

"Don't let him get to you, Kellerman," said Charlie. "Collins is just jealous of our twenty-four-hour cafeterias and free buses."

The truth was, of course, that every Oak Ridge scientist in the room was green-eyed over Artie's being down there with Oppenheimer, Fermi, Teller, Compton, and Bohr. That was the big show, and they all knew it.

"The lunch hall is truly open all night long?" asked Artie.

"Truly. People work around the clock for your . . . you know what."

Artie grinned. "Well, what do you know? I feel a bit hungry now." A few minutes later, the whole lot of them was headed out to the cafeteria, led on an adventure by Artie, just like at Princeton.

By the end of the evening, they had made their way to the canteen, having moved on from the cafeteria. They were sitting around a table, and Artie was telling a story about Sam's falling asleep in their old laboratory, ribbing him in a good-natured way, and everyone laughed. "You keep an eye on this man, June," Artie said, nudging him. "He can't quite take care of himself."

Sam hung his head in mock shame. Even though he hadn't wanted June to come, Sam was glad that she had. He hoped Charlie would go home tonight and tell Ann all about it. You see? June was capable of holding her own with physicists, he might say. Maybe she hadn't shared her thoughts on Freud, but she had listened and been charming. He wasn't mad to love her, after all. Her cheeks were rosy from the beer, and her eyes glowed in the dim electric light as she laughed at Artie's jokes. Sam put his arm around her, feeling happy and protective.

The next day at work, he got a phone call asking him to report to a private meeting with Dr. Armstrong. He had the sensation of being called to the principal's office for bad behavior—although Y-12 had been running smoothly as of late. Sam lit a cigarette as he sat down at Dr. Armstrong's desk. Sunlight streamed through the window, forcing the men to squint.

"Well, Cantor . . ." Armstrong leaned back in his chair, deeply inhaling from his own cigarette. "I'm going to be leaving you."

Sam wasn't sure how to take this, or even what it meant. Was he leaving Y-12? Oak Ridge? Was he dying? "I'm sorry to hear that" seemed appropriate for any of the possibilities.

"Yes. I'm a bit sorry myself. This crazy place has become dear to me." He straightened his back, and his voice became more practical. "Anyway, I'm not going far, and I'm sure I'll be in Y-12 periodically. Actually I've been promoted and am moving to the main offices. I'll be overseeing work at different sites here, but of course, most intensely involved with Y-12."

"In that case, congratulations."

"Thank you. Now, Cantor, if you're interested, I've discussed it with my superiors, and we think you should be promoted, too."

Sam took the cigarette out of his mouth, surprised.

"You won't be at quite my level. The idea is that you and Houser will both be given greater responsibilities and will take over my position between the two of you. It's a decision from above; no offense to either of you, but you're not quite senior enough—you know how the Army is about hierarchy. And before you get too excited—let me warn you, it's mostly going to be administrative work. Honestly, we've gotten through the hardest times of getting the place up and running, as I'm sure you realize. They wouldn't be moving me otherwise."

"Of course not."

Armstrong leaned forward and stubbed out his cigarette in a large glass ashtray on the desk. "But that doesn't mean congratulations aren't in order for you, either. You've come by this through your own dedication to Y-12 and practical, innovative thinking. There will be a substantial pay raise, and you will get one of these big offices as well as a secretary."

"Will Glenda be my secretary?" Sam asked, referring to the matronly blonde currently assisting Dr. Armstrong.

"Oh, no. I'm afraid I'm taking Glenda with me."

* * *

"BUT I *CAN'T* type," June said for the second time.

"Don't worry. I just told them you'd taken a course, and that you're overqualified to be working on the calutrons. Which is true."

Her face was pinched with anxiety. "Maybe. But I can't type."

She was sitting on the edge of his bed, across from him in the chair. "Honestly, how hard can it be? You're smart."

"Do you know how?"

Sam had typed plenty of papers in grad school, but had only ever utilized his index fingers in the process. "Not really, but I can use a typewriter."

She made a whimper and put her head in her hands. He had thought she'd be thrilled at the prospect of getting away from those tedious machines and becoming his secretary, but ever since he'd mentioned the typing test she'd have to take, June had been miserable. He was becoming annoyed. "You know, I've pulled strings for you. I'm trying to help you."

She gave him a limp smile. "I know. Thank you, honey."

He came over to the bed and put his arm around her, which inevitably led to kissing. Before it led to anything more, she gently pushed him away. "Ann's here, isn't she?" June whispered.

Sam let out something between a sigh and a moan. Of course Ann was there, so they mustn't. Goddamn Ann. He released June and lay back flat on the bed. This evening wasn't going anything like he planned. He wanted to celebrate his promotion with June. He thought she'd be thrilled about his arranging this interview for her, too, but instead she was just worrying herself sick over it. His head was beginning to ache.

June stroked the back of his hand with her fingers. "You hungry?"

"Not really."

"I'm starved. Why don't we walk over to the cafeteria? You'll work up an appetite on the way." She stood and straightened her skirt.

He got up slowly, still with half a mind to stay in bed. But he didn't want to upset her. He collected his jacket and hat from the desk and began putting them on. "I don't understand it," he said, opening the door for her. "You're usually so optimistic about things. I thought you'd be thrilled for this opportunity."

"Honestly, Sam, I am thrilled. I'm just nervous, too, you know. I wish I knew how to type."

The smell of cooking meat wafted from the kitchen. Ann was sitting on the living room sofa reading *Time*. "Hello, June. How are you?"

"I'm good, thanks. And you?"

"Fine."

Sam ignored her as per usual these days and continued toward the door. "I'm sure we can find someone to teach you," he continued.

"Do you know anyone with a typewriter?"

"I have a portable typewriter," Ann interposed.

Sam stopped in front of the door. She was beaming at them from the sofa, the magazine laid across her lap.

"Really?" asked June. "Can you type?"

"Oh, yes. I typed all of Charlie's papers at Princeton. Do you need lessons?"

"Desperately! Could you teach me? We'd be so grateful." Sam's head was pounding now, and he wished June would stop squealing.

"I'd be delighted to help." Ann was smiling broadly and gave Sam a look that he couldn't interpret. Was she gloating? Proud to be able to help a simple girl like June? "When do you need to learn by?" she asked.

"Next week."

"Then we should start immediately."

"I could come back after dinner."

"Nonsense! Stay here for dinner. There's plenty for both of you." Sam felt trapped; there was no way out of this. He took off his hat and hung it by the door.

"Thanks, Ann," he said. "It's really swell of you to help out."

It wasn't long before Charlie was home, and Ann served them beef hash and potatoes. She was so kind and pleasant throughout the meal that Sam found it hard to maintain his anger, though he wanted to. She seemed to take a special interest in June, and they chatted and laughed about feminine matters, like lipsticks and skirt length. Charlie grinned at Sam, rolling his eyes at the women in his good-natured way. After dinner, Ann got out the typewriter and began teaching June how to use it at the dining room table. Charlie and Sam went to the living room for a game of chess. The sound of female voices combined with the typewriter's rat-a-tat-tat made Sam feel like he was in a secretarial school.

The next day he came home to find June already there, practicing as Ann knitted beside her. And so it went the whole week; June and he shared dinner with Charlie and Ann, and June spent every free moment pounding on the typewriter. By the weekend, he was carrying on conversations with Ann again and realized that without either one of them saying anything, they had made up. June was gaining confidence with her typing, and Ann said she was getting the hang of it. Sam had found out as much as he could from Dr. Armstrong's secretary about what June could expect at her interview on Monday. One thing he hadn't counted on was a lie detector test. It struck him as ridiculous for a secretary, especially since the machines were notoriously unreliable. But June panicked again when he told her about it.

"But I'll have to lie when they ask me what I know about Y-12!" She was sitting at the typewriter. It was Saturday afternoon, and Charlie and Ann had gone out to the movies, so they had the house to themselves. He'd been hoping to get June into bed, but so far hadn't managed to pull her away from the typewriter. He saw now that mentioning the lie detector had been a tactical error.

"There's no need to worry. The machine can't really tell if you're lying. It just measures your blood pressure and pulse. If you remain calm when they ask you questions, it should be fine."

June's eyes were wide, and Sam was afraid her blood pressure was spiking right now.

"Let's practice," he said, dragging his chair beside her. He put his hand gently on the nape of her neck and felt the thumping of her heart.

"Is your name June Walker?"

She giggled. "Yes."

"How long have you worked at the Clinton Engineer Works?"

"Um . . . five months."

"Have you ever spoken with anyone about the nature of your work?"

"No." Her heartbeat seemed steady to him, though it was difficult to tell.

"Have you ever had sexual relations with any of your superiors at the CEW?" Her heart sped up for sure that time.

She looked him in the eye, with a mischievous grin. "No."

He kissed her and a couple of minutes later managed to get her away from the typewriter after all.

* * *

JUNE WAS ALLOWED a day off from work for her interview. She woke up before her alarm had a chance to ring and went down to the bathroom to wash and take the curlers out of her hair. She had made sure her best dress, red with white buttons, was clean and pressed and had bought a smart jacket at the department store in town to go with it. Mrs. Ransom's lecture from her first day at Oak Ridge rang in her ears as she applied eyeliner and a touch of rouge, borrowed from Cici. Look attractive, but not *too* attractive.

Cici was on the night shift and still in bed. June was glad she didn't have to talk to her this morning. She'd told her a couple of days before about the interview and could tell Cici didn't like it. June couldn't really blame her. It wasn't fair, and she felt guilty to have this opportunity just because of her man. On the other hand, if anyone should understand, shouldn't it be Cici? She, who so blatantly hunted for a rich husband and showed off Tom's presents?

June dropped by the cafeteria for breakfast but ordered

only one slice of toast to dull her hunger pains. She knew she should eat something but was afraid anything more would make her ill. Her stomach seemed to have a mind of its own, and she was glad the lie detector couldn't measure her level of nausea, which would surely give her away. She practiced typing even as she ate, thinking of a word such as *toast* and moving the correct fingers to pretend-type it in the air. Her fingers moved fast, and she no longer had to think consciously about where the keys were. In fact, she liked typing. It was basically as mindless as the work in her cubicle, but she enjoyed racing with herself to go faster and faster, the satisfaction of the *clack, clack, clack,* and the finished product of bold black-on-white words.

She reported to the bullpen, where she'd spent her first few days in Oak Ridge. Back in November, this plain rectangular office building had seemed daunting; she'd been so unsure of where to go or what would happen to her. She knew Oak Ridge so well now, it was difficult to imagine ever having been so intimidated by this place. It truly felt like home.

The receptionist gave her a pile of forms to fill out. The woman moved with assurance and spoke with a bright smile. June watched her enviously and hoped that soon she, too, could be an administrator. The working women in the movies she watched at the Ridge Theatre seemed to live glamorous lives. It was usually just a matter of time before their bosses seduced them, but this, of course, wouldn't be a worry for June because Sam would be her boss. She wanted to smile for visitors, answer phones with a syrupy voice, tell people to wait one moment, and take exquisite messages. Besides, it was a career that could take her beyond Y-12 and the war, which was surely winding to a close.

Yesterday, Hitler had killed himself, and now all anyone was talking about was when the Germans would surrender. The papers were filled with news of triumph—yet there were more horrors still. The Americans and Russians had found vast camps where human beings had been made to live like animals and then were slaughtered like animals as well. The horror of it could hardly be contained in a newsreel. Pictures showed American soldiers giving food to starving men and women who looked more dead than alive, their bones visible through their taut, sickly skin. These images stayed with June. Every time she thought she had a handle on, at least an understanding of, this war, she realized she had no idea. She would never have any idea, really, safe here in Tennessee. In future years, on occasions when she had encounters with veterans and a handful of Europe's displaced persons, she would always know that they had seen sights she would never be able to imagine and had known things about people she couldn't begin to understand. Attending dinner parties populated with the wounded men of her generation or chatting with the shy foreign woman who worked in the market, June would remain horrified and humbled by the suffering she knew was beyond comprehension.

Another woman came out to tell June her typing test was about to commence. A big green typewriter waited for her on a desk; beside it was a document holder with the letter she was to type, and a stack of paper. June breathed deeply, sat down, and loaded the paper into the machine.

"Ready?" asked the woman.

"Yes, ma'am."

"All right. Start!"

She got off to a flying start, a sprinter bursting off the starting block. Then she ground to a halt as she watched herself type HTE twice in one sentence. Her heart was beating faster than she was typing, but she forced herself to concentrate, go slower, more carefully. Gradually she built up speed once again. *Clack, clack, clack* went the keys, and she was back in control, her fingers bounding around the keyboard. In a flash, the five minutes were over. She had filled up just over half the page, single spaced.

Next, she had an interview with Sam and someone called Sergeant Johnson. Once she'd gotten the job, it wouldn't matter if people knew they were going together, but Sam thought it would hurt her chances of being hired if the Army thought he'd requested her only because he found her attractive. She had to pretend that she and Sam were just casual acquaintances, which was nerve-racking. Even so, with the typing test over, she felt relaxed. She shook hands with Sergeant Johnson and Sam and took a seat across from them at a small, round table.

Sergeant Johnson's demeanor was friendly. "Nice to meet you, June," he said, shuffling through the forms she'd filled out earlier.

"Miss Andrews tells us you did well just now on the typing test," he continued and looked up. "Know what you scored?"

She shook her head. "Sixty-eight words per minute, with two errors. That's very good. Where did you learn to type?"

"I took a course in Knoxville a couple of years back." This was the lie that Sam had come up with and they'd practiced again and again. She kept focused on Sergeant Johnson to avoid Sam's eyes.

"Why didn't you apply for a secretarial job here?"

"Well, sir, I never actually finished that course. I didn't know if I'd be qualified."

"Oh, with this typing speed you should be fine. Now, I think Dr. Cantor has a few questions for you."

Sam nodded and took out a legal pad on which he'd scribbled his questions. Of course she'd already seen them and practiced answering them with him the night before. He spoke in an authoritative voice, and his stare was cold. Later they would kiss and cuddle and laugh about it all.

The rest of the interview went smoothly, and Sergeant Johnson didn't seem to suspect a thing. Finally it was time for the lie detector test. Miss Andrews led her down a hall to another small room. A large black box sat on a table, wires and cables coming out of it in different directions. June repeated in her mind, *Don't be scared, you're in control,* as Sam had suggested to her. It felt silly, but it did seem to calm her.

A man in a lab coat told her to take a seat. "Please don't be nervous, June. You understand because of the sensitive nature of this job, all potential employees have to undergo a polygraph test."

"Yes."

He explained that he had to attach the polygraph components to her, but it would be totally painless. She nodded, and he asked her to untuck her blouse and unbutton it slightly at the top. He took two of the tubes connected to the machine and attached one to her chest and one to her stomach, just above her skirt, with sticky patches that tugged at her skin.

Next he attached small metal plates to the index and ring fingers of her left hand. Then he asked her to roll up her sleeve and placed a blood pressure cuff around her upper arm.

"Is your name June Walker?"

"Yes."

"Where are you from?"

"Blount County, Tennessee."

"What is your mother's name?"

"Rose."

"Have you ever lied to her?"

June was startled by this and wondered if the machine could tell. "Yes," she said.

"What did you have for supper last night?"

"Um . . ." Again June faltered; she realized she was getting more and more nervous. She couldn't remember. Ann had cooked, but what had it been?

"Chicken stew!" she said over-triumphantly, relieved to have remembered.

After that, she managed to keep calm. *Don't be scared, don't be scared,* she kept telling herself. The test went on for over an hour, more mundane questions, then on to the serious ones.

"Have you ever discussed with anyone outside of your job what you do here at Oak Ridge?"

"No." *You're in control,* she thought, *don't be scared.*

"Have you ever witnessed another employee revealing classified information?"

"No."

Finally it was done. He helped her out of the tubes and told her she was free to go. As she stood up, she glanced at the machine and the chart of lines created by her responses. She didn't know if they were good or bad.

* * *

SAM HAD LUNCH with Sergeant Johnson, a good guy who said he didn't see any problems with hiring the girl as long as she passed the security test. When they got back to the bullpen, Johnson's secretary told them that Mr. Geary, the polygraph administrator, was ready to see them.

"The girl looks perfect from a security perspective. Sweet little country thing as far as I can tell."

The polygraph man lit up a cigarette and offered his pack to the other men. Sam took one, feeling celebratory.

"Just between us, the lie detector test's a joke. Miss Walker passed all the security questions, but failed when I asked if she knew how to type."

Sam laughed just a bit too loudly at that, his anxiety released all at once and replaced with a rush of sweet relief.

* * *

IT WAS ONLY June's second week at her job, when the news that everyone had been waiting for finally came in. She'd just arrived at the office and was feeding paper into the typewriter on her big wooden desk when the phone rang.

"Dr. Cantor's office," she answered.

"Hello there," said a woman's voice. "I'm calling from the central office to let everyone know that victory has been declared in Europe."

Even though she'd been waiting for it for weeks, it still came as a shock.

"Please give everyone in your area the news. But also stress to them that they must keep working. No one is allowed to leave their post. Remind them that the war is not over, and we still have a vital job to perform here."

"Of course."

She hung up and went to Sam's office. He was smoking by his window, looking down at the parking lot, and had obviously already heard. A large truck was driving through the parking lot, and a man was shouting the news through a megaphone out the window: "Victory declared in Europe! Germany surrenders! Please do not leave your posts! We still have to fight a war with Japan. Whose son will die in the last minute?"

Sam turned to her. "We got the Germans," he said, his voice and face oddly blank, reflecting none of her own jubilation.

Later, when trying to understand his reaction, June would think of only one explanation. Already he was thinking past the victory to the consequences of their work. There was no longer a race with Germany for a bomb; whatever they were building would be destined for Japan.

(Courtesy of the Department of Energy)

Chapter 16

JOE PUSHED HIS MOP DOWN A LONG HALLWAY, WHISTLING SOFTLY under his breath. This section of the building was all offices, and most folks had left for the day. It was quiet save for an electric hum in the background, and the hallway was dark and stuffy. Cleaning the offices was easy work, just a bit of sweeping usually. The laboratories were a different story, and the toilets were the worst. But none of it was the strain that construction had been.

This was Joe's third summer in Oak Ridge, and the hutments never had gotten any cooler or the mosquitoes any less vicious. But now that he had Moriah and his babies with him, it seemed more bearable. Between the two of them, they were making more money in a year than they would have seen in three in Alabama. The children were starting school in the fall and would be able to attend full days for the entire school year, unlike back in Alabama. They had moved into their own hutment—still a wretched place to live, but his and Moriah's all the same, all to themselves and the children. It was a kind of bliss to come home after his late shifts and find her there, half asleep in the bed, waiting for him, and then in the morning to wake to the smell of bacon frying on the stove and see Moriah standing over the frying pan, little Ben at her feet.

Nevertheless, he worried about the girls, especially Ellie. This was hardly a respectable place to bring up children, and they might be better off back on the farm, away from the gambling and violence of the hutment area. Ellie was almost thirteen now, old enough to get into trouble, with all these rowdy men. The thought of it twisted Joe's guts. Luckily, she was tall but quite skinny, still gawky in a girlish way that he hoped wouldn't give anyone any ideas.

After their talk, the foreman had written a note to the officials at Roane-Anderson and arranged for Moriah to come work as a cook in one of the cafeterias. Joe had taken the bus to Knoxville to meet her and the children. He'd gotten to the Greyhound station two hours early, because he wanted to be sure to be waiting when they arrived. He bought three cups of coffee, drinking them slowly on a hard wooden bench by the window of the colored waiting area. Buses came and went; he watched tearful farewells, soldiers getting hugged and kissed hello, and travelers who had no one to say goodbye or hello to.

He saw Becky first, hopping down the steps at the front of the bus in a pink dress and pigtails. Joe ran outside, waving, his coffee forgotten on the bench. By the time he got to Becky, Ellie was beside her, and Moriah was carefully climbing down the stairs, holding Ben, already three years old. Moriah's face was as familiar as his own reflection and yet a miraculous surprise. She plopped Ben onto the ground and held out her arms. He embraced her, squeezing right through her flimsy cotton jacket, pressing his hand against the felt hat crowning the back of her head. "Moriah . . ." he whispered.

"I'm here," she said. "I'm here."

He could feel the contours of her body against him, just as he remembered them. He didn't want to let go but knew the girls were staring up at them, anxious. They were bashful at first. Ellie was almost as tall as Moriah now, a skinny thing, all legs and big, wide eyes. Becky was softer, still insulated in baby fat, not quite a young woman yet, thank goodness. He said their names, "Becky, Ellie," and they forgot their shyness and attacked from both sides, hugging his waist and legs. He kissed both their heads, then scooped up Ben, and stared into his son's eyes. The child stared at him suspiciously, and it hurt Joe to know that he must not remember his daddy at all. Joe blew air onto Ben's cheek, an old trick that he remembered amused the girls when they were little, and the boy laughed.

The Army had begun allowing colored families to live together only a month earlier, finally caving in to the demands from the Colored Camp Council. Negro families could apply for their own hutments now, and a small school for colored children had been set up. Even so, Ralph and his friends weren't content. Joe thought they might quit while they were ahead, but they continued meeting once a week, and Ralph had even gone to a labor meeting on the other side of town, too. There was no talking him out of it. Joe was certain Ralph would get laid off, but so far he hadn't been. Even this didn't make Ralph happy. He said it was because the bosses thought it would look bad to fire him after he'd made all that fuss.

Joe couldn't see what difference it made. A paycheck was a paycheck.

Folks knew who Ralph was now, and other men looked up to him, even with his crippled arm. Still, he was hardly more than a boy. His cheeks remained childishly plump, his eyes clear and hopeful. Joe felt bad having to leave him on his own in the hutment while he moved to the family area with Moriah. Ralph was awfully quiet that day as Joe packed up his stuff. He'd been sitting on his cot, watching Joe gather what few possessions he had. Finally, when Joe was snapping his footlocker shut, Ralph muttered, almost under his breath, "You remember Alabama?"

A silly question. Joe had lived there for forty-five years, hadn't he? "Yeah."

"When I first got to the farm, I didn't know nobody."

"You looked like something the cat drug in."

"Reckon I did. But you and Moriah were real friendly to me."

Joe put down the locker and turned to him. "You weren't no more than a boy."

"Even so . . ."

"You're always welcome in our house."

Ralph had nodded without looking at Joe, embarrassed by the emotion in his voice.

Moriah suggested inviting him and Shirley over for supper once they had their hutment set up. It was her day off from cooking in the cafeteria, but nevertheless she spent hours over her own woodstove, trying to make a nice stew out of scraps from the cafeteria. The girls were tasked with keeping the hutment neat—it was all but impossible to keep dirt out, but they dutifully swept and dusted as their mother cooked. Joe set up a table outside where they could eat in the fresh air.

Ralph arrived promptly in his fancy hat and tie, with Shirley on his arm. She was wearing a dark green dress that fit her perfectly. A small black hat and big smooth curls framed her face. Becky and Ellie peered out from the doorway at her. "Come on outside, girls, and say hello."

Ellie jumped down the steps and put her hand out toward Shirley. "Hi. I'm Ellie."

Shirley shook Ellie's bare hand in her delicate, gloved one. "Hi, Ellie. Nice to meet you."

Becky stood behind her big sister, shy.

"This is Becky," Ellie said for her.

"Say hello, Becky," urged Joe.

Becky silently stared up at Shirley. "Hi, Becky. My name's Shirley."

Becky glanced up at her sister, then cautiously smiled.

"Come on over and have a seat." Joe motioned to the makeshift table he'd constructed from some spare boards left over from hutment construction. Somehow Shirley looked elegant, even in this ridiculous setting, smoothing her skirt as she sat at the rickety table.

"Ellie, fetch some water for our guests."

Moriah leaned out the doorway. Ralph stood politely, as he always did around her. "Hello, Mrs. Moriah."

"Hi there, Ralph. What do you think of our new house?"

Ralph looked around at the dusty jumble of hutments and shook his head. "All I can say is, at least you're together as a family."

"Thank God for that," added Joe.

Ralph motioned to Shirley, who was still seated. "This here's Shirley Crawford from Atlanta, Georgia."

Moriah stepped out of the hutment, followed closely by Ben. "Hi, Shirley. I'm Moriah."

Shirley extended her hand. Moriah shook it and turned back to the hutment. "I better finish getting supper ready."

Ellie returned with glasses of water. "What's Atlanta like?" she asked as she set the glasses in front of Ralph and Shirley.

"It's nice—a real big city. We've got streetcars, and new buildings going up all the time."

"Sounds like Oak Ridge," said Joe.

"It's nothing like Oak Ridge. Atlanta's a real, proper city, with all sorts of people in it."

"How you like Oak Ridge, Ellie?" asked Ralph.

Ellie shrugged. "There's lots to see. But Daddy won't let us leave the hutments."

"Your daddy just wants you to be safe," said Ralph. "This ain't like living in the country."

"Ain't that the truth!" Moriah came back out, carrying a steaming pot.

Joe called the children to the table, and they all joined hands to pray. Moriah began serving stew out while Ellie passed around peas and potatoes.

"How are you finding it here, Moriah?" asked Ralph.

"I miss the farm. Only place I ever lived. But I'm glad to be making money, and I'd have moved just about anywhere to have my family all together again."

Moriah spoke sincerely. Her face was thinner than when Joe had left her in Alabama, with a few new lines around her mouth and eyes. She looked tired most of the time. Joe knew living here wasn't easy for her, and living without him in Alabama hadn't been, either.

"I'm glad you here," said Ralph. "And I'm real glad you all get to live together. But I'm ashamed it has to be like this, in these here hutments."

Becky and Ellie could hear the anger in Ralph's tone. They watched the adults attentively to see what would happen next.

"It's a roof over our heads, and we're all together. That's what matters." Moriah smiled and instantly looked young again.

"You are too accepting," said Shirley. The girls' eyes were glued on her now. "Do you know that the Army actually planned to build slums here? Can you imagine that? When else in history have people created slums on purpose?"

"I ain't thought of it that way," said Moriah.

Ralph turned to Ellie. "You still got your harmonica?"

Ellie beamed. "Yes! Mama, can I play a song?"

"After we through with supper." She shook her head. "This girl loves music!"

"I can dance!" Becky chimed in.

Ralph sat back in his chair. "Well, I think after dinner, we'll just have to have a little concert!"

"You'll have to sing for us, Ralph," said Moriah. "You got about the nicest voice I've ever heard."

"Thank you, Mrs. Moriah. If Ellie will play her harmonica, I'll surely sing."

Ellie was good at squawking out melodies, and Ralph kept his word and sang along. The girls attempted to tap-dance less successfully, but Joe clapped and cheered for them all the same. They could do so many things they couldn't when he'd left them to come up here. Later, when Ralph and Shirley had gone and the children were in bed, Joe found Moriah outside at the sink, washing the dishes. He took the rag she'd slung over her shoulder and began drying them.

"That girl sure has a lot of opinions," she said.

"Shirley?"

"Mmm-hmm." Moriah mocked: "Shirley Crawford of Atlanta, Georgia."

"She's a real city girl."

"She's a real know-it-all if you ask me."

"Ralph's crazy for her."

"Well, she's good-looking, I'll say that much."

"Is she? I hadn't noticed." Joe grinned at his wife, who put down the dish she was holding. He leaned over and kissed her on the mouth. "You're the most beautiful woman I know."

"I know that ain't true. But I like to hear you say it."

* * *

UNLIKE RALPH AND Shirley, Joe didn't feel too much like complaining. For the first time in his life, he wasn't working out in the sun. He was in charge of cleaning two corridors of the factory building. He pushed the large flat broom down the hallway and thought it was just in time, too. His knees ached when he walked up the stairs, and his back ached all the time.

The scrawny secretary who worked for Dr. Cantor walked past and smiled. "Hi, Joe."

"Hello, Miss Walker. Don't tell me Dr. Cantor's got you working this late?"

"I'm just finishing up a couple of things for him."

"Well, you better hurry on up and get out of this place. It a beautiful summer night. You go on and enjoy it."

"I will. Good night, Joe."

She went into Dr. Cantor's office and shut the door behind her. Joe continued down the hallway; he'd have to remember to come back to the office later. For now he had the ladies' restroom to deal with. He whistled louder now, his tune echoing in the small, tiled room.

* * *

JUNE FOUND THAT not only was she a good typist, she also had a knack for organization. Each evening Sam would leave an explosion of papers and trash on his desk, and then in the morning June would set about arranging it into neat labeled piles. Her own desk was tidy, with a calendar on one side, where she kept her running to-do list, and orderly piles along the other end. She would go over her to-do list for the day, make coffee for herself and Sam, and prioritize the day's tasks. By the time Sam got there, she was already hard at work.

In the first weeks on the job, it became obvious that June needed to learn dictation. Sam was kind about her ineptitude, of course, but she realized she couldn't hold this position without learning the skills required. She found a guide at the small library, and after some careful observation of the other secretaries on the floor, determined that Sophie, a sweet, chubby girl from Ohio, would be understanding if she asked for help. Sophie met with her at lunch a few times and helped June practice dictation until she had the confidence to follow Sam around, jotting down his words just like a proper secretary.

Sam was less happy with his new position. The Army required large amounts of paperwork, and he missed his laboratory. Often he told June that he didn't know what he'd do if she weren't there with him—lose his mind, probably. It made her glad that he appreciated her presence, but she worried about him. She was so much happier as a secretary and hated that he had to be so miserable, as though her happiness had been traded for his. His bad moods made her anxious. She worried about him, but worried too that he might take out his frustration on her. And she couldn't help but wonder why she wasn't enough to satisfy him anymore.

Today, though, she could see that Sam was excited. His old boss from California, Ernest Lawrence, was visiting. Sam's usual cynicism had dropped away, and he seemed genuinely eager to impress Lawrence. June thought it was sweet. As best she could tell, Y-12 was running smoothly these days, so hopefully Lawrence would be pleased with Sam's work.

Officially, she was not supposed to know about Lawrence's visit. She had to follow all sorts of special protocol to maintain secrecy. Many of the letters and memos she typed were coded so that she didn't actually know what they meant. Sam assured her that it was nothing worth knowing, just dull administrative matters. Classified letters had to be sealed in double envelopes with a sealing wax that would make tampering evident. She also had a special wastebasket for any secret information. Every time she picked up the heavy black phone, a red insert was revealed on the base, which reminded her to "Avoid Loose Talk."

In truth, she and Sam barely spoke about the war these

days. They had all but exhausted the subject of atomic bombs. Now that they worked together, when it was time to go home, all they really wanted to do was leave the office behind, go to the movies, listen to the radio, discuss anything besides Y-12.

It was the middle of summer, and June's windowless office was already stuffy when she arrived in the morning; by the afternoon, the air became muggy and oppressive. She inched the small electric fan on her desk closer and closer to her face, forced to use spare change and heavy pens as paperweights for whatever might be in the path of its breeze. The dorm was miserable, too, and never seemed to cool down at night. She had taken to wearing her lightest slip to bed and using only a sheet, her feet sticking out from under it. Still, she would wake in the middle of the night, sweating, her feet throbbing in the heat.

The absolute worst place to be on a summer afternoon was on one of the buses. If folks opened the windows, dust came blowing in. If they didn't open them, the bus was suffocating. The still air smelled of sweat, and when the buses were crowded, which was always the case at shift changes, you had to sit or stand uncomfortably close to other damp, sticky bodies. This was one reason that June had taken to staying late at work with Sam. She was supposed to clock out at five, but if Sam wrote a request for her to stay late, she could present it at the clock alley. They tried to avoid the rush on the buses and the busiest times at the cafeteria. Sam genuinely did need to stay late most days; he never seemed to get a handle on all the forms he had to fill out, letters that had to be signed. Often he got distracted in the afternoons, wandering back to his old lab to see how things were going there. June's work was almost always finished by five, but she didn't mind staying to keep him company. If she did leave without him, it was usually to go to the movies by herself, time alone in the dark that she cherished. Sam didn't care for the pictures the way she did, and she didn't need him sitting beside her to enjoy the stories on the screen.

She'd slowly been improving her wardrobe, making little purchases from Miller's—new boots here, a jacket and scarf there—in an effort to look smarter, less like a country girl. Now that she was a secretary, this seemed even more urgent. She wanted to dress the part. But it was difficult in this heat to get excited about putting on any clothes. Even lipstick and rouge felt hot on her face. Two simple cotton dresses she'd made herself were the coolest things she owned, and she wore them as much as possible. Stockings were hard to come by these days, so luckily, she didn't stand out by not wearing them.

She'd bought a satin slip, telling herself a working woman needed proper undergarments in addition to the more noticeable accessories. One day when Cici was at work, June tried it on in front of their small mirror. She had never dared look at herself naked before. Sometimes she felt wicked to have let Sam make love to her. With Ronnie she had felt obligated, but with Sam she had no real excuse. She figured he didn't know, but she was always nervous when they managed to get the house to themselves. He would expect her to give in to him, and she could hardly tell him no now. Sometimes she didn't know how to react to him—if she was holding her body in the right position, what sounds she was supposed to make. Even when she felt pleasure, it was usually eclipsed by her anxiety. Still, she loved how Sam looked at her when she was naked. She never knew she could have that effect on a man. Slowly she'd drawn her hand across her belly, the fabric deliciously smooth, her skin hot underneath. She was wearing the slip that day in the office as well; it swished against her legs when she walked, and her every step felt sophisticated.

She got a call from the front security checkpoint announcing Mr. Lawson's arrival. "Lawson" was a code name for "Lawrence." A few minutes later, she let in Dr. Armstrong and "Mr. Lawson," a tall man with glasses. She was surprised by how youthful and athletic he looked, not at all what she'd expected. In Sam's office, the men were all smiles and vigorous handshakes, jolly in one another's presence, and she closed the door on them. A few minutes later, they emerged, and Sam told her not to expect him back in the office until after lunch.

One problem with being good at organization and prioritizing was that by midday she'd often run out of things to do. Sometimes she would type things just for herself, almost to herself, like a journal. Most of the time, she ripped them up when she was done, but every once in a while she'd fold them and put them in her purse. Today she wrote:

Bored, bored, but why should I be bored? I can do anything I want really. Hope S. becomes happy. Does my happiness depend on his happiness? Is that good or bad? It would make him angry if I said that. He doesn't like to think I'm too dependent. But if you love someone, how can you be happy if they are not? Truly, completely happy, anyway.

She stopped typing, stood up, and paced across the room. She had a novel in her purse for reading on the bus, but it seemed too blatantly recreational to take it out here. Strange that she should be paid more money now to do less work. She went back to the typewriter, deciding she would use the time to write her parents another letter. They were so impressed by her typing.

Sam didn't get back until after five o'clock. By that point, June had given up all pretense of work and was reading the book. As he opened the door, she tossed it into her open pocketbook on the floor. Not that Sam would really mind, yet still she felt guilty. But he didn't notice at all. He had a goofy smile, and she wondered if he was drunk.

He closed the door behind him and grinned at her. "I did well today."

"Good!" she said, standing, genuinely pleased.

He came to her and put his arms around her waist. "Lawrence was very happy. He wants to get dinner tonight. Is that all right? I know we had plans."

"It's fine. I've been wanting to go to the movies anyway."

He patted her bottom and went toward his own office. "Thanks, honey. I'll make it up to you. We'll go out tomorrow. Oh, I almost forgot. I actually have some work for you to do and need you to stay late tonight. You might still have time for the movie, though."

"Sure. If not, I can catch it another time."

He stopped in the doorway and turned back. "Thank you, June. I really don't know what I'd do without you."

He held her gaze for an extended moment, his eyes shining with gratitude and affection. She felt her cheeks, already rosy from the heat, redden even more. He still had the power to look at her and make her feel like an altogether more capable, exciting, *better* person than she had ever felt herself to be before. One look like that, and a hundred petty grievances and worries would disappear. And maybe this approval from Lawrence was what he needed to cheer him up.

Once he was gone, she got to work on the letters he'd left behind for her, and the time went by quickly. The hallways became quieter and quieter as everyone left for the day, until the only sound was the rhythmic clatter of her typewriter.

(Courtesy of the Department of Energy)

Chapter 17

TOM WAS NEVER LATE. IN FACT, HE MADE A HABIT OF ARRIVING early wherever he went, which sometimes irritated Cici when she was running behind herself, taking an extra five minutes to do her hair, knowing he was waiting for her outside the dorm. Cici glanced at her watch again. Ten minutes late! She sat on a bench by the entrance to the rec center, dabbing at her face with a handkerchief to try and hide her perspiration. She wasn't worried—with another guy, she might have wondered if he was losing interest or stepping out on her. But Tom was devoted.

He had written to his mother about Cici, and Mrs. Wolcott had actually sent Cici a letter. She had read it dozens of times. Everything about it was elegant: the return address was stamped on the flap of the envelope, Mrs. Wolcott's penmanship was excellent, and even the paper was softer, smoother than normal. The letter was short and formal but kind.

Dear Cecilia,

    It is unfortunate that due to the circumstances of this terrible war, we cannot meet at the present time, except via correspondence. I look forward to the happy day when you can travel with Tom to New Jersey and be introduced to our family in person.

    Since he was a boy, Tom has been an excellent judge of character, so I trust him when he tells me you are a young woman of superlative character and innumerable charms. A mother cannot help but have strong opinions on the type of woman her son should marry. Having no daughters of my own, perhaps I feel this even more strongly than most. If his accounting is true, Tom would be lucky to have a girl like you by his side.

    The Wolcotts are a welcoming family. I can assure you life amongst them is exceedingly comfortable, though not without its responsibilities. I hope you will accept my guidance should you become a member.

With warmest regards,
Eleanor Wolcott

Cici had to go to the library to look up *superlative* and *innumerable* in the dictionary. It was as though one of the fancy Nashville ladies she used to greet as a hostess had written her a letter, and was in fact inviting Cici to join her family. This had always been her objective, yet Cici could hardly believe she was this close to crossing the finish line.

She looked around idly. Out of habit, she found herself

assessing the array of soldiers on hand. None were intriguing, not that she was tempted to step out on Tom, anyway. Things had progressed past the point of creating any useful jealousy; the key now was merely to keep steady, on course. She saw June and Dr. Cantor coming through the entrance. What a nuisance to have to make small talk with them. June had been a fine girl, but she had changed around that awful scientist, smiling up at him constantly, seeking his approval. Cici had never fawned over a man that way. And June was putting on airs. Not the useful kind that Cici had cultivated in herself, but foolish pretensions. She talked about the news and the war with this knowledgeable air that Cici knew was fake.

"Hi, Cici. Meeting Tom?"

"Mmm-hmm. You two have fun."

Luckily, they went on past her without any further conversation. She knew Dr. Cantor didn't like her, though Cici couldn't care less about his opinion. He'd gotten June a job as his secretary, which was infuriating. Cici had thought about reporting their relationship to the Army. The trouble was she couldn't prove they were doing anything against the rules, even if it was tacky for Dr. Cantor to get his girlfriend promoted. Now June wore suits and only had to work day shifts. Not that Cici particularly wanted to be a secretary. That was short-term thinking. She was going to be a wife.

She saw Tom walking toward her on the boardwalk before he noticed her. His head was down, and he was walking fast, distracted. She waved, but he didn't see until he was standing practically in front of her. He looked at her with an expression she'd never quite seen on him—his brow creased, mouth clenched. "What's wrong?" asked Cici.

"I've had a letter from Bobby," said Tom. Cici had heard all about Bobby, Tom's best childhood friend who was in the Navy.

"What did he say?"

"He's been injured." Tom didn't elaborate.

"How serious is it?"

"He's been in the hospital for weeks. He was burned."

Cici began to understand the look on Tom's face. She put her hand on his.

"I'm so sorry, Tom."

"His face is burned. Can you imagine?"

Cici shook her head. Tom looked close to crying. "Poor Bobby," he said. "He'll never look normal again."

"We don't have to go inside. Do you want to go home?"

Tom stared at the ground and said nothing. Cici watched him, unsure of what to do next. She usually knew just what to say to a man, but then again men were usually happy around her. After a long silence, Tom seemed to become energized and grabbed Cici's hands. He looked her in the eye and began speaking quickly, as though in a rush to get his thoughts out. "Let's get married, Cici! I'm sorry—I know this isn't how I should propose. I promise when the war is over I'll get you a proper ring and a white dress, too, if you want. But let's get married now, right now. I don't want to wait any longer. Will you say yes? Will you marry me?"

Cici was shocked. She had never known Tom to be impulsive. She was about to get everything she wanted, and the feeling was almost too much for her to bear. "Of course I want to marry you. But we can't even live together."

"I know, I know. But listen, if anything happens to me—"

"What would happen to you? You're perfectly safe here."

"If I get sent to Japan. When we invade."

"You think that will happen?"

"I don't know."

Cici thought of the letter from Mrs. Wolcott and squeezed Tom's hands. "I'll marry you, Tom. But you should tell your family first. I don't want to go behind their back or get off on the wrong foot."

Tom's shoulders dropped as though relieved. "You're right. Of course. I'll write to your aunt as well to ask her permission."

Cici dreaded forging a reply to Tom from her mythical aunt, but at least she had Mrs. Wolcott's letter to guide her now. "That would mean a lot to dear Aunt Faye."

"I love you, Cici."

He kissed her fiercely, and the pressure of his mouth on hers made Cici feel like she couldn't breathe. When he finally pulled away, she put a hand to his cheek. "I love you, too."

It was the first time in her life she had said those words. Her family had never been given to emotional declarations, and they felt ill suited to her mouth.

Tom gave her a squeeze. "Cici Wolcott. How does that sound?"

"It sounds wonderful."

They went to the canteen and the roller rink, Tom telling everyone they saw along the way that they were engaged. His mood had completely transformed. Bobby was forgotten, and he wanted to celebrate. Finally she had to send him off to bed, but not before a long session of necking on the boardwalk, more than she'd ever let him get away with before.

She went straight to bed when she got to the dorm. They'd stayed out too late, and she was exhausted. Still, she found she was unable to sleep. She had done it. He would marry her tomorrow if she said the word. It was everything she wanted. Her future was secure—there would be no hunger, no hand-me-down dresses, no tobacco harvesting, no Baptist preachers.

Yet she didn't feel quite happy. Success was unsettling. She had expected something more, something deep and satisfying. Instead, she felt empty. For so long, she had devoted all her energy to achieving this goal, and she hadn't the faintest idea how she would occupy herself now.

* * *

IT WAS SAM'S idea that they go on a real trip together. They could get only one day off from work, so they couldn't go far. But he'd heard colleagues talk about going to Gatlinburg for the weekend, a little town at the edge of the new Great Smoky Mountains National Park. Ann and Charlie had gone themselves a couple of months earlier and recommended a hotel. Sam made all the arrangements and told June all she had to do was meet him at the bus depot Friday morning with a suitcase.

He'd put it in romantic terms, saying it would be a chance for them to have some time to themselves, not at Y-12 but in a lovely mountain chalet next to a burbling brook. Still, June knew there was more to Sam's urgency than he was letting on and suspected his main motivation was to get her into bed. He was always coming up with strategies for getting her over to the house when Charlie and Ann were out. The night before the trip, however, her monthly period came.

She didn't know how to tell Sam. It was all she could think about that morning, waiting at the depot, her abdomen knotted in pain. It was a hot, hazy day already at eight o'clock, and she wanted to find a seat on the bus, hopefully by a window.

"Hello, gorgeous," said Sam, putting an arm around her.

"Ready for our adventure?" she asked, and he nodded.

At least he seemed happy. Lawrence's visit had cheered him briefly, but as soon as the physicist left town, Sam's mood had turned sour. It was obvious he didn't like his new job. He was irritable and short-tempered, snapping at June over the smallest things. He was also drinking more, and she was no longer able to distract him from his whiskey.

They had to take one bus to Knoxville, and then transfer to another that would take them the eighty miles to Gatlinburg. June leaned on Sam's shoulder when they sat down.

"You all right?" he asked.

"Mmm-hmm. Just sleepy." The perfect opening for her to tell him, but she couldn't.

They had time to kill in Knoxville, and Sam suggested a big breakfast at the bus stop diner. June ordered scrambled eggs and toast.

"Come on, is that all you want? It's my treat. Sausage? Pancakes?" He was in such a jaunty holiday mood that she hated to disappoint him.

"I'm just not that hungry." She smiled weakly.

The bus to Gatlinburg was only about half full, and they sat in the back, away from the other passengers. He put his arm around her and whispered in her ear, "Do you know what I'm going to do first thing when we get to the hotel?"

She didn't want to hear about it. "Why don't you wait and tell me about it when we get there?"

He leaned back into the seat to doze. She looked out the

window as they crossed the Tennessee River. Two men were fishing off the side of a boat. It would be nice to be down there, able to jump right in the river for a swim, about the only way a person could cool down these days. Soon the buildings of the city gave way to farmland, and then a mountain rose up in the distance. The bus stopped in Sevierville, where the driver pointed out the historic courthouse with a tall clock tower in the middle of town. The majestic Mount Le Conte loomed in the distance, its muted blue standing out against the hazy summer sky.

Gatlinburg was hardly more than a village, populated with a few new inns and restaurants meant to cater to national park visitors. The park had been completed less than a decade earlier, and parts of it came over into Blount County, not that far from where June grew up. It had been another government project that forced people out of their homes. But June liked the idea of it better than that of a dam or bomb-building factory. The land had to be kept exactly as it was to be a gift to future generations. It was a comfort to know there were still places that no one could touch.

Their hotel overlooked the Little Pigeon River, and though the room was furnished simply, it did have a balcony with two rocking chairs, where you could sit and watch the water burble by. Sam seemed satisfied by it, and as soon as they had a look around, he tossed June on the bed. She had to speak now. "Honey . . ."

His eyes were closed, and he was kissing her neck, working his hands up her thigh. He paid no attention to her voice. "Honey, I have to tell you something."

His hands were on her breasts, his mouth approaching her lips. "Sam!"

She had his attention, and he opened his eyes.

She swallowed. "I have bad news."

"What?"

"My monthly period started last night."

He sat up straight. "Oh. Do you not feel . . . up to it?"

"Um, I don't know. Does it bother you?"

"Not if it doesn't bother you." He began kissing her neck again.

But the further his lovemaking progressed, the more she realized it did bother her.

When his hand tried to make its way between her legs, her muscles clenched almost involuntarily. She felt awkward and dirty. "I don't want to ruin the sheets," she said.

"I'll get a towel." He went into the bathroom and returned with one, a pristine white.

"It'll ruin the towel."

He tossed it on the bed. "What if we do it in the bath?"

"In the bath?" June wasn't sure exactly how that would work.

"Sure, it'll be fun."

Her flesh pressed into hard porcelain, horribly self-conscious about the blood, June was sure that their romantic weekend was off to an inauspicious start.

They ate lunch at a nearby diner, both too embarrassed to make much conversation. June wondered if he was disgusted by her. As they finished their sandwiches, the afternoon loomed in front of them like a threat. June suggested they walk to the national park.

They walked in silence through the town, both lost in thought. June wondered what was going through his mind. She wanted the weekend to be good, wanted to think of some way to salvage it. She picked black-eyed Susans from along the side of the road as they walked, making a bouquet.

"We should look for a nicer place to get supper tonight," she said. Sam nodded.

There was a small visitor's center at the entrance to the park, and they browsed separately. June was relieved to have a few moments to herself, away from the oppressive silence that had dogged them ever since they left the hotel. It was already getting to be late afternoon, and when they got back to the hotel, she suggested a nap. They lay next to each other on the bed, fully clothed, but June wasn't able to sleep. She knew this wasn't what Sam had planned and wished she could will her body to cooperate.

She got up off the bed, deciding to take a bath instead. She ran cool water into the tub and dropped her hot body into it, savoring the chill it brought to her skin. When she got out, she put on her favorite summer dress, a delicate pink with a full skirt and little sleeves that just skimmed her shoulders. She filled a coffee cup with water and put the black-eyed Susans in it on the dresser.

"How do you like Gatlinburg?" she asked that night over their respective chicken and pork chop. She was determined to sustain a conversation.

"Not much of a town, but the mountains are beautiful."

"I've never been here before. Funny, 'cause I grew up so close. I'm glad they built the national park."

"It looks lovely. It'd be nice to see more of it."

The discussion continued along those lines. It was as if they had run out of things to say to each other. When they were done, they trudged back to the hotel room and Sam took a bottle of splo from his suitcase and went out to the balcony.

She was fairly certain he'd already been into it before supper as well. She didn't like it. It hurt her that he needed to drink that awful stuff, even on their romantic weekend. Why was she no longer enough to make him happy? She wanted to say something but knew if she did it would probably cause trouble. Idly she picked up one of the flowers from her bouquet and began ripping off the petals. *He loves me, he loves me not.* She felt she knew the answer without having to rely on a flower to tell her so.

For a moment she watched him. He was standing by the rail, looking down at the small river. She went out and stood beside him. He offered her the bottle, but she shook her head. The dark outline of the mountains was illuminated by an almost-full moon.

"You shouldn't drink so much, Sam."

"Why not? Because it's sinful?" He was laughing at her.

"No. Because it makes you unhappy."

"I'd be unhappy without the liquor. Drinking just makes the unhappiness easier to take."

"Is your life really as bad as all that?" she said, accusing.

"Don't worry. It's not your fault, June."

She didn't know what to say to him and tried to think of a way to change the subject, soften the mood. "Daddy always says you can see God in the mountains."

Immediately she regretted saying this, knowing Sam would think that sort of thing was silly. He didn't laugh but replied, "They're big and beautiful, but I don't see God in them."

"Well, it's an idea, you know. You're not really supposed to see him, I suppose."

"I get it." It was hard to get a good look at his face in the darkness, but his voice sounded mean.

"I think because the mountains are beautiful, you're supposed to see God in them."

"I get it. But I don't see God."

"Don't you have the same god?" she asked, hoping he didn't find the question stupid.

He took a big gulp of the splo. "Do you mean do Jews have the same god as you Christians do?"

"Yes, I guess."

"I guess as a Christian you'd see it that way."

"I'm sorry, I didn't mean any offense."

"None taken. But if you want to discuss theology, you've got the wrong man."

"What do you mean?"

"I don't believe any of it. I'm only a Jew because my parents were Jews. I don't have a god."

"You mean you don't believe?"

"Believe in what?"

"God."

He took another drink and looked away. "What God? What God do you think there is in this world? My whole family in Europe is dead!"

He turned to her, his voice rising, and she took a step back. "Dead! Aunts, uncles, cousins, dozens of human beings. All over Europe, a generation disappeared. Do you know how many dead? How many in Russia? Or China?"

She was shaking her head, but he paid no attention. "Not just dead," he ranted, "tortured and raped as well. Do you know how many we've killed with our bombs in Dresden and Tokyo? And how many thousands more will die when this bomb that we, you and I, work on every day is finished? It will kill indiscriminately—babies, mothers, the elderly, whatever is in its path. What God is there in this world? Where do you see God?"

Sam had never spoken to her like this. He seemed off-kilter, capable of anything—cruelty, violence even. "Why are you shouting at me? I didn't mean to make you angry."

"Just shut up then! Stop rambling on about God like a country hick!"

"Why would you call me that?"

"I don't know, June! Because I'm not nice! I told you the first time we met, but you didn't listen."

"Why are you acting this way?"

"Christ, I just told you! I am a bad man. I'm not nice!"

Tears were streaming down her cheeks.

"I'm going out," he said, grabbing his hat and taking the bottle with him out the door. She stumbled back into the room, to the bed, and lay there in her dress, crying until she fell asleep.

Sam didn't come in until around four o'clock, and he passed out in the bed almost immediately, snoring drunkenly. He was still deeply asleep when June awoke the next morning. She went out to the balcony and closed the door behind her.

She watched the clear water form white lines as it passed over rocks. If she stared at it long enough, it looked still, even though it was rushing past. *I should leave him,* she thought. This wasn't right. She shouldn't be in a hotel with a man she wasn't married to. Especially a man who drank like that. He shouldn't drink like that. He shouldn't speak to her that way. But she couldn't imagine her life without him. If only she could help him. Not that long ago, she thought she had. He'd stopped drinking during their first months together. During the winter and spring, they had done everything together, in sync, happy together. He'd often told her that she made his life better, but he never said that anymore. She didn't know what had changed or what she could do to get back to those times.

She'd been sitting like that for a long time when Sam opened the door and walked out beside her.

"June . . ." His voice was soft and faltering, so different from last night. "Don't be sad, June."

She didn't know what to say, so she just kept looking down at the water.

"I'm sorry about last night. I've just been so frustrated lately. I shouldn't have taken it out on you."

She turned. He looked awful, still in his clothes from yesterday, his hair sticking out in all directions and dark shadows under his eyes. "You shouldn't drink like that," she said.

"I know. I'm sorry."

His eyes pleaded with her. She knew he was sorry. She had thought his behavior was unforgivable, but after one minute of his apology, she relented. He looked so lost and sad, and she wanted more than anything to be in his arms, to be comforted and to comfort him in turn.

"Why don't you take a bath?" she asked. "We can get some breakfast and go for a walk in the mountains."

"Okay."

She smiled faintly, a gesture to reassure him.

"I love you, June."

"I love you, too." Her voice was hushed, almost a whisper. He turned to go back inside to the bathroom. It was the first time she'd said it aloud.

As the day progressed, they began to relax around each

other. Soon they were laughing again like normal, holding hands as they walked. The despair from the night before was melting away. They walked to a waterfall and stood, still and silenced by the roar of tumbling water. Everything around them was green and damp, the air so thick with moisture that June felt as though she couldn't quite catch her breath.

"Should we go in?" Sam shouted over the blare.

She looked quizzical, but he had already bent down to take off his shoes and roll up his pant legs. She followed his lead, kicking off her sandals and slipping her feet into the icy river. The intensity of the cold made her squeal out loud. Sam gently kicked water onto her shins, and she laughed, all the tension of the past twenty-four hours evaporating as she playfully splashed him back. He grabbed ahold of her tightly around the waist, and they kissed. She gave herself over to the moment fully, the feel of his lips, the sound of the falls, the cold of the water, the heat of the air.

But on the bus ride back to Oak Ridge, Sam dozing beside her, June couldn't shake the feeling that something had been broken in Gatlinburg and would never be the same. All couples fight, she knew, but they hadn't really fought. It was more like Sam had exploded, and this unpredictable side of him frightened her. Even if it didn't reappear, she knew now that it was there inside him, waiting.

It was late afternoon when June returned to the dorm. She carried her suitcase up the stairs to her room, the effort dampening her with perspiration. The room was stifling, oppressive. Cici sat on her bed, painting her fingernails, and the sharp smell of nail polish hung in the still air. She looked up at June, waving her hand in the air to dry. "Where've you been?"

The fact that June hadn't even told Cici she was going away just went to show how far their relationship had deteriorated. They hardly ever went out together anymore, each spending most of her time with her respective boyfriend.

"Sam took me away for the weekend to Gatlinburg."

"Oh, I suppose you can take time off whenever you want now that he got you that fancy job."

June couldn't stand the whininess of her tone. She felt altogether too hot and irritated for Cici this afternoon. "It was just one day off. You can get that, too."

Cici blew on her fingers now, making far more elaborate gestures than seemed necessary. "Tom isn't so desperate to get me into a hotel room as all that."

"Cici!" June felt something snap. "You have no right to talk to me that way!"

Cici walked over to her vanity and dropped the nail polish into her toiletry bag. She turned to face June. "I'm just being honest. I thought we were friends and could be honest with each other."

"If you were really my friend, then you'd treat me with some respect."

Cici's mouth tightened. "I'll give you the respect you deserve."

June was yelling now. "You just can't stand that there's a man in the world who prefers me to you!"

Cici let out a short, loud breath. "I'd rather die than be touched by that dirty Jew!"

June was driven by pure emotion, her mind floating somewhere above her rage-filled body. She'd never slapped anyone, hardly knew how to slap someone, but found her hand hitting Cici hard across the face.

They were both stunned. Cici's mouth opened, and she stared at June, motionless. She picked up her pocketbook and turned to the door. She opened it wide and slammed it hard behind her. June slumped over to her bed and lay back, staring up at the ceiling. Her eyes welled with tears. She wished Cici would never come back. She had no idea at all how they had ever been friends.

(Courtesy of the Department of Energy)

Chapter 18

THE HOUSE WAS EMPTY WHEN SAM GOT IN THAT AFTERNOON, AND he was relieved, eager for some time to himself. He was sweating through his shirt and tossed his hat and jacket on the back of the sofa, then collapsed onto it himself, lying stretched out across its length. He watched the ceiling fan spinning above him and willed it to send down cool breezes. The weekend had left him exhausted. He'd behaved horribly. He'd been in a foul mood for weeks now and had hoped the trip would help shake it, but it had seemed only to make it worse. God, it had been awful. He'd gotten truly drunk but still remembered the fear in June's face as he had yelled, and the sadness the next morning, the terrible way she'd looked at him, like a small, hurt child. No matter what happened between them now, he would not be able to forget making her look at him that way. He wished he could take it all back, start back at the beginning on that bus headed to the mountains. Be a gentleman. Show June a good time. She deserved it. She tried so hard all the time—to do a good job at work, to make him happy. She deserved better. He'd tried to make it up to her. After the awful night, her sadness, the look, all he'd felt like doing was getting drunk and staying drunk, but he'd followed her through the forest and the ridiculous backwoods town and hadn't had a sip of liquor for the rest of the weekend.

Which made him think, now was the perfect time for a drink. He found a bottle hidden under his bed, happily still half full. He stumbled back to the sofa with it and searched his pockets for cigarettes. Once the smoke was lit and his mouth gently tingled with the sour alcohol, he felt a sense of calm wash over him. It was almost happiness.

But he couldn't forget that look. And the thought nagged at him: *She deserves better.*

The door opened. He tossed the bottle into his suitcase and sat up. With relief, he saw that it was only Charlie, alone.

"Hello there. You just get back?"

"Yeah. Sorry for the mess." Sam motioned with the cigarette at his suitcase and jacket.

"Oh, don't worry about it."

"It's too damn hot to move."

"Tell me about it." Charlie slumped in the chair across from him, looking uncharacteristically dispirited. "If you just got back, then you probably haven't heard."

"Heard what?"

Charlie was lighting his own cigarette and inhaled deeply before answering. "It's done." Charlie spoke softly, almost in a whisper, though they were all alone in the house. "They tested it this morning in New Mexico."

Sam felt his stomach contract. "What happened?"

"It worked. Beautifully."

Sam nodded slowly. It had been only a matter of time until the wretched thing was ready. Still, after all this time, working and waiting for this moment, he found it hard to believe it had really happened. "What have we done, Charlie?"

Charlie shook his head. "Created a monster, I suppose. You don't happen to have any of that bootleg whiskey on you, do you?"

Sam pulled the bottle out of the bag and passed it to Charlie. He drank from it directly, wincing as the fiery liquid hit his mouth. Sam took a gulp after him. Charlie motioned for more. Before he drank, he held the bottle up, as though to make a toast. "To the Age of Fission. The Atomic Era."

Sam had never heard his upbeat friend speak with such irony. It was almost more frightening than the news. He went to Max to commiserate, but depended on Charlie to put a positive spin on things.

They drank for a while, and when Ann got home, Sam went out to the canteen. Max wasn't there, so he drank by himself. If he'd been in a bad mood before, the news had sunk him into something deeper than words. It was always going to come to this, of course. He must have known. Some possible scenarios would have absolved him of guilt—they couldn't get the bomb to work, the war ended before it was used (which was of course still possible, though hardly likely)—but he had never really believed they would come to pass. Still, his pessimism hadn't prepared him for this feeling. It was just a matter of time until they could get another bomb together, decide on a target, and so forth. Nothing to do but wait for it. Wait and wonder how this had ever seemed a sensible thing to do—to any of them. Not to the Army, of course—building weapons was their bread and butter—but to the scientists, him and his colleagues. They had known exactly what they were doing and had all gone ahead together, telling themselves they had to beat the Germans to it, had to end the war.

He forgot to eat supper. By the time he stumbled home, he was completely drunk and had almost reached the state of oblivion he desired. Not quite, though—as his head hit his pillow, so came the evil, drunken dreams of fire, smoke, and blinding light.

The next day was worse, of course, because he had a hangover to deal with on top of his black mood. He kept the door to his office closed, telling June he had a lot to catch up on, unable to face her and sure if they spent too much time together, she would notice the telltale signs of his condition. He sent her off to the movies by herself after work, complaining he had a headache, which was true enough. On the hot, dusty bus, his head began to pound. He must get to his bed as soon as possible. Maybe a nap would set him right or at least prevent him from being sick.

He was opening the door to his bedroom when Charlie called out to him. His friend appeared completely recovered from the previous day's depression. He was talking in his usual fast, smooth way. It took Sam a moment to focus enough to understand his words. He was saying something about a petition.

"Szilard started it in Los Alamos, and now we've started one here as well. There's a meeting tonight at Kellerman's house, eight o'clock. You'll come, won't you?"

Sam rubbed his forehead with his thumb and index finger. "Yeah, I'll come. But do you really think this is going to do any good?"

"It's worded carefully and doesn't demand too much. We just ask that we give the Japanese a warning—explode one of the things at sea or on some unpopulated island to show them its power and give them a chance to surrender before we use it on a city."

"And who will the petition go to?"

"All the way to the top. President Truman. You know, Szilard started this all. He was the first one to try to get the government involved in fission. Maybe he can finish it, too." Leo Szilard was the eccentric Hungarian physicist who had championed the cause of the bomb program back in 1940, even enlisting Einstein to write a letter to President Roosevelt explaining the implications if Germany was developing a bomb. Now he was crusading against the bomb, but Sam couldn't quite blame him for his change of heart, when he was guilty of the same.

"Would have saved a lot of time and money if he and Einstein had never gotten the government involved in the first place."

"We have a chance to end the war without costing any more lives."

Sam didn't really believe it could work. The Army and the president would have to go for the plan, and the Japanese would have to actually surrender for it to work. But of course he would go to the meeting. It was the best they could do to make themselves feel better.

"Can you get hold of Max?" asked Charlie. "He'll sign, won't he?"

"Yeah. I should be able to find him. He'll be sympathetic." Max had expressed his doubts about using the bomb the first time Sam had ever met him.

"Good. Then I'll see you at eight. I'm going out to make a few house calls, make sure everyone's got word."

It was no cooler outside when Sam left the house an hour and a half later, the humidity capturing the sun's heat and holding it in the air, even as it began its descent toward the horizon. Sam felt a bit better. His headache was gone, and he felt flickers of hunger. If Max wasn't at the canteen, he'd head over to the cafeteria for some supper before the meeting at Kellerman's.

But Max was in their usual spot, nursing a beer. Sam waved, and Max raised his glass in salutation. "Hello, old friend. Haven't seen you around in ages."

"I was here last night."

Max lowered his voice, though they were in the corner, far away from other patrons. "So you must have heard the news?"

Sam nodded.

"Let me get you a beer," Max said, and before Sam could refuse his offer, he was at the bar, ordering. Might be just the thing, anyway, hair of the dog.

"So we've accomplished what we set out to do." Sam couldn't classify Max's tone, if he was meaning to be sarcastic or sad. His inflection was even, matter-of-fact.

"Max, there's a petition going around. Have you heard about it?"

"Yes."

"Then you'll come with me to this meeting at Dr. Kellerman's house tonight."

"Afraid not. I have a date."

"Have you signed it already?"

"No."

"Then you must come. We don't have much time."

Max took a gulp of beer and looked Sam in the eye. "I'm not going to sign it."

"I don't understand."

"If I were the president, I'd use the bloody thing."

Sam felt bewildered and betrayed. "You must be joking. I thought we were of the same mind. You always talked about what a nasty business this is."

"War is a nasty business. Personally I don't enjoy it and worry about men who do. But surely you agree that in this case it has been unavoidable."

"The war was unavoidable. Using this weapon is not."

It was madness to be speaking so openly in public, but Sam was hardly thinking straight. Max was calmer. "Why don't we step outside?"

Sam followed him, still reeling from his friend's position. "Now, Max, I know there's not much chance of this thing doing any good, but we have to give it a shot."

"We certainly do not. I've given five years of my life to this project. Why in the world would I try to sabotage it at this stage?"

"But you've misled me about your beliefs."

"No, I've never lied. It is one thing to have misgivings, another to give up on the thing completely. Either one of us could have quit at any time. Why did you work so hard on something you've now decided shouldn't be used for its intended purpose?"

They were behind the canteen, and no one was around. The building backed onto a small patch of woods, which had somehow survived the cycles of construction, and the setting sun cast shadows through the branches, stretching over to where they stood. Sam was too tired for eloquence and too surprised by this argument to make his point effectively. But he was also too riled up to let it go.

"When you started you must surely have thought that the Germans were doing the same thing."

"What difference does it make? Would it be more just to have used it on the Germans if they were building their own bomb? They committed atrocities enough as it is, no? Would you have minded so much using it on Hitler?"

"We would have been killing innocent Germans, just as we'll kill innocent Japanese. My own family could have been killed by our bomb."

"Forgive me, Sam, but we both know the chances of your family in Germany still being alive."

"Christ, Max!"

"What about your immediate family? When the Japanese surrender, your brother can come home. This thing could save his life."

"But how many innocent people will have to die?"

"Innocent people have died by the legion in this war. Let's end it, for God's sake."

Sam couldn't think of a reply. He stared down at the dusty ground, not wanting to look Max in the eye.

"Look, mate, scientists were never meant to be bomb makers. Most don't take to it well."

Sam had to struggle not to yell. "I took to it too well, that's the problem! I enjoyed it too much!"

"You enjoyed the physics. That doesn't make you a monster. Go easy on yourself and all of us. You didn't enjoy the idea of killing. None of us do."

Max gave him a pat on the back, which made Sam feel ridiculous. "Let's forget it and finish our beers."

So the subject was dropped, and they went back inside, each aware that their friendship, based on the false presumption of a shared viewpoint, would never be the same.

(Courtesy of the Department of Energy)

Chapter 19

JOE COULDN'T SLEEP AND HAD GONE OUT TO THE FRONT OF THE hutment to smoke. The August air was still and hot, though it was past midnight. He had a bad feeling. It had been two whole days since he'd seen Ralph, which was unusual. They usually met up in the afternoon, when Ralph was getting off his shift and Joe was headed to his. Joe would drink coffee, and Ralph would eat his supper. Sometimes they hardly even spoke, each tired from hard work and good enough friends that the silence didn't worry them.

The first day Ralph didn't show up, Joe hadn't worried too much. He reckoned he had taken the day off or was working overtime. But the next day bothered him. It didn't feel right and wasn't like Ralph not to be in touch. He wasn't the type to make Joe and Moriah worry, and there were simply too many ways Ralph could get himself in trouble. He might have been fired. If you lost your job here, it meant you also lost your housing, so a man would have to pack up and leave immediately. Still, wouldn't he have written to let them know

what had happened? That brought Joe to a worse possibility—he had gotten in a fight and been hurt. Ralph wouldn't
have provoked it, but he also wouldn't back down if threatened. Of course, there were simpler explanations. Maybe he
was sick, maybe he was just being rude and careless. He
couldn't quite get himself to believe that, though; the bad
feeling had lodged in his stomach and stayed there.

The last time they talked, Ralph had mentioned that the
few remaining construction workers might strike. Joe had
told him to give up such foolish notions. They'd been in the
cafeteria, Ralph shoveling mashed potatoes into his mouth.

"If we get the white workers together with the colored
workers, they'll have to pay attention."

"There's a war on. Folks got better things to worry themselves about. You lucky to have these here jobs. Don't you know
nine out of ten of the construction workers been laid off?"

Ralph put down his fork and shook his head slowly. If Joe
hadn't known him better, he would have thought the boy was
angry with him. Ralph looked him in the eye. "We got to stop
acting like we lucky when we're being treated like animals.
Men deserve more than jobs. They deserve decent places to
live. We're doing our part for this country, and what's this
country doing for us?"

Joe gulped at his coffee, even though it was burnt and
bitter. It was no use talking to Ralph. The boy looked off
past him, and Joe turned to follow his stare. Shirley had just
walked into the cafeteria.

Ralph waved her over.

"Hi there, Joe," she said, sitting beside Ralph.

"How you doing, sugar?" Ralph asked her.

"I'm all right. You coming with me tonight?"

"Can't tonight," said Ralph. "But I'll be there Friday."

"What's on Friday?" asked Joe. He knew it must be some kind of trouble she'd gotten him into.

"Union meeting," said Ralph, his voice preemptively defying whatever Joe might have to say about that.

"That a white man's union. You ain't got no business there."

Shirley spoke, "No one's said Negroes aren't allowed."

"They ain't got to say it."

"I know some of the organizers," said Ralph. "They're expecting me."

"You don't belong on that side of town, boy."

Ralph straightened up, and Joe felt bad for calling him a boy in front of his woman. "Just be careful," he said, a kinder but no less urgent command.

But the boy never listened. He was good but wild, always doing what he thought was right—which was dangerous. Truth was, Joe had never known a man like that before. No one back at the Hopewell farm had been that full of guts—or foolishness, depending on how you looked at it. Most men carried anger and hatred around with them, but it took a man like Ralph to do something about it, and most men weren't like Ralph.

He knew the boy pitied him. He hadn't always, but lately, since he'd gotten involved with Shirley and the other hotheads, the boy had started looking at Joe differently. Ralph hadn't said anything, but Joe saw it in his eyes. He looked at Joe like the old man he was becoming. He thought Joe was afraid, and that was true enough. Joe knew the boy loved him, but Ralph had moved past him in some important way. He was going somewhere Joe couldn't follow, and the older man feared that the boy was already gone, out of his reach.

Joe swatted at an invisible buzzing by his head. Didn't know why he even bothered trying to kill the beasts; he'd wind up bitten no matter what.

"Joe?" Moriah was behind him in the doorway, eyes droopy with sleep, her hair in rollers.

"Sorry, honey. Couldn't sleep."

She closed the door and sat down by him. "You all right?"

He slapped at the mosquito on his leg. "I think Ralph may have got himself in real trouble this time."

Her face softened. "I swear you worry 'bout that boy like he your own son." She placed her palm on the back of his hand.

"You happy, Moriah?"

"Got you here beside me. My babies is safe. Sure I's happy."

He put his big rough hand on her smooth cheek. "Let's go back to bed."

She started to get up, but he reached his arm around her before she could, leaned over, and kissed her firmly on the mouth.

He was calmer in the morning. Ralph was a grown man, after all. He had to stop thinking of him as the frightened boy with the broken arm. Still, he headed to the cafeteria before taking the bus to work, hoping he might run into Ralph. Instead, Shirley was waiting for him at the door to the dining hall. She looked lovely as always, somehow unaffected by the intense heat. He nodded when he saw her.

"Can I speak to you for a minute?" she asked. Her voice was less assured than usual, nervous even. All his worries came rushing back.

"You want to go inside?"

"No, I'm not hungry. I was hoping to find you here and have a word."

"Of course," he said. She led him away from the cafeteria, walking slowly, aimlessly.

Finally she spoke. "I'm worried about Ralph."

"When the last time you saw him?"

"Friday evening, at the union meeting."

"What happened there?"

"Nothing. I mean, I don't know really. There were some white men at the meeting who didn't look too kindly on Negroes joining in."

Joe said nothing. There was no pleasure in saying *I told you so.*

"I know you don't approve of us."

"I just worry, is all."

"I know. I know you care about Ralph, and he looks up to you."

"You leave the meeting together?"

"Yes. But those men—there were three of them in particular. They followed us onto the bus. They were making crude comments, laughing, jeering, that sort of thing. I didn't think it was serious . . . but now I don't know. We got off in the colored village, and they were still on the bus, so I thought it was over. Ralph walked me as far as he could, then headed back to his hutment. And I haven't seen him since." Her eyes were shining with the barest hint of tears.

"I'll find him, Shirley."

"There's another union meeting tonight. Can you go? Ask around? Maybe someone knows something."

"Of course."

They had wandered a ways from the cafeteria, and he didn't have time to get coffee now. He would have to get straight on the bus to work, and he better get there on time so he could leave quickly come evening to get to the meeting before it was over.

He'd have hell to pay from Moriah if he missed supper, but he didn't see any way around it. He might just leave Shirley out of his explanation, though. Moriah really couldn't stand the girl. She thought Shirley looked down on them as ignorant country folk. Joe knew this wasn't true, but he knew better than to defend the girl to Moriah. That was one battle he didn't need to fight.

* * *

JUNE SAT BY herself in a corner of the canteen, fanning her face with the *Knoxville Journal*. She'd already read the paper—about the Potsdam Conference, how the Allies were to punish and govern Germany now, and the Army was preparing to invade Japan. It was nothing new and more useful as a fan than reading material.

Sam was supposed to have been here twenty minutes ago; by now all the ice in her Coke had melted, and her legs were stuck to her seat with sweat. She hated waiting around, and the heat was making her especially irritable. Perhaps he had forgotten they were meeting, though they had arranged it only three hours earlier when June left work. He was awfully preoccupied these days, and she didn't know what to say to him half the time. He made himself miserable, worrying about his work, the war, the bomb. To make matters worse, two days ago he'd gotten a telegraph from his sister in New

York saying that his mother had collapsed at home and was now in the hospital. He was drinking more and more—kept a stash in the office now, and got flat-out drunk most nights. Sometimes she chided him over it, but she hated to sound like a nag or a broken record and usually kept her mouth shut. Some days he would bury his head in her arms and beg her forgiveness. Then she would tell him he was a good man, assure him that she wasn't angry, that she would help him give up the drink.

He *was* a good man, she thought, but she could never quite convince him of it. He was so hard on himself, so angry with himself, it was impossible to get him to relax the way he used to when they were first going out. It must be a phase, and surely, he would return to normal soon, like he was in those early, happy days. She just had to keep loving him and helping him.

She blew bubbles in her Coke out of boredom, like a child. It was nearly dark out, but the air didn't cool. How long should she give him before she gave up and went back to the dorm for another night of sweaty, stifling sleep? She would be lucky if she could get to sleep before Cici got home. Cici was on the day shift this week, making them all the more likely to run into each other. They hadn't spoken since the night June slapped her. June hadn't told anyone what had happened. Sam would have been livid and embarrassed, she suspected, though he wouldn't have admitted it.

No, the thought of going home was unbearable. She could go see a movie by herself—why not? She would wait an hour, though, give him a chance to show up. If only she had a magazine or something to read.

He walked in ten minutes later, casually, in no apparent

hurry. He kissed her on the cheek and sat beside her. "Awfully hot in here."

"You're late."

"Sorry about that. Got stuck talking to Charlie and lost track of the time."

She didn't believe him. She could smell the whiskey on his breath and suspected he'd been drinking—perhaps with Charlie but more likely by himself. "You want to stay here or go out? We could go to a movie."

"Maybe in a bit. Let me get a beer first. You want another Coke?"

She pushed away the flat beverage and shook her head. He went up to the counter, and she glared at his back. They would miss the movie if he stayed in this hot room drinking that disgusting beer. He had already gulped down half of it when he returned.

Perhaps she was still glaring without realizing it. "What's gotten into you?" he asked.

"What do you mean?"

"You seem quiet."

"I'm just hot."

He gulped down the rest of the beer. "Should we get some air?"

She nodded and followed him outside. But the humid air wasn't refreshing. Breathing it felt like being underwater.

"God, I hate the summers here," he said and stumbled slightly as he stepped up onto the boardwalk. He was drunker than she'd realized. "You still want to go to the movies?" he asked.

"I don't know."

"Well, do you or don't you?"

"Do you?"

"Not really. What's the point? It's always the same old beautiful people with the same old ridiculous problems."

"What do you want to do?"

"Nothing. I don't know. Let's just walk."

So they did, wandering aimlessly through the Townsite. For a moment they were silent. Then Sam spoke again, "You know what I hate?"

"What?"

"When you know something awful is about to happen, but it's too late to stop it. You know what I mean? Like watching a train wreck in a film. You can see the disaster coming, but the thing's built up so much momentum. There's nothing you can do."

June was glad it was dark now, because hot tears were filling her eyes. She knew exactly what he meant, but she hadn't expected to hear him say it aloud. Of course she sensed how doomed their relationship was. But she hadn't thought there was nothing they could do to fix it. "Is that how you really feel?"

"Right now, yes! I'm sick, June. I can't sleep at night. The whole thing, this whole goddamned place makes me sick."

"What do you mean?"

He motioned to the town buildings around them, indicating with his gesture that they were in public and he couldn't speak freely. "The war. All the death that is yet to come."

She had misunderstood; he wasn't talking about their relationship, but worrying about the bomb. Though she should have felt relieved, it only irritated her. Here she was worried about their relationship. Why wasn't he? He didn't notice, didn't care that she was angry and unhappy. "What are you upset about?" she heard herself saying, in a voice harsher than she had intended.

"The tragedy of it all, for God's sake!"

"Oh, please! What do you know about tragedy? You haven't killed anyone! You have both your legs! You're alive!"

She was yelling now and had stopped walking. She had never spoken to him this way before. He stopped to face her, his face slackened with shock.

"What do you mean? Just because I'm not in the Army, I'm not supposed to care about what's going on?"

"No, of course not. But you're not supposed to care this much. You're not supposed to let it ruin your life—when you're lucky enough to have a life!"

He was still staring. Then his face shifted upward into an angry grin. "You don't know the things I do. You have no idea."

His smile enraged her. He wasn't listening, wasn't taking her seriously.

"Yes, I do! You've told me all your secrets. You know, I just realized how stupid you think I am, like those birds you can teach to talk, but you don't think I *understand* anything. Well, I do understand! I understand just as well as you do what this bomb means!"

His smile collapsed and his eyes widened as the same thought went through both their minds. Despite the heat, she felt her face go cold as she looked around to see if anyone had heard her. A couple of shadowy figures stood by the cafeteria, about ten yards away. Could they have heard?

Sam spoke in a low, controlled voice, sobered by her outburst. "June, get ahold of yourself."

He put a hand on her shoulder, but she shrugged it off. "I have to go," she said, turning from him.

"June, wait!" he called after her, but she didn't turn. The need to get away from him was urgent. She walked quickly along the boardwalk, though she had no destination in mind. All she knew was that she wanted to put space between herself and Sam, that it would be impossible to think straight until she was away from him, by herself.

* * *

CICI WATCHED JUNE go from behind the wall. Cici had been walking home from the cafeteria when she saw them. At first she crossed the block so she wouldn't run into them. They hadn't noticed her; they were talking loudly—arguing, it occurred to Cici, as she passed with her head down.

"What are you upset about?" June was saying in a strident voice, the same awful shriek she had used on Cici before slapping her last month.

Cici had spoken to some other girls she worked with about moving into their house; hopefully it would all be arranged next week. But in the meantime it seemed useful to be aware of any fighting between her terrible roommate and Dr. Cantor. Maybe she should have kept walking along the boardwalk to the dorm, but she turned and followed a few paces behind them.

Dr. Cantor was saying something about tragedy; Cici couldn't quite catch it. "Oh, please! What do you know about tragedy!" June screeched.

They stopped moving and were facing each other. Cici stood across from them under the awning of a drugstore and fiddled about with a cigarette to look casual. Her heart pounded with the thrill of playing spy.

Sam talked quietly. His back was to her, and she couldn't make out the words. But soon June was at it again. "You're not supposed to let it ruin your life—when you're lucky enough to have a life!"

Cici didn't know what June was going on about, but her voice was loud and her tone angry. Sam said something inaudible and June yelled back, "Yes, I do! You've told me all your secrets. You know, I just realized how stupid you think I am, like those birds you can teach to talk, but you don't think I *understand* anything. Well, I do understand! I understand just as well as you do what this bomb means!"

June stopped, and both their bodies seemed to freeze on the spot. June looked over her shoulder, as though to see if anyone had heard, and Cici turned to face the wall.

Bomb. Yup, that is certainly what June had said, Cici thought as she sucked on her cigarette. She blew the smoke out, wondering how best to use this information. It was only then that she noticed the colored man walking toward her. He had just passed June and Sam as well, and must have heard the same thing she had.

"Hey!" Cici called out. At first the man didn't seem to hear her and kept walking.

"I'm talking to you, boy! What's your name?"

He turned to her. "Beggin' your pardon, miss. I'm just on my way home and don't want any trouble."

She couldn't stand his cowardly tone. "What's your name?"

"Joe Brewer, miss."

"Did you hear that girl yelling just now?"

"Please, I don't want no trouble."

Cici's voice rose. "Did you hear her?"

"I wasn't intending to listen in on any conversations. I just happened to hear her as I walked by."

He was practically cowering before her, pathetic. "Well, get on out of here, then."

"Yes, miss. Good night, then." He scurried off.

Cici got out another cigarette and began walking toward the rec hall. She hardly ever went there without Tom anymore, but she wasn't ready to face June at home and needed some time to think through what she'd just witnessed.

* * *

THE UNION MEETING was over by the time Joe found the rec hall where it took place. Shirley had told him where to go, but he wasn't used to this side of town. And it wasn't an official union anyway—even white folks lied about what they were getting up to there to avoid trouble with the Army, so he couldn't ask anyone where to go.

He had to walk through a gymnasium where young people were dancing to find the spare, cinder-block room where the union met. He knew folks were staring at him, and he was waiting for trouble at any minute, but none of the young girls or soldiers said anything about a Negro janitor wandering into their dance party. Two white men were still in the meeting room when he got there, sitting at a table, talking in low voices. They looked up as he knocked on the open door.

One of the men, middle-aged and thin, spoke up, "Can we help you?"

"Excuse me for interrupting. I's looking for a friend, name of Ralph Hitchens. He comes here to the meetings sometimes."

The two men exchanged a glance. The second one, who wore thick glasses, replied, "I know Ralph. He was here on Friday."

Joe took a deep breath, wondering if these men were sympathetic or not. "I heard some folks here didn't like Ralph coming round."

The man with the glasses nodded. "I'm sorry to say that's true. There were a couple of young fellows who gave your friend some trouble that evening."

"Ain't no one seen him since then. I's just trying to find out if anyone here knows why."

The thin man stood up. "Now, see here. I don't appreciate you throwing accusations around."

"I'm sorry, sir. I don't mean to accuse nobody."

The man with the glasses sighed. "I haven't seen Ralph or those men since that evening. None of them were here tonight."

The thin man sat back down, eyeing Joe suspiciously. But the man with glasses had a kinder expression. "I'm sorry. I wish I could help you. If Ralph does show up here, we'll be sure to tell him you're looking for him."

"Thank you, sir. I appreciate that."

He went out the door, feeling worse than he had all day.

(Courtesy of the Department of Energy)

Chapter 20

SAM NEEDED COFFEE BADLY BUT WAS AFRAID OF ASKING JUNE TO get him any more. How had it not occurred to him what a bad idea it was, having your girl be your secretary? He couldn't stand the idea of facing her again, at least not until he had to leave for lunch.

He rubbed his aching temples and stared down at the pile of unforgiving paperwork in front of him. He was in no mood for this. He should have called in sick; then he could have avoided seeing June altogether. He cared for her—loved her even. But they were making each other crazy. Lately she was always in a bad mood, always nagging him about drinking. She was right, of course. She was right about all of it, which was the worst part. He was drinking too much. He took her for granted. Why did she want to be with him at all? He didn't understand why she didn't just leave him. It would be the best thing for her. Find a nice boy her own age. Or go away to school—she was smart enough. He wanted the best for her, wanted to help her. He used to think that he was helping her, but now he knew that he was not. The truth was that the kindest thing he could do for her would be to end it himself.

On top of everything else, there was this business with his mother. His sister said the doctors were running tests to figure out what was wrong. Meanwhile, he needed to write and send some money for the hospital.

The phone rang, and June's line lit up. He let it ring three times. "Yes?"

"You've been called to an emergency meeting, Dr. Cantor." She always addressed him formally in the office. "It's in five minutes, in meeting room D."

"Thank you." Just what he needed on a day like this.

June was typing away at her desk. He nodded slightly to her as he went out the door, and her lips rose in the slightest of smiles.

Most of the high-level scientists and administrators in his area were gathering around a large conference table. Dr. Armstrong sat at the head. Even before Sam had found a seat, Armstrong began talking. "Gentlemen, there's no point in delaying this further. Some of you may have already heard. The announcement went out on the radio ten minutes ago."

Sam felt his stomach shift uncomfortably as he guessed what Armstrong would say next.

"This morning an atomic bomb was dropped on the city of Hiroshima."

Armstrong stopped for a moment, and the room was completely silent. The men seemed shy, afraid to look at one another. Sam had the terrible notion that he might start to cry, even though he hadn't cried in years. He heard a voice from someone beside him. "We did it!"

With that, the silence was broken, and everyone began laughing and shaking hands. Sam felt a friendly slap on the back.

"Yes, gentlemen, we did it. That bomb was chock-full of CEW uranium. We did it."

Now there was applause. Sam wasn't sure who started it, but soon they were all clapping, a couple fellows even cheering. He looked down to see his own hands taking part in the celebration.

Finally Armstrong motioned for silence. "You should all be very proud, and there will be time for a great deal of celebrating as the day continues. But we do need to talk about how you will explain this to the rest of your staff. An announcement has already gone out on the radio and no doubt begun to spread across town. President Truman made a statement, a copy of which I have before me."

Armstrong tapped some papers on the table before him and began to read. "'Sixteen hours ago an American airplane dropped one bomb on Hiroshima, an important Japanese army base. That bomb had more power than twenty thousand tons of TNT. It had more than two thousand times the blast power of the British "Grand Slam," which is the largest bomb ever yet used in the history of warfare.'

"The president goes on: 'It is an atomic bomb. It is a harnessing of the basic power of the universe. The force from which the sun draws its power has been loosed against those who brought war to the Far East.'"

Sam stared at the wood grain of the table. He'd remember this day forever, he knew—this room, these people. This was history.

Armstrong looked up. "He goes on to explain the genesis

of the atomic bomb program, then gets a bit more specific: 'We now have two great plants and many lesser works devoted to the production of atomic power. Employment during peak construction numbered 125,000, and 65,000 individuals are even now engaged in operating the plants. Many have worked there for two and a half years. Few know what they have been producing. They see great quantities of material going in and they see nothing coming out of these plants, for the physical size of the explosive charge is exceedingly small. We have spent two billion dollars on the greatest scientific gamble in history—and won.

"'But the greatest marvel is not the size of the enterprise, its secrecy, nor its cost, but the achievement of scientific brains in putting together infinitely complex pieces of knowledge held by many men in different fields of science into a workable plan. And hardly less marvelous has been the capacity of industry to design, and of labor to operate, the machines and methods to do things never done before so that the brainchild of many minds came forth in physical shape and performed as it was supposed to do. Both science and industry worked under the direction of the United States Army, which achieved a unique success in managing so diverse a problem in the advancement of knowledge in an amazingly short time. It is doubtful if such another combination could be got together in the world. What has been done is the greatest achievement of organized science in history. It was done under high pressure and without failure.'"

Armstrong put the papers down and grinned across the table. "That, gentlemen, was the president of the United States, congratulating you all."

More applause. Sam didn't clap this time. He wanted

nothing more than to know what he was supposed to tell his staff and then to go tell them. He wanted out of the smothering self-congratulation of this room, and fast.

"Truman also goes on to name Oak Ridge as the location of one of the bomb-making facilities. Newspapers have been sent more thorough press releases going into some detail about the workings of the CEW, such as number of employees, exact location, and that magic word we've all been unable to utter to our wives and mothers for so long: uranium."

"Uranium!" the redheaded engineer said with a goofy smile. A few other men repeated the word with guilty grins, like children who'd said a bad word. "Plutonium!" said a scientist across the table, laughing hysterically. Sam felt himself begin to laugh, too. He felt wrong, horrified with himself even—nothing about this was funny—but even he had to admit, it was an extraordinary release to let go of the secrecy. He wanted to scream at the top of his lungs: "Uranium, uranium, uranium!"

"So, boys, you'll return to your departments and spread the good news." Dr. Armstrong held up a stack of papers. "I have official statements here for all of you, which go over exactly what you can tell employees. You can talk about atoms, uranium, et cetera. However, I shouldn't have to tell you that the specifics are still strictly off-limits. Don't forget to thank and congratulate them all. This is a day for us all to feel proud."

* * *

JUNE WAS EVEN more efficient than usual this morning. She'd been in a sort of trance since the argument with Sam the night before. After she'd left him, she'd walked aimlessly for a while, ending up at the movies after all. It was a musical about sailors with Gene Kelly, not what she was in the mood for; still, she was enthralled by the dancing, moved by the music, and transported. She must be awfully miserable, she knew, deep down, but on the surface, she remained calm. She didn't even feel sad, though she suspected that was coming later and would be devastating. Though she hadn't exactly said it last night, in her heart, she had broken things off with Sam. It had been coming for a long time. She wasn't happy; he wasn't happy. He would never change. The night she had met him, he had been drunk and miserable. Perhaps loving her or being loved by her had cheered him briefly, but now he was the same drunk, miserable man as in the beginning.

Another realization had crystallized in her mind overnight, and when she woke up, it had become a clear certainty. She used to love the way he looked at her, and wanted to be the girl he saw. But now she knew that she *was* that girl and always had been. She was thankful to him for seeing more in her than she had recognized in herself and helping her to also see it. But he wasn't responsible for it; she alone was responsible for who she was.

Her concentration was broken by a cautious tapping at the door. "Come in!" she called, and Barbara, another secretary from down the hall, appeared, an expectant look on her face.

"Have you heard?" asked Barbara.

"Heard what?"

"It's all over the radio. An atomic bomb"—June's eyes widened despite herself—"has been dropped on a city in Japan. It's the most powerful weapon ever created and it's what we've been working on here at Oak Ridge. We can talk about it now! President Truman has told the whole world about Oak Ridge. And they say this will end the war."

Barbara's enthusiasm boiled over into giggles. June was standing motionless, her mouth half open, a tingle rising up through her body out toward her limbs. It was just as Sam had told her. Something was happening, something *big,* and she was a part of it.

A smile broke out across her face. Barbara, whom she hardly knew, ran over to her desk and embraced her. June hugged Barbara back, and it didn't feel strange at all to be in the arms of a practical stranger.

Barbara pulled away. "It's why they called the emergency meeting. I think we'll all be called into a meeting soon. But I've gotten calls from two girlfriends about it already. Everyone in town has already heard."

Barbara left, and June sat down at her desk. There was no returning to typing now; she was too wound up. All this time, all this work, all the secrecy, and it was finished. They had done it. The war would be over.

There was in fact a meeting. Sam stood in front of a crowded room and read from a statement. The president congratulated them all and thanked them for their hard work. At first the employees were quiet, but then someone began shouting, someone else laughed, others clapped, and the room erupted in noise. Sam smiled politely, but June could see the distress in his eyes and knew he'd be into the whiskey as soon as possible.

The celebration moved outside. No one bothered to clock out; June asked Barbara if they should as the crowd swept them past the clock alleys, but Barbara just laughed. "No one's clocking out. Look!" There were girls and men everywhere, all rushing out of Y-12 into the parking lot, everyone headed to the bus stop. Work had unofficially been called off; people wanted to get home, to their families and friends. Everyone wanted to celebrate with someone they loved.

June hadn't bothered looking for Sam after the meeting. She'd gotten caught up with the crowd and decided to stay close to Barbara for some protection, just in case they did get in trouble for leaving early. Part of her wanted to be with Sam right now, sure, but a more persuasive part didn't want the excitement of the moment and these people to be ruined by his guilt and melancholy. Maybe she could try to find her sister, though she didn't really know how that would be possible. By the time she had squeezed onto a bus, it was clear the whole town was on the streets.

Church bells were ringing. Strangers on the bus were patting each other on the back, singing "God Bless America." As they drove into the center of town, the bus had trouble getting through the crowds of pedestrians clogging the streets. Two boys on bicycles rode down the sidewalk waving huge American flags and cheering. A man and woman were necking right on the side of the street for everyone to see. Almost everyone had a newspaper and was reading it or waving it in the air.

The newsboys were ready at the bus stop. "Extra, extra, pictures of Oak Ridge!"

"I'll take one," said June, without even looking to see which paper it was.

"One dollar," said the boy.

"Really?"

"That's the price today."

June found a dollar in her purse and took her copy of the

Knoxville News Sentinel. "Atomic Super-Bomb, Made at Oak Ridge, Strikes Japan," it read in huge block print. Above that in smaller letters, "Oak Ridge has over 425 buildings."

She read the paper and walked, smiling at strangers, nodding to everyone. It was like Christmas, when everyone's friendly with everyone else. She heard snippets of conversation as she walked: "I *knew* it was a bomb!" "But what *is* uranium?" "As far as I'm concerned, we keep dropping them until Japan is wiped off the map."

June stopped and stared at the girl, no older than herself, who'd made the last comment. They made eye contact, and June didn't disguise her contempt. "What?" the girl said. She had a sharp, rodent-like face. "The Japs killed two of my brothers, don't you look at me like that!"

The two other girls she was talking to put their hands on her shoulders and muttered calming words; June turned and kept walking. The euphoric feeling which had carried her thus far was gone. She wanted to cry. Mostly, though, she had a sudden and urgent desire to find Sam.

It took her almost an hour to walk to his house through the crowds. She knocked on the door, and he answered himself. He was wearing just his undershirt and trousers, his hair disheveled as though he'd been in bed. And of course he was drunk.

She followed him to his room and sat on the bed in silence. He offered her his flask and she took a sip. The whiskey burned her throat, and she almost coughed it up.

"Well, it's finished," he said.

"How are you feeling?"

His red-rimmed eyes considered, and he let out a long breath. "I knew this day was coming."

"I guess the war will be over soon."

"Yes." He took a long drink from the flask. "Do you know what this Hiroshima must be like right now?"

"Sam, don't—"

"For those who are still living, it must be hell on earth. It would almost be better if we could truly destroy an entire city, you know, make it cease to exist. But of course, it can't work like that. There has to be pain and suffering."

She put a hand on his cheek, more to force him to quit talking than anything. To her surprise he grabbed her hand forcefully and pulled her toward him. He began kissing her—it might have seemed passionate to someone looking on, but she knew it was desperate, angry.

They made love that way, wordlessly. She tried to push out all her thoughts as it was happening: the bomb, Hiroshima, Sam, his drinking, the end of their affair. When they were done, they lay next to each other in silence, the sounds of distant cheering and celebration drifting in through the open window.

* * *

CICI LEFT WORK with all the other girls, happy enough for the chance to celebrate, hugging and singing with them, though she didn't really count any of them as friends. She looked out for Tom, but didn't see him. She wondered what would happen now, how soon the war would be over and they'd all be asked to leave Oak Ridge. The girls around her seemed hysterical suddenly, stupid even, repeating the same lines over and over—how amazing this bomb was, how incredible that they'd made it possible. She left them quietly and walked briskly over to the main administration building on the hill.

Cici didn't think of it as anything so petty as revenge, and knew she wasn't acting out of self-interest. When she'd threatened Lizbeth, the situation was different. She'd been exploiting the girl's carelessness to get what she wanted, which certainly didn't cause Cici any moral qualms, but admittedly was a selfish act. She had nothing particularly to gain from reporting June. The war would be over any day now, and they surely wouldn't be roommates or even acquaintances for much longer, anyway.

She wasn't being selfish, and it wasn't retribution. It was something more basic than that. Her duty, plain and simple. Cici was doing the right thing, just as she'd been instructed by the Army over and over again since first arriving in Oak Ridge. She was helping June, in fact, by teaching her a lesson. June had lost her way following Dr. Cantor. Cici had tried to talk to her reasonably, but it hadn't done any good. The girl's obstinacy had driven her to take extreme measures.

Cici wasn't sure if she was in the right place, but she went up to the receptionist boldly. Even here, they were celebrating. Three girls were huddled behind the counter at reception, talking and laughing over a copy of today's *Knoxville Journal*.

"Excuse me," said Cici.

They looked up. A girl in a bright crimson dress said, "Yes?"

"I need to talk to someone regarding a security issue."

"What kind of issue?"

"I've heard someone say something that violates the security code."

The girl snickered, "Well, everyone's saying things today. It's in the paper!" She held up the *Journal*. Cici felt like reaching over the counter and giving her a smack.

"This was yesterday."

"All right. You just wait over there, and I'll find someone."

Cici sat on a hard metal bench. She resented the receptionist for doubting the seriousness of her case. For all that hick knew, June was a Jap spy.

The girl came back and directed her down two hallways and up a staircase. At the top of the stairs was a large sign: MANHATTAN DISTRICT INTELLIGENCE AND SECURITY DIVISION. Cici went up to a secretary and explained herself again. This woman was older, more serious. "Right this way," she said.

She wound up across a large, wooden desk from Douglas Milton, an equally serious man with dark, bushy eyebrows. "Thank you for coming in, Miss Roberts. Please tell me exactly what you heard."

"June, my roommate, was a sweet girl when we first met. But she's . . ."—Cici paused for dramatic effect—"become involved with a man and changed."

"All right. And who is this man?"

"He works at Y-12, name's Dr. Cantor. He even got her a job as his secretary."

"What exactly did you hear this Dr. Cantor saying to June?"

"It wasn't him, it was her. I heard them talking last night, but I didn't quite piece it together until today, you know, with the news. She said 'this bomb.' They were having an argument and she said she understood what 'this bomb' means."

Douglas Milton wrote something on a piece of paper. "All right, then. Was there anything else in their conversation which made you suspicious?"

"No, sir, except they were fighting in public. Disgraceful."

"Is there anyone else who heard the comment?"

"Yes. A colored man named Joe Brewer."

"Is this Mr. Brewer an acquaintance of yours?"

"No, of course not! I just saw him there and asked him his name."

"I see." Milton wrote something else, then looked back up at Cici and cleared his throat. "Miss Roberts, you realize accusing someone of breaching security is a serious thing. If this is about some roommate squabble or over a man—"

"Mr. Milton, I am offended! I'm a good Christian girl. I did everything I could to help June. Only now I'm beginning to realize that maybe I should never have become her friend." To her own amazement, Cici felt her eyes begin to well with tears.

"Of course, I didn't mean to judge your character, but I have to ask these sorts of questions of anyone who comes in. I understand this is difficult."

He produced a handkerchief from his pocket, and she delicately dabbed at her eyes. "Is there anything else you need to know?" she asked.

"Not now, but I will be in touch if we need any more information."

He rose, and she handed him back his handkerchief.

"If you don't believe me, you can ask that—" She paused to stop herself from using the slur she'd grown up using, struggling for the correct term in polite society. "That Negro." Cici turned and let herself out of the office.

(Courtesy of the Department of Energy)

Chapter 21

*E*VERYTHING WAS CHANGING OR ABOUT TO CHANGE. OAK Ridge's identity transformed overnight from the Secret City to the Atomic City. And though obviously most residents still had no idea what atomic energy was, they surely were proud to be a part of it. Even after the excitement of the first day died down, all the talk on the bus or at the drugstore remained focused on atoms, Hiroshima, and then three days later, the news of a second bomb and another city destroyed, Nagasaki.

June wanted the war to end as desperately as everyone else. She was impatient for it, frustrated every day by the newspapers and radio that still broadcast no news of peace, though everyone knew it must be coming. She felt stuck in place, waiting to find out what would happen next. No one talked about it yet, but once the war ended, most people in Oak Ridge would lose their jobs. If Sam and she managed to keep struggling along together, then he would have to make a choice about where he was headed, and she would have to decide if she was going with him.

They never talked about what happened the night before the bomb was dropped. June had been sure then that their relationship was over, but they continued going out, necking, all of it. She didn't have the heart to break it off now. He recoiled at any mention of the bomb or Hiroshima, became irate when he saw people celebrating, and after the news of Nagasaki came in, stayed drunk for a whole day, even missing work. June was the only person he could stand to be around. Some days it seemed like the only things he consumed were whiskey and cigarettes, and he was losing weight. He seldom took a lunch break anymore, and she would bring a sandwich to his office and urge him to eat.

She tried to cheer him. As they walked off the bus, past a group of girls giggling about atoms, June gave his hand a squeeze. "They just don't understand."

"They understand well enough." He took his hand from her to light a cigarette.

"They say the war will be over any day now."

"How many more bombs will we drop first?"

She hated that he refused to be happy. But the truth was that she, too, was filled with anxiety. Cici had been acting even more unpleasant than usual, for one thing. June felt like Cici was staring at her sometimes, and her roommate asked odd, pointed questions about where June had been during the day, what she'd done. The newspapers were all endless speculation about when the Japs would surrender. When she'd gotten on the bus that morning, folks said that the Japanese had sent a message to the Allies in the middle of the night, but by the time they got to Y-12, the radio in the clock alley said it wasn't true.

In the cafeteria, June sat alone, eating a tuna sandwich, lost in her thoughts. It took her a moment to notice the man in front of her. He stood at the other end of the table, staring down at her.

"June Walker?" he asked in a deep voice.

"Yes?"

"I'm from Intelligence and Security." He tapped the badge on his jacket. "I need you to come with me."

June put the sandwich down. "What's this about?"

"We'll talk about that in the administration building."

"But I've got to get back to work."

"Don't worry about that. Arrangements have been made." His face was stern. June's stomach twisted, and she wished she hadn't eaten the tuna.

"Can I take this sandwich up to my boss? I told him I would." She pointed to the still-wrapped sandwich she'd bought for Sam.

"I'll have someone take it to him." He handed the sandwich to another secretary and told her where to take it, all the while keeping an eye on June. When he came back, he took June by the arm and began leading her toward the exit.

"What about clocking out?" she asked as they passed the clock alleys.

"It will be taken care of." He didn't look at her as they walked. There was a car waiting at the front of the building, and he opened the door for her.

They were both silent during the trip to the administration building. June thought of the rumors she'd heard about security—stories of people disappearing, losing their jobs, their homes, just like that. Of course she had breached security dozens of times, talking with Sam. But they'd always been careful. What if it was Sam who was in trouble? He'd been so upset lately, maybe he'd done something foolish.

The man led her into the building, up a staircase, into the Intelligence and Security division, to a small windowless office and told her to take a seat at a table. He left her alone in the room. The white walls were bare. June tapped her fingers nervously on the wooden table as she waited. It was stuffy and her armpits felt damp.

Finally, another man came in. He was heavyset with thick eyebrows. "Hello, June, my name is Douglas Milton."

He gave her hand a firm shake, sat down across from her, and took out a notebook and pack of cigarettes. "You've been brought in here because a very serious accusation has been made about you."

Her heart jumped. She stared at him wide-eyed, not knowing what to say.

"I'm going to ask you some questions. Please respond honestly and keep in mind it will only make your situation worse if you lie."

She nodded. "Have you been romantically involved with Dr. Samuel Cantor?"

June gulped. Of course, plenty of people knew about her and Sam, so it would be pointless to lie. "Yes."

He jotted something down in his notebook.

"Were you with Dr. Cantor the evening of August 5?"

"Um . . . I can't remember."

"It was nine days ago, Miss Walker. The day before Hiroshima."

"Oh, yes." And suddenly, everything clicked into focus.

The day before Hiroshima. The night she and Sam had the awful fight, and she had yelled about the bomb in the middle of town.

"Were you with Dr. Cantor that evening around eight o'clock?"

"Yes, sir. I believe I was."

"Tell me about what you did."

"We met up at the canteen, then went for a walk. We got into a fight, actually. Nothing serious, just a silly argument. I wound up walking by myself, then going to the cinema." She gained confidence as she spoke. Whatever he asked, she could just pretend not to remember.

Mr. Milton wrote something down. June glanced at the notepad but couldn't make out his handwriting.

"What was your argument about?"

"Nothing in particular. He was late meeting me. It was hot, and we were both short-tempered."

"Did you say anything that would have aroused suspicion in passersby, Miss Walker? I remind you that the best way to handle this is by being completely honest with me now."

"I don't know what exactly I said. I was angry, not thinking straight."

Mr. Milton shifted his weight in the chair and stared at her in silence for a moment. He cleared his throat. June thought maybe she was convincing him. "Miss Walker, before August 6, did you know anything about the nature of the work being done here at Oak Ridge?"

"Only what I had observed at my jobs at Y-12, sir."

"So you had no idea what was going on at Y-12, what the ultimate aim of the work was?"

"Of course not."

"Dr. Cantor never let anything slip to you about his scientific work?"

"No." June thought back to the lie detector test and tried to stay calm as she told these bald-faced lies.

"What if I told you, June, that we have a witness who heard you talking about a bomb to Dr. Cantor that night?"

June scrunched her eyebrows together, trying her best to look confused. "I don't know why I would have mentioned a bomb, sir. I don't remember everything I said."

"Tell me about your relationship with Cici Roberts."

Now her confusion was real. What did Cici have to do with anything? "Cici's my roommate."

"Do you consider her a friend?"

"Well, we used to be quite close but have drifted apart recently."

"Did you have a falling-out?"

"You could say that. She doesn't like Dr. Cantor."

He wrote something down. There was a knock at the door. "Yes," Mr. Milton called out.

The man who had picked June up stuck his head in. "I've got Mr. Brewer here, sir."

"Thank you, Pete. Send him in, would you?"

Joe, the Negro janitor from work, appeared in the doorway. June looked at Mr. Milton for some clue as to why he was here. Mr. Milton was motioning for Joe to come in, though he didn't offer him a seat. Joe was holding his cap in his hands, staring down at it.

"Mr. Brewer, do you recognize this young woman?" asked Mr. Milton.

"Yes, sir. I know Miss Walker from work."

"Have you ever seen her outside of work?"

"I don't recollect such a thing, sir. I stay in the colored area when I'm off work."

"Do you remember where you were on the evening of August 5?"

Joe was twisting his cap nervously. "Yes, sir. I was in the Townsite that night looking for my friend Ralph Hitchens. He's been missing for two weeks now, ain't showed up to work or church."

"While you were in Townsite, did you see Miss Walker?"

"I can't recall."

"Lying about this would be a serious mistake, Joe. This is a matter of national security."

"I might have seen her walking with Dr. Cantor, sir."

Joe's eyes darted down to meet June's. She wasn't sure, but thought he looked apologetic. She wished she could put him at ease, but of course her own blouse was drenched in sweat now, her heart thumping.

"Mr. Milton?" Joe asked.

"Yes?"

"Do you know anything 'bout my friend Ralph? Ralph Hitchens? I been looking for him for two weeks."

"Try to stay focused, Joe. We're talking about the night of August 5."

Mr. Milton lit a cigarette and blew out a plume of smoke in June's direction. She decided that she hated him. He leaned back in his chair. "Do you remember hearing anything that Miss Walker said?"

"No, sir, I wouldn't listen in on folks' conversations."

"She was yelling."

"I don't remember."

"We have another witness." Mr. Milton looked at June

now. "She heard Miss Walker say something rather remarkable and claims that you heard her, too, Joe."

June's increasing antipathy toward Mr. Milton was building up her courage. She felt less afraid and more angry—angry at the way he was badgering and condescending to Joe. Angry that he wouldn't let the poor man sit down and was blowing smoke in her face. She was beginning to feel reckless.

"I don't recollect, Mr. Milton. That was over a week back. I ain't been thinking about much else besides finding Ralph."

Mr. Milton slammed his fist down on the table and its loud thud reverberated within the small room.

"Well, try to think back, Joe! You were in Townsite, just outside the pharmacy. A real pretty white girl was standing beside you, and Miss Walker was yelling at Dr. Cantor. What did she say?" He was screeching, his face turning crimson.

"I don't know!" Joe unclasped his twisted cap and let his hands fall to his sides. He looked Mr. Milton right in the eye.

"I don't like your tone, boy."

"I'm sorry, sir. But I don't recollect what Miss Walker—"

Mr. Milton stood as he spoke, then shouted in a trembling voice, "Think harder!"

"Stop!" said June, and without meaning to, she realized that she was also standing now. "I'll tell you what I said, Mr. Milton. I said, 'I understand what this bomb means,' all right? Leave him alone."

Mr. Milton sat back down. "Well, well, Miss Walker. You've changed your tune."

"I didn't want to say before because I was scared. Look, I hardly knew what I meant when I said it. I guessed we were making a bomb, that's all."

"You guessed?" He was sarcastic, disbelieving.

"Yes. I guessed it was a bomb. I asked Dr. Cantor, but he wouldn't tell me anything. Still, I could tell I was right by the way he reacted." She was shocked by the sound of her own voice, strong and smooth. Lying was coming so easy.

"What do you mean you could tell?"

"You know, a woman can tell things about her man. I knew his looks. It was foolish, I know. I never talked about it with anyone else."

"But what were you referring to, when you said 'what this bomb means'?"

"Just that working here, on this bomb, was all that was holding us together. Me and him, I mean. I thought we were about to split up."

Mr. Milton shook his head, as though deeply disappointed. Without looking up at him, he motioned Joe away. "All right, Joe, you can leave."

"Thank you, sir." Joe put on his cap and started for the door.

"Oh, your friend Ralph . . ."

Joe stopped and swung back around. "Yes, sir?"

"He's dead. Stabbed in a knife fight two weeks ago. Apparently, he was cheating at cards. You should watch who you hang around with."

Joe's mouth had fallen open; June could see that his hand trembled. "Yes, sir," he said softly, and went out the door.

* * *

JOE DIDN'T KNOW how he wound up at the rec hall. He'd walked out of the administration building and kept walking—one foot after the other with no thought to where he was going, no thought to going back to work, where he was due for his shift, no thoughts at all, really. Just walking.

He couldn't think. No, that wasn't right. He knew he shouldn't think, because if he did, it would become too much, too painful. That bastard's words would begin to have meaning, a meaning that of course he already understood—had in fact already assumed and dreaded—but if he thought about the words and the meaning, then he would have to think about Ralph, which he shouldn't do. He would have to think about the way that man looked at him, the way he spoke to him, the way Ralph hated men like that. But no, he shouldn't think about Ralph right now. He shouldn't think.

He walked through the town, not making a conscious decision to head back to the colored area, but going that way anyhow, pulled back toward home like a lost animal. It was far, but he must have been walking fast. Or maybe not; he had no real sense of time going by, no real sense of anything except for the need to keep walking, the need to keep not thinking. Things were pretty quiet at the rec hall when he got there. Some men played poker in the corner. Others stood around a radio, listening to a replay of some boxing match. It was almost unbearably hot. He watched the men playing poker. One with a long face and red cap asked if he wanted to join in. Joe shook his head.

It was impossible to know how long he'd been standing there when the radio began beeping, the boxing match interrupted. The men listening to it groaned and cursed.

"Breaking news, breaking news," said a newsreader's urgent voice. "The war in Japan has ended—"

The newsreader went on, but it was impossible to hear

what he said. Everyone in the room had begun cheering and stomping. He was perfectly still and quiet against the wall, watching them all slap each other on the back and toss their cards in the air. Suddenly Joe hated these men. He hated them more than he had ever hated anything in his life. He hated them more than the bastard from the administrative building even, because they were here, and they were loud, and they were so goddamn happy. An engine turned inside his chest, he felt the physical force of rage propelling him forward, and just like that, his fist connected with the red-capped poker player's chin, knocking him right down to the ground.

The yelling stopped. The other men were too stunned to react, and suddenly Joe wasn't angry at all, but deeply sorry and deeply ashamed. The president was on the radio: "I have received this afternoon a message from the Japanese government in reply to a message forwarded to that government by the secretary of state on August 11 . . ."

Joe felt the unfamiliar sensation of tears filling his eyes. "I'm sorry," he mumbled.

The man in the red cap suddenly lunged up off the ground, growling. Joe wanted to be hit. He felt the man's fist in his stomach, the air knocked out of him, a sick, dizzy feeling in his head. The man stood back, waiting, it seemed, for Joe to make the next move. As soon as he had his breath back, Joe repeated, "I'm sorry."

He turned and walked to the door, aware the man and his friends might come for him again from behind. But no one moved. Joe escaped the rec room and breathed deeply of the wet August air. He walked toward home, toward his family.

* * *

THE QUESTIONS WENT on all afternoon, but June slowly seemed to wear Mr. Milton down and convince him of her story. She had guessed it was a bomb, Sam had never told her anything. After four hours, he left her in the room alone. She laid her head on the table. She hardly cared what happened to her anymore; she just wanted out of this room to take a shower, put on a fresh dress, eat some supper.

Another half hour passed. The man who had picked her up at work came back in. "You are being dismissed from your job immediately. Consider yourself lucky, Miss Walker. You won't face any criminal charges. However, you have to leave the Manhattan Engineer District. I will escort you to the bus stop, and your belongings will be sent to you. You will not be permitted into Oak Ridge again."

She wasn't exactly surprised by the news, yet still it was shocking. His words felt like physical slaps against her skin. "Where will I go?"

"That's up to you, ma'am. There are hotels in Knoxville."

She would have to take the bus to Knoxville, then try to get in contact with her family.

"Follow me, please," the man said. And that was that.

They were in the entryway to the building, when June first noticed a distant roar like steady thunder. As they neared the doors, she realized it was a human sound, a crowd screaming. They walked out into the late-afternoon light, and she saw people filling the street in front of the administration building—women, soldiers, children—all cheering, singing, laughing. A man ran up to them, waving a newspaper. "Have you heard?" he yelled just for the pure pleasure of it, then ran back to the street. The giant headline read: "WAR OVER."

June felt her eyes become hot. She stole a glance at her

stern escort. A broad grin had spread across his face. He was smiling and she was crying—yet she knew they were feeling the same thing.

The moment was over quickly. He noticed June looking at him and regained his composure.

"Come on," he said, taking her firmly by the arm. She wiped her eyes with her free hand.

It was difficult to get through the crowd, but he led her with single-minded purpose. Girls were screaming and crying together, hugging, kissing one another's cheeks. A soldier threw his hat into the air and let out an ear-piercing shout. The newspapers were once again everywhere, waving in the air. All the while, her escort pulled June along.

A bus was preparing to leave for Knoxville, but no one was on it; everyone was in the street celebrating. The man led her all the way on and watched her sit. "Your badge," he said.

She took it off her blouse and handed it over. He gave her a nod and hopped off the bus. The driver turned back to her. "Why ain't you joining in the party?"

She shrugged. "Got to get to Knoxville."

"I don't blame you. This town is a mess."

She had enough money for a room in the Andrew Johnson Hotel for the night. The phone lines were all busy; she tried again and again to get through to Mary or Sam, but it was no use. Knoxville was just as mad as Oak Ridge had been. People were out on the streets late into the night, carousing. She couldn't blame them. She ate supper at a diner, then sat by the window in her room, watching the revelers outside. She kept the newspaper she had bought spread on her lap, as though to remind herself it was real. The headline took up half a page, though it was only a single word: "PEACE."

* * *

TELLING MORIAH WAS easy compared to telling Shirley. Joe didn't have to say a word when he got home; Moriah took one look at him and knew. The children were playing outside, like most everyone in town. The night was noisy with honking cars, blasting radios, shouts and calls, like the biggest Fourth of July party you could imagine.

Moriah led him through the doorway, shut it behind them, and held him tight. He clung to her. After a moment she took off his shirt and wet a cloth to wash him with. He felt like a child, and it felt comforting, peaceful.

When he was in a clean shirt, drinking the water she'd given him, Joe finally spoke. "The Army man said Ralph been stabbed."

Moriah squeezed his hand. "That boy was like an angel. Too good for this world."

"I got to find Shirley."

Moriah nodded.

"Can you tell the girls? Later, when they come inside?"

"I'll break it to them gentle."

"Good." He put on his hat and went to the door.

It took an hour to find Shirley—back at the rec hall, where a huge crowd had gathered. She was laughing in a circle with her girlfriends, but when she saw Joe across the room, her face became serious. She walked to him.

"Mind to step outside for a minute?" he asked.

She nodded and followed him. It was hard to find anyplace with privacy. He led her around the side of the building, a few feet from a group of men who were smoking by the wall. When Joe stopped walking, Shirley looked at him, expectant.

"I'm so sorry to tell you this. Ralph is dead."

She nodded. She looked calm, almost unaffected. He wondered if he should take her hand, but felt too awkward.

"I've been looking for him for days. I finally got someone from the Army to talk to me."

Shirley said nothing.

"The Army man told me he been stabbed. Over a game of cards."

"They lie!" she exclaimed, the sudden fierceness of her voice startling Joe.

"I kept telling him not to go to that white folks' union . . ."

"I told him *to* go." She was staring out at the twilight, not seeing Joe. He never said the right thing with Shirley.

"We were going to get married," she said, softer. "After the war. Get married and go back to Atlanta . . ."

Joe took her hand. Despite the August heat, it felt cool. She didn't react. They stood like that, her staring off, him feebly holding her hand, until he gently put it down.

"You need me to walk you back inside?" he asked.

She shook her head.

"I know he loved you."

She didn't seem to hear.

Joe walked away from the rec hall, feeling useless. Back at the hutment, the girls were in bed, but Ben was awake, toddling around on the ground.

"He's seen all the excitement outside," said Moriah. "Little boy can't sleep."

Joe picked up his son and swung him in the air. Ben chortled with delight and clamored for him to do it again. Joe picked him up and swung him higher, again and again, until they were both worn out.

(Courtesy of the Department of Energy)

Chapter 22

THE NEXT DAY JUNE FINALLY SPOKE TO MARY, WHO PROMISED TO send Bill to drive her home if she could hold on for one more night in Knoxville. He would even be able to bring her clothes. She was thankful, though nervous wondering what Bill would think of her. She found she wasn't that upset about having to leave Oak Ridge; in fact, the thought of spending the night in her parents' house was wonderful. But she was terrified of what they, Mary, and everyone else would think of her.

She wandered around Knoxville all day. The city had a festive atmosphere; everyone was smiling at one another on the street, as though they were all at the same party. She sat by the river for a long time, watching boats go by. She would miss certain things for sure—the spaghetti in the cafeteria, the roller rink, the movies.

She tried not to think about Sam. When she heard his voice, calling her name in the lobby of the Andrew Johnson, she had to look up and see him standing across from her to believe her ears.

"What are you doing here?"

"I've quit my job," he said. "Come on, come out with me. Let me get you dinner."

She led him back to the diner where she'd eaten the night before, but he insisted on something nicer. "Someplace with tablecloths," he said.

He seemed in good spirits. She had so many questions for him but waited until they were sitting down.

He leaned forward. "Are you all right, June?" His voice was tender with concern.

"Yes."

"But you lost your job?"

"Yes. Someone heard me that night. When I said 'bomb.' Don't worry, though, I told them you never told me anything."

He nodded. "I figured you must've. They gave me a pretty harsh talking-to, but that was all. I decided to quit on my own."

"Why?"

"You know I've been unhappy. I'm going back to New York."

"Oh." She hadn't known if she would ever see him again, but it still hurt to hear that he was leaving her.

"It's just temporary. My mother is sick, and I need to see her. But eventually I'll get a job at a university again. That's where I belong. June, you know, I don't think I would have survived my time here without you. I mean that."

She couldn't quite look him in the eye. "I know."

"I do love you, you know—"

"Please, stop." She looked up. "Let's just have a nice dinner. There's no need to say any of those things."

They ate steak and chatted about mostly mundane topics— the peace treaty, the future of Japan, the weather, his train trip in the morning. Later she would reflect that after all that time they had been forbidden to talk about certain things, when they were finally free to speak however they wanted, it was as though they had nothing to say.

They walked back to the hotel together. On the street outside the entrance, he kissed her on the mouth. "Do you want to come to my room?" he whispered in her ear.

She shook her head. "No. Let's say good-bye here."

She could see this surprised him. He looked stricken, truly sad. "Good-bye, June."

"Good-bye, Sam." She turned before anything more could be said and went up the stairs before him.

* * *

JUNE HAD BEEN wearing the same wrinkled dress for three days when Bill finally came to drive her home. She fidgeted next to him in the car and stared out the window. He tried to make conversation. "It's cooled off a bit, thank goodness. They say we might get some rain this afternoon."

"I hope you don't have to drive back in it."

"Don't worry, I'll be fine."

"Thanks for giving me a ride."

"It's my pleasure."

June felt too ashamed to look at him.

"Are you all right, June?"

"Oh, I'm fine."

"You sure?"

"Yes. I just feel bad. You must think I'm awful."

He shot her a glance. She tried to stare straight ahead at the road as if she didn't notice.

"Look, June, I'm sorry you got into this mess. And I've got to tell you, I wouldn't mind giving that Dr. Cantor a piece of my mind. But you're just a kid. I know you didn't mean anyone any harm."

"I didn't, Sergeant—"

"Call me Bill, please! I'm your brother."

"I didn't mean to hurt anyone. It was silly, so silly. I was just curious, really."

"Well, anyway, the war's over now, so what does it matter?"

She felt relief spread across her face in a wide grin. Bill smiled back at her.

Rose was sweeping the porch when they drove up to the house. June hadn't had any way to get word to them about her dismissal, so when Rose saw the car, she dropped her broom and ran to them in a panic. June got out as quickly as she could to reassure her. "It's all right, Mama, everything's all right. Bill's just given me a ride home. I've quit my job."

She looked back at him, and he nodded to let her know he wouldn't give away her lie.

Rose looked calmed though confused. "What you want?" came Jericho's voice from the doorway, directed at Bill. The old man hobbled toward him with his usual angry expression.

"I'm just dropping off your granddaughter, sir," said Bill in his friendly voice. "I don't mean you any harm."

Jericho showed no sign of comprehension, walking past them toward the barn. The old man didn't even know that a town called Oak Ridge existed.

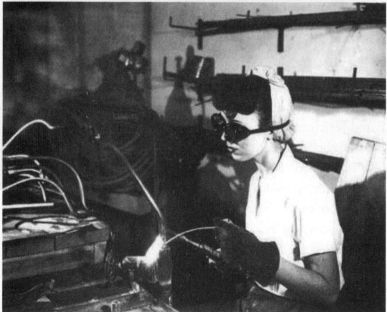

(Courtesy of the Department of Energy)

Chapter 23

THE FIRST FEW DAYS HOME DRIFTED BY IN A PLEASANT HAZE. JUNE helped out with chores just as she used to, went for walks in the afternoon, and listened to the radio in the evenings.

But she knew it couldn't last. Cici had been right, after all; with the war over, she needed a husband or a job. So she began scouring the newspapers for secretarial work. When she saw an ad for a secretary in the biology department at the University of Tennessee, she figured she'd be a perfect fit.

Mama helped her sew a new blouse for the interview, where June felt calm compared to when she had to take the lie detector and typing test at Oak Ridge. She managed to find the right office and waited patiently for Dr. Houston. She wished she'd brought something to read and tried hard not to stare at the secretary, who was typing away. Would she be replacing her?

Finally the door to Dr. Houston's office opened. He was younger than she'd expected, looking to be just barely in his thirties, lightly freckled with closely cropped red hair. He wore a gray suit and dark blue tie. "June Walker?" he asked.

She nodded and stood. He shook her hand firmly. "Timothy Houston. Come in."

He motioned her into the office, which was cluttered with stacks of books overflowing from the shelves. She sat across from him as he looked down at her application. His face was wide and expressive, but he seemed distracted as he asked her a series of straightforward questions. She described her experience in detail, but he wasn't even looking up at her.

"But I don't understand. When did you attend secretarial school?"

"I didn't. But I learned everything I needed to know working at the Clinton Engineer Works."

He took off his black-rimmed glasses and rubbed his temples. "Yes, but why in the world did they hire you with no experience?"

She wanted to burst into tears. His tone made it clear that he had already made up his mind about not hiring her. "I don't know, sir."

"And you quit on V-J Day. That seems awfully abrupt."

She inhaled deeply. She figured there was no point in lying. "I was dismissed because of a suspected breach in security."

"I see." He shook his head. "Thank you for coming in, Miss Walker. That will be all."

She stood and turned, anxious to get out of the office as quickly as possible. As she reached for the door, she heard him behind her. "And to think you never had any idea what you were even doing there."

His condescension was too much. She turned around. "Excuse me, sir, but I knew exactly what I was doing."

He looked up from his papers. "Yes, but you didn't know what it was all about."

The anxiety of the interview followed by his swift rejection had left her feeling reckless, like she had nothing to lose. "But I did."

He gave a little snort, but she could see she finally had his attention. "You're telling me that you knew about the atom bomb before any of the rest of us?"

She nodded.

"But you couldn't possibly have understood how it worked."

June took a deep breath and spoke with a confidence that was new to her. "I was a secretary at Y-12, where uranium was enriched using the electromagnetic method. Uranium-235 was separated from natural uranium using calutrons, a kind of mass spectrometer. The uranium was bombarded with electrons, which caused it to become positively charged ions. These were accelerated and sent through a magnetic field, which separated out the lighter 235 ions. Those were used in the bomb they dropped on Hiroshima."

His smirk was gone, and his voice became sincere. "How on earth did you know all that?"

She looked him in the eye, the corners of her mouth upturned ever so slightly. "I breached security," she said, and turned to go.

Tim Houston watched the girl in amazement. He had barely registered her when she had first walked in, looking like every other country girl from these parts in her homemade skirt and drugstore lipstick. But something had happened to her face as she spoke. Her eyes lit up, she had a half-smile, and even though he knew she was laughing at him, he thought that she looked beautiful. For years to come, he would swear that at that moment the thought crossed his mind: This is the woman I am going to marry.

"Wait, Miss Walker!" he called out, and chased her down the hallway.

(Courtesy of the Department of Energy)

Epilogue

CICI AND TOM WERE MARRIED AS PLANNED A MONTH AFTER THE war ended at a simple ceremony in Knoxville, attended by only one of Tom's Army friends. It wasn't until a year later that he was finally demobilized, and they were able to travel together to New Jersey, so that Tom could begin working in his father's bank. Tom's mother Eleanor took three days to decide that Cici was a classless fraud. Eleanor made the decision to keep silent on the matter, on the grounds that a divorce from a manipulative gold digger would be more humiliating for the Wolcott family than a marriage to one, which she hoped could be managed.

Tom, blinded by love, didn't realize the truth about Cici until almost a decade later. By then it didn't matter—she was a Wolcott through and through. As soon as they had taken up residency in Morristown, Cici began studying, just as she had when she first arrived in Nashville. She knew Eleanor hated her, but Cici admired her mother-in-law, and both women realized it was in their best interest for Cici to learn from her. Eleanor would never have admitted it, but she was impressed with Cici's ability to absorb the rites and customs of the gentry and convincingly reproduce them. In no time, Cici was setting up accounts at Bonwit Teller and Saks, arranging charity auctions for the historical preservation society, serving with confidence on the tennis court, and developing a taste for old-fashioneds. Even Cici was surprised by how naturally it all came to her. She was meant for this life, and she looked gorgeous wrapped in mink, walking arm in arm with Tom down Fifth Avenue on their way to meet other bankers and their wives for drinks and dinner.

She bore Tom three children, further securing her place in the family. Mothering did not come naturally to her, but luckily, nurses, nannies, and tutors were all provided. Only decades later would her husband and children turn on her, frustrated by years of emotional distance and neglect. By that time, Cici had taken up permanent residence in the summer house and could be found most evenings on the balcony with a cigarette and glass of brandy, staring out at the Atlantic Ocean, still beautiful in her chic bob and perfect makeup. If there were times when she allowed her mind to wander back through the years, questioning the decisions she'd made and actions she'd taken, you would never know it by looking at her, perfectly composed with a carefree elegance. And if she regretted any of her earlier behavior, she certainly never said so or let the thought linger very long in her mind. Even after the divorce, when two of her children had stopped speaking to her, Cici considered herself a success. She had gotten what she had wanted.

* * *

SAM GOT BACK to New York just in time for his mother's funeral. A week later, a telegram arrived for her with the news that his brother Jon had died of complications from malaria. Sam stayed with his sister Sarah in Brooklyn for the next four months. They had never been close, but with the rest of their family suddenly gone, the siblings clung to each other in silent grief. He stopped drinking altogether and even went along with his sister's family to their synagogue.

As soon as the veil of mourning lifted, Sarah set about finding a suitable Jewish girl for Sam to marry. He was too worn down to resist. Three months later, he married Esther Lieberman, twenty-six, his nephew's third-grade teacher, who had given herself up for an old maid years before. They got along well enough, and she didn't know about his drinking. He wasn't particularly attracted to her but appreciated her common sense and practicality. She was happy to leave Brooklyn with him to return to California that winter. They had one son, Jonathan, named after Sam's brother.

Sam went back to work at Berkeley. Though he regained something of his old enthusiasm for research, Sam never fully lived up to the promise he'd shown as a young scientist. Eventually Esther came to realize he drank, often secretly and often too much, but she found ways to protect herself and little Jon from the worst of its effects. She was a good mother, and in most of the ways that matter, they had a good life together. Occasionally Sam would think of June, wonder what had become of her, and remember the good times. In retrospect, he realized she was the only woman he had ever been in love with. Esther found a photograph of June in Sam's study once, but never asked about it.

* * *

JOE WORKED AS a janitor at Y-12 for almost thirty years. The labs gradually emptied out, and the pace of work and life in the city slowed to a less urgent speed. He watched as most of the men he'd known from the war days drifted off, back to their farms or to northern cities, and eventually the old hutment area was razed. The Brewers moved into a small house in Scarboro, the Negro section of the new, more permanent town.

A Negro elementary school was opened for Becky and Ben, though Ellie had to take the bus to Knoxville for high school. The Scarboro School finally added high school classes in time for Becky's sophomore year. And in 1955, *Life* magazine came to Oak Ridge to take photographs as Ben and forty-one other Negro students showed up for school at Oak Ridge High School, the first desegregation in the South.

By that time, Ellie was married with children of her own, but Becky followed a different path. Her teachers at the Scarboro School were impressed enough with her abilities to help her apply for a scholarship to Fisk University in Nashville. When she returned home to visit after a year at Fisk, Joe and Moriah were shocked to find that she had become an independent young woman and a dedicated political activist. Becky became involved in the Nashville student movement, participating at sit-ins and traveling around the South to protest, against Joe and Moriah's terrified wishes. Joe was reminded for all the world of Shirley Crawford, a decade earlier, and sure enough, Becky even ran into her once in Montgomery, where Shirley was organizing for the Southern Christian Leadership Conference. Every sit-in, every boycott, every protest made Joe think of Ralph, and he could hardly stand the worry he felt for his daughter.

But Becky managed to stay out of harm's way. Eventually she settled into a career in social work. Ben also went to college and became an accountant. And as he relaxed into old age, Joe felt blessed beyond reason when he thought about his three lucky, striving children, all living lives he had never dared to imagine for them.

* * *

JUNE WORKED FOR Dr. Timothy Houston until January of 1948, when they were married. They both loved spending time outdoors, discussing current events, and traveling, which they did much of together, around the United States, Mexico, and later Europe. They had two children. Annie took after her father and had a wild streak that June could never quite figure out. Peter was more like his mother—calm, quiet, always observant, and deeply curious.

In 1965, with the children growing older and needing her less, June enrolled in the University of Tennessee to study education. Tim encouraged her and saw to it she always had time for her studies. Upon graduating, she took a job at a Knoxville high school teaching physics. Occasionally students would ask how she'd come to teach physical science, noting that it was unusual for a woman. June would tell them she had worked at Oak Ridge and had met a physicist there who first sparked her interest in the subject. Then she would sweetly remind them that a great many things had been un-usual for women not long ago, and the usual was changing fast.

When they were old enough to understand, June's children asked her questions about her wartime work. They were raised on air raid drills and learned to duck and cover in school. By the time of the Cuban Missile Crisis, Annie was thirteen and already forming her own opinions about nuclear proliferation. It was around that time when she first asked her mother in a somewhat accusatory tone if June had understood what the bomb was when she was working on it. June told her that she didn't think anyone had understood really. Oppenheimer, Bohr, Teller, and all the rest might have appreciated the physics, predicted the destruction, feared the political repercussions. But no one really understood until August 6, 1945, and even then the understanding was just beginning. The thing was too awful and enormous to truly comprehend until it existed. And through the years, June's understanding had increased; first with the stories from Hiroshima—the firestorm and black rain, the people without skin, the radiation poisoning, the shadows victims left behind—and later with the news of the Soviet bomb and all the buildup, speculation, and fear that followed. The new vocabulary—cold war, fallout, hydrogen bomb, nuclear winter—brought with it more horrible understanding.

June tried to explain life during the war to her daughter, but as the politics of the sixties swept her up, Annie came to see her mother as a pathetic pawn in the government's evil game. She wanted to ban the bomb and give peace a chance, and June was endlessly proud of her. She hoped that if she had been her daughter's age now, she would be out protesting the same things. But Annie was too young to understand that the right thing to do could change through the years. Different times call for different actions, and June was old enough to know better than to waste energy regretting her own.

Peter was more sensitive than his big sister and had recurring nightmares about atomic war. June would hold him next to her in the darkness and whisper comforts into his ear, solace false and true at the same time. She couldn't promise that humanity wouldn't destroy itself. But she had to teach him to believe it, just as she had taught herself in order to get through life. June was no better equipped for this than any other mother—she had no special knowledge, and her experience was limited to a few months in front of a panel turning knobs and checking meters.

She couldn't explain that time to her children. All she could say was that she had entered the atomic age just a moment before the rest of the world.

About the author

About the book

Insights,
Interviews
& More . . .

Meet Janet Beard

About the author

Bradley Cummings

Born and raised in East Tennessee, JANET BEARD moved to New York to study screenwriting at New York University and went on to earn an MFA in creative writing from The New School. Her first novel, *Beneath the Pines*, was published in 2008. Janet has lived and worked in Australia, England, Boston, and Columbus, Ohio, where she is currently teaching writing, raising a daughter, and working on a new novel. ∽

Behind the Book

Growing up nearby in East Tennessee, I first learned about the history of Oak Ridge at age seven, on a field trip to the city's American Museum of Science and Energy. About half the of AMSE was a typical children's science museum with a focus on energy where we could do things like touch a ball that would make our hair stand up with static electricity. The other half told the history of the making of the first atomic bombs, and that half freaked me out. I don't know if I knew what atomic weapons were before that visit, but I remember being deeply concerned about them after and even asking my dad that night how we knew that some other country might not drop a bomb on us at any moment. This would have been the twilight years of the Cold War, but I didn't know enough to have specific concerns about the USSR. Mine was the more general anxiety of beginning to grow up and realize that the world is full of horrors.

Throughout my Tennessee youth, Oak Ridge remained a local symbol of that anxiety, as well as scientific achievement—the two halves of the museum. But when I returned to the Oak Ridge story as an adult, it was the more personal narratives that drew me in. I happened on a TV ▶

3

Behind the Book *(continued)*

documentary about the "Calutron girls" who manned the Y-12 laboratory during World War II, unbeknownst to themselves, enriching uranium. My childhood fascination returned, along with a new interest in these women's stories. I read everything I could about Oak Ridge during the war. I revisited the city, where only fragments of the temporary wartime architecture remain, save for the mostly still off-limits (for those without security passes) labs. And I talked to my own grandmother, who I found out for the first time had worked for the Manhattan Project in Knoxville, typing documents for what purpose she never knew, while her sister worked in Oak Ridge.

Their experiences were typical of that generation in East Tennessee. The scope of the project was so large that it affected the entire community—particularly young women, who were entrusted with much of the U.S. war effort on the home front. And for me it was this massive collision of everyday lives with the combined forces of history, science, industry, and war that made me want to write a novel. Ordinary individuals from a wide variety of backgrounds came together to assist in the creation of one of history's greatest and most horrible achievements, while bearing witness to the birth of the United States

as a superpower. And all in my own
native unassuming hills of Tennessee,
no less. That was a fascinating story—
or rather, a fascinating premise for
hundreds of mostly forgotten stories.
This book is my effort to bring a
handful of those stories to life. ⟡

Time Line of Events

Manhattan Project Event
World War II Event
'The Atomic City Girls' Event
....

1937
July   Japan invades China.

1938
March   Germany annexes Austria.

December   Otto Hahn and Fritz Strassmann discover the
                    process of fission in uranium in Germany. Lise
                    Meitner and Otto Frisch confirm the discovery.

1939
August   Physicist Leo Szilard writes a letter that Albert
                    Einstein signs to send to President Roosevelt
                    warning of the possibility of Nazi development
                    of atomic weapons and urging that the U.S.
                    begin its own nuclear research program.

September   Germany invades Poland. Great Britain and
                    France declare war on Germany, and World War II
                    begins.

October   Roosevelt commissions the Advisory Committee
                    on Uranium.

1940
March   John R. Dunning and his colleagues at Columbia
                    University verify Niels Bohr's hypothesis that

fission is more readily produced in the rare uranium-235 isotope than the abundant uranium-238.

April	*Germany invades Norway and Denmark.*
May	*Germany initiates attacks on Western Europe and soon takes control of the Netherlands, Belgium, and France.*
June	*Italy enters the war, joining the Axis powers.*
July	*Germany begins air attacks on Great Britain.*

In response to a memorandum from University of Birmingham scientists Otto Frisch and Rudolf Peierls concerning the possibility of creating an atomic bomb, Winston Churchill establishes the MAUD Committee to further investigate.

In the U.S., the Advisory Committee on Uranium becomes part of the newly established National Defense Research Committee (NDRC).

1941

February   Glenn Seaborg's research group discovers plutonium.

June   *Axis forces invade the Soviet Union.*

Roosevelt creates the Office of Scientific Research and Development (OSRD), which is headed by Vannevar Bush and absorbs the NDRC. ▸

Time Line of Events *(continued)*

July   The MAUD Committee issues a report
                  concluding that an atomic bomb is feasible.
                  Bush receives a copy.

October   Bush briefs Roosevelt on the MAUD Report.
                  The president approves a project to confirm
                  the findings.

December   *Japan attacks Pearl Harbor, and the U.S. enters
                  World War II.*

                  First meeting of the S-1 Uranium Committee
                  (part of the OSRD) dedicated to developing
                  nuclear weapons.

1942
January   Roosevelt authorizes production of an atomic
                  bomb.

February   *Japan captures Singapore.*

April   *The U.S. strikes Japan from the air for the first
                  time.*

May   *Japan captures the Philippines and Burma.*

                  Allied bombing of Germany begins.

June   *The Allies defeat Japan in the Battle of Midway.*

                  The S-1 Executive Committee is formed,
                  consisting of Bush, James Conant, Arthur
                  Compton, Ernest Lawrence, and Harold Urey.
                  Roosevelt approves their recommendation to

move to the pilot plant stage and build piles to produce plutonium and electromagnetic, centrifuge, and gaseous diffusion plants to produce uranium-235.

Production pile designs are developed at the Metallurgical Laboratory at the University of Chicago.

August   The Manhattan Engineering District is established by the Army Corps of Engineers.

September   Colonel Leslie Groves is appointed director of the Manhattan Engineering District and promoted to brigadier general.

The Army Corps of Engineers moves to acquire 56,000 acres in East Tennessee.

November   *The Allies defeat Japan in the Battle of Guadalcanal.*

Groves chooses J. Robert Oppenheimer to head the research into the design of a weapon. Together they decide on Los Alamos, New Mexico, as the site for the laboratory.

June's grandfather is forced to sell his farm to the U.S. Army.

December   The first nuclear reactor goes critical at the University of Chicago, creating a self-sustained nuclear reaction, under the direction of Enrico Fermi. ▶

Time Line of Events *(continued)*

1943

January	Groves selects a third Manhattan Engineering District site, Hanford, Washington, for plutonium production.
February	*The Soviets defeat Germany in the Battle of Stalingrad.*
	Construction of the electromagnetic separation plant Y-12 and pilot plutonium production plant X-10 begins in Oak Ridge.
April	The laboratory at Los Alamos begins operations.
May	*Axis forces in Tunisia surrender, ending the North African campaign.*
July	*Allied troops invade Sicily.*
	Joe and Ralph arrive in Oak Ridge.
September	*Italy surrenders to the Allied forces.*
	Construction of the gaseous diffusion production facility K-25 begins in Oak Ridge.
November	*U.S. forces invade Tarawa.*
	The X-10 graphite reactor goes critical.
	Sam arrives in Oak Ridge.

1944

February	**Y-12 sends 200 grams of enriched uranium to Los Alamos.**
May	June's friend Ronnie joins the Army and asks her to marry him.
June	*Allied forces invade Normandy on D-Day.*
August	*The Allies liberate Paris.*
September	June's fiancé Ronnie is killed in Saint-Malo, France.
October	*U.S. troops land in the Philippines.*
	Cici arrives in Oak Ridge.
November	June arrives in Oak Ridge.
December	*Germany launches its last major offensive, the Battle of the Bulge.*
	Cici and Tom meet.
	June and Sam meet.

1945

March	*The Allies capture the Japanese island of Iwo Jima.*
	K-25 begins production. ▶

Time Line of Events *(continued)*

April

Roosevelt dies, and Harry Truman becomes president.

Joe is offered a job as a janitor.

The Soviets encircle Berlin, and Hitler commits suicide.

May

Sam is promoted, and June becomes his secretary.

Germany surrenders, bringing an end to the war in Europe.

Joe's family joins him in Oak Ridge.

June

The Allies capture Okinawa.

Cici becomes engaged to Tom.

July

Los Alamos scientists successfully explode the first atomic bomb at the Trinity test in Alamogordo, New Mexico.

Truman informs Stalin that the U.S. has an atomic bomb, unaware that the Soviet leader has already learned of the nuclear program through espionage.

The Allies issue the Potsdam Declaration, demanding Japan's surrender.

August   Ralph disappears.

The B-29 *Enola Gay* drops Little Boy, a uranium weapon, on the city of Hiroshima.

The Soviet Union declares war on Japan.

Fat Man, a plutonium weapon, is dropped on the city of Nagasaki.

Japan surrenders, bringing World War II to an end.

June leaves Oak Ridge. ∿

Playlists

Music was a vital part of life in Oak Ridge. Radios were almost always on, both in public and private spaces. And live performances, whether by professional bands at dances or amateurs entertaining themselves and others in the recreation centers, were commonplace. These playlists give a taste of what might have been playing.

Big bands, inflected with swing jazz rhythms, ruled the airwaves, often accompanied by big vocals. The war informed the popular music of the 1940s as it did all aspects of life. Many songs dealt directly with world events ("G.I. Jive," "When the Lights Go On Again") and love songs were preoccupied with separation and faithfulness ("I'll Be Seeing You," "I'll Walk Alone").

Strong folk traditions flourished in the rural communities where many Oak Ridge workers originated, though change was in the air. Old time or "hillbilly" music was still played throughout the South at the same time as modern country and bluegrass were being born. Meanwhile, African American blues, jazz, and gospel were blending and evolving into what was soon to become rock and roll.

"Chattanooga Choo Choo"—
Glenn Miller & His Orchestra
"Long Ago (And Far Away)"—
Dick Haymes & Helen Forrest
"G.I. Jive"—Johnny Mercer with Paul
Weston & His Orchestra
"I'll Be Seeing You"—Bing Crosby with
John Scott Trotter & His Orchestra
"Boogie Woogie Bugle Boy"—
The Andrews Sisters with Vic
Schoen & His Orchestra
"I Don't Want to Walk Without You"—
Harry James & His Orchestra,
featuring Helen Forrest
"Don't Get Around Much Anymore"—
The Ink Spots
"When the Lights Go On Again"—
Vaughn Moore & His Orchestra
"Kiss the Boys Goodbye"—Tommy
Dorsey & His Orchestra, featuring
Connie Haines
"What a Difference a Day Made"—
Andy Russell with Paul Weston & His
Orchestra
"Besame Mucho"—Jimmy Dorsey & His
Orchestra, featuring Bob Eberly &
Kitty Kallen
"Sentimental Journey"—Les Brown &
His Band of Renown, featuring
Doris Day
"Don't Fence Me In"—Bing Crosby &
the Andrews Sisters
"I'll Walk Alone"—Dinah Shore ▶

Playlists *(continued)*

"Paper Doll"—The Mills Brothers
"I'll Get By"—Harry James & His
  Orchestra, featuring Dick Haymes
"Moonlight Serenade"—Glenn Miller &
  His Orchestra
"Accentuate the Positive"—Johnny
  Mercer & The Pied Pipers

THE "COLORED" RECREATION CENTER

"Tippin' In"—Erskine Hawkins & His
  Orchestra
"Lover Man"—Billie Holiday
"What's the Use of Getting Sober"—
  Louis Jordan & His Tympany Five
"I Wonder"—Cecil Gant
"I Will Be Home Again"—The Golden
  Gate Quartet
"Stormy Weather"—Lena Horne
"In Love Again"—Lonnie Johnson
"Don't Stop Now"—Bonnie Davis
"35th and Dearborn"—Jimmy Yancey
"Trav'lin' Light"—Paul Whiteman &
  His Orchestra, featuring Billie
  Holiday
"Me and My Chauffeur Blues"—
  Memphis Minnie
"Straighten Up and Fly Right"—The
  King Cole Trio
"Do Nothin' Till You Hear From Me"—
  Duke Ellington & His Famous
  Orchestra
"Who Threw the Whiskey in the
  Well"—Lucky Millinder & His
  Orchestra

"When My Man Comes Home"—
Buddy Johnson & His Band, featuring
Ella Johnson
"Into Each Life Some Rain Must Fall"—
Ella Fitzgerald & The Ink Spots
"Take It and Git"—Andy Kirk & His
Clouds of Joy
"See See Rider Blues"—Bea Booze
"Hamp's Boogie Woogie"—Lionel
Hampton & His Orchestra
"Somebody's Gotta Go"—Cootie
Williams & His Orchestra
"Five Guys Named Moe"—Louis Jordan
& His Tympany Five

CHARLIE'S HOUSE

"Cotton Tail"—Duke Ellington & His
Famous Orchestra
"Blues in the Night"—Cab Calloway &
His Orchestra
"Clarinet a la King"—Benny Goodman
& His Orchestra
"God Bless the Child"—Billie Holiday
"Woodchopper's Ball"—Woody Herman
& His Orchestra
"Snowfall"—Claude Thornhill & His
Orchestra
"Jumpin' at the Woodside"—Count
Basie & His Orchestra
"Nuages"—Django Reinhardt & the
Quintet of the Hot Club of France
"Flying Home"—Lionel Hampton & His
Orchestra ▶

Playlists *(continued)*

"Why Don't You Do Right"—Benny
  Goodman & His Orchestra, featuring
  Peggy Lee
"Take the 'A' Train"—Duke Ellington &
  His Famous Orchestra
"Stardust"—Artie Shaw & His Orchestra

JUNE'S PARENTS' HOUSE

"Keep on the Sunny Side"—The Carter
  Family
"New San Antonio Rose"—Bob Wills &
  His Texas Playboys
"Smoke on the Water"—Red Foley
"Mule Skinner Blues"—Bill Monroe &
  His Bluegrass Boys
"I'm Walking the Floor Over You"—
  Ernest Tubb
"At Mail Call Today"—Gene Autry
"They Took the Stars Out of Heaven"—
  Floyd Tillman
"Poor Wayfaring Stranger"—Burl Ives
"I'm Wastin' My Tears on You"—Tex
  Ritter & His Texans
"When the World's On Fire"—The
  Carter Family
"You Are My Sunshine"—Jimmie Davis
"Rocky Road Blues"—Bill Monroe & His
  Bluegrass Boys ∿

Discover great authors, exclusive offers, and more at hc.com.